She Was A Fly In The Wrong Soup

She Was A Fly In The Wrong Soup

by *Anita Dixon Thomas*

She Was a Fly in the Wrong Soup
Copyright 2020 by Anita Dixon Thomas

Published by Anita Dixon Thomas-Loose Associations

Book Cover Design by William Calhoun
Edited by Monique Huenergardt
Book Design by Maureen Cutajar

She Was A Fly in The Wrong Soup is a work of fiction. Names, characters, places and incidences are byproducts of the author's imagination. Any resemblance to actual events, locales, or persons, living or dead, is entirely coincidental.

ISBN: 978-1-7331688-2-3 (print)
ISBN: 978-1-7331688-3-0 (ebook)

I dedicate this body of work to my beautiful mother,
JUANITA DIXON,
a loving and gracious spirit who is my truest and greatest fan.

Acknowledgements

I owe a debt of thanks to my sisters, Cheryl and Crystal; my best friends, Patty Weathers-Brownlee and Paula McGuire Turner; and my daughter, Tierri. Finally, the love of my life, "D" as well as my social work colleagues Melissa Collis-Abdulla and Amanda Wagner. They all showed me such love and support as I recreated this fascinating, entertaining story by giving me their invaluable, needed, constructive advice at a moment's notice.

All of you deserve credit for the success of this project. Last but not least, a special thanks to Dr. Viorca Peneca for inspiring the title of this novel. She had no idea that her witty, hilarious comment during one of our conversations would end up being the title of this comical, dramatic masterpiece.

"Truth is stranger than fiction."
– MARK TWAIN

Prologue

Early Spring

It was midday at Saint Mary's Cemetery in the town of Salter's Point. The sun, a raging ball of fire, hung in the bright blue sky, and substantial evergreen trees swayed in the light cool breeze. Twigs blew around gravesites, and black crows howled and swooped back and forth. A huge black cat with fiery golden eyes crept among the gravesites, oblivious to the noises around him.

It had rained all night, and everything in the universe was damp. The cat didn't care. With each measured step, he navigated around the cold gray tombstones, wet hilly inclines, and slippery rocky paths. He knew where he was going. He was heading to his favorite place, the lonely gravesite beneath the big evergreen tree.

This had been his daily routine since the horrible day he's lost his mistress three years ago. He now made his home on the cliff inside the trunk of a large evergreen tree in the woods behind the hospital. He leaves his home when the sun is high in the sky, runs by the iron gate in front of the hospital, and pauses to linger in front, looking through the iron bars. Then he runs down the winding road to the town at the bottom of the cliff, not stopping until he safely reaches the cemetery and the tombstone with the letters "JL." There he always finds a warm bowl of soup left by the old groundskeeper who watches from a respectful distance.

The cat sat in front of his bowl of chicken soup and observed three flies creeping along the rim. Faint scratchy melodies floated from the flies rubbing their tiny silver wings while the soup's spicy aroma drew their nosy antennae inside the bowl. Annoyed, the cat swiped the pan with his massive midnight paw, spilling the contents onto the ground. Two flies flew off, leaving one squirming and wiggling in a sea of soup. The unlucky fellow struggled to save himself, and after a brave fight, he shook himself off and flew away on his way. The cat lapped up the remainder of soup, and when he was finished he laid in front of the tombstone until dusk.

When twinkling stars showed in the dark sky and the moon came out from behind the clouds, he lurched up and slowly crept away, trotting back to the cemetery entrance. He ran out the gate and up the winding road back to his home on the cliff. There he rested and mourned, his faint eerie cry a whisper in the wind. When the sun rose again, he repeated the same routine, traveling the same route, going to the same destination. His only purpose was to lie on the grave underneath the evergreen tree, watching another hungry fly teeter on the edge of his bowl of soup. Just as his mistress had been, it was always a fly in the wrong soup.

Chapter One

Mid-October 1984

I t was almost midnight, and the moon loomed like a big orange pumpkin in the dark, clear sky. Curled on the hard, narrow bed in a fetal position with a blanket over her, Susan Cole gazed at the moon's reflection through the octagonal window eight feet above her. Depending on how she moved her head, the unevenness of the safety glass stretched and squeezed the moon's image, much like a carnival mirror. Susan was struck by the moon's brilliance, gazing at it until she saw black spots. She squeezed her eyes shut, and when she opened them again, the black spots were gone. She detected footsteps coming down the hallway and suddenly halting at her door. Bob, the charge nurse, was making his final rounds for the night.

The door opened, and a bright light shone in her face. Susan lifted her head and squinted into the light from the hallway, then pulled the blanket over her head. The door closed, and for a minute or two Susan listened as Bob walked down the hall. Once his footsteps faded, Susan sat up, wrapping her blanket around her, and stared at the light shining underneath the door. When the light finally went out, Susan knew Bob had settled in for the night at the nursing station.

Now safe to move about, Susan threw off her blanket and hopped out of bed. She stooped to the floor, reached under the bed,

3

and pulled out a shopping bag. She set it on the bed carefully and opened it, trying hard not to rattle the crackling paper. In the bag, she kept three outfits along with a pair of Reebok tennis shoes. She took out her jeans and a black sweater and quickly dressed.

Happy to be rid of the dull tan pajamas she'd had to wear since arriving at the hospital two weeks ago, Susan lingered on the edge of the bed and slipped on her Reeboks, tying the laces into neat bows. Leaping to her feet, Susan tiptoed to the closet, opened the door, and took out her black coat and matching wool hat. She threw on her jacket, buttoning it to her chin. With her hat in her hand, Susan tiptoed back to the bed, and sat on the edge. She twisted her curly blond hair into a bun, and pulled her hat over her head.

Then she sat there staring at the door, twiddling her thumbs while she waited on Doctor George Benny. He was her knight in shining armor, her psychiatrist, and her new lover. He promised to whisk her away from this crazy, awful place she'd found herself in. He promised her a better life from the dreary world she had always known.

While she waited, Susan found herself reflecting on the events that brought her to Salter's Point Regional Hospital. She didn't know if she'd been born cursed, or if her perpetual bad luck was a result of her father abandoning her to be raised by a drug-addicted mother. On welfare and high on crack most days, her mother just didn't seem to care about her, so Susan learned to fend for herself. She came to hate herself as much as her mother seemed to, and acted out by sleeping with men and making superficial cuts on her wrists with a small switchblade. She never intended to seriously injure herself; the cutting just made her feel better. She always treated the cuts and wrapped her arms with thick white gauze, and she wore shirts and sweaters with long sleeves to hide the damage. Except for the nurses and doctors at the psychiatric hospitals she often stayed in, Susan never told a soul about her terrible secret.

Eventually, the cutting and sleeping around no longer soothed her, and she graduated to suicide attempts. She would take a bunch of pills and end up in a hospital getting her stomach pumped. Her intention was never to kill herself; she was just desperate for someone, anyone to care about her.

Hoping to leave her troubles behind her, Susan had moved from California to Salter's Point six months earlier, but things didn't go as she'd planned. She couldn't make enough money waitressing to pay her rent. She lost her apartment and found herself on the streets. Despondent, homeless, and broke, Susan resorted to her old bad behavior. After overdosing on Tylenol, a man found her lying on the town sidewalk moaning in pain and called 911. After spending time in a local hospital's ICU, Susan's doctor committed her to Salter's Point Regional, her tenth commitment on record. Susan was saved, guaranteed free room and board for the duration of her stay.

It was at Salter's Point Regional that Susan met Doctor George Benny. He was working the late shift when she was transferred in, and he assigned himself as her doctor. Susan immediately fell in love with him. When he spoke, she hung on his every word. The doctor's marginal good looks and charming personality reminded Susan of her estranged father. Caught up in his seductive web, every day they would make love in the doctor's office. Susan was ecstatic when George offered her a place to stay.

Together they planned Susan's escape, and now, finally, the night had arrived. Susan was eager to begin her new life and leave the old one behind. So, with her hands clasped tight in her lap, Susan waited for George. The shopping bag with her two additional outfits sat on the floor next to her feet. Susan stared at the door for some time, and when it opened, George entered the room. Susan's eyes lit up, and she dove off the bed. She fell in his arms, almost knocking him over, and clung to his waist like an expectant child, gazing lovingly at him with bright blue eyes.

"Whoa," he laughed, "slow down!"

"I thought you'd never get here!" Susan giggled like a schoolgirl. "I've been waiting all day!"

"I'm here now. I told you I would come." George smiled. He was tall and slender with silver-gray hair and a mustache. George's eyes were intense and sparkling blue. Years of smoking pipes every day left the doctor's smile with mustard-yellow teeth.

George embraced Susan and kissed her forehead, then released her and pointed to the bed. "Get your bag. We need to go. We don't have much time."

"What about my medication? I need my pills. They keep me calm."

"Did Bob give you medication this evening?"

"Yes," Susan said, snatching her shopping bag and following George to the door.

"No need to worry. I have plenty of medication at home." He stopped for a moment and looked in both directions down the hallway. Satisfied the coast was clear, he and Susan tiptoed toward the unit exit. When they passed the nursing station, Susan busted out laughing at Bob's loud grizzly bear snore.

George became incensed. "Be quiet! You're going to wake Bob up!"

As soon as those words left his lips, Bob's snoring stopped. George and Susan held their breath as they stood frozen in place. Susan's heart thumped hard in her chest as they watched Bob smack his lips and yawn. Seconds later, a soft snore rumbled from his lips, and a stream of clear liquid dribbled from his mouth. Susan felt George squeeze her hand, causing her to cringe in agony.

"Ouch! That hurts!"

"You almost got me in trouble," George sneered.

"I didn't mean to," Susan whined as she poked her bottom lip out. "Bob looks so funny sleeping there."

"Just be quiet and let's go!" George dragged her down the hall. Sweat dripped from his face. He fiddled with the key ring, dropping it, and it clanged on the floor. George moaned in exasperation and glanced down the hall to see if anyone was coming. "Shit, I just can't get it together!"

Susan stooped over and picked up the key, handing it to George. "I think you need some of my medication. You're a nervous wreck." George cut his eyes at Susan, and she made a face. "Don't look at me like that! I was only kidding!"

"If you say so," George snapped as he unlocked the door. He hurled his slender body against the door, shoving it open. George grabbed Susan's hand, and together they stepped out. After he closed the door, it automatically locked. The two lovers sprinted through the lobby and out the main entrance. The cold, crisp wind stung Susan's face as they ran across the lit parking lot. They slowed down to a brisk walk as they made their way to George's red Porsche.

While Susan waited for George as he fumbled with his keys to unlock and open her door, she looked back at the hospital. Dense white fog hung over the hospital, and its gloomy appearance reminded her of a haunted house. In the clock tower, a small light flickered on and off every three seconds, illuminating the clock's sizable white face. The clock's black hands crept to the numeral twelve, and Susan heard the clock chime twelve times.

Startled by the sound, bats that were hanging off the clock's wooden ledge took off with their wings roaring like rushing water, swooping back and forth over the clock tower. Once the chiming ended, the night creatures settled on the clock's narrow ledge, lined up like big black crows on a picket fence. One by one, they flipped upside down with their naked bodies suspended in midair as if posing for a Halloween portrait. Susan shuddered, turning back around as George opened the car door.

"It's creepy around here," she mumbled under her breath.

Susan slipped into the soft leather seat of George's Porsche while he dashed around the car and got into the driver's side. They snuggled together briefly, then George zoomed out of the parking lot with lightning speed, passing through the open iron gate and down the road. Susan suddenly realized she hadn't seen John, the security guard, in the lobby when she and George left the hospital.

"Honey, I didn't see John when we left. Do you know where he might be tonight?"

"Who cares where he is? Be glad we didn't run into him. Do you want me to go to jail?" George quipped as he stepped on the brake, slowing his vehicle down.

Susan withered in her seat. She hated when George snapped at her. "No, George, I was just asking. He's usually around."

George remained silent as he navigated down the sharply curving road that snaked through the town of Salter's Point. Susan gazed out the window at the tall evergreen trees that lined each side of the street. Salter's Point Regional sat on a cliff, and on the right side of the road was a deep, vast valley. Susan lurched up and strained her neck, trying to look down. All she saw was darkness, and a cold chill rippled through her spine. The whole scene was eerie, and it gave her the creeps.

Susan sighed heavily and sat back in her seat. She glanced at the clock on the dashboard and realized they'd been driving for fifteen minutes. Eager to see her new home, she cleared her throat. "Humph, excuse me, George, do we have far to go?"

"Just another fifteen minutes," he smiled.

"Cool, I can't wait!" Susan laid her head on the headrest and gazed out the window, counting stars in the midnight sky.

Fifteen minutes later, the car came to a stop, and George announced, "We're here."

Susan straightened in her seat. George's home took her by surprise. Instead of a mansion like she'd imagined, his house was a modest white bungalow. It had two front windows with windowpanes painted black. Thick fescue grass grew in the front yard, and red roses crept along the white picket fence. A cobblestone sidewalk led up to the porch, with four steps going to the front door. The door was red with a white wicker chair on each side. Susan sighed with disappointment. *Very cute! No mansion. Oh, well.*

"What are you waiting for? Let's go!" George said as he flipped the lock and opened the car door. He stepped out, opened the rear door, and grabbed Susan's bag. As George shut the door, Susan was already out of the car.

"I like your home," she fibbed.

"Thank you," George said as he reached over and pulled Susan to him. She, in turn, wrapped her arms around his waist. George lowered his head and planted a wet, passionate kiss on her thin lips.

He pulled back and stared into her eyes. "Darling, welcome to your new home. I hope you'll be comfortable here."

"Don't worry. I'm sure I'll be fine." Her lips erupted into a childish grin. George opened the gate and Susan followed him in. They walked up the steps and George unlocked the door, twisting the knob and opening it. He flipped the light switch on the wall and a ceiling light came on. Susan heard soft jazz playing in the background as she followed George inside. He shut the door, and Susan looked around wide-eyed. "I hear music. Where is it coming from?"

"I have built-in speakers wired throughout so I can play music all over the house."

"So cool." Susan smiled, taking in the ambiance of George's home. In the living room along the back wall sat a black leather couch. A few feet from the couch was a matching chair. Next to the chair, a CD Player with CDs stacked on each side sat on a cherry wood entertainment console, and a large abstract oil painting with red, blue, and orange colors hung over the console. Across the room, a huge stone fireplace with ash residue on the hearth sat between two front rectangular windows with white blinds. *So, simple!*

Double glass French doors separated the living room from the dining area. George opened the doors and stood to the side so Susan could go in. The dining room was decorated simply with an oval oak table and four chairs with black upholstery. On the wall hung another abstract painting with black and burgundy colors. This particular painting caught Susan's attention.

"George, I love this painting. The colors are so striking."

"I collect abstract art. I find it interesting."

George passed through an archway leading into the kitchen. Susan followed him and was shocked by the kitchen's small size. The black refrigerator and stove took up a lot of space along the wall. On the other side of the kitchen, there was a shiny black sink with granite counters. Black painted cabinets hovered over the counters.

"George, is black your favorite color?"

"Black is a masculine color. I like decorating with it."

"Oh, I can see that." Susan followed George out of the kitchen, passing through the dining room and out the French doors. George turned left, stepping into a short hallway with wood stairs.

"Time to show you my room." He ran upstairs with Susan on his heels. George pointed to a small room as they walked down the short hallway. "This is one of the two bathrooms. The other one is in the master bedroom."

"Oh," Susan said, taking note. At the end of the hall was another set of French doors. The doors opened into the master bedroom, and when George opened them, there sat a king-sized bed with a black comforter. On the wood floor was a black fur rug, and to the right was the bathroom. The walls were bare, except for the rectangle window facing the front of the house.

George dropped Susan's bag and closed the blinds. Susan plopped her behind on the bed and looked around. George walked over and gently pushed her back on the bed. He covered her face with sloppy, wet kisses, and Susan wiggled and giggled with delight. Hopelessly excited, Susan knew she had arrived. Despite all the bad things that had happened in her life to this point, finally she could be happy.

Chapter Two

The Next Day

Rachel Thomas tossed and turned in her queen-sized bed. She didn't get much sleep last night because her anxiety was working overtime. At eleven o'clock, she would at last be interviewing for a real, professional job with decent pay. Her current social work job at the nursing home barely paid the monthly bills.

Fidgety and wide awake, Rachel laid on her back and stretched her legs. She wiggled her toes and repeatedly yawned, each yawn louder than the last. She drew circles with her index finger around each red dot on her pajamas, a nervous habit she'd had since childhood.

She rolled over and sat on the side of the bed. Her eyes drifted to the alarm clock on the nightstand glowing in the dark, and the time was five minutes to eight. Rachel never set her alarm. She relied on her internal clock and the grace of God to wake her up on time every morning. Because of her faith in God's timing, she was never late for work. Rachel scooted across the bed and switched on the lamp.

Her dark brown eyes settled on a photograph of her and Picasso Cooper, her ex-fiancé. They looked happy together, hugged up in front of the Golden Gate Bridge with Picasso planting a kiss on her cheek. She could still feel his warm lips and tight embrace. Rachel smiled as she reminisced fondly over the memory. Soon her smile dwarfed into a frown. Sadly, they parted ways because of his infidelity.

Although he hurt her badly, she kept the photo of them together next to her parent's picture on the nightstand. An only child, she considered Picasso to be family. She had known him most of her life. They met in high school and she thought they would be together forever, but it wasn't in the cards.

Rachel stood on her feet and trudged over to the window. She opened the blinds and noticed the clouds were dark and angry, threatening rain. She wondered if the rain would even come because it had been bitterly cold for the past few days. Rachel hated the rain, a common occurrence in Seattle especially during the winter and spring months. She preferred the dry, freezing winter weather of her native California.

When the sun was out, Rachel could see Mountain Rainier from her one-bedroom fourth-floor apartment. Although having the view made her rent more expensive, she had no plans to give up her place. Her bedroom was her favorite refuge, her escape. African art decorated the walls, and green ivy plants hung by the bay window. In a corner next to her full-length mirror sat her favorite red velvet chair with fluffy black pillows.

Disappointed she couldn't see the mountain, Rachel turned away from the window and hopped onto the bed. She grabbed the remote from the nightstand and turned on the television. A reporter on KIRO News was reporting on Salter's Point Regional Hospital. A patient with a history of suicide attempts had escaped from the locked unit. Rachel's mouth sagged open and she sat straight up on the side of the bed. She turned the volume up and listened more intently.

"My word, this is terrible!" she gasped and shook her head. "I hope they find her before she ends up killing herself."

Rachel sighed heavily and turned off the television. In preparation for her interview, she'd read about the hospital's sordid past.

In the 1940s, Salter's Point Regional had a reputation for performing frontal lobotomies and using ice baths and electric shock treatments on their patients. Although in later years the hospital had cleaned up its act, Salter's Point Regional remained a horrifying place to be admitted. Rachel wasn't bothered by the hospital's history and reputation. Her career goal was to add mental health experience to her resume. One day, she hoped to start her own mental health practice.

Rachel looked at the clock and panicked. Time was ticking away. It was eight-thirty, only two and a half hours until her interview. Rachel leaped to her feet and darted around her apartment. She ran to her closet and threw suits, dresses, and sweaters on the floor. Fifteen minutes later, Rachel finally settled on a cream blouse, a red suit, and two-inch brown pumps. She stood there for a minute, admiring her selection. When she wore red, compliments would always follow.

Again, Rachel glanced at the clock. It was now eight forty-five. She ran to the bathroom, turned on the shower, and moved to the sink. She carefully unraveled the rollers from her hair, placing them in the vanity drawer. She slipped out of her pajamas, slid on her shower cap, and stepped into the shower.

Twenty minutes later, Rachel was out of the shower, drying herself off with her fluffy red towel. She wrapped the towel around her slender, curvy body and stood at the sink staring into the mirror. Rachel twisted her long black curly hair into a bun, leaving a dangling curl in her face. She later wrapped it around her right ear as she hurriedly applied her makeup, being extra light on the foundation. Rachel applied bronze eye shadow and deep blue mascara to bring out the dark brown color in her eyes. She topped off the look with a hint of blush and smiled, admiring herself.

Rachel hurried out of the bathroom and down the hall to her bedroom. She looked at the clock again, and it was now nine ten. She hurriedly dressed, slipped on her heels, and gave herself an inspection in the full-length mirror, spinning around three times to make sure there were no wrinkles. After a close examination, she dashed to the kitchen. Her upcoming interview came to mind, and she felt her stomach getting jittery. "I need a strong cup of coffee to calm my nerves," she muttered out loud.

Rachel made herself a pot of Starbucks Caffe Verona coffee, and she microwaved a Danish cheese roll, her favorite. Within minutes she was sitting at the kitchen table, a graduation gift from her parents, enjoying her meager breakfast. By nine-thirty, she had finished eating, so she rose from her chair and placed her dishes in the sink. Rachel dashed to the bathroom and hurriedly brushed her teeth. Once she finished, she applied her red lipstick. A brief glimpse in the mirror made her chuckle. Although she was determined to nail the interview, she was nervous as hell. It felt like her heart was about to burst out of her chest as she stood over the sink, breathing deeply.

Fifteen minutes later, she felt calmer, checking her watch for the time. It was ten o'clock. Rachel rushed to her closet and opened the door. She snatched her raincoat from a hangar and slipped it on. Next, she grabbed her handbag and umbrella and, satisfied she had everything with her, Rachel opened the door and walked out.

As Rachel cranked up her red Toyota, the gray sky opened up and hail the size of mothballs bounced off her windshield. Backing out of her parking space, she whipped the car around and drove out of the apartment complex. Even with the wipers swishing back and forth full force, an icy, slushy maze zigzagged across the front windshield, hampering her view. The traffic was tight, bumper to bumper as she crept along Interstate Five. As she merged into traffic, the rain and hail assaulted her window.

Rachel kept a steady snail-like pace as she cruised along the freeway. She turned on the radio, and Prince's hit song "When Doves Cry" blasted over the airwaves. Rachel sang along, bopping her head to the music. Soon the freezing rain tapered off into a drizzle, making it easier for Rachel to see. She stepped on the gas and zoomed down the freeway.

Thirty minutes later, a sign scripted with Salter's Point appeared on the highway. Rachel exited the freeway and made a sharp right. She drove down a long stretch of highway crossing over railroad tracks, and soon the road snaked along Puget Sound. The water's rough waves splashed up on the rocky beach below. On Rachel's left, tall evergreen trees lined the road, their green needles dusted with silver-white dew glistening on the branches. The sky brightened as the sun's red rays burned through the clouds, chasing huge clusters of gray away.

Up ahead, a man wearing red sweats, a knit striped hat, and brown-tinted sunglasses rode a ten-speed bicycle. When she whipped by the man, he seemed to be too focused on the road ahead to notice her.

It wasn't long before she was driving up a winding mountainous terrain. Rachel struggled with the stick shift as her Toyota chugged uphill around the sleek curves. Evergreens were everywhere. Their majestic beauty decorated the mountain embankment, and the sun's intense warmth dried out their water-logged branches.

"So beautiful," Rachel whispered to herself as she took it all in.

After a while, a few yards up the road, Rachel saw the iron gate of Salter's Point Regional. A guard stood in a glass booth trimmed in black wood with an archway. He caught Rachel's attention as she near the entrance. Dressed in a black uniform and clunky combat boots, the guard looked like Darth Vader. Rachel smirked to herself, amused by his peculiar, dark look. His bushy gray eyebrows hung over his deep-set blue eyes, and the fixed lines in his face disappeared into his thick gray mustache. The lines on his face reminded Rachel of one of those complicated Atlas road maps back in the day.

The guard signaled Rachel to stop. She stomped on her brakes, bringing her Toyota to a screeching halt. Rachel turned off the ignition and rolled down the window as the guard approached her vehicle. Rachel smiled, but the guard's face remained as hard as a rock. Tension rumbled in her stomach.

"Good morning, sir," she greeted him in a breathy, quavering voice. "I've got an eleven o'clock interview with Beth Jones."

The guard poked his head in the window, and Rachel could smell tobacco on his clothing. She leaned back, shifting in her seat, surprised by his lack of personal space.

"You here to see who?" he asked in a gruff voice.

"Beth Jones," Rachel repeated, wide-eyed.

"Young lady, I need to see your ID!"

Rachel carefully pulled her wallet out of her handbag, unzipped it, and took out her driver's license. Her hand trembled as she handed it to the guard. He snatched it from her, flashing her a look of disdain. The guard whirled around and hiked back to his glass booth. Rachel watched him as he made a phone call. As her heart quivered in her chest, she contemplated whether to ask him for directions, scared of what he might say. However, by the time he returned to her vehicle, she had mustered up enough courage. With her voice trembling, she asked, "Sir, do you mind directing me to South Campus?"

Frowning, the guard handed her back her license and turned around, glaring ahead. Pointing his thick crooked finger at the gate, he growled, "Go through this gate and past North Campus Hospital. When you reach the top of the hill, you'll see a gray building on the right. That building is South Campus Hospital. Now get!"

The guard backed away from Rachel's Toyota, turned around, and headed back to the booth. He stood in the archway and flipped a switch, and the gate slowly opened. The guard beckoned for Rachel to go through, and with her face twisted up, Rachel muttered, "What an asshole!"

Once she drove through the gate, Rachel noticed red and black rose bushes blooming on each side of the road. On her left, there were clusters of white cottages scattered on the well-manicured green lawn. On her right sat Salter's Point Regional, a massive brick building with the words *North Campus* on the front. Above the roof, a clock tower trimmed in gold loomed over the building. The clock's huge white face had black hands and large Roman numerals. It reminded her of one of the clocks in the olden days. The clock's impressive architectural design added to the hospital's mystique. Amazed by the hospital's glamour and lush landscape, Rachel declared, "What a beautiful campus!"

She drove over the hill, and her eyes rested on South Campus Hospital. It was a large gray stone building, not as pretty as the North

Campus building, and it was nestled in a grove of evergreen trees. Two men dressed in blue overalls stood outside in front of the hospital's entrance smoking cigarettes. Jittery, with her heart pounding in her chest, Rachel carefully checked the men out while she parked her Toyota. She sat there for a moment, fiddling with the dangling curl in her face. She slapped down the sun visor and checked her makeup in the mirror. Satisfied with her appearance, Rachel slapped the sun visor in place. Grabbing her shoulder bag, Rachel opened the car door, eased out, and slammed the door shut.

Rachel strutted to the entrance at a clipped pace. The two men, quiet as church mice, moved aside without looking at her as she stepped to the sliding glass door. Rachel tapped the button, and the door slid open. Relieved, Rachel hurried inside. Her eyes grew big when she stepped to the reception desk. In front of her on the counter sat six white wig heads wearing black witches' hats. They were sitting in a perfectly straight line with thick yarn for hair. Each wig head had large black dots for eyes. Below the eyes, someone made a red smudge for a nose and drew two crooked lines creating lewd, sinister grins. Rachel chuckled, amused by the scene.

On the other side of the counter, a woman with a beehive hairdo sat with her back to Rachel, tapping away on an Emerson typewriter. Oblivious to Rachel's presence, the woman's stubby little fingers clicked keys on the typewriter in a staccato tempo, and her silver hoop earrings jingled with the rhythm. The receptionist wore a plain white blouse, and her black polyester pants fit snug on her full behind. Clearing her throat, Rachel took a deep breath. "Um…Madam, hello?"

The receptionist, still consumed with her typing, didn't hear her, so Rachel snapped her fingers and shouted in a high voice, "Hello there, my name is Rachel Thomas!"

The receptionist spun her chair around so fast she almost flipped out of it. Her brown eyes darted back and forth like a wild animal as she patted her chest. "Oh, my goodness…I'm sorry, have you been standing there long?"

"No, I just got here," Rachel smiled warmly. "I didn't mean to scare you. I'm here to see Beth Jones."

"I'm Joyce Smith. I'm the secretary here." The chair squeaked as she shifted her plump bottom. "Please have a seat. I'll tell Beth you're here."

"Thank you." Rachel turned away and found a seat on the sofa in front of the bay window. She gave the lobby a once-over, deciding the place was as drab as a prison. The white walls were void of pictures, and there were black marks on the tile floor. The lobby was sparsely decorated with four end tables with ashtrays filled with cigarette butts, and a sofa and four fluffy tan chairs sat in a rectangle on the opposite side. *Messy!* Rachel thought as she scooted back on the sofa.

Three male patients dressed in tee-shirts, jeans, and sneakers with no shoelaces came through double doors on the left side of the lobby. Mumbling to themselves as they paced back and forth like robots, each soul methodically paraded in front of her, the smiles on their faces wiped away by the drugs they were being given. Rachel cringed and her stomach bubbled. She wondered if she made the right choice in accepting an interview at such a peculiar place. She decided it was. After all, the job paid well, and the extra income would come in handy.

Rachel glanced to her right and noticed steel gray double doors with the sign *Admissions Unit* overhead. It wasn't long before she heard a lock click, and a woman came through the doors. She was short and chunky and wore a free-flowing glittered orange dress and flaming green high-heeled shoes. Her thick curly gray hair cradled her round chipmunk face, and round framed bifocals sat on the tip of her pudgy nose. The bifocals magnified her big green eyes, and she looked like a jaybird staring through a window. At first, Rachel thought the woman was a patient, but when the woman wobbled over to her, she wasn't sure. The keyring on the woman's belt jingled like a pair of cowbells.

"Good morning, I'm Beth Jones. You must be Rachel Thomas," she grinned.

18

"Yes, I am." Rachel offered her hand and smiled. As the two women shook hands, Rachel worried her hand was clammy with perspiration, but Beth didn't seem to notice.

"Glad to meet you, young lady. Follow me." Beth took off, waddling like a duck through the lobby, and Rachel followed her two steps behind.

Beth stopped in front of the steel gray doors and snatched the keyring from her belt. She flipped through the keys like a deck of cards until she found the one she wanted. Beth leaned into the door while jamming the key into the lock, turning it until it clicked open. With a slight shove, Beth opened the door and stepped into the unit. Rachel followed her inside, and Beth allowed the steel door to slammed so hard and loud, the weight of it rattled the walls.

Thick gray cigarette smoke greeted them in the hallway, and huddles of patients stood nearby, staring at them and puffing on cigarettes. With no fresh air to speak of, Rachel gagged and coughed. Beth didn't seem bothered by the smoke, and Rachel wondered how she could stand it. Beth apparently read her mind.

"The patients are entitled to four smoke breaks a day," she explained. "I'm a smoker. The smoke doesn't bother me."

"I see," Rachel coughed.

Beth's office was a few feet from the steel doors. Patient bedrooms lined each side of the hallway, and Rachel saw patients moving in and out as she waited in front of Beth's office. On the door hung a large black sign with words scripted in white ink *Enter at Your Own Risk*. Amused, Rachel wondered what could be so risky in Beth's office. Beth quietly unlocked the door and slowly pushed it aside as if unveiling something scary. She stepped inside. "Come in," she demanded.

Rachel followed Beth in, and her eyes grew big. She slapped her hand over her mouth as she viewed the messy, cluttered scene. Books, papers, and patient charts were stacked high on one side of the desk. Cardboard boxes sat in corners and empty Coca Cola cans were scattered on the floor. Anchored on the wall behind Beth's chair was a deer head with a snide toothy grin. White panties and pink socks hung off the deer's antlers. And the stench…oh, it reeked of rotten eggs. Stale cigarette smoke took Rachel's breath away, and she wanted to puke.

"Miss Thomas, have a seat," Rachel heard Beth say. Speechless and queasy, Rachel found an empty chair and sat. As soon as her bottom hit the seat, Rachel lurched right up. She looked down and noticed fine cracker crumbs all over the seat.

"Oh my," she gasped, but Beth didn't say a word. Rachel discreetly wiped the crumbs off the chair and sat again. With her handbag in her lap, she stared at the supervisor as Beth lit a Marlboro cigarette. Beth reviewed Rachel's resume, puffing on her cigarette until it was spent. When she was finished, she placed the cigarette on the edge of the ashtray, then opened up her desk drawer and took out a Snickers candy bar. She tore the wrapper off with her teeth and gobbled it up in a matter of seconds. Beth's fat cheeks bulged like a chipmunk as she chewed, swallowing and licking her thin lips. After the candy was gone, Beth peered over her bifocals, staring at Rachel with intense scrutiny. Bewildered, Rachel held her breath.

"Honey, why do you want to work here?" Beth asked in a sharp tone.

"Um, um." Rachel cleared her throat. "I'm very interested in the mental health field. I think this hospital will be a good place to get some experience."

"You don't say." Beth reached for another cigarette and lit it up. "Tell me why you think so."

Beth puffed smoke rings into the atmosphere while Rachel told her story. Beth's fiery green gaze through the haze of smoke made Rachel so nervous she thought her heart was going to jump out of her chest.

"After I finished graduate school, I decided to stay in Seattle. I like the area and thought I could begin my career here." Rachel's voice trembled.

"I see you graduated from the University of Washington," Beth stated in a gritty voice.

"Yes, ma'am."

"What makes you suited for this job?"

"Well, I worked in a nursing home and ran a caregiver's support group while there. I also took psychology classes in college."

Beth snuffed her cigarette out in the ashtray and popped out of her seat like a jack-in-a-box. Rachel lurched back, blinking her eyes erratically.

"Honey, this is no nursing home! These folks are off their rockers! Are you willing to work with a bunch of crazy folks?"

Shocked, every nerve ending in Rachel's body twitched, and she longed to leave. Too scared to move, Rachel sat there at a loss for words. Beth cocked her head to the side, looking like a big jaybird with big glaring green eyes.

"Honey, does the cat got your tongue?"

Rachel fidgeted in her seat and her face was warm with embarrassment. "I'm sorry…yes, ma'am, I can work with crazy people."

Beth grinned, clapping her hands. She swayed back and forth, from side to side like an excited fan at a football game. Rachel cringed. Beth's demeanor scared her as she waited for the woman to stop clapping. Finally, Beth settled in her seat, grabbing Rachel's application. This time, she studied it. After some minutes, Beth popped out of her chair again, and Rachel patted her chest with her mouth sagging open, frightened.

"The salary is forty-five thousand a year. Honey, do you accept this salary?"

"Yes, ma'am." Rachel was burning inside. She resented Beth calling her *honey*.

"Very well then, you can start in two weeks on Monday morning at eight."

"Thank you."

"You'll work with Doctor Michael Louis on the Admissions Unit."

"Great, I look forward to working with you and Doctor Louis." Beth's thin lips parted into a sardonic smile as she stepped to the door. Rachel took this as a clue the interview was over and was relieved. Beth swung the door opened and stepped into the smoky hallway. Rachel followed her out, and Beth locked her office door. When they both reach the unit exit, Beth unlocked the steel doors and shoved it open.

"See you November fifth, Monday morning, eight o'clock sharp," she grinned.

Rachel stepped out into the lobby and smiled at the supervisor. "I look forward to it."

Beth released the door, and it slammed shut, rattling the walls. Alone in the lobby, Rachel sighed with relief. She strutted toward the exit, shaking her head at the craziness of it all. Glad to be free from the smoky environment and Beth's nasty office, Rachel wondered if the second-hand smoke would make her ill. *Lord, I don't want to develop lung cancer*. It was an awful thought that she immediately put out of her mind.

Suddenly, Rachel heard a man yelling in the reception area. She stopped in her tracks and whipped around. A hippie-looking, middle-aged man with a red, bloated face was cursing and pounding his fist on the counter. He looked scraggy with his long matted blond hair hanging on his shoulders and a prickly mustache and beard covering his bulldog face. On the tip of his nose, he wore wire-framed glasses, and the sleeves on his wrinkled white shirt were rolled up to his elbows. Hanging on his back was a twisted striped tie, and he wore tan high-water pants with black loafers. The man had on no socks.

Joyce, teary-eyed, stood crunched over the counter with the wig heads, tolerating the man spewing obscenities in her face. "Hell, stop crying, woman! What's wrong with you? Hiram needs his damn patient report!"

Joyce mumbled something that Rachel couldn't hear. Out of the blue, the man punched each wig head onto the floor. He jumped and stomped on each one as tiny pieces of foam flew in the air. Joyce ducked for cover under the counter, and Rachel, who'd had enough of this unseemly crazy place, made a mad dash to the exit. Two security guards rushed through the main entrance from outside and ran past her. They pounced on the man and wrestled him to the floor.

"Get the hell off Hiram, you sons of bitches! Get the hell away!"

"Hold down that son of a bitch!" yelled one guard. "Hold him down!"

Rattled and outdone, Rachel made it to her Toyota. She unlocked the car, threw in her handbag, and climbed in. She cranked the ignition, backed up, and whipped her car around. She sped out of the hospital parking lot as fast as she could. Once safe on the main road, Rachel wondered who the looney man was, and why he was so angry.

Chapter Three

Monday, November 5th

Rachel hated Mondays with a vengeance. Getting up early to be somewhere on time after a relaxing weekend got on her nerves. She wished the weekend could last longer than the two days allotted. However, this Monday was different. She was starting a new job. Thrilled and nervous at the same time, a smile came over Rachel's face. She was glad she had a full-time professional job that paid well. She no longer had to pinch pennies to pay her bills.

This morning brought more fog and rain to the town of Salter's Point. A thick white mist hovered over the road forcing Rachel to turn on her headlights. As she navigated the slippery road, she could see South Campus Hospital ahead. Eager to start her day, she was excited about her new job. By the time Rachel reached the hospital and parked, the rain had ceased, but the fog was so thick only the outline of the building was visible. Dark outside, the sun wouldn't rise until eight o'clock, a common occurrence in the Great Northwest.

Rachel turned off the ignition and sat in her car as she prepared her mind for the day ahead. Feeling flushed, Rachel reached up and touched her forehead. She slapped the visor down and peered into the brightly lit vanity mirror. Beads of perspiration glistened on her face. She reached in her handbag and took out a tissue. Being careful not to mess up her foundation, Rachel lightly dabbed her face. She closed her eyes, momentarily inhaling deep breaths. Her anxiety was getting the best of her, and she desperately needed to calm down.

Soon Rachel felt calmer. She slapped the sun visor in place and opened her car door. When she stepped out of the car, the damp air felt cool against her face. With her handbag on her shoulder, she buttoned up her coat. Rachel grabbed her umbrella and locked the car door. She strutted to the hospital entrance with her high-heeled pumps clicking hard on the charcoal pavement. When she arrived, Rachel reached up and rang the buzzer instead of using the button. She waited for the sliding door to open. The door didn't move, so Rachel grabbed the handle, trying to pry it open. The door still wouldn't budge. Rachel pressed her nose against the cold glass door. She stared into the lobby and noticed Joyce sitting at her desk.

Rachel pounded on the door, but Joyce ignored her. Irritated, Rachel pounded on the door even harder.

"The doors don't open until eight," came a rough booming voice from behind her. Rachel spun around so quick, she almost lost her balance and fell on the ground. Catching herself, her eyes fell on a tall, slender man about six feet tall, wearing blue sweats and a knit wool hat. He was in the process of chaining his ten-speed bike to the rack. The man's sparkling blue eyes complimented his silver-gray mustache and beard. "You need a key to get in after hours," he added.

"Oh, okay," Rachel replied. She recognized him as the man she saw riding his bike on her way to her interview two weeks ago.

"Are you here for an appointment?"

Rachel cleared her throat. "Um, yes. I'm Rachel Thomas, the new social worker for the Admissions Unit, and this is my first day."

"Well, it's nice to meet you, young lady. I'm Doctor George Benny," he smiled, exposing a mustard-yellow grill. Rachel lowered her eyes, unnerved by his smile.

"Nice to meet you, too." *Damn, he looks like an overgrown Cheshire Cat, grinning like that!*

The doctor walked over. "I heard you were coming. We need a lot of help around here. Where are you heading?"

"To Beth Jones' office."

"Allow me to accompany you there."

"Well, thank you." Rachel smiled as she stepped aside to allow Doctor Benny to unlock the sliding glass door. He pulled the door open and stepped inside, holding it back until Rachel safely walked through. When he released the door, it slammed shut. Rachel followed him as he walked wide-leg across the lobby, and he waved as he passed Joyce's desk. Rachel refrained from waving, still sore Joyce had ignored her earlier.

When they arrived at the Admissions Unit, Doctor Benny unlocked the heavy steel door. He shoved the door open, moving to the side so Rachel could walk in. The door slammed hard behind him, and the floor shook beneath them. Rachel walked alongside Doctor Benny the short distance to Beth's office. Rachel coughed repeatedly, bothered by the strong cigarette smoke in the hall. George looked over at her with pity on his face. "Are you all right?"

"I'm afraid I'm allergic to cigarette smoke," she explained.

"That's too bad. Smoking is a common habit around here with staff and patients. I hope you can get used to it."

Annoyed, Rachel coughed again. The doctor's lack of concern for her health irritated her. *How dare he say that? He can get used to it! This smoking is for the birds!* Fuming, Rachel decided that during smoke breaks, she'd go outside. She didn't mind the cold. She'd rather breathe fresh air than die from smoke inhalation or, much worse, lung cancer.

Soon they were standing in front of Beth's office, and her door was slightly ajar. Cigarette smoke crept out of her office, causing Rachel to cough again. George banged on the door, but Beth ignored him. She was sitting in her high-back swivel chair with her feet propped on the desk, puffing on a cigarette. Her lime-green knee-high granny boots matched her low-cut flowing dress. Pinned on the left side of her head was a flaming lime-green hat. Beth looked like an evil leprechaun in a horror flick, and it took everything in Rachel's power not to laugh out loud. George pounded on the door again and waited a couple more moments. He grimaced and took the liberty to enter, clearly irritated by Beth ignoring him. He charged into her.

"What the hell is your problem this morning? Didn't you hear me knocking?"

"You called that knocking? It was more like pounding," Beth quipped as she flashed her big green eyes at him.

George gave her an icy stare. "You're so despicable at times," he mumbled under his breath.

"No more despicable than you," she shot back. It was clear to Rachel that these two didn't like each other. Beth smashed her spent cigarette in the ashtray and slid her feet to the floor. Straightening up in her chair, Beth gave Rachel an annoyed look as if she didn't want her there. "Good morning, young lady, I see you made it."

"Good morning, Beth. I'm excited to be here," Rachel replied with big eyes. Scared out of her wits, she wondered if a bomb was going to drop soon. Rachel flinched when Beth popped out of her chair wildly waving her hands.

"Take a seat. You don't have to stand there looking like a scared goose!"

George rolled his eyes. "Beth, you've no class," he mumbled. Beth glared at him, giving the doctor the silent treatment.

Jittery, Rachel pulled off her coat and sat in a chair across from Beth's desk. She was glad this time the seat was free from cracker crumbs. Styling in a red Liz Claiborne dress with matching two-inch pumps, Rachel realized she was overdressed compared to her new supervisor and Doctor Benny. *Tomorrow I'll wear something more casual.*

Sitting like a soldier, erect and straight, Rachel clasped her hands in her lap. Noticing her posture, Beth slyly teased, "Are you okay? You seem stiff."

"Yes," Rachel answered, her cheeks warm with embarrassment. She softened her shoulders and crossed her legs. Doctor Benny stood in the doorway, leaning against the frame, looking fierce.

Beth zeroed in on him. "Doctor Benny, have you heard from your patient Susan Cole? It's been two weeks since she disappeared from this unit."

The doctor scowled, curling his lips, and he snarled at Beth, "Don't you start with me! I haven't seen that patient nor heard from her!"

"Huh, huh, I bet." Beth rolled her eyes heavenward, not convinced. She sucked her teeth as she mockingly looked him up and down.

Doctor Benny jerked his head back. "What do you mean, you bet?"

"Come on! Susan Cole didn't leave this unit by herself. She had help, and I think you had something to do with it."

"Hell, you're speculating as usual!" he growled. "You don't know what you're talking about!"

Beth hissed at the doctor with narrowed green eyes, "The ethics committee is looking into this..."

"The ethics committee can kiss my ass!" Doctor Benny's face was red and contorted.

Beth stood up. "How dare you speak to me like that! Do you know how serious this is?"

The doctor stepped inside and slammed the door. Beth and Rachel drew back, startled. His nostrils flared, and the sparkle in his deep blue eyes disappeared, replaced with a fiery, steely gaze. Doctor Benny gritted his yellow teeth and sneered, "Get off my case! I have no idea how that woman got off this unit. So, again, you and that ethics committee can kiss my royal ass!"

Beth flung her hands on her hips. "There's nothing royal about your pasty ass!"

Rachel snickered, slapping her hand over her mouth. Doctor Benny looked wolfish, kicking the trashcan against the wall. He swung the door open with such force, it hit the wall and a screw popped from the hinges. The doctor stormed out with Beth yelling, "You damaged my door, you big pasty turkey!"

Beth stared at the doorway as if she expected him to return. When he didn't, she wobbled over and closed the door. She sat in her chair and reached for her half-spent cigarette. She puffed out several drags, and Rachel held her breath.

Beth spoke a minute later. "I know he's got something to do with that woman's disappearance! I know it! He's too damn defensive."

Shrugging her shoulders, Rachel had no idea what to say, so she said nothing. She found it odd that Beth suspected Doctor Benny. After all, he seemed professional enough. *Why would he risk his career to help a patient escape? What's in it for him?*

Beth interrupted her thoughts as she peered over her bifocals, snuffing out her cigarette. "How much do you know about Susan Cole's disappearance?"

"I heard it on the news." Rachel fidgeted in her seat. "I never knew her name until now."

Beth's gaze was stern. "What goes on in this hospital, you need to keep it in this hospital. Do you understand?"

Rachel felt her stomach knot up. "Yes, I understand."

Beth's demeanor softened, and she changed the subject. "Today, you're going to hang out with Jamie Lee. She works with that asshole Doctor Benny, but she knows the rules and will show you the ropes."

"Okay," said Rachel, forcing a smile. She was stunned by Beth's choice of words. *This woman has got some screws loose!* Rachel wondered if she could deal with Beth over the long haul.

"Are you still with me? You seem preoccupied." Beth's gaze was heated.

"Yes, ma'am, sorry," Rachel's face was hot with embarrassment.

"Then pay attention!"

Rachel sank in her seat, even more embarrassed.

Beth continued. "First, I'm going to take you to your new office so you can settle in. Then I'll take you to meet Jamie Lee."

"Okay," Rachel murmured.

Beth bolted from her seat and gestured for Rachel to follow. She opened her office door and took off. Rachel followed the supervisor out and walked alongside her as they made their way down the hall. Oodles of black eyes stared back at them from a sea of thick, white smoke. The patients' morning smoke break was underway, and Rachel gagged and coughed until they entered the dining room. A smoke-free area, Rachel reveled in the fresh air, taking deep breaths.

A woman dressed in a puffy, high-collared red dress with a paper crown on her head came up to them and curtsied, with a big, cheesy smile on her face. Her eyes drifted to Rachel.

"Hi, my name is Mary, Queen of Scots." She sounded like a squeaky mouse. "Madam, what's your name?"

Rachel pursed her lips, stifling a laugh. "Rachel Thomas, your new social worker," she managed to say.

"Pleased to meet you." The woman curtsied and cocked her head to the side. "Did you know honeybees hum in the key of F?"

"No," Rachel replied.

"Well, they do." The woman curtsied three times and spun in a circle. Facing Rachel again, she giggled. "And did you know flies have x-ray vision?"

Beth stepped in, rescuing Rachel. "Ellen, that's enough. You need to eat your breakfast before it gets cold."

"Sure," Ellen beamed as she hurried away, turning around once to glance back at Rachel. Beth leaned in close to whisper in Rachel's ear. Her breath smelled like stale cigarette smoke and chocolate candy. Rachel cringed, backing up a little.

Unfazed, Beth explained, "Ellen dresses in seventeen-century clothing because she's delusional. Her mother makes her costumes. Last week she thought she was Marie Antoinette."

Rachel chuckled. "I see."

They watched Ellen struggle with her big puffy dress as she attempted to sit at the table, knocking several breakfast trays onto the floor. Patients sitting at the table groaned with frustration as nursing staff ran over to clean up the mess. Laughing, Beth and Rachel exited the dining room. They passed Doctor Louis' office, and Rachel's was next to his. Doctor Louis' door was closed, and Rachel wondered if he was in there.

Beth read her mind. "Doctor Louis is out this morning. You'll meet him this afternoon."

"Good, I look forward to it." Rachel felt uneasy that the supervisor could read her thoughts.

Beth reached in her pocket, taking out two gold keys. One had green plastic trim around the top. "Here are your keys. The one with the green trim around it is your office key. Now open the door."

Rachel took the keys and inserted the green one in the lock, turning it clockwise. The door clicked opened, and Rachel stepped inside. It was dark, so she left the door open so the light from the hall could shine through. She patted the wall for the light switch, discovering it on the right side, and flipped it on. Her eyes widened in surprise as she gave her new office the once-over. The only furniture was a cherry wood desk and a high-back swivel chair. The space looked dreary because the office lacked windows. *I guess I'll need to spruce this place up with some wall paintings.*

Rachel stepped to her desk and sat in the chair. She spun it around, visualizing decorating her new space. Loud tapping came from behind her, and Rachel swung around. Her mouth flew open when she saw Beth in the doorway with both hands on her hips.

Beth glared at her, tapping her right foot. "Are you finished?"

Rachel scrambled out of her chair. "I'm sorry...I was just..."

Beth whipped around and left, cutting her off. Embarrassed, Rachel ran to the door. She shut the door behind her, and in two minutes she was walking alongside Beth. They walked together in silence, and Rachel welcomed it. Relieved she wasn't going to be scolded, she pondered what lay ahead. Soon they stopped at an office door with a placard scripted with the name *Jamie Lee, MSW* on it. Beth knocked and entered at the same time, and Rachel saw a woman with her feet propped up on the desk reading the Seattle

Times newspaper. Dressed in black, the woman was plain-looking with no makeup, and she had a jazzy salt-and-pepper pixie haircut. Rachel noticed her sad, light brown eyes reflected a life of pain.

The woman dropped her newspaper and flashed them a crooked smile. "Good morning, my people, what's up?" As she slid her feet to the floor and stood up, her eyes drifted to Rachel. "So, who do we have here?"

"This is Rachel Thomas, our new social worker. She'll be working with you here on the Admissions Unit."

Jamie offered her hand, and Rachel grabbed it. Jamie jerked her forward, gripping her hand so tight Rachel winced in pain. Jamie didn't seem to notice. "Hi there, and welcome. I'm Jamie Lee."

"I'm Rachel. Nice to meet you, too," Rachel squeaked as intense pain jolted through her hand and arm.

Jamie let go, and Rachel took a deep breath, rubbing her sore hand and arm as she glanced around the room for a place to sit. Every seat in Jamie's office was stacked with books, magazines, and newspapers. Rachel had no choice, so she remained standing. Beth wobbled over and handed Jamie a sheet of paper.

Squishing her face up, Jamie looked annoyed. "What's this?"

"Instructions. Show Miss Thomas the ropes and see to it she gets a picture ID."

"Will do." Jamie sighed, rolling her eyes. "Is there anything else besides what's on this paper?"

"No, just show her how things are done around here."

"Okay."

Satisfied, Beth wobbled out of Jamie's office, slamming the door behind her.

Jamie made a face. "I can't stand that woman. She gets on my damn nerves."

Jamie saw Rachel looking around the room and pointed to the sofa. "Shove those papers on the floor and have a seat."

"Thank you." Rachel gathered the stack of newspapers and set them on the floor, then sat on the sofa, making herself comfortable. Suddenly her eyes teared up, and she felt a tickling sensation in her nose. Rachel sneezed repeatedly, unable to stop as she inspected the sofa. Black fur covered the cushion where she sat, and the place reeked of stale alcohol and musty newspapers. The combination of cat hair and odors was wreaking havoc on Rachel's allergies. After five minutes, she was able to stop sneezing, but she sniffled, rubbing her nose hard.

"Are you all right?" Jamie asked, looking concerned.

"Do you...do you...aaaaachooo! Do you have a cat?"

"Yeah, why?" Jamie wrinkled her brow.

"I'm allergic to cats," Rachel squeaked.

Jamie grabbed a Kleenex box off her desk and gave it to Rachel. "I'm sorry, I didn't know..."

"I know..." Rachel sneezed again. She snatched a tissue from the box and blew her nose hard. It sounded like a foghorn.

"Damn!" Jamie said. "Are you trying to blow your damn brains out, girl?"

Rachel's laugh was weak. "I'm trying to make sure I get all the snot out."

Jamie shook her head. "Believe me when I say, there is no more snot in that nose!"

They both laughed out loud. Rachel liked Jamie immediately.

Jamie pointed to a wood chair by the door. "Move those books and sit in that chair. There's no cat hair there."

Rachel got up and moved the books to the floor. She sat, crossing her legs with both hands clasped around her knees. Jamie returned to her desk, looking apologetic. "I'm so sorry about your allergies, but the cat is my pet. I bring him to work with me sometimes."

"I understand." Rachel blew her nose again and threw the soiled tissue in a nearby wastebasket. Feeling a little better, Rachel peppered Jamie with questions. "What's the deal with Beth? What's her story? How is she as a supervisor?"

"Whoa, girl, one question at a time," Jamie chuckled.

"Sorry, I'm just curious." Rachel fell back in her seat.

"No problem. Let me tell you, Beth is basically bitchy and controlling, arrogant and rude. Slamming my door like she just did earlier is definitely her typical behavior."

34

"My goodness!"

"Yeah, she thinks she knows everything, likes to have it her way. When she came to Salter's Point Regional ten years ago, it was rumored she'd tried to kill her psychiatrist husband for running off with some scrawny young thing in his office!"

"You're kidding me? Is that true? How old was she when this happened?" Rachel sniffled, wrinkling her nose. The tickling sensation still bothered her.

"In her forties, not really sure. When I asked her about it, she denied it, cursing me out."

Rachel leaned forward, wide-eyed. "She really cursed you out?"

"Yup!" Thrilled she had a captive audience, Jamie ramped up the gossip. "It's also rumored that instead of shooting him and risk going to jail, she fought back another way."

"What did she do?" Rachel scooted to the edge of her seat, mesmerized.

"She drained his bank account, left town with their two teenage boys, got a job, and later went back to school to become a social worker."

"Well, she triumphed at the end. She got her revenge," Rachel sniffled.

"Yep," Jamie agreed.

"So, where are her two sons? Do they live here in Washington State?"

"Yes, they do. She helped them get through law school, and now they have families of their own."

Rachel uncrossed her legs and folded her arms across her chest. "Beth's weird, but you got to admire her tenacity and determination. How old is she now?"

"She's been a social worker for twenty-some years, so I think she's about sixty-three years old." Jamie paused, rubbing her forehead.

"Wow," Rachel answered, impressed.

"Girl, did you know she has a crush on Doctor Louis?" Jamie laughed, tilting her head back. "She tries to seduce him by wearing low-cut dresses, but he pays her no mind."

"Nooo…" Rachel's eyes were as big as an owl's.

"Now listen, girl, that Doctor Louis likes young pussy. He's married to a woman twenty years his junior."

Rachel squealed with laughter, slapping her hand over her mouth. "That's freaking hilarious," she replied with a muffled voice.

Jamie laughed, checking her watch. "I've got a meeting with Doctor Benny in an hour. Let's get started."

"You're assigned to Doctor Benny?"

"Yep. Beth didn't tell you?"

"No, she didn't. What's Doctor Benny like?" As far as she could tell from Doctor Benny's and Beth's disturbing interaction earlier, his reputation around the hospital was murky. She wanted to learn more about his alleged involvement with Susan Cole's disappearance.

"He's all right. He can be a bit eccentric at times." Jamie's face turned solemn. "When he gets angry, he becomes extremely passive-aggressive. Did you hear one of his patients took off from the unit two weeks ago?"

Bingo! She walked right into it! "Yes, I heard on the news that a patient escaped, but I didn't know the patient was his," Rachel fibbed with her eyes on Jamie.

"Yep, the patient is his, and her name is Susan Cole. The woman was diagnosed with a borderline personality disorder, and her escape is shaping up to be quite a mystery," Jamie said, lowering her voice.

"From what I read in the literature about patients with borderline personality disorder, they can be difficult to manage," Rachel whispered back.

"You're right. Between attention-getting suicide attempts and sabotaging their own treatment plans, they can be quite a challenge."

"Do you have any idea how she managed to escape?" Rachel scooted to the edge of her seat.

Jamie shook her head. "No ma'am, but it's rumored she and Doctor Benny were lovers, and he may have helped her escape."

Rachel fell back in her chair, floored. "Oh, my goodness!" she gasped. *Beth's rude behavior toward Doctor Benny now made sense. Surely the doctor isn't capable of committing such an act, messing around with a patient. That's unethical.*

Jamie changed the subject. "So, I hear you're going to be working with the Colonel," she said.

"The Colonel?" Rachel raised an eyebrow.

"Yeah, the infamous Doctor Louis."

"Why do you call him the Colonel?"

"Because he's a retired Army colonel and runs the Admissions Unit like a damn boot camp!"

Rachel giggled. Suddenly the hinges on the door rattled like a bag of old bones. Someone was pounding on the door.

Jamie stood up, frowning. "Who in the hell is banging on my door like a damn lunatic?"

The door swung open and hit the wall with a thud. A man burst in and stood in the middle of Jamie's office, scowling. Rachel immediately recognized the scruffy-looking man who had attacked the wig heads two weeks earlier. She popped out of her seat and parked herself behind Jamie Lee, spooked. Jamie twisted slightly around to glanced back at Rachel.

"I'm okay. I was trying to get out of the way."

Jamie shook her head and focused her attention on the scruffy man. She folded her arms across her chest. The man stood in front of her, posing with his hands on his hips, blinking his long eyelashes.

"Dude, what is it?"

"Hiram wants your list of patients for court tomorrow," he growled. He reached back and scratched his behind.

"What?" Jamie's face contorted into the shape of a pretzel.

"Hiram wants your list of patients," the man demanded again.

Seething with rage, Jamie handed the man her list. With the list between his right index finger and thumb, he stared at the paper, dropping it on Jamie's desk.

"The patients on this list are nothing but flies in the wrong soup!" the man said, flipping his blond locks to one side. Pissed,

Jamie shook her finger at him, and Rachel jumped back with her eyes big as saucers.

"Damn it, Hiram! Stop acting like a nitwit and talking in the third person! You're so ridiculous! Where are your manners? Don't you see our new social worker standing here? Introduce yourself!"

Hiram looked at Rachel and gave her a big silly grin. "Miss…"

"It's Rachel Thomas, sir," Rachel politely blurted.

"Well, hello, missy. My name is Hiram Gottchalks. I'm the attorney for the poor souls unjustly locked up in this hell hole," he calmly replied.

Rachel fell out laughing. She couldn't help herself. The man was a spectacle and hilarious. "You can't be serious," she muttered, pursing her lips.

"What? Hiram didn't hear you." He reached up, flipping his earlobe forward. Rachel regrouped.

"Did you say you're an attorney?" she politely asked.

"Yeah, missy, and what's it to you?"

"Forgive me. I don't mean to offend you." Rachel struggled not to laugh. She kept her eyes fixed on the floor to avoid eye contact.

"No problem," Hiram said with his eyes drifting back to Jamie. He poked his chest out, staring at her as if she had horns on her head. With a cunning expression on his face, Hiram told Jamie. "Please forgive me for my rude manners, my sweet Sugar Tits, but you, my little witch, are as rude as they come!"

Jamie lunged at him. "Get the hell out of my office, you weasel of a troll! I've had enough of your shenanigans!"

"My, aren't we bitchy this morning?" he teased with a wicked gleam in his eye. He sniffed the air like a dog as he backed up toward the door. "You smell like a pissy bottle of liquor! Have you been drinking again, Miss Lee?"

Chili-pepper red, Jamie grabbed her empty coffee cup and threw it at Hiram. He ducked, and the cup sailed over his head. It hit the floor, breaking into a million pieces. Hiram laughed like a hyena. "Sugar Tits, you missed!"

"You son of a bitch!" Jamie screamed. She grabbed another cup and charged the crazy attorney with Rachel following closely behind. Hiram bolted out the door, almost falling on his behind as he turned the corner and dashed down the hall. Jamie twisted her face as she stood at the door. She threw the cup at him and missed, and it landed on the floor in big chunky pieces.

"If you come to my office again, you little shit, I'll kill you!" she screamed. "Do you hear me, you little shit? I'll kill you!"

Hiram made it to the exit and stopped. He spun around and flipped Jamie the finger. Jamie lurched forward with her hands on her knees, breathing heavily. "Your shitty little troll!" she gasped under her breath.

"Not as shitty as you, Sugar Tits!" Hiram unlocked the steel gray door to the Admissions Unit and ran out. It slammed hard behind him.

Rachel stood over Jamie, rubbing her back, trying to comfort her. "Are you okay?" she asked, feeling worried.

Jamie was silent, still stooped over, her breathing ragged. She stood up and looked at Rachel with her face etched in pain.

"My lungs are shot. I stopped smoking a few months ago, but I still get short of breath." Jamie took a step and stumbled. Rachel grabbed her before she fell to the floor. Jamie leaned on Rachel for a few seconds until she regained her composure. Still unsteady, Jamie held onto Rachel's arm as the two women trudged back to Jamie's office. Once they were safely inside, Jamie separated herself from Rachel, stumbled to her desk, and plopped down in her chair. Rachel returned to her chair and remained quiet, waiting for Jamie to speak first.

As Jamie ducked under her desk, Rachel heard rustling papers and wondered what she was looking for. To her bewilderment, when Jamie sat up she held a half-full bottle of Jack Daniels. "I need a little nip. It's been a stressful morning."

Jamie twisted the cap off and put the bottle to her lips, turning it up. She gulped down the brown liquor with her throat pulsating violently. Jamie stopped a minute and took a breath. She winced and wiggled her nose. "Ahhhh," she moaned. She finished the bottle and tossed it in the wastebasket.

Rachel was stunned. She wondered what she'd gotten herself into by accepting a job at Salter's Point Regional. Not only was the hospital's attorney a full-blown maniac, but her social worker colleague was a drunk. *How did these two crazy people land a job in a psychiatric hospital? Can I work with these people?* She shook her head in amazement, resigned to her predicament. *I'm here now. I guess I can make it work.* Rachel glanced at her watch. She was already exhausted, and it was only eleven-thirty in the morning. *Is it time for a break? Boy, did she need a break!*

"Are you all right, sweetie?" Jamie asked with glassy eyes, interrupting Rachel's thoughts.

"Just tired," Rachel sighed.

Jamie left her seat and walked to the coffee pot sitting on an end table. She grabbed a cup and poured herself some coffee. "My dear, would you like some coffee?"

"No, thank you," Rachel calmly replied. She twirled her thumbs. "What's the deal with Hiram? He seems a little weird."

Jamie walked back to her desk and sat, sipping on her coffee. "He's more than a little weird. That weasel of a troll isn't normal. He's simply out of his damn tree!"

Rachel laughed. "Well, he's quite an interesting character, so tell me about him."

"To be truthful," Jamie sighed, "Hiram is quite intelligent. He graduated from Harvard at the top of his class, and instead of going into corporate law, he decided to be a defender for the little man."

"How compassionate, I'm impressed." Intrigued by the unusual attorney, Rachel then asked. "How old is he and has he ever been married?"

"Boy, you sure are nosey!" Jamie laughed.

"Social workers are trained to be nosey."

"Well, if you must know, nosey girl, Hiram is forty-five years old and divorced. The man is a nut! Always talking in the third person. It gets on my damn nerves."

"I noticed that. Why does Hiram do that?"

"Who knows. Two weeks ago, he went to a beauty supply store

and bought a bunch of wig heads. He painted their faces, put witches' hats on their heads, and lined them all up on the counter in the lobby."

"I saw those wig heads when I came for my interview. I wondered why they were there. What possessed Hiram to do such a thing?"

"Crazy," Jamie chuckled. "He thought the lobby needed sprucing up. He threatened to sue Joyce if she tried to take them down."

"Well, the lobby is very drab. It could use a makeover."

"Yeah, you're right."

"The first time I saw Hiram, I thought he was a patient. He was having a hissy fit in the lobby. He punched the wig heads onto the floor and stomped on them. He scared the holy shit out of me!"

Jamie laughed. "The man is a knucklehead, but I feel bad for him. I think he suffers from manic depressive disorder."

"How do you know?"

"Just the way he behaves."

"Has he ever been diagnosed?"

"No, not as far as I can tell."

"How does he get away with being so crazy?"

"I don't know," Jamie wearily groaned. "He just does."

Rachel wanted to know more. "Why does he look so dirty? He reminds me of a homeless man."

Jamie howled. "Hiram has money, but he chooses to live like a pauper. He lives in a garage in an old auto shop near the beach."

"I see. What did he mean when he made the comment about flies in the wrong soup?"

"Let me explain something to you." Jamie leaned forward, folding her arms on the desk. "Hiram believes the patients in this hospital don't belong here. He believes psychiatric institutions don't help them. He thinks patients fare better in the community with outpatient mental health than institutionalized and held against their will. So, he fights for them in court by getting their cases dismissed. Most of the time he's unsuccessful, but sometimes he's not."

"So, he works for the system, but he doesn't believe in it. The man sounds conflicted."

"You got it."

Satisfied for now, Rachel changed the subject. "I'm hungry. When is lunch?"

"Let's take a break. Meet me back here at one, and we'll go to personnel for your photo ID," Jamie suggested.

"Cool." Rachel stood on her feet and left Jamie's office. Within minutes she was back in her office. She sat in her swivel chair, opened her desk drawer, and took out her lunch bag. Rachel tore into it, took out her peanut butter and jelly sandwich, and took a bite, savoring the thick, nutty taste. She thought about Hiram and Jamie and how insane they seemed to be, amused by the craziness of it all. Rachel took another bite of her sandwich, chewing hard. She swallowed and muttered to herself, shaking her head. "Damn, this is one crazy place! I sure hope I can do this."

After lunch, Rachel returned to Jamie's office. She knocked and entered at the same time, and a big furry ball sailed past her. Rachel screamed, backing up. "What the hell is that?"

Jamie laughed. She stooped over and scooped the feline intruder into her arms. The cat's body was the size of a bobcat's, and its eyes were an eerie, penetrating bright yellow.

"He's not going to hurt you," Jamie tried to reassure her. "This is Peepers, my cat. I gave him the name because of his golden yellow eyes."

Rachel slowly closed the door, and her voice trembled. "That cat needs to be in somebody's zoo or a scary movie!"

Jamie laughed. "I know his size is intimidating, but he's harmless."

"What type of cat is it?" Rachel moved behind a chair, distancing herself from the feline.

"He's a Siberian. These cats are usually bigger than the average domestic cat."

"Just keep him away from me. He's too big for my taste!" Rachel sneezed, stooping over, covering her nose with her right hand. "Remember, I'm allergic to cats," she gasped, trying to catch her breath.

"Boy, don't I remember," Jamie smirked, laying the cat on the couch. The cat sat upright on his hind legs, licking his long black fur. He hesitated and stared at Rachel, his piercing gaze both hypnotic and mysterious. Rachel wondered what secrets Peepers harbored behind those golden yellow eyes.

"Jamie, you've got a creepy cat. He scares me."

"You'll get used to him. Everybody does eventually."

Jamie handed her a Kleenex box, and Rachel took a tissue and blew her nose. Although she was allergic, Rachel thought the exotic-looking cat was stunning with its thick black fur and sheathed claws. She could tell from his neatly trimmed coat that he was well-groomed and spoiled.

"Girl, let's go to personnel so Tran can make you a picture ID."

"Splendid," Rachel said as she kept an eye on Jamie's cat.

Peepers leaped to the floor and followed Rachel and Jamie out of the office and down the hall. When Rachel dared to look back, the exotic cat was gone. Rachel panicked.

"Girl, where is your creepy cat?"

"Stop worrying about my cat. He's out hunting for his dinner," Jamie teased with a wicked gleam in her eye.

"Ooo, gross!" Rachel moaned with disgust.

On their way to personnel, a man's scratchy voice boomed over the loudspeaker. Rachel looked up at the ceiling with her heart pounding wildly in her chest. The man's voice vibrated so loudly, it sent chills up her spine.

"Ladies and gents, can I have your attention, please? Can I have your attention, please? Butt Patrol is needed on Unit One. Butt Patrol is needed on Unit One."

Rachel grabbed Jamie's sleeve, stopping her. "Did he say..."

"Yup, you heard it," Jamie answered, giggling.

Rachel fell out laughing with her mouth stretched open. "Butt Patrol? What's a Butt Patrol?"

"It's a committee for sweeping cigarette butts off the floor," Jamie calmly replied.

The man repeated the announcement. "Ladies and gents, can I have your attention, please? Butt Patrol is needed on Unit One. Butt Patrol is needed on Unit One now."

Rachel giggled hysterically, looking at Jamie like she lost her mind.

"Girl, don't look at me like that. I can explain," Jamie insisted.

"I'm listening." Rachel was giggling so hard she barely got the words out.

"The patients throw their cigarette butts on the floor after they finish smoking. The charge nurse got tired of cleaning up after them, so he recruited some patients and named them the Butt Patrol Committee. Now they clean up their own butts."

Rachel bowled over with laughter. "That's the most ridiculous shit I've ever heard. Excuse my French!"

"Well, it's the truth," Jamie chuckled.

"This place is so unbelievable!"

After Rachel had her new ID clipped to her dress, the two women descended on Beth's office. The door was open, and they walked in. Glad to see them, Beth grinned, showing jagged brown teeth. Rachel inwardly cringed. *Beth, please stop smiling. You look ridiculous!*

"Ladies, how has your day been?" Beth asked in a syrupy sweet voice.

"Fine," Rachel fibbed. The truth was she'd been having a terrible day. Between her allergies, the cat, and the cigarette smoke, she was done with this place. She wanted to quit right there, but she needed the money. *Lord, help me find a way to get used to this job, please!*

Jamie grinned foolishly, choosing not to answer Beth's question. Irritated, Beth tore into Jamie with a salty vengeance. "Jamie, what the hell are you up to?"

"Why do I have to be up to something? You're so paranoid!" Jamie jerked her head forward, blinking her eyes in an exaggerated manner.

Beth scoffed. "Whatever!" Her flashing green eyes drifted to Rachel, and her voice turned syrupy sweet again. "Doctor Louis called out sick for the rest of the day. He'll be here tomorrow."

"Okay," Rachel answered, feeling relieved. She'd had enough of this crazy place. Rachel longed to go home where sanity awaited her.

To her surprise, Beth read her mind. "If you like, you can leave early. I don't have anything else planned for you today."

Hallelujah! Thank the Lord! I can't believe it! I'm done for the day! This time she didn't mind Beth reading her mind.

Rachel didn't waste any time telling everyone goodbye. She hurried to her office, unlocked the door, and grabbed her coat and handbag. Rachel stepped back in the hall and locked her office door. She practically ran down the hall. She couldn't wait to leave this looney bin. Unlocking the gray steel door with the key Beth gave her, Rachel shoved it open and stepped out into the lobby. She heard the door slam behind her as she made a mad dash to the hospital exit. Pressing the button, the sliding door open and Rachel walked out. Strolling briskly to her Toyota, Rachel searched her handbag for her car keys. She'd found them by the time she reached her car, unlocking the door and hopping in.

Rachel cranked the engine, backed out, and sped out of the parking lot. Could she work in such a crazy, unusual place? The people who worked at Salter's Point Regional were definitely looney, not the typical coworkers she was used to. Despite her reservations, Rachel found herself drawn in, fascinated by the challenge. She cracked up laughing when she remembered something Beth said in her interview two weeks ago.

"Lady, you're absolutely right. The people at Salter's Point Regional are definitely off their rockers. But, my dear sweet woman, they're not the patients, not even close!"

45

As soon as Rachel arrived home, she slipped out of her raincoat, dropping it on the floor. She tossed her handbag on the coffee table, flopped on the couch to call her dad. DeWayne Thomas, a psychology professor at San Francisco University, encouraged Rachel to pursue the mental health profession. She'd already told him about her crazy interview and her reservations about working at the hospital. Although he understood her anxiety around working with odd coworkers, he still felt the experience would be beneficial for her career growth. After bantering back and forth about the issue, Rachel had reluctantly given in to her father's reasoning. She'd promised to call him upon completion of her first day of work.

Still traumatized over the day's crazy events, Rachel grabbed the phone from the end table next to the couch. She welcomed the familiar buzzing, the only normal activity she had experienced all day. It wasn't long before she heard her father's husky voice on the line.

"Professor Thomas speaking."

Relieved he'd answered the phone, Rachel fell back on the sofa, crossed her legs, and shook one foot as she talked. "Dad, this is Rachel. I've got so much to tell you."

"I'll bet," he chuckled. "So, how was your first day?"

"Very crazy," Rachel sighed.

"Tell me about it."

"Dad, you're not going to believe this. My supervisor and one of the doctors got into an argument, and later the social worker training me drank whiskey right in front of me!"

"How do you know it was whiskey?"

"I saw the bottle. It was Jack Daniels."

"Damn!"

"I know. Then this same social worker got into a fight with the hospital attorney…"

"A fistfight?"

"Almost. She threw her coffee cup at him!"

Her father's laugh sounded shaky. "Sounds like a bunch of lunatics work there."

"I tried to tell you." Rachel hesitated, taking a deep breath. "And you know what's weird? When the hospital attorney talks to you, he refers to himself in the third person."

"Sounds like he's not wrapped too tight," he laughed heartily.

"Dad, I told you, this place is crazy. I feel so out of my element. I don't know if I can work with these people. They aren't normal," Rachel groaned.

"Look at it this way, sweetheart. At least you'll be entertained while you're learning new skills. After all, didn't you tell me you wanted to specialize in mental health?"

"Yes, but…"

"But what?"

Rachel dropped her shoulders, sighing heavily. Her father was right. He liked giving people advice. "I prefer to work with normal people. Professionals who are seasoned and have sense."

Her father cracked up again. "Sweetheart, give it a chance. Life, in general, is not tied up in a neat bow. There are variables, gray areas, and episodic bouts of pure insanity intertwined. You will gain valuable experience at Salter's Point Regional. You'll learn how to communicate with all types of personalities, including your crazy coworkers. Stay for a couple of years, get the experience, and move on."

"A couple of years?" Rachel yelped. "I'll be half crazy by then!"

"I promise, you won't," her father laughed. "As an old psychologist once told me, just do your eight every day and hit the gate!"

Rachel rolled her eyes. "Bye, Dad."

"Keep me posted."

"I will." Rachel hung up.

She sat for a while, thinking about her crazy new job. Her father had a point. She would be more marketable as a mental health professional if she stayed at the hospital for at least two years. Maybe she could be a supervisor like Beth or manage a whole department. With solid experience behind her, the sky was the limit.

Suddenly Rachel was more hopeful. *I'll stay put for now. The sacrifice is worth it. I can do this.* Rumbling in her stomach caught her attention and Rachel leaped to her feet, heading to the kitchen. "I'm starving. I need to find me something good to munch on."

Chapter Four

Friday, November 9th

By mid-week, a bruising storm-ravaged Salter's Point forcing the townsfolk to remain inside. The only time anyone dared to venture out was to go to work or to the grocery store. For two whole days, heavy rain assaulted the town. Muddy debris mixed with broken branches, paper, and dirt clogged the drains along the roads. Soon water overflowed into the streets, making driving in the area unsafe. Refusing to stay at home, Rachel took her chances and navigated the treacherous roads. Each day, she witnessed fire personnel dressed in yellow jackets shoveling twigs and muddy debris off the streets. By Friday, the rain retreated and a drier, more cooling front crept in with the sun's rays warming the area.

For the first time in a week, Rachel was able to see Mountain Rainier. The snow-capped fourteen-thousand-foot rock wonder looked terrific against the deep blue sky. The mountain stood in Puyallup, a city forty minutes from Salter's Point. Rachel drove through town on her way to work, admiring the oak trees with their dazzling red and yellow leaves. She chugged up the road toward the hospital and noticed pumpkins sitting on the porches of the residents' homes. With the rain gone and Thanksgiving only a week and a half away, town residents were looking forward to a festive holiday season.

At precisely seven forty-five, Rachel arrived at the hospital, waving at the stoic guard as she passed through the gate. He didn't smile, but he waved back, a welcome change from his usual demeanor. The parking lot at South Campus Hospital was almost full, forcing Rachel to park several yards from the entrance. Once she found a spot and parked, Rachel grabbed her shoulder bag and got out of her car. She locked the door, and the cool breeze whipped around her. Shivering, Rachel swore the temperature was twenty degrees instead of forty. Rachel strutted across the parking lot, zipping her black coat to her neck. To her right, she heard soft cooing. She looked and saw pigeons fluttering their wings and hovering over grainy piles of brown mush.

Rachel stepped over a pile of mush herself, rubbing her nose when she smelled the rank odor. She stopped and stooped down to inspect the unusual substance. *What is that? It sure does stink!* Bothered by the smell, Rachel stood upright and kept going. She reached the entrance and tapped on the button, and the glass doors slid open. When Rachel strutted into the lobby, she couldn't believe her eyes. The place had been transformed overnight.

Strings of paper pilgrims decorated the front of the reception area, and giant pumpkins with rustic glittery wreaths sat on each end of the counter. Bright orange lights hung over the bay window, across the ceiling, and over chairs and end tables. The floor was clean and shiny and smelled like fresh lemons. Rachel sneezed, bothered by the strong scent. Joyce heard her sneezing, and she came from the back and stood at the counter. Wearing a brown pilgrim dress with a shiny black belt buckled tight around her waist, Joyce's ample behind appeared two inches larger.

"Good morning, Rachel. Are you all right?"

"I'm fine. I'm allergic to wax. Hell, I'm allergic to anything with a strong scent," Rachel laughed.

"I'm sorry, dear, but the place needed brightening up."

"I know. It's about time." Rachel gave Joyce the side-eye.

"Joyce, why are dress like that? Thanksgiving is still a few days away."

Joyce frowned. "Does it bother you?"

"Oh, no, I don't mean to offend you. I was just curious, that's all."

"I like dressing up for the holidays. I'll be wearing something like this every day."

Rachel chuckled. "I see. Well, you looked festive."

"Thank you."

Warm perspiration beaded on her forehead. Rachel unzipped her coat, opened her bag, grabbed a tissue, and dabbed her forehead.

"Joyce, do you know when Doctor Louis will be back to work? I'd like to meet him."

Joyce slapped one hand over her mouth, shaking her head. "Oh, you don't know, do you?"

"Know what?" Rachel's eyes widened.

"Come here," Joyce whispered, looking around. "I don't want to say this too loud."

Rachel stepped to the counter and leaned over. "Okay, I'm all ears. What's going on?"

"Doctor Louis..." Joyce paused, scoping out the lobby again.

"Joyce, will you hurry up! I want to hear about Doctor Louis."

"Okay, I just want to make sure no one overhears me."

Rachel laughed. "Joyce, it's just you and me in this lobby. No one is going to overhear you."

"You're right. Doctor Louis is out ill," she whispered.

"Huh, huh."

"The poor guy had a heart attack one evening while having vigorous sex with his young wife, Sierra."

Rachel's mouth flew open. "Rigorous sex, you don't say."

"No one else knows," Joyce whispered. "He's home recuperating. His wife, a registered nurse, is looking after him, you know."

"Very interesting."

"I'll say."

The sliding doors opened and a tall woman with auburn red hair in a bun pranced in from the outside. She was plump, wearing a black raincoat with matching balloon slacks and toeless heels.

Her long fake eyelashes blinked erratically over her bright green eyes, and Rachel noticed she had a big shiny diamond on the fourth finger of each hand. *Who is this?*

"Good morning," she quipped in an English accent as she checked out the lobby. "It's about time someone did something to this dreary, awful lobby. Very festive, indeed."

"Thank the housekeeping staff for their hard work. How was your vacation?"

"Marvelous! My hubby and I went to the Oregon Coast and had a grand old time." The woman zeroed in on Rachel. "So, who is this young lady?"

"Our new social worker. She started over a week ago," Joyce said, glancing at Rachel.

Rachel stepped forward and held out her hand. "I'm Rachel Thomas."

"Sally Dobbins. Pleased to meet you." She shook Rachel's hand. "Where are you working?"

"On the Admissions Unit with Doctor Louis."

"Well, I'm the head nurse on that unit. Glad to have you." Sally leaned over, placing her elbow on the counter. "Speaking of Doctor Louis, I hear he almost met his maker the other day."

Rachel snickered, and Joyce jumped in. "Yeah, I heard that too."

"Well, at least it will be pleasant around here for a while. That man's personality is despicable." Sally looked at Rachel. "Is your office on the unit?"

"Yes, ma'am, it is."

"Let's walk." Rachel walked alongside Sally as she talked. "Dear, tell me where you're from."

"San Francisco."

"I love San Francisco. It's just a lovely place. Married? Have any children?"

Boy, she's nosey! "No, ma'am."

"So far, how do you like working here?"

"It's okay. I'm still settling in."

Sally stopped in mid-step and looked at Rachel, her brow deeply furrowed. Rachel wondered why the grim expression. "Miss Thomas, most people working here are a little bit touched in the head." Sally tapped her temple with her index finger. "Some of these workers need to be hospitalized."

"Why? What do you mean?" Rachel placed her hand over her chest, glad to hear someone other than herself thought some of the employees were a little crazy.

"They're nuts. Nuttier than your average fruitcake! But don't fret, dear. A few of us here, like myself, are very sane, indeed," she softly chuckled.

Rachel giggled. Sally was funny, and she liked her immediately. As the two women headed to the Admissions Unit, a man in an electric wheelchair whipped by, beating them to the door. He stopped and waited for them. Bald with thick black hair around his temples, the man had bushy black eyebrows and a handlebar mustache. Black-framed glasses covered his almond-shaped dark brown eyes, and he wore a candy-striped shirt with a black bow tie. His slacks and shoes were black, and Rachel struggled not to laugh out loud at the man. *Man, he's peculiar looking. He looks like one of the Marx Brothers...that dude Groucho!*

"Good day, ladies." His voice was pitchy.

"Good morning, Doctor Beebe," Sally said. "Have you met Rachel Thomas, our new social worker?"

"No, but was aware she's here," he smiled, glancing at Rachel. "Sorry, I haven't gotten around to meeting you yet. It's been quite busy lately."

"Nice to meet you, Doctor Beebe."

"Have you settled in yet?" Rachel swore he wiggled his eyebrows like Groucho Marx used to do.

"No, not yet. I have a few things to get for my office."

Doctor Beebe leaned forward. "What do you need? We may have it here."

"A couch, a rug, and a coffee stand would be nice," she smiled.

"I'll have maintenance to bring those items to your office today. We want you to feel at home here."

Sally raised an eyebrow. "Really, Doctor Beebe, this looney bin is a far cry from feeling like home!"

"Missus Dobbins!"

"I speak nothing but the truth, sir." She winked at Rachel. Sally unlocked the unit door and shoved it open. Doctor Beebe whipped through with Sally and Rachel walking in behind him.

"Good day, ladies," he said as he took off down the hall.

"I gather he's the medical director," Rachel surmised.

"Yes, he is. Doctor Beebe is a workaholic, committed to his career. He never married or had any children."

"Why is he in a wheelchair?"

"He had a stroke a few years ago. He whips around the hospital like he's in a race. It's a wonder he never runs into anyone."

Rachel laughed. "Sally, where's your office?"

"On the ground floor. Every morning, I stop by the nursing station to get a report before going to my office." Sally glanced at her watch. "And I'm late. Listen, if you have any questions about this looney place, feel free to ask."

Rachel placed one finger on her lips. "I do have a question."

"What's that, dear?"

"That brown mushy stuff on the ground in the parking lot. What is that? It sure does stink."

Sally cracked up. "My dear, it's bat poop."

"Bat poop?"

"Yes, bats hang out in the trees around the hospital, and at night, they like to hang upside down in the clock tower on North Campus."

Rachel sighed, dropping her shoulders. "This place never ceases to amaze me."

"Just wait," Sally laughed. "You haven't seen anything yet."

Later in the afternoon, Maintenance came to Rachel's office, bringing her a tan couch, a red rug, and a taupe metal coffee stand. Pleased Doctor Beebe kept his promise, Rachel had the men placed the sofa on the far wall. After they left, Rachel inspected the couch. The armrests were slightly worn, but otherwise the furniture appeared to be in good shape. She placed the rug on the floor in front of the sofa and stood back. *The sofa needs some color. I'll stop by Pike Place Market this weekend and buy some bright, pretty pillows to jazz it up.* After she placed the metal coffee stand in the corner, Rachel heard a knock on her door.

"Who is it?"

The door opened and Jamie stuck her head in. "Hey there, girl. Can I come in?"

"Oh, sure," Rachel grinned, waving her in.

Jamie stepped inside and closed the door, looking around. "Well, you've been here a week, and you still haven't decorated this dreary office. What gives? Do you plan to stay awhile?"

Rachel cracked up laughing. "Of course, silly. Maintenance came by a few moments ago and delivered this couch, rug, and coffee stand. I have an extra Mister Coffee pot at home. I plan on bringing it in. This weekend I'm going to Pike Place Market to shop for a few things. I'll have this place looking top-notch before you know it."

"Good." Jamie sighed, heading to the couch. She plopped her behind on a cushion and crossed her legs. "Well, Thanksgiving is coming up. Are you going home?"

"No, I'm going to hang out here. On Friday, after the holiday, I'm meeting a friend in Victoria."

Jamie blinked her eyelashes. "Um, is this friend, a man?"

"Yes…" Rachel hesitated. She turned around and sat in her chair. "He's a good friend, nothing romantic."

"Darn," Jamie chuckled, slapping her knee. "I wanted to hear some juicy details."

"Sorry to disappoint you," Rachel laughed. "And you, what are your plans? Anyone special?" Rachel's chair squeaked as she leaned back in her seat.

"I live with my girlfriend. We usually stay home, watch movies, and argue," Jamie snickered.

"Now that's boring," Rachel joked.

"Anne is boring, and of course she gets on my damn nerves. But I love her all the same."

"So, her name is Anne."

"Yep."

Nosey, Rachel had to ask, "Why do you two argue? It seems counterproductive."

Jamie shrugged her shoulders. "We're two different peas in the same pod."

"Never heard it put like that before."

The two women sat in silence for a brief moment. Rachel twiddled her thumbs, thinking about her planned trip to Pike Place Market. Then her thoughts switch to Thanksgiving again.

"Hey Jamie, I have a question."

"What is it?"

"Does the hospital cook Thanksgiving dinner for the patients who can't go home for the holiday?"

"Girl, girl, girl, Beth didn't tell you about the hospital's big Thanksgiving feast?"

Rachel rolled her eyes. "No, she didn't. It seems people around here like to withhold information. So, tell me."

"Every year, the hospital holds this big Thanksgiving feast for patients, their families, and staff who work the holiday. There's plenty of food and fun activities to do. A lot of the staff love this event. They sign up to volunteer. I, myself, prefer to stay at home."

"Sounds like fun. Can I volunteer?"

"Sure, help yourself. Just make sure Beth knows so you'll be paid for working the holiday."

Rachel's face brightened. "Cool, more money!"

Jamie stood to her feet and headed to the door. "I've got work to do. Let me know if you have any more questions. We certainly don't want you flailing around in the dark."

Rachel giggled. "Very funny, but I do have another question."

"What?" Jamie twisted around slightly with her left hand poised on the doorknob.

"I noticed some of the patients wear pajamas and some wear street clothes. Why the differences?"

"The nurses have the patients change into pajamas as soon as they're admitted. We don't want them wearing any clothing that can be used as a weapon. For example, taking a shoelace and trying to choke themselves or somebody else with it."

"That makes sense."

"After they've been here a week taking medications and participating in treatment, the doctor moves them to phase two. They're transferred to an unlocked unit, free to come and go during the day when not in a group, and allowed to wear their own clothes."

"Very good. Thanks for the clarification. I guess since I'm on the Admissions Unit, all my patients should be wearing pajamas."

"Unless they refuse to change into them. Sometimes, psychotic patients do. They want to be the one to make the decision."

Rachel took a deep breath. "I can imagine."

"Anything else?"

"Nope, I'm cool." Rachel swung her chair back and forth, and Jamie opened the door.

"See you later. Call me if you have any more questions."

"Don't worry, I will." Jamie walked out and shut the door behind her.

Rachel swung around in her chair, thinking about what Jamie shared. "Boy, I have a lot to learn," she sighed.

Saturday, November 10th

Rachel hopped on the metro in front of her apartment and rode downtown to Seattle's Pike Place Market. It was a cold and sunny morning with not a cloud in the sky. Wearing her favorite wool red jacket, Rachel wore a matching red hat and scarf. When the bus turned left on First Avenue, Rachel tugged the bell cord and got off. On the sidewalk a block away from the market, Rachel checked out the bustling scene.

The area was lively. Buses and cars whizzed by. People bundled in coats and hats hurried up and down the sidewalk or across the street. Wrapped in a tattered Seahawk blanket, Rachel noticed a homeless man sound asleep in a nearby corner. She wondered how he could sleep so soundly with all this bustle and cold. Rachel shoved her handbag over her shoulder and headed to the market.

She passed a couple of boutiques as well as an outdoor eatery. Men and women huddled around small wood tables, shivering in the cold. Some rocked back and forth, trying to keep warm while waiting on their breakfast. Others were already eating breakfast while others finished with their meal and enjoyed a cigarette. Rachel kept going until she arrived on the steep hill leading down to the market. Turning right, she slowly trudged down the slope gazing out at Elliot Bay in front of her. Small sailboats bobbed along the sharp waves while speed boats racing each other clipped pass them. Seagulls soared in the sky, and Rachel marveled at the breathtaking scenery.

Finally, she made it to the bottom of the hill. Her calf muscles ached from walking down the steep incline. Rachel stopped to stretch her legs, then continued on her way. The market was vibrant, as usual, crowded with hundreds of farmers, craftspeople, shops, and small businesses. People moved in and out of booths along the cobblestone street, either purchasing items or looking. A robust and nutty whiff of coffee caught Rachel's attention. Several people gathered in front of Starbucks, and Rachel hurried over to get in line. Cold, but not freezing, Rachel yearned for a hot cup of coffee to warm her insides.

After standing in line for eight minutes, Rachel received her coffee. She paid for it and left the store. Rachel sipped her beverage as she waded through the thick crowd to the fish market. Rachel always stopped there to watch the fishmongers throw salmon back and forth to each other. People seemed to slow to a standstill by the time Rachel reached the fish display. Rachel could hear the fishmongers shouting, but she couldn't see for the crowd. Rachel looked around and spotted a wood banister. She fought her way through the crowd, and once there, Rachel climbed up on it and sat down. A huge sign hung from the rafter that read *Caution: Low Flying Fish*.

Rachel watched men with ruddy faces and soiled rubber overalls throw salmon back and forth over the crowd. The crowd cheered and clapped their hands. The fishmongers threw fish all day as long as the people kept buying. For twenty long minutes, Rachel watched the fishmongers throw fish back and forth. Eager to get to her shopping, Rachel slid off the banister and then took off up the stairs to the second level.

The shop she liked, Hands of the World, was known for its funky home décor. When Rachel entered the shop, she smelled cinnamon in the air. On the counter next to the cash register, a brown candle burned in a glass vase. A woman with dark onyx eyes stared at her as she approached. Rachel noticed how different she dressed. She had on a purple pleated peasant skirt with a low-cut vintage lacey black blouse. Tacky glittery jewelry hung from her neck, and the woman wore large hoop earrings. She had a purple scarf wrapped around the crown of her head with tangled black hair hanging on her shoulders. Bangle bracelets dangled on each wrist, and every time she moved the jewelry tingled. *This woman looks like a gypsy.* Rachel walked over.

"Hi, your shop smells so good."

"It's the candle," the woman replied in a husky voice, turning the vase around. "Cinnamon is a scent that is warm and puts out good vibes." The woman grinned, and Rachel noticed a massive gap between her two front teeth. "Ma'am, can I help you? Are you looking for anything in particular?"

Rachel twisted around, scoping out the place. "As a matter of fact, I am."

"Tell me." The woman walked around the counter.

"I started a new job, and I need to spruce up my office."

"Congratulations on your new job. So, what do you have in mind?" She tightly clasped her hands, staring at Rachel with piercing determination.

The woman's unrelenting stare creeped Rachel out. "Let me look around for a minute. If I find anything, I'll let you know."

"Very well. If you need anything, my name is Roma."

"Okay, thank you." Rachel watched the woman returned to the counter and sit on a wooden stool. She kept her eye on Rachel as she moseyed around the shop. Rachel took her time, picking up items and inspecting them, then placing them back on the counter. Soon Rachel found two red pillows, a lampshade, and two colorful paper-mache clowns. Rachel examined the clowns and chuckled to herself. *These clowns fit the bizarre place I work.* Rachel carried the items to the checkout counter.

"I see you found something you like," Roma grinned.

Damn, she's scary looking. I wouldn't want to meet her in a dark alley. Rachel smiled back. "Yes, but I'm not finished. Can I leave these here? I want to take a look at your posters."

"Sure."

Rachel moseyed over to the poster rack and fingered through the prints. She noticed an eleven-by-seventeen sized poster of the space needle and took it out of the frame rack. Rachel checked it out and decided to buy it. She stood it up against the rack while she searched through the rest of the posters. It wasn't long before Rachel found another with a picture of Mountain Rainier on it. She grabbed the two posters and went to the checkout counter.

"I think I'm done," she smiled. "I don't see anything else right now."

"Wonderful! I'm glad you're pleased." Roma rang up the items while Rachel looked at pictures on the wall behind the counter. A big poster with the words *No Smoking* scripted on the top caught her attention. Right below the terms, a woman's bright eyes peered out from a haze of thick, white smoke. She had thick bushy eyebrows and a lit cigarette dangling from her pale, pursed lips. Rachel laughed out loud at the poster's humor, and Roma flinched violently, startled.

"What's so funny?" she croaked.

"That poster right there!" Rachel could hardly contain herself.

She giggled, shaking her index finger as she pointed at the poster on the wall. "I've got to have that poster! I hope it's for sale!"

Roma whirled around to look at the poster. "Oh, you like it?"

"I love it!"

"Then it's yours for ten dollars."

Rachel was stunned. "Why so cheap?"

"Everybody who comes in here and sees that poster hates it. I've had it for three years. Nobody wanted to buy it until now."

"Well, I love it! It will go perfectly in my office. Smokers where I work look like the woman in the picture."

"Then it's yours." Roma took the poster off the wall and slid it into a paper bag. "This poster is a guaranteed conversation piece. You won't have to worry about anyone smoking in your office."

"That's the point," Rachel giggled. "I know exactly where I'm going to put it."

Roma finished ringing up the items and placed them in a shopping bag. Rachel paid for her merchandise and happily walked out of the shop. Her stomach growled as she hurried down the stairs. *I think I'll stop by Pike Place Chowder and get me some of that good old clam chowder before I go home.*

Chapter Five

Tuesday, November 13th

Rachel walked into the lobby and saw a large white rubber turkey with juicy red lips propped between two giant pumpkins on the counter and made her way over. Joyce was staring hard at the turkey with both hands on her hips. She was wearing her pilgrim dress. *My goodness, what's gotten into her?*

"Good morning, Joyce. What's wrong?"

"Don't you see this mess?" she pouted. "This rubber turkey has ruined my pumpkin display. I worked so hard on it."

Rachel's eyes widen. "This turkey isn't yours?"

"It sure in the hell isn't!"

"Then whose is it?" Rachel poked the turkey's stomach then picked it up.

"Put that down. Hiram will have a fit!"

Rachel placed the turkey back on the counter, squealing with laughter. "How do you know the rubber turkey belongs to Hiram?"

"Who else would do something so damn silly?" Joyce frowned.

"Joyce, come on, where's your sense of humor? I think it's creative and quite funny."

"Oh, please. I don't appreciate Hiram moving my pumpkins around to make room for this ugly rubber turkey!"

"Oh, relax, he's just having fun. If you don't like it, tell him to move it."

Joyce shook her head violently. "I wouldn't dare ask him to move his precious rubber turkey. I don't want that man yelling at me."

Rachel giggled, nodding her head in agreement. "Well, you're right about that. He's a pistol when he's mad."

Joyce waddled to her chair and flopped her ample behind in the seat, folding her arms.

Rachel sighed, shaking her head. She took off, waving at Joyce. "You and that rubber turkey have a nice day," she teased.

"Not funny!" Rachel heard Joyce yell. She cracked up laughing as she hurried through the lobby.

At her office, Rachel unlocked door, opened it, and stepped inside. She flipped on the wall switch, turning on the light. On the back wall, her *No Smoking* poster with the lady engulfed in smoke hung over the couch. *I couldn't have picked a better spot for that poster! Now everyone will see it when they first walk in. No smoking is allowed in this girl's office.* Rachel smiled, proud of herself.

On each end of the couch were two red pillows. The red rug was sprawled on the floor in front of the sofa. On the right side of the office, Rachel arranged her desk and swivel chair in a diagonal slant so she could view the door more easily. The red lampshade she bought at the market matched perfectly with the gold lamp base she'd brought from home. The lamp sat on the right side of the desk, and the two paper-mache clowns sat on the left. A few feet from the door, a coffee stand sat in a corner. A Mister Coffee pot sat on the top shelf, and a bag of coffee, three red mugs, and a box of crème and sugar packs were stored neatly on the bottom.

Craving a hot cup of coffee, Rachel shut the door and hung her coat on the rack. She went to her desk and opened the bottom drawer. Rachel dropped her handbag in the drawer and closed it. She made a pot of Caffe Verona, and soon her office smelled like fresh coffee. Rachel's mouth watered. Feeling impatient, she eagerly poured herself a cup before the pot stopped gurgling. After she put the crème and sugar in her coffee, Rachel took a sip, closing her eyes. *Ahh, so good. So very good.*

Rachel returned to her desk and sat in her chair, sipping on her coffee. She thought about Jamie and wondered if she'd had her morning brew. Rachel decided to give her a call. After all, she had plenty of coffee to share. Rachel set her cup on the desk and dialed Jamie's number. When Jamie didn't answer, she hung up. She checked her watch, and it was eight forty. *The admissions meeting is going to start in twenty minutes. I need to go early and get me a seat. There are never enough seats to go around in these meetings.*

Rachel tucked her pen behind her ear and grabbed her coffee and notebook. She left her office and hurried straight to the conference room. When Rachel walked in, she heard sobbing. Rachel found Jamie slumped over the table with her arms around her head.

"What's the matter with you?" Jamie raised her head, and Rachel noticed her eyes were puffy and red.

"Anne is messing around on me," Jamie whined, laying her head back on the table.

"Really? How do you know?" Rachel pulled out a chair and sat.

"Anne came home at six this morning! She refused to tell me where she was! We had a huge argument, and she threatened to leave me. She thinks I'm possessive!"

"Are you?"

"I don't think so," Jamie bawled with her shoulders jerking up and down. Rachel scooted her chair closer to Jamie and patted her back. A whiff of stale alcohol tickled her nostrils. Wrinkling her nose, Rachel spoke in a soft voice.

"Listen, give Anne some space for a couple of days. Once you're less emotional and calmer, bring up the subject again."

"Okay," Jamie sniffled. She raised her head again and looked intently at Rachel with red, tear-filled eyes. "Do you think God is punishing me?"

Rachel's eyes widened, caught off guard by the question. "What do you mean?"

"Some people think I'm committing a holy sin by having a romantic relationship with a woman."

"I wouldn't worry about what other people think, but I do believe your relationship with Anne causes you a lot of grief."

"You're right. It's not healthy." Jamie took a deep breath and fell back in her chair.

"You and Anne spend a lot of time fighting. It's time for you to evaluate whether you want to stay in this relationship. Besides, do you want someone cheating on you?"

"I guess not." Jamie poked her bottom lip out as she wiped tears from her face. She gave Rachel a puppy-dog look and whined, slinging snot from her nose. "But, I love Anne!"

Rachel frowned, annoyed with Jamie's poor manners. "You may love her, but it's not fun living with someone you can't trust. Believe me, I know."

"What are you saying?"

"I'm just making a point." Rachel wasn't willing to tell Jamie about her own bout with betrayal. To her, it was still too raw and painful to talk about.

"Well, I guess you're right. I've got a lot to think about." Jamie stood on her feet, swaying forward on the verge of losing her balance. She steadied herself and moved toward the door.

"Are you okay?" Rachel asked, feeling very concerned.

"I'm okay, just feeling a little woozy. I'm going to the bathroom. I'll be right back."

"Be careful," Rachel said.

Jamie left the conference room, and at nine o'clock the nursing staff trotted in, congregating around the conference table for the admissions meeting. Before long, Sally Dobbins strode in, taking her seat at the head of the table. Sally was forty years old, and she looked her age. She smoked like a chimney, a habit she adapted to calm her nerves. Her auburn hair was pulled into a thick bun as always, and she wore an extra-large flowery blouse over black slacks with a pair of black heels. A vain woman, Sally strutted around the hospital like a peacock, blinking her long fake eyelashes and showing off the diamond rings her retired general husband gave her. Despite her bragging and pompous demeanor, Sally was witty and a compassionate soul. Celebrated as a good nurse, the patients of Salter's Point Regional loved her.

"Good morning, my beautiful people!" Sally playfully shouted.

"Good morning!" Everyone smiled at one another as they shifted in their seats.

"It was a full moon last night," Sally declared. "Some interesting characters were admitted to the hospital."

"Tell us about it!" Jamie strode in looking chipper and glassy-eyed. She wrenched a chair away from the table and sat down, signs of her previously upset no longer there. Rachel wondered if Jamie had a few drinks while holed up in the bathroom.

"Well, let's see." Sally took a deep breath. "Last night, an engineer was brought in for throwing his computer equipment out a three-story window and giving away thousands of dollars to random people on the street."

"Where was I when this crazy fool was giving away thousands of dollars?" someone hollered from the back. "I could've used that money to get my freak on at the strip joint!" He laughed at his own joke while his colleagues twisted around, glaring at him. Stone-faced, Sally pressed on.

"Two schizophrenic men in their early twenties were also admitted to the hospital last night. One thinks he's Jesus and almost drowned while trying to walk on water in Puget Sound. The other complained he hears female voices telling him to flip somersaults every five minutes."

"I know he's tired as hell," Rachel smirked. Everyone cracked up laughing, shaking their heads while Sally stared at Rachel with disgust. Rachel scooted down in her seat, twiddling her thumbs, grinning from ear to ear. Sally's disapproval didn't faze her one bit.

Sally continued. "Finally, we have a high school teacher in her early thirties claiming to have multiple personalities."

"How many personalities does she have?" asked a nurse.

"Her family reports she often changes into three personalities, a four-year-old girl, a professor, and a prostitute."

"Damn, what a combination!" Jamie chuckled.

"Yeah, this chick is definitely messed up!" Rachel agreed. Everyone howled with laughter.

"So, what personality is she this morning?" Jamie asked.

"Well, she's dressed like a prostitute this morning." Sally leaned back in her seat and folded her arms across her breast. "The principal at the school where she teaches called the police after receiving complaints from parents that she was seducing their teenage sons during class."

"Damn, this chick is a trip! I bet her interview will be a blast!" Jamie wickedly cackled.

Sally, unamused, cut her eyes at Jamie. "Get serious! We need to get our ducks in a row before taking these patients to court. Hiram will fight us all the way."

Rachel laughed out loud. "Oh, please! Hiram should be committed himself!"

Loud laughter erupted around the table, and Sally joined in. "You've definitely got a point," she giggled. "But we're stuck with him, so we must deal with him and his crazy antics."

"Ugh, he makes me ill!" Jamie snapped.

"He's funny to me," Rachel giggled.

Jamie rolled her eyes. "You would think that!"

Sally jumped to her feet. "Well, people, that's all I've got this morning! Everyone enjoy your day at the nuthouse! Meeting adjourned."

Sally pranced to the exit with several nurses following behind her. When the last nurse had left the conference room, Rachel and Jamie were alone. They sat together, not talking, both engaged with their own thoughts.

After a few moments, Jamie's gritty voice broke the deafening silence. "I'm so behind in my paperwork. I need to catch up. Will you handle the interviews with Doctor Benny this morning?"

Rachel took a deep breath. She knew full well Jamie was lying. Rachel was keenly aware that Jamie wasn't over her argument with Anne, and when upset, she avoided seeing patients. Reluctant but feeling she had no choice, Rachel sighed heavily.

"I'll cover. Don't worry."

"Thank you so much!" Jamie looked away, fidgeting in her seat. "Look, let's get lunch later, my treat."

"Okay, cool. What time?" Rachel slid out of her seat with her notebook and coffee mug and headed to the door.

"Is noon okay?" Jamie hollered.

"Fine with me," Rachel said as she walked out the door. She balled up one fist, frowning as she hurried down the hall to Doctor Benny's office. "Does Jamie expect me to do her work and mine too? What nerve! I better have a chat with this chick before I lose my religion," she grumbled out loud.

Before long, Rachel knocked on the doctor's door. She opened it and stepped into his sparsely decorated office. Other than his desk, a lamp, and his swivel chair, the only other furniture in the office was a worn dark brown leather loveseat and a folding metal chair. The lack of pictures on the wall made his office cold and unwelcoming. Hunkered down at his desk with his bald head buried in a chart, the doctor dictated notes into an antiquated tape recorder.

"Good morning, Doctor Benny!" Rachel greeted him in a cheerful tone as she shut the door.

The doctor looked up and broke out into a huge grin. He clicked off his recorder, looking like a hyena with his dingy yellow teeth. "What's up?"

"I've been directed to assist with interviews this morning. Jamie doesn't feel well. She and Anne had a spat, and she's out of commission." Rachel set her notebook and coffee mug on the doctor's desk and snatched the stress ball. She squeezed it tightly with twisted, exaggerated anguish on her face.

Doctor Benny's blue eyes crinkled at the corners and he growled with laughter.

"What's so funny?" Rachel said, frowning.

"You seem stressed out."

Rachel forced a smile. "I'm just irritated."

"I can see that. You're squeezing that ball pretty tight." He leaned back in his chair, clasping his hands together behind his head. "So, you say Jamie and Anne are on the outs again."

"Yep! Jamie is in her office sulking, and she had the nerve to ask me to cover for her."

Doctor Benny's brow furrowed as he peered over his wire-framed eyeglasses. "You're aware Jamie is self-absorbed and a problem drinker," he calmly reminded her.

"Yeah, but..."

"But what?" he asked, raising one eyebrow.

"Jamie's not an alcoholic. She can stop drinking anytime," Rachel argued.

"That's bullshit, and you know it. Her drinking is out of control. One day, it will be the death of her."

Fuming inside, she knew he was right. Unwilling to let on she agreed with him, Rachel insisted otherwise. "She'll get it together. You'll see."

"I hope you're right. But I must warn you, past efforts to get Jamie to stop drinking failed. I admire your loyalty, but I'm afraid you're wasting your time."

Rachel frowned, drawing in a deep breath. "Doctor Benny, you're certainly entitled to your opinion."

Doctor Benny blew out his cheeks and promptly changed the subject. "I understand we have four admissions to see this morning."

"Yep, which one do you want to see first?" Rachel asked, still squeezing the stress ball.

"How about Lola, alias Mary Peters? Her story sounds pretty interesting, with her claim of multiple personalities."

Rachel dropped the stress ball in a box on the doctor's desk. "Can I see her chart?"

"You certainly can." Doctor Benny gave Rachel a rectangular metal folder. She leafed through the progress notes, pausing at an old psychosocial history Jamie wrote three years ago. Mary, a newlywed at the time, taught high school in Bellevue, Washington, ten and a half miles outside of Seattle. On her thirteenth birthday, her favorite uncle raped her behind her father's shed. The sexual trauma adversely affected her ability to cope when under stress, no matter how minor. A different personality emerged like a character in a movie or play, and Mary changed her voice and physical appearance to avoid facing her perceived stressor. Her immediate family grew used to her episodic bouts with mental illness, but her husband, although he loved her, never adjusted.

Rachel grew more intrigued as she read Mary's history. She learned Mary was going through a messy divorce, the underlying reason for the sudden change in personality. Rachel understood that behaving like a prostitute helped Mary to cope with her new stress. Sighing heavily, Rachel closed the chart, feeling sorry for Mary. She looked at Doctor Benny and softly said, "I'll find Mary and bring her to you."

"Great, I heard she's in the patients' lounge."

Rachel opened the door and walked out, leaving the doctor's door wide open. On her way, she ran into a man in tan pajamas performing somersaults in the hall. Moving fast in her direction, Rachel jumped out of his way as he flipped by. He stopped for a moment, and their eyes met. Rachel could see the agony in his frightened onyx eyes. Dropping her shoulders in remorse, Rachel recalled the flippant remark she made about the man during the morning meeting. *Girl, shame on you! How could you be so insensitive!*

The man flipped again, and Rachel watched him perform somersaults in the hall until he disappeared around the corner. Inhaling deeply, Rachel trudged on until she walked into the patients' lounge. Rachel stood in the entrance with her brown eyes searching the room for Mary. She found her sitting with her legs crossed at the knees on the armrest of a tattered plaid sofa. Definitely a lady of the night, Mary seductively licked a lollipop. Her brown hair hung on her shoulders like a messy mop, and she wore a low-cut, see-through pink blouse, a black leather mini skirt, and fishnet stockings with matching stiletto heels. Mary swung her leg back and forth with one high heel hanging off her foot. The bright red lipstick she wore along with the blue mascara on her long eyelashes added drama to her light brown eyes.

Rachel took a deep breath, making her way over. "Good morning, Miss Peters!"

"Please, the name is Lola. Good morning to you, sweet cakes!" Mary's deep scratchy voice sounded like a man's, which Rachel found unsettling. She didn't like being called "sweet cakes" either.

"The name is Rachel Thomas. I'm your social worker today."

"Okay, Raaa-chell," Mary flippantly enunciated each syllable in Rachel's name.

Rachel kept her poker face. "Doctor Benny and I want to interview you."

"Sure, Raaa-chell!"

Rachel rolled her eyes heavenward, turning her back on Mary. "Come with me. Let's go to Doctor Benny's office."

Mary slid off the armrest and followed Rachel through the lounge. Rachel heard whooping and hollering and swiftly turned around. A group of men huddled in a corner were gawking at Mary. They whooped and hollered when she switched her hips right and left, and she puckered her lips and blew out some kisses.

Irritated by what she saw, Rachel gave Mary a tongue lashing. "Stop teasing the male patients! It sends mixed messages!"

Mary's smile was wicked. "If you say so, sweet cakes! Don't mean any harm."

Rachel shot Mary the evil eye. They walked together in silence all the way to Doctor Benny's office. Mary sashayed in and flopped her behind on the love seat. She licked her lollipop, twirling a strand of hair around her pinkie finger. Rachel closed the door, unfolded the metal chair, and sat. The doctor left his seat and dragged his chair to the front of his desk, sitting across from Mary and crossing his long legs.

"Miss Peters, my name is Doctor Benny. I've read your chart and know why you're here, but I would like to hear your story."

Mary stopped licking her lollipop and winked at the doctor. She slowly opened her legs, showing her crotch. She was wearing red panties. "What's shaking, handsome?" she crooned.

"Tell me your story. I know you have one." Doctor Benny leaned forward.

"Are you a trick?"

"No, Mary, I'm not," he managed to reply in a calm voice. Mary lifted her bottom and shoved her skirt up. Water beaded on the doctor's forehead as he twisted around in his seat to grab Mary's chart. He laid the chart on his lap, pressing down on it, and fidget in his seat unable to keep still.

Rachel stared at the doctor, checking him out. Something felt off to her. He was acting pretty strange. Rachel gasped with horror when she saw the hard ridge in his pants. *I don't believe this shit! Is he for real?*

Spell-bounded, Rachel held her breath, keeping one eye on the doctor and the other eye on Mary. Unnerved by Mary's sultry grin, Rachel kept quiet, deciding to let Doctor Benny handle the interview for now.

"Are you feeling hot, doctor?" Mary seductively asked as she swung her left leg back and forth.

"Let's stick to why you're here," Doctor Benny redirected her. "I understand you're a schoolteacher…"

Mary interrupted him, frowning. "This old geezer of a trick arrested me for messing around with the younger tricks!"

"Whom are you talking about?" Doctor Benny half chuckled.

"The principal!" Mary said, raising her voice. She continued to spout off, twirling her lollipop in her fingers. "He's just jealous! What makes him think I want his old crusty butt? I prefer a good-looking trick like you!"

The doctor rubbed his forehead and groaned. "Mary, do you realize the tricks you're speaking of are minors, teenage boys? You can go to jail for such behavior."

"You don't say? No wonder the old fart was so upset." Mary rolled her leather skirt to her waist and spread her legs wide. She scooted further down on the sofa, swinging her thighs back and forth, sucking on her lollipop, looking wide-eyed. Perspiration rolled down Doctor Benny's face. Rachel, not sure what to do, looked on with big eyes. *Damn, can't he control himself? What's wrong with him? Do I need to intervene?* Frozen in place, Rachel sat there. She cringed when Mary blew Doctor Benny a kiss.

"You can partake of this anytime, handsome. I promise you won't be disappointed," she replied in a silvery voice.

"Uh, uh…" The chart on Doctor Benny's lap slid to the floor. Rachel saw that the bulge in his pants formed a large tent, and her eyes popped out. *You've got to be kidding me! Do something, girl! You've got to stop this!*

Mary kept on, batting her long eyelashes. "Honey, I see by the looks of your Peter you want some of this!"

Cherry red, Doctor Benny shook his head violently. "Now, now, young lady, that's not nice."

"Not nice? Man, I can make you come better than a good shit in the morning!"

"You're so naughty!" Doctor Benny seductively snarled, curling his upper lip and showing the top row of his yellow teeth.

"Naughty, indeed, and I know you like it!"

Rachel had enough. She bolted out of her chair, glaring at the doctor with her hands on her hips. Refusing to speak to him directly, she focused her anger on Mary. "Mary, close your legs now!"

Mary rolled her eyes and obeyed. She lifted her bottom and pulled her skirt down with one hand, then sat back on the sofa, slurping on her lollipop.

Rachel returned to her seat, taking over the interview. "Tell me more about Mary. Where is she today?"

"Mary?" Mary's eyes widened as if hearing her name for the first time. She shrugged her shoulders, twisting up her face. "That woman is a prude!"

"A prude? What do you mean?"

"The bitch doesn't 'prove of my lifestyle. She hates sex. She's boring as hell!"

"Where is Mary now?"

"Who cares where she is? Why do you care?"

Momentarily stumped, Rachel racked her mind for an appropriate response. Rachel's abrupt silence wasn't lost on Mary.

"What happened, sweet cakes? Has the cat got your tongue?"

Rachel gave Mary a dirty look. She looked to Doctor Benny for help, and he obliged.

"Are you done with interviewing Mary? I am."

"Excuse me," Mary interrupted, batting her light brown eyes. "Hey, handsome, let's kick this nosy, hard-ass chick out of here so we can get it on. You know you want to! I can tell."

Rachel shot out of her seat again, furious. "Doctor Benny, you need to end this interview now!"

"Rachel is right. This interview is over." Doctor Benny straightened in his chair, looking sheepish.

Mary's light brown eyes glistened with tears. "You're treating me so bad," she whined.

Rachel snatched a tissue box from the doctor's desk and gave it to her. "We're not treating you bad. You're sick and need treatment. You're going to court tomorrow. We're requesting that the judge commit you to the hospital."

"Why?" Mary whined like a little girl, wiping her nose with the tissue as tears streamed down her cheeks.

"Apparently, your past trauma makes it hard for you to function right now. You need extensive therapy so you can get better."

"How long will I have to be here?" Mary tilted her head sideways.

"At least two weeks," Rachel said. "Expect a visit from Hiram Gottchalks, the state attorney. He'll prepare you for court. Do you have any more questions before you go back to the unit?"

"Noooo," Mary whined as she wiped her eyes like a little girl.

"You're excused." Rachel opened the door. Mary didn't budge. She sat there, wiping her eyes, ticking Rachel off. *If this little hussy doesn't get up and leave this office, I swear I'll grab that mop of hers and throw her out myself!*

Fighting back the urge to do just that, Rachel snapped her fingers and pointed to the doorway. "Mary, let's go!" she demanded. Mary glanced at Rachel with tear-filled bloodshot eyes. Rachel remained silent as she pointed to the door. Mary rose to her feet and sashayed to it. She hesitated in the doorway, then whirled around. She broke out into a wide grin, her eyes on Rachel.

"Sweetie, you need to lighten up a bit, and get yourself something sweet and hard to suck on!"

Rachel's blood curdled in her veins. She wanted to shove Mary out the door. "Miss Peters, we're done here. It's time to go."

Mary stepped into the hall and hollered, "Goodbye, Doctor Benny, you handsome trick!"

Rachel slammed the door, then spun around and glared at the doctor with hawk-like eyes. "I can't believe what just happen! You were so out of line! You flirted with a patient!"

"I'm sorry! The situation got out of control." His watery blue eyes peered over his eyeglasses, looking pitiful.

"Sorry? What possessed you to behave like that?"

"I don't know. I guess I got turned on."

"Turned on? You can't be serious. Good gracious, man, you're a damn doctor! You're not supposed to get turned on! What's wrong with you?"

He immediately clammed up, embarrassed, and folded his arms on his chest like a little kid. Silence engulfed the room. Except for the ticking clock on the wall, no one spoke or uttered a sound. Five minutes passed before Doctor Benny was brave enough to break the deafening silence. He spoke in a low voice.

"Listen, let's keep this between us. I promise it will never happen again."

However, Rachel wasn't ready to let him off the hook. "Don't placate me!" she huffed.

"I'm not. Please don't tell anyone! It will ruin me," he pleaded.

Fuming, Rachel stared at the doctor with fierce disgust. He didn't deserve her loyalty. His behavior was despicable and unethical and must be reported, but Rachel saw the pitiful expression on his face and felt sorry for him.

"All right, I'll keep your secret for now. But you better not do this again!"

"Don't worry, I won't!" Doctor Benny sighed with relief.

Rachel stepped swiftly to the door. "I need a break. I'm taking forty-five."

"No problem," Doctor Benny replied. As Rachel opened the door and walked out, she heard Doctor Benny faintly mutter under his breath, "Thank you."

Rachel slammed the door and headed to her office with disturbing questions swirling around in her head. *What if Beth is right about Doctor Benny's role in Susan Cole's disappearance? Were they lovers like Jamie suspected? Did he use sex to manipulate Susan?*

Rachel spent her break drinking coffee and making phone calls. After a while, she felt better and left her office. Rachel took her time going to Doctor Benny's office and found a note on his door. She snatched it off and read it. "Meet me at the nursing station. I'm interviewing patients in the dining room." Rachel crumpled the note up and jammed it in her pants pocket. She stepped briskly to the nursing station and saw Doctor Benny sitting at a table interviewing a male patient in the dining room. The patient's expressive onyx eyes stared at Doctor Benny, taking in every word as the doctor took his time giving him feedback. He was a small man with a round face full of freckles, and his red curly locks fell on his shoulders. Dressed in tan pajamas, the man was animated, talking fast with pressured speech, blurting out words telling his story. Rachel recognized him. *Isn't he the same man I saw earlier doing somersaults in the hall, unable to stop?* He sat in the recliner with his legs underneath him, calm and cool as a cucumber. Shocked and leery of the man's changed behavior, Rachel wondered. *Who is this man trying to fool?*

Rachel reached over the wooden gate and opened it. She walked into the nursing station and sat in one of the black swivel chairs at the white laminated counter. Charts were scattered everywhere. The tile floor had black and white specks. Eight round tan tables about sixty inches in width sat in the dining area in a vast circle. Patients sitting in gray metal chairs around the tables quietly played board games with each other. Across the room in front of a sizable double-paned window was a burgundy couch with four fluffy cushions.

Four female patients dressed in denim overalls sat on the couch with their legs crossed in the same direction. Silent as snow, the women whipped their heads back and forth, watching patients with zombie-like faces pace in front of them with their slippers scratching the laminated tile. The constant pacing was either due to boredom or being over-medicated. Despite the annoying behavior, most patients loved congregating in the dining area. Meals, smoke breaks, naps, and exercise activities were often held there. Even psychiatry and social work staff used the area to meet with patients or run groups.

The screeching telephone rang off the hook, grating on Rachel's nerves. The nurses were in the dining room giving out medications leaving her to answer the phone. Rachel placed the caller on hold, then she raised on her tiptoes and leaned over the counter, searching for a nurse. Candy appeared in her line of vision, and Rachel grabbed the microphone, turning it on. "Candy, there's a call for you," Rachel's voice boomed over the loudspeaker.

Candy looked up with bright blue eyes. She locked her medication cart and shoved it to the nursing station. Sporting a bushy red ponytail, Candy was a woman who usually took her sweet time. However, today, she was in a hurry, busting through the gate and snatching the phone. Candy didn't say much, just listened and nodded her head, grunting. Rachel plopped her butt in a nearby chair and waited for Candy to finish her call. After three minutes, Candy hung up.

"That was quick," Rachel noticed.

"It was Doctor Beebe. He needed to confirm an order," Candy solemnly replied.

Rachel glanced across the room. "Who is that patient with Doctor Benny?"

"Oh, that's Robbie Banks."

"Thanks." Rachel searched for Robbie's record on the counter, finding it underneath a stack of papers. Rachel flipped the file open to the admission sheet and found Robbie's mother's phone number. Scooting her chair closer to the phone, Rachel called the woman.

Full of information, Robbie's mother gave her the lowdown on her son's psychiatric history. According to her, Robbie took Haldol, a magical cure for his unsettling predicament. Two months ago, Robbie stopped taking the medicine. Feeling better, Robbie believed he didn't need the medication because his voices were gone.

After a long conversation, Rachel thanked Robbie's mother and hung up the phone, then documented the call in Robbie's chart. Doctor Benny, finished with his interview, appeared in the nursing station and pulled up a chair. He sat next to Rachel, grinning like a Cheshire Cat.

"I'm taking Robbie Banks to court. He needs to stay here in the hospital. He has voices commanding him to do weird things."

Rachel raised an eyebrow. "Like what?"

"Well, he told me he's getting tired of the voices telling him to flip when he's standing up. He says he's exhausted and needs rest."

"I bet. What else did Robbie say?"

"He said the voices don't bother him when he's eating, sleeping, or using the toilet." The doctor chuckled softly.

Rachel laughed out loud. "Oh, come on, you can't be serious!"

"I'm just telling you what the man told me," he replied, flashing his yellow grill again.

"I called his mother," Rachel said.

"Oh, what did she say?"

"Haldol seems to be the magic drug that makes Robbie's voices go away."

"I already have him on a low dose. Maybe he needs a higher one. I'll update the order."

Rachel handed him Robbie's chart. As she reached in the chart rack for another record, Rachel heard a woman loudly cursing in the dining area. "You sorry little fucker, watch where you're going!"

Rachel and Doctor Benny rose out of their seats to see what was happening. A woman was sitting on the floor, and Robbie was performing somersaults around her as she scowled at him, curling her lips. George twisted around and signaled for Candy. She pranced over, easy-like, taking her sweet time.

"Yes, Doctor?"

"Give Robbie five milligrams of Haldol right now."

"I'm on it!" Candy ran to the medication cart, unlocked it, took out the medicine, and locked the cart back up. Candy and Doctor Benny ran out of the nursing station over to Robbie and persuaded him to sit down, then Candy injected him with Haldol. A few minutes later, Robbie's eyes closed, and his head bounced forward.

"He should be okay for a while," George surmised as he returned to the nursing station.

"Good, I certainly hope so," Rachel answered, feeling relieved.

They both settled in for the afternoon reviewing charts and interviewing patients. As they wrapped up their interviewing for the day, a heated argument broke out in the dining area. Rachel and Doctor Benny whirled around to see who was causing the commotion. An elderly man with fiery gray eyes was puffed up like a blowfish. Bald at the top of his head with white clumps of hair curled around his temples, he yelled and shook his wooden cane at the nurse.

"I don't want that pink pill! Pink is for girls!"

Steve was trying to give Harry his afternoon medication.

"Don't worry about the color, Harry. The pill makes the voices go away."

"I don't care! I'm not taking it! It's poison!"

"Harry, it's not poison."

"Yes, it is! You can't make me take it!" Harry's face was red as a cherry.

Getting angrier by the minute, Steve drew in a sharp breath, trying to explain. "Harry, if you don't take it, you'll have to stay longer in the hospital."

"The hell I will! I'm not staying in no damn hospital!" Harry aggressively shook his wooden cane in Steve's face.

Steve backed up with his brown eyes widening. "Harry, give me your cane," he calmly said.

"No! This is my cane!"

"Give me your cane before you hurt somebody with it." He took a step closer to Harry.

"No! Get your own damn cane!"

"If you don't give me the cane, I'll have to call security," Steve warned.

"The hell you will! You better stay away from me!"

Steve's face was stern. "Harry, give me the cane right now!"

Harry swung his cane and whopped Steve in the head. A nasty gash appeared on his forehead, and blood dripped down onto his nose. Steve's brown eyes darted around the room. "Somebody call security now!" he yelled. Bewildered and shaken, Rachel grabbed the phone. As she quickly dialed the number, Rachel noticed her fingers felt like butter. Sweat beaded on her forehead as the phone rang and rang in her ear. Feeling sick that there was no answer, Rachel hung up. Then a thought came to her mind, and she picked up the phone again. This time she paged security overhead. "CODE NINETY-NINE, SECURITY NEEDED ON THE ADMISSIONS UNIT! CODE NINETY-NINE, SECURITY NEEDED ON THE ADMISSIONS UNIT!"

Harry went buck wild. "You damn whippersnapper! How dare they call security on me!" Harry beat Steve down like a dog, his cane hitting Steve's head, shoulders, and arms. Steve managed to jerk the rod out of Harry's hands, and Harry fell backward, landing on his butt on the hard floor.

"You son of a bitch! Give me my cane!" Harry yelled as he raised himself off the floor. He rubbed his butt, glaring at Steve.

Out of nowhere, a large figure with long, wiry blond hair flew like superman through the air, hopping over a dining room table and a couple of chairs. Hiram landed on his feet and sucker punched Steve in the face. Steve fell on the floor and Hiram fell on top of the nurse, slapping him on his head and growling like a wild animal.

"Get off of me, you big turkey! What's wrong with you?" Steve grabbed Hiram's hair, twisting it around his fingers.

"Ouch, you bully! Let go of Hiram's hair!" Hiram pried Steve's fingers loose, and a watery mist sprayed from his mouth. "Hiram'll teach you not to bully patients!"

"Stop spitting on me, you son of a bitch! Somebody get this asshole off of me!"

Three husky male nurses came to Steve's rescue. They pulled Hiram from the badly beaten nurse, shoving him aside. Hiram fell on the floor, rolling like a dog. He hopped on his feet, tightening his fists. He glared at Steve, and Steve glared back. The nurses assisted Steve to his feet, who balled his fists, ready to fight.

"You want this?" he growled. "Be a man and do it right!"

Hiram cranked his neck and flexed his muscles. "Let's duke!" he shouted.

Steve made a mad dash at Hiram, shoving him down. Hiram slid on his butt across the floor. He hopped on his feet and sprinted at Steve with his head down like a defensive halfback, colliding into him and knocking Steve straight to the floor. Hiram sat on the nurse's stomach, beating him in the head with his fists. The male nurses joined the brawl, falling on top of Hiram like football players in a scrimmage. They rolled on the floor, wrestling each other until Steve managed to break free. He rose to his feet, groaning.

"Damn," he said, limping to the nursing station.

Hiram and the nurses kept fighting, knocking over tables, chairs, and ashtrays. Soon a circle of patients surrounded them, whooping and hollering and egging them on. They jumped up and down, clapping like a bunch of munchkins chanting, "Fight, Fight, Fight!"

"Damn, security is taking too long to get here. Rachel, page them again!" Doctor Benny said as he scrambled out of his seat to join the fight. Rachel grabbed the phone and saw Hiram punch Doctor Benny in the jaw, knocking him to the floor. *Oh, my goodness, this is bad!* She snatched the phone and paged security again. Doctor Benny grabbed his jaw, moaning, falling on his back. Hiram stood over him.

"Hiram is sorry, man. Hiram didn't mean to hit you! Are you all right?"

"No, I'm not, you jerk!" the doctor hollered. He sat up, grimacing and rubbing his jaw.

"Hiram said he was sorry."

Just then, Steve swung Hiram onto the floor and pulled his hair. The nurse sat on his chest, refusing to get up. Hiram screamed, "Get off Hiram's chest, you jack ass!"

"I'm not finished with you yet!" Steve pinned Hiram to the floor, and Hiram pinched Steve's hands until he let go. "Ouch!" Steve hollered, hopping up and taking off. With his adrenaline in full force, Hiram leaped to his feet. He ran after Steve overtaking him, body-slamming him against the wall.

"Ugh! Are you trying to kill me?" Steve gasped with the wind almost knocked out of him.

"That's what you get for pulling Hiram's hair, you jack ass!" The attorney curled his lips, grimacing. He backed away, flexing his muscles.

"You're crazy!" Steve's voice was hoarse.

"You haven't seen nothing yet!"

By this time, Doctor Benny had returned to the nursing station and he called security again while Rachel, a nervous wreck, looked over his shoulder. He slammed the phone on the receiver and rubbed his throbbing jaw.

Rachel asked. "Are they coming?"

"Yep! They're on the way."

A male patient with dreadlocks plopped on the counter, hollering like a hyena. Rachel jerked back, mortified. She wildly gestured for him to move, screaming. "Get down from there, right now! I said, get down now!"

"I want to see the fight! I can see it better from up here," he grinned with his dark pupils dancing.

"Get down, I said." Rachel stared defiantly at him. The patient slid off the counter, flipped her the finger, and sprinted across the room.

At the same time, the unit door flew opened, and five men in black fatigues stampeded into the dining area. One guard grabbed Hiram and held him in a headlock while another guard blew on a bullhorn. "Stop fighting now and line up against the wall!"

"Someone, please escort these patients to their rooms!" a third guard yelled. Two nurses stepped forward and ushered the patients to their rooms.

"That was a hell of a fight!" a patient said as he followed the nurse down the hall.

Two female patients giggled their hearts out as they walked to their rooms. "That was a hell of a fight!" one said.

"A hell of a fight, indeed!" agreed the other.

The guards released Hiram after he promised to calm down. Steve sat on the floor, nursing the fiery red lump on his forehead. Above his right eye was a white piece of gauze. Rachel felt sorry for him. *He looks terrible. I hope he's okay.*

Suddenly Hiram made his way over, and Rachel gasped in horror. *Oh, no! He's lost his mind!* Rachel gripped the phone, ready at a moment's notice to call security. She sighed with relief when she saw Hiram pull up a chair and sit next to the badly beaten nurse.

"Look, man, Hiram is sorry. He got out of hand." Hiram wrinkled his nose and sneeze.

Steve glared at Hiram out of the corner of his eye. "You're crazy, but I think you know that!"

"Yeah, Hiram is a little nutty." Hiram hung his head low, avoiding eye contact.

Steve leaned over and nudged Hiram's shoulder. "Apology accepted."

"Good, Hiram is glad." Hiram lifted his head and grinned. "Is there anything Hiram can do for you, man?"

"Yep! Take me to the ER."

"Man, no problem." Hiram sneezed again and stood on his feet, helping Steve up.

"Are you allergic to something?" Steve asked.

"Huh, huh, it's the rubbing alcohol you nurses use all the time."

"Oh, I see. Sorry about that."

The two men embraced each other as they limped down the hall toward the exit. With his free hand, Hiram rubbed his butt while Steve winced, groaning from the pain.

"There's something else I need you to do for me when we get to the ER."

"What's that?"

"Pay my damn bill!"

Hiram and Steve roared with laughter. They exited the unit leaving everyone watching with their mouths sagged open.

Chapter Six

Wednesday, November 14th

Susan was in the kitchen preparing breakfast for Doctor Benny. She wanted to surprise him with her culinary skills, and she had gotten up early, tiptoeing around trying not to wake him. Susan was worried about George. Last night when she asked about the purple bruising on the left side of his face, he shrugged it off, mumbling to himself. He barely spoke two words to her during dinner, and he tossed and turned all night, heightening her anxiety.

Disturbed by it all, Susan scuffed around the kitchen on the wood floor in her fluffy pink house slippers, tying the belt around her waist on her long pink robe. Although warm heat blew hard from the ceiling vent, the house still felt chilly. She turned on the oven, adjusting the dial to 400 degrees. *This will chase the chill out of the kitchen.*

Within minutes, Susan had bacon sizzling in a skillet, and she grabbed a carton of eggs from the black double-door refrigerator. She carefully cracked five eggs into a ceramic bowl, added salt and pepper, and then whipped the eggs until they were light and frothy.

Susan made a pot of coffee, and seconds later the robust nutty scent competed with the sweet smell of crisp, cooked bacon. Susan closed her eyes, raising her face to the ceiling, breathing in the decadent odors. It felt like she was participating in an immoral, erotic moment of pleasure. *I love the smell of bacon and coffee together. It makes me feel sinfully toasty and naughty.*

Susan turned off the stove, grabbed a spatula, and transferred the bacon to a plate lined with a paper towel. On the granite marble counter to her left sat a pan of homemade biscuits ready to go into the oven. *I'll bake these once George gets up.* While she waited for George, Susan set the table.

Finally, he appeared in the doorway, grinning sheepishly at her as he glided into the kitchen. "Good morning, my love! It sure smells good in here. What are you cooking?"

Susan twisted around slightly and smiled. "I made homemade biscuits, just finished frying bacon, and now I'm going to cook some scrambled eggs. Thought you might like breakfast before taking off to work."

"Homemade biscuits? You made homemade biscuits! I'm impressed!"

"Honey, sit down," Susan laughed. "I'll bring you a cup of coffee."

Dressed in his usual attire, a blue suede sweat suit with white tennis shoes, George wrenched a chair and sat at the end of the table. Susan poured him a cup of coffee and placed it in front of him. George's smile was wide and glaring. "You remembered."

"Yes, honey, I sure did. You like your coffee black."

"That's right, my sweet." He picked up his coffee and sipped it.

Thrilled that George was pleased, Susan giggled. She scurried to the counter, picked up her pan of biscuits, opened the oven door, and shoved the biscuits on the rack. She closed the door, flipping on the oven light. Susan grabbed the skillet off the stove and scuffled to the sink. She washed the skillet with soap and water, dried it off, and returned it to the stove.

"George, darling, I noticed you were restless last night. Was something worrying you?" Susan dropped two slices of butter into the skillet and turned on the stove.

"No," George grumbled, staring at the table.

Susan twisted around to look at him. She noticed the wrinkles on his forehead were more pronounced than usual, and his face looked grave and haggard.

"Are you all right? You look pale and tired."

"I told you, I'm fine!"

Startled by his rough tone, Susan withered inside. She turned her back on him and didn't say another word. Susan grabbed the bowl of eggs and dumped them in the skillet, stirring them until they were done. Then she opened the oven door to check on the biscuits. They were brown and even on the top. Susan grabbed a potholder, took out the pan of biscuits, and placed it on the stove.

George glanced at his watch and rose to his feet. "The newspaper should be here. I'll be right back."

Susan kept her mouth shut, still hurt by his rough tone. He left the kitchen, and Susan dumped the biscuits in a clothed-lined basket. She placed the basket on the table along with a jar of jelly and a stick of butter on a plate. On her way to the stove, Susan grabbed the skillet of eggs. She returned to the table, shoveling out eggs in equal portions on each plate. Susan dropped the skillet in the sink and returned to the stove to grab the plate of bacon. She set the plate on the table, then poured herself a cup of coffee and sat.

George walked in carrying his newspaper. He sat at the table in front of his plate of eggs.

"This looks and smells good. Thank you for breakfast."

"You're welcome." Susan sipped her coffee, staring off into space.

George frowned. "Now, what's wrong with you?"

"Nothing."

"What do you mean nothing? You looked angry."

"I guess I am." Susan softly replied as she placed her coffee cup on the table. She folded her arms and glared at the doctor.

"Do you mind telling what you're pissed about?"

"I always tell you my feelings, but when I ask about yours, you either snap at me or put me off. I don't think you're being fair."

George groaned. "Susan, I deal with a lot of issues, issues I can't discuss with you. Besides, you can't help me anyway. It's work related, so don't worry about it. I'll handle it."

"Oh, so you're keeping secrets from me. Keeping secrets is not good for the relationship."

George grabbed a biscuit and two slices of bacon, placing the food on his plate. "Let's eat before your wonderful breakfast gets cold." George buttered his biscuit, unfolded his newspaper, and started reading.

"Is that it? Is that all you have to say?" Susan fumed.

George ignored her. Instead, he ate his biscuit and read his newspaper.

Burning up inside, Susan snatched her cup of coffee, stood on her feet, and walked out of the kitchen without saying another word.

Rachel arrived at work to find Hiram's and Steve's infamous brawl had spread like wildfire throughout Salter's Point Regional, over-shadowing Susan Cole's disappearance and forcing Doctor Beebe to put the investigation aside. For the next few days, staff would be focusing on workplace violence, fitting in scheduled seminars whenever they could during work hours. Rachel found the idea of adding the seminars to her busy schedule quite stressful. She'd have to miss lunches trying to keep up with everything.

At mid-afternoon, Rachel, Hiram, and Doctor Benny were in her office reviewing the court docket for the next day when, out of the blue, Hiram threw a hissy fit.

"You're taking Robbie Banks to court? Why? He should be discharged!" Hiram paced the floor like a rabid dog.

"Will you stop all of the antics! Yes, I'm taking him to court!" Doctor Benny sneered, showing his yellow grill.

"Damn you! Are you God or something? Let the man go home."

"No, Hiram! My call, not yours! I'm the damn doctor!"

"A sorry one at that! You're despicable! I'll see your long, tall ass in court!"

"I can't wait."

Hiram stomped around Rachel's office like a toddler. Frightened, Rachel stood up and ran to the door, yanking it open. Instead of her leaving, Hiram darted past her and out the door.

"See you later, missy! Hiram is done with that fool!" He waved as he danced down the hallway like a jackrabbit.

Rattled, Rachel slammed the door and locked it. She took a deep breath and shook her head in disbelief. "That man is so damn twisted and out of his tree. Talking to him is like talking to a wall."

"I agree." Doctor Benny peered over his eyeglasses as he glided to the door, unlocking it. "I'm taking a break. I need to recover from this."

"I hear you, see you in a few." After Doctor Benny left, Rachel shut the door and locked it. She sat at her desk and reached for the phone. She called Jamie, who answered on the first ring.

"What's up?"

"I need to talk," Rachel said in a hurry. "Can I come by?"

"Sure, I'm not going anywhere."

The two women hung up, and Rachel grabbed her coffee mug and ran out the door. Five minutes later, she was knocking on Jamie's door and entering at the same time. Cigarette smoke slapped her in the face, sending her into a coughing spell. Sally, laid back on the couch, was smoking her cigarette with Peepers stretched out beside her. Red in the face, Rachel struggled to breathe. Peepers stared at Rachel with pity in his golden eyes. Rachel took a deep breath and groaned in a raspy voice.

"Girl, you need to get rid of that cigarette! The smoke is suffocating me!"

Sally huffed. "All right, I'll put the damn thing out." She smashed her cigarette in the ashtray on her lap. Coughing her head off and wheezing, Rachel stumbled to the coffee pot. After she helped herself to some coffee, she sat in a chair close to the door. Rachel sipped on her coffee, trying to relax. A few minutes later, her wheezing subsided. "I suppose you guys heard about the fight in the dining room yesterday."

Sally giggled. "We sure did. I told my husband about it, and now he wants me to quit. He thinks this job is too dangerous for me."

"Well, the man has a point," Jamie piped in.

"I know, but I like working here in this chaos. You're never bored. Besides, I'd miss you guys if I leave," Sally grinned.

Rachel brightened. "Oh, what a sweet thing to say."

Jamie rolled her eyes. "So, Rachel, what's on your mind?"

"Speaking of the fight, you should've seen Hiram with his crazy self pretending to be some sort of superhero. Jumping over tables and chairs, rolling on the floor like a damn dog!"

Jamie hollered with laughter. "That man is a straight-up maniac! He needs to be committed."

"Hiram could use some days in the hospital," Sally chimed in.

A sharp pounding on the door interrupted their conversation. The three women flinched, and Rachel almost spilled coffee on herself. The door flew open, hitting the wall, and a picture fell on the floor, breaking the glass frame into tiny pieces.

Beth stood in the doorway, looking like an overgrown Easter Bunny, sparkling bright in her fluorescent pink dress and Nike tennis shoes. With one hand on her hip, Beth tapped her foot, glaring at them. "Tell me something, what are you ladies up to?"

"Is there something you need?" Jamie frowned, rising from her chair.

"I asked you ladies a question! What are you up to? Don't you have work to do?" she demanded with her green eyes flashing.

"We do. However, we're taking a break," Jamie smugly replied.

"A break? There's no time for idle breaks when you've got work to do!"

Jamie walked to the closet and took out a broom and dustpan. She swept the broken picture frame in a pile and shoved the debris into the pan. "Damn, you're worrisome sometimes!" she griped under her breath.

Beth ignored her. "Rachel, I have a doctor out here I want you to meet. She does the physicals for our patients." She turned her back, waddled to the door, and poked her head out. "You can come in now," she called.

A tall woman in a white lab coat sashayed into Jamie's office. She had a stethoscope around her neck and cherry blond curls hanging on her shoulders. Rachel gave her the once-over. She noticed thick dark hair growing on the woman's bare legs, and on her feet she wore a pair of old, decrepit brown sandals. Rachel shook her head when she saw the pink polish cracking on the woman's toenails. She decided the woman was too tacky for a healthcare professional.

Suddenly a musky odor gripped the air, and everyone cringed, wrinkling their noses. Unfazed by their reaction, the woman introduced herself.

"I'm Doctor Grace Hornsby. Pleased to meet you." She stuck out her hand, and Rachel stood on her feet and shook it. She immediately recoiled from the clammy touch.

"Glad to meet you, too," Rachel mumbled under her breath.

Rachel's reaction wasn't lost on the doctor. "I washed my hands earlier, but I didn't dry them well. Sorry."

Rachel felt like throwing up. She wiped her hand on her pants leg as she sank into her chair. Feeling faint, she fell back, closing her eyes. The place smelled like a herd of billy goats.

"Rachel, are you okay?" Jamie asked with her brow wrinkling.

"I'm fine," Rachel replied, opening her eyes and straightening up.

Jamie wrinkled her nose, making sniffing noises. She zeroed in on Grace with a wicked gleam in her eye. "Damn, it stinks in here!"

Sally snickered. "Yep, it's ripe in here, all right!"

Grace was clueless. "I hope you two don't run Rachel away with your silly antics. Girls, do you remember what happened to the last social worker we had?"

Jamie whipped her head back, scrunching up her face.

"Why the face?" Grace's question caught Jamie off guard.

"I'm trying to figure out why I have such an awful stench in my office."

Grace chuckled. She still didn't get it.

"Tell me what happened to the last social worker." Rachel butted in, changing the subject.

"She quit. She only worked for three months. This place was too crazy for her."

Beth shot Grace a dirty look. "What are you trying to do? Run my new social worker away?"

"No, Beth, I just thought…"

Beth cut her off in mid-sentence. "Ignore her. Doctor Hornsby has a wild, crusty hair up her ass!"

"And a stinky one, too," Jamie added under her breath. Rachel slapped her hand over her mouth and snickered. Sally, tight-lipped, stared at the ceiling, trying not to laugh out loud.

"Let's go before you say anything else you've no business saying," Beth said, shoving the doctor out the door. "Ladies, talk to you later." Beth walked out and slammed the door.

After Beth and Grace left, the women cracked up laughing.

"Ew, that woman stinks!" Sally said, fanning her nose.

"Someone needs to introduce her to some serious soap and water! She smells like a sour mop!" Rachel said, pinching her nose.

"Apparently, she's allergic to bathing. She smells like that most of the time," Jamie observed.

"Did you see those hairy gorilla legs? Doesn't she believe in shaving?" Rachel asked, rubbing her nose.

"Apparently not," Jamie grinned.

"Why haven't I seen her around? Where does she work?" Rachel asked.

"Her office is on North Campus. But she spends most of her time over here doing physicals for the newly admitted patients," Jamie explained.

Rachel gasped. "Ewe, I wouldn't want her touching me!"

"Neither would I," Sally agreed.

"What's her story? I know she's got one, and Jamie, I know you know." Rachel made a face.

Jamie grinned mischievously. "What makes you think that?"

"You know everything that goes on around here. So, spill the beans." Rachel rose out of her seat. She moseyed over to the sink and poured out her cold coffee.

"Doctor Hornsby has a checkered reputation," Jamie said.

"Yeah, I bet she does." Rachel returned to the coffee pot and refreshed her mug with hot coffee. She stood by Jamie's desk, waiting for her to finish.

"To put it bluntly, the woman's a damn slut!"

Sally frowned. "Jamie, why so harsh? We don't know that for sure."

"Please. The woman has fucked every security guard in this hospital. She manages to get more sex than anyone I know!" Jamie laughed.

"Smelling that bad?" Rachel was floored.

"Yeah, girl. Despite her stinky ass, she's one hot momma!"

"Those men just want to get some. They don't give a damn about the smell," Sally added.

Rachel shook her head in disbelief. "So disgusting! Has anyone ever caught her in the act?"

"Nope," Jamie flatly said.

"Well, I'll be damned." Rachel was flabbergasted.

Sally stood on her feet. "Well, ladies, it's been nice, but I have to get back to work. I've got to finish my documentation before I go home this evening."

"Me, too," Rachel sighed, dropping her shoulders. She followed Sally to the door. "See you tomorrow, Jamie."

"Will do."

After they left Jamie's office, Rachel returned to hers. Settling in for the afternoon, she worked on her documentation until six thirty. With her stomach growling, Rachel glanced at her watch. *Gosh, the cafeteria closes in twenty-five minutes. I better get me some dinner.*

Rachel jumped up, grabbed her wallet, and hurried to the cafeteria. She made it there just before it closed and bought a salad and a large cup of iced tea. With her wallet tucked under her arm,

Rachel carried her salad in her right hand and held her drink with the left.

On the way back, Rachel ran into Peepers. He was in front of the employee lounge, growling and flashing his pearly white fangs and clawing the door. "What's going on here?"

Rachel stopped at the door, and Peepers looked up at her. His golden eyes looked fierce, and Rachel stooped to her knees, placing her salad and tea on the floor. She gently caressed the cat's fur, trying to comfort him. No longer allergic, she was able to lean close and whisper in the cat's ear, "Peepers, what's wrong?"

A man's voice growled from behind the door. The fur on the cat's back sprung up, prickly like a porcupine. Rachel heard the man moan like he was being tortured. "OOOO, OOOO, shit woman, give it to me! That's it, that's it, that's it! Damn, I can't take it! Stop! I can't take it!"

Rachel's mouth gaped open. She recognized the voice of John Easley, the nightshift security guard, hollering like a banshee. Curious, Rachel stood up, cracking the door open. She peeked inside and almost lost it. John and Grace, naked as jaybirds, rolled back and forth on the floor, wrapped up like a couple of weasels. The room reeked of old dirty diapers. Rachel shut the door in a hurry and fell against the wall, gagging. "Oh, my goodness, I don't believe this. It stinks to the high heavens!"

Peepers sat, staring at the door and growling. Rachel stooped over, petting the top of the big cat's head. "Hush, Peepers, you're making too much noise. They can hear you."

The cat ignored her, hissing softly. Without warning, loud barking erupted from the lounge. Peepers stood on all fours with his back arched, his piercing eyes narrow slits. He hissed and clawed at the door, leaving deep scratches.

"Stop it! Let me handle this," Rachel fussed, using her foot to push the cat away. The barking grew louder and more intense, and Rachel wondered if a dog was trapped inside. *Maybe I didn't see the poor thing in my state of shock.* Feeling brave, and with her hand poised on the doorknob, Rachel held her breath and cracked the door. She gasped, almost urinating on herself when she saw John's pasty white butt moving up and down between Grace's thick hairy legs. Dripping with sweat, John hollered as his face contorted into a pretzel. "Give it to me, woman! Give it to me right now!"

Grace dug her pink fingernails into John's hairy back as she held on for dear life. She barked and screamed, scaring the holy hell out of Rachel. "Woof, woof! Take it all, woof, woof, take it all!"

Turned on, John growled. "I love it when you bark!" John slapped her on the butt, and she barked again.

"Woof, woof! Do it again! Woof, woof!" John slapped her butt again, and Peepers tried desperately to force his massive head inside. Rachel took her foot and nudged the cat out of the way. She shut the door.

"I can't believe this woman is barking like a damn dog. She's flipped her wig!"

Rachel kneeled to the floor, grabbing her salad and iced tea. "Peepers, let's go." She turned and hurried down the hall. Reluctant to leave, Peepers stayed back. He hissed at the door and Rachel whirled around. She set her tea on the floor and inserted two fingers in her mouth, whistling. "Peepers, come on, I don't have all night!"

Rachel grabbed her tea and left. Peepers crept behind her, taking his sweet time. By the time Rachel reached the lobby, Peepers was trotting alongside her. Instead of going to her office, Rachel decided to sit in the lobby and eat her dinner. She plopped her butt on the sofa in front of the bay window and tore the plastic wrapping off her salad. With John's and Grace's sex scene fresh in her mind, she closed her eyes, breathing deeply. Peepers hopped on the sofa and sat next to her. He licked his black fur and fell on his side, stretching his legs and pointing his massive paws. Rachel opened her eyes, grabbed her fork, and dug into her salad.

Questions swirled in her head as she thought about the past two months. Many of the incidences she experienced were just plain crazy. She thought about John, Doctor Hornsby, and Susan Cole's disappearance. *I wondered if John and Doctor Hornsby were having sex the night Susan Cole disappeared? It's possible. She got away somehow!*

97

Rachel looked at Peepers. His mysterious golden eyes met hers, and she wondered how many secrets were behind the cat's stare. Convinced she might be on to something, Rachel carefully thought out the pieces of the puzzle. Doctor Benny, for his own selfish reasons, could've helped Susan Cole escape. His flirtation with Mary Peters crossed her mind again, and she realized she must tell Beth about it right away.

As soon as I arrive at work in the morning, I'm going straight to Beth's office.

Chapter Seven

Thursday, November 15th

Precisely at seven-ten, Rachel's red Toyota zoomed into the parking lot. She parked directly under a streetlight a few yards from the hospital entrance. Rachel yawned, feeling exhausted from not getting enough rest the night before. She'd been up all night worrying about talking to Beth about Doctor Benny's scandalous behavior and Doctor Hornsby's sexual escapade with John Easley.

As Rachel struggled with her feelings, she reminded herself that it was the right decision. Doctor Benny must be confronted and disciplined as soon as possible. When Madonna's hit song "Borderline" came on the radio, Rachel welcomed the distraction. Turning the volume up, Rachel swayed and snapped her fingers to the melodic beat. As she grooved to the music, an orange glow shone through her front window. The sun was rising over the hospital, and its bright rays sizzled on the paved parking lot.

The blazing sun forced the bats out of surrounding pine trees, and the night creatures hightailed back to their cave. After the song went off, the news came on and Rachel turned the volume down. She glanced across the parking lot and noticed an African American man about six feet two inches tall sporting a colossal afro. He glided like a panther as he walked to the hospital entrance. Rachel thought his outfit to be quite odd. Dressed in an army jacket with blue jeans, the man wore dark sunglasses and combat boots. *Why the army clothes? Where is he going dressed like that?* Her question was immediately answered. The man used a key to unlock the sliding glass door, and he glided in, disappearing into the building. Rachel was floored. *Oh, my goodness, he works here! Go figure!*

Determined to find out the man's name, Rachel turned off the ignition. She opened the car door and hopped out. She hurried to the hospital entrance, unlocked the sliding door, and pushed it open. Rachel went inside and found Joyce sitting in her usual spot. Rachel looked around and caught a glimpse of the man's afro as he slipped through the Admissions Unit door. *Who is this guy?*

"Good morning," Joyce sang.

Rachel winced when she heard Joyce's voice. "Oh, Good morning!"

"Are you okay?" Joyce's brown eyes were huge.

"I'm fine. Did you see a man with a big afro walk by here?"

"Yeah."

"Who is that?"

"Oh, that's Doctor Everett James. You haven't met him?" Joyce's eyes were wide.

"Apparently not," Rachel grimaced.

"Well, he's the assistant medical chief, and his office is on North Campus. He only comes around when he has a meeting with one of the doctors or if he has to cover for one of them."

"I see. Does he always dress like that? It's not very professional."

Joyce chuckled. "Rachel, honey, this is a looney bin. If you stay here long enough, you'll see many weird styles. Besides, Doctor James is good looking. The women around here don't care how he dresses."

Rachel let out a long sigh. "Joyce, please, it's not professional for a doctor to dress like that. Certainly not a man with his position."

"When you meet him, you won't care, believe me." Joyce winked.

Rachel rolled her eyes and took off, stepping briskly to the Admissions Unit. By the time Rachel walked onto the floor, the tall man was nowhere in sight. Frustrated, she went to her office. She unlocked the door and stepped inside. Moving like lightning, Rachel locked her handbag in the desk drawer. She took off her coat and flung it over her swivel chair. Then Rachel walked out, closing the door behind her. Rachel planned to visit Beth, but she decided to go to Jamie's office instead. Rachel needed advice, and Jamie always knew what to say and do.

A minute later, Rachel was at Jamie's office, banging hard on the door, and she could smell cigarette smoke. Rachel turned the doorknob and went inside. Jamie was sitting at her desk reading the newspaper, and Sally was perched on the sofa smoking a cigarette.

"Good morning, you two!" Rachel said as she closed the door.

"Good morning to you," Jamie mumbled, not looking up.

Sally immediately stamped out her cigarette in the empty coffee cup she was holding. "You're early this morning, dear."

"Yeah, I know. I have a full agenda today." Rachel wrinkled her nose, nauseated by the lingering cigarette smoke. "Geez Sally, you smoke this early in the morning?"

"Sometimes!" Sally quipped in her English accent.

Jamie frowned as she laid her newspaper on the desk. "You're always so damn chipper in the morning. It gets on my nerves!"

"And you're always in a sour mood," Rachel laughed.

"So, girl, what's up?" Jamie leaned forward, folding her arms on her newspaper.

"You're not going to believe what I saw last night," Rachel said, flopping on the sofa.

Jamie huffed, rolling her eyes heavenward. "Okay, what did you see, a wicked witch?"

Sally laughed. "Very funny!"

Rachel made a face. "Don't talk like that! You're going to like this!"

"Would you please stop talking in circles and get on with it!"

"If you insist," Rachel said. Inhaling deeply, Rachel spoke in a raspy, strained voice. "I saw John Easley and Doctor Hornsby getting it on in the employee lounge last night."

Jamie let out a small scream and clapped her hands over her mouth, her eyes looking like light brown buttons dancing in their sockets.

Sally scooted to the edge of her seat and howled. "Girl, you're lying to us!"

"Girl, no, I'm not. The man humped her like a dog, like this!" Rachel leaped off the sofa and began jerking and wiggling her body. Jamie and Sally howled with laughter.

"That's not even the best part," Rachel said. "Every time he yelled, *give it to me, woman,* she barked like a dog! The woman sounded like a yelping Chihuahua, *arf, arf, arf, arf!* It was weird as hell."

Jamie was beside herself. She laughed so hard tears leaked from the corners of her eyes, and she almost fell backward out of her chair. "Damn, damn, damn! I don't believe it!"

"That's some crazy mess!" Sally giggled hysterically.

"Jamie, didn't you tell me Doctor Hornsby has sex with the security guards? Why don't you believe me?"

"I do." Jamie sighed, wiping her face with a tissue. "That slutty woman barking. Now that's precious."

Rachel frowned. "It's disgusting and uncouth…who does that?"

"She does," Jamie laughed as she reached inside her desk drawer and pulled out a bottle of Jack Daniels. "This requires a celebration. This is too good!"

Jamie placed the bottle on her desk, and Rachel and Sally twisted up their faces. "Really, Jamie? A drink? It's not even eight thirty in the morning yet!" Rachel commented.

"Pipe down. I just need a little sip to celebrate. Doctor Hornsby barking like a Chihuahua is too good to be true!" Jamie screwed the cap off and turned the bottle upright to her lips. She took a sip of the brown liquor and coughed. "Ahhh, that's good!"

Silent, but seething with rage, Rachel watched Jamie put the bottle of whiskey back in her desk drawer. Rachel glanced at Sally, rolling her eyes again. Sally sat there stone-faced with her mouth clamped shut. Rachel adored Jamie, but she despised her constant drinking. Drinking on the job was not only an ethical concern, but it was against hospital policy. However, she knew reminding Jamie of this fact was a complete waste of time, so she refrained from chastising her, keeping the focus on Doctor Hornsby instead.

"I've got an epiphany," Rachel blurted out.

"What's that?"

"I think John Easley is responsible for Susan Cole's disappearance."

Jamie's eyes widened. "How so?"

"He wasn't at his post the night Susan disappeared because he was in the employee lounge having sex with that barking Chihuahua Doctor Hornsby!"

Jamie fell out laughing. "I think you've got something there."

"Good point," Sally agreed.

"Do you think I should tell Beth about my theory?" A crease develolped on Rachel's forehead.

"Why not? It's something to think about," Jamie snickered.

A faint scent of cinnamon drew Rachel's eyes to the half-filled coffee pot on Jamie's end table. She walked over, grabbed an empty mug from the table, and helped herself to some coffee. "I hope you don't mind." Rachel inhaled the sweet scent. "I need a cup of Joe to settle my nerves.

"Go ahead..." Jamie trailed off, annoyed.

Rachel paused a second and sighed. "Then there's that nasty Doctor Benny."

"What do you mean?" Sally's eyes were big.

"Doctor Benny and I interviewed Mary Peters two days ago, and he flirted with her. In fact, he came on to her." Rachel twisted her face up as she set her coffee mug on the end table.

"Really, you don't say," Jamie chuckled as she exchanged knowing glances with Sally.

Their nonverbal exchange wasn't lost on Rachel. "What was that look about?"

"What look?" Sally asked, looking like a deer caught in headlights.

"That look the two of you gave each other. Don't play with me!"

"Well, I'm not one to spread gossip, but Doctor Benny has a reputation of being flirtatious with the women."

"Even with patients?" Rachel asked in a high-pitched tone.

"Even with patients," Sally confirmed.

Rachel violently shook her head. "I don't believe it!"

"Well, it's true," Sally said.

"Let's not get off the subject." Jamie leaned back in her seat, clasping her hands behind her head. "Finish the story, please."

"Okay, here it goes." Rachel became solemn. She fell back on the couch, her forehead furrowed, feeling distressed. She spoke in a measured tone, taking her time. "Mary Peters flirted with him, and his dick got hard. He even told Mary she was a naughty girl."

Jamie cracked up laughing. "What a dog, what a dog!" Her eyes narrowed haughtily. "So, how do you know his dick was hard?"

"I could see it protruding in his pants. His crotch looked like a tent!"

Jamie and Sally howled with laughter. Hyperventilating and red in the face from laughing so hard, Sally stood up and took long deep breaths. Jamie left her seat to rub Sally's back.

"You guys, don't you think Doctor Benny was unethical coming on to Mary Peters like that?" Rachel sharply asked.

"Yes, dear," Sally said, between halting, short breaths as she sat back on the sofa. "I just can't get over his hard-on looking like a tent!"

Rachel shook her head, frowning. "I'm sorry, I don't see the humor."

Jamie sat between Rachel and Sally and leaned in close. As Jamie talked, Rachel wrinkled her nose. Jamie's breath smelled like stale alcohol and cigarettes.

"I'm going to tell you something, but you have to promise to keep it between us," Jamie urged.

"Okay, I promise," Rachel said with big eyes, rubbing her nose.

"Doctor Benny has been married and divorced eight times."

"You're kidding!" Rachel squealed.

"Yes, girl. And years ago while he was living in Texas, he married one of his patients."

Rachel's mouth flew open as Sally looked on. "Girl, you're lying to me!"

"No, honey, I'm not!"

"Tell me more." Rachel twisted her body away from Jamie. Her bad breath was getting on her nerves.

Animated, Jamie kept talking. "His business partner was so disgusted by his behavior, she reported him to the licensing board. After a month in jail, the judge dismissed the case."

Rachel bolted from the couch, slapping her hands on her hips. "Are you saying he got away with this crap?"

"Yup, that's what I'm saying!" Amused by Rachel's reaction, Jamie added more fuel to the fire. "In Texas, spouses can't testify against one another in court. That's how he got away with it. You see, Doctor Benny is one smart, slippery old dog!"

Sally laughed. "I agree he's an old dog, but a smart one...that's a stretch. He's just good at covering up his shit!"

Rachel and Jamie howled with laughter. "Girl, that's a good one," Jamie giggled, barely getting out the words.

"So, who else knows about this?" Rachel flopped on the couch, grabbed her coffee mug, and took a sip.

"No one except Anne."

"Does Anne know him?" Rachel asked, raising an eyebrow.

"Yes, she was his partner. She's the one who reported his horny ass."

"Damn, what a story. So, what happened to his crazy wife?"

"She skipped town with his money and was never heard from again."

"Serves him right!" Secretly pleased Doctor Benny's wife got revenge. Rachel finished her coffee. The three women sat in silence, thinking, thinking, thinking of what to say to each other next.

Finally, Jamie stood up and walked to her desk. She fell in her chair, grabbed her newspaper, and leafed through the pages. She made faces, sipping on her coffee, which was now icy cold.

"Don't need no more of this," Jamie said as she set the mug on her desk.

Rachel's voice was hoarse. "Since we're telling secrets, I have a secret to share."

Jamie raised an eyebrow as she fiddled with her newspaper. "My, you are full of news this morning. What now?"

"Yeah, share," Sally piped in.

"First, I'd like to say, I think Beth is right."

"Right about what?" Jamie leaned back in her seat and picked up her pencil. She chewed on the pink eraser, rocking back and forth.

"About Doctor Benny," Rachel said.

"Go on," Sally urged.

"I didn't think much about it at the time, but I witnessed Beth grilling Doctor Benny about Susan Cole's disappearance as if he had something to do with it."

Jamie put her pencil down. She leaned forward and placed her elbows on the desk, cradling her chin in her hands, looking wide-eyed. "Really?"

"Huh, huh! After Beth grilled him, he became so angry he left her office and slammed the door."

"Wow," Sally said, blinking her eyes. "I would've liked to have been a fly on the wall and seen that!"

Jamie's short, pudgy fingers methodically tapped the desk. "Keep talking. I think I know where you're going with this."

"Doctor Benny's past indiscretions, Susan Cole's disappearance, and his outrageous behavior with Mary Peters are all related. He's guilty as hell and he should go to jail!"

"Hold on," Sally cautioned. "We don't know if he's responsible for Susan's disappearance. Doctor Beebe is still investigating the situation."

Rachel hung her head low, looking up at Sally with puppy-dog eyes. "I know, but should I tell Doctor Beebe about Doctor Benny's behavior with Mary Peters? It might help shed light on his investigation."

"I think you need to tell Beth first," Sally advised.

Rachel mulled over her thoughts for a brief moment. "I suppose you're right. I should follow the chain of command."

"You got it," Sally smiled.

"I sure hate this. Lord knows I don't want to cause Doctor Benny any trouble." Although Rachel despised Doctor Benny's behavior, she was worried he would lose his job if she tattled on him. Hesitant, but with a strong desire to do right, Rachel looked to Jamie for guidance, and Jamie didn't waste any time giving her some.

"You have to tell Beth. You can't keep this a secret. This behavior has to stop!"

"I know." Rachel's face darkened, and a cold shiver rippled up her spine. "Jamie, will you go with me to tell Beth? That woman really scares me!"

Jamie laughed. "Sure. I wouldn't dare leave you alone with that witch! Girl, we're a team!"

"You're a gem!" Rachel beamed with a broad smile on her face. She got up and headed to the door. Jamie left her seat and joined her there. "Sally, we're going to Beth's office.

"Good luck. Keep me posted." Sally rose to her feet, followed them out the door, and returned to her office. Rachel and Jamie headed to Beth's office, planning their strategy along the way.

"I think I should start the conversation," said Rachel. "After all, I witnessed the incident. You can jump in if I leave anything out."

"Good idea."

"I hope Beth listens and doesn't give us a hard time." Rachel didn't like talking to Beth about anything. The woman scared her. Beth could be so intimidating.

"Girl, stop worrying. She'll listen. Beth hates Doctor Benny."

As soon as they arrived at Beth's office, cigarette smoke hit them in the face. The door was slightly ajar, and Jamie shoved it wide open, stepping inside. "Beth, we need to talk to you. It's urgent."

"What do you mean, urgent?" Beth asked, puffing on her cigarette. She glared at Jamie and Rachel with bloodshot eyes.

"Urgent is urgent," Jamie said as she sat in a chair across from Beth. Too scared to enter, Rachel stood in the doorway, her eyes big as a spotted owl's. Beth took one look at her and frowned. "What are you standing there for? Bring your little behind in here and sit down!"

Rachel did as she was told, shutting the door behind her. She sat in a chair close to Jamie. Her seat felt funny, and she could've sworn it was wet. Empty soda cans, juice bottles, and dried red spots were on the floor around her. Rachel tried to shift her body weight, but her butt wouldn't budge. Stuck to the seat, Rachel panic. *Oh, my goodness, there's something sticky on this damn chair!*

Beth smirked. "Are you all right over there? You looked uncomfortable."

"No, no, I'm fine," Rachel lied.

Beth leaned back in her chair, folding her arms on her breast. "So, what in the hell do you two want?" Beth's eyes reflected shades of green through her large bifocals.

Rachel's eyes were wild, and her heart pounded in her chest. "I...I...I have to tell you something," she stuttered.

"Get on with it!" Beth demanded. Before Rachel could say another word, Jamie stood on her feet and patted her butt, making a face. "Um, what's this wet sticky stuff in the chair?"

Rachel was relieved she wasn't the only one with the problem. Beth ignored Jamie as if she never asked the question. "I'm waiting to hear this urgent message."

Jamie shook her head and sat. She scooted around in her seat, cursing and mumbling to herself. Rachel attempted to move again, but her behind still wouldn't budge. Her brown eyes made contact with Beth's fierce glare. Rachel knew she better start talking. Panicky inside, perspiration beaded on Rachel's forehead.

"Yesterday, Doctor Benny and I interviewed Mary Peters," she said in a soft voice.

"Yessss..." Beth crooned with the word gliding off her tongue. She held her cigarette in her fingers, inhaling each puff, pursing her lips every time she blew smoke out. "Go on."

"She flirted with Doctor Benny, and he responded in kind. I thought his behavior was unprofessional."

"Huh, huh, I see." Beth leaned forward on her desk, and she put her cigarette out in the ashtray. Her green eyes narrowed as she stared at Rachel.

"He called her a naughty girl, and I noticed he had..."

Beth pounded on the desk and shot out of her chair like a jack-in-the-box, causing Rachel and Jamie to violently jerk back. "Honey, stop muttering and speak up!"

Rachel felt tears coming on. She knew this would happen.

Perturbed and far from being intimidated, Jamie made a bold move and lit into the supervisor. "Beth, what's wrong with you? You're scaring the hell out of us! Why are you acting so damn ridiculous! Rachel is trying to tell you something important, so damn it, listen!"

"Fine!" Beth's face softened along with her voice. "Sorry if I scared you, but speak up so I can hear you."

"Okay," Rachel meekly answered. Her heart raced in her chest, and it took a minute to get her bearings. After taking some deep breaths, Rachel continued with her story. "When Mary spread her legs wide open, I noticed Doctor Benny had, had..."

"Had what? Speak up!" Beth snapped.

Rachel's eyes watered. "I'm sorry, but I'm too embarrassed to tell you."

"Just say it!"

"Doctor Benny had a hard-on when Mary opened her legs!" Rachel blurted out.

"A what?"

Jamie glowered with anger. "Beth, come on, you're not freaking deaf! She said the man had a hard-on! A damn erection for goodness sakes!"

Beth gave Jamie an evil look. "Jamie, I get it," she hissed, rolling her eyes to Rachel. "Are you sure about this?"

"Yes, I am." Rachel blurted out, feeling a sense of relief. Her crazy supervisor finally got it, and now Rachel thought they could move on, but she miscalculated. Beth bombarded her with more questions.

"Did you confront the horny devil?"

"I did, but he blew me off."

Beth's voice was high-pitched. "What do you mean he blew you off?"

"He minimized the situation, and he immediately apologized," Rachel said with her stomach in knots. Again, she attempted to leave her seat, but she was stuck. Fear came over her. Her behind was glued to the chair. *How in the hell will I get out of here?*

"That horny devil," Beth murmured. She fell into her chair, opened a drawer, and pulled out her handbag. "I need another cigarette," she announced. After searching her bag, she found one and lit it up. "Damn him!"

"I know," said Jamie. "We thought you should know. You realize he flirts with some of the female patients around here, especially the attractive ones."

"I'm aware," Beth softly replied. The three women sat in silence, alone in their thoughts. Beth blew puffs of cigarette smoke into the air causing Rachel to cough. Beth put her cigarette out and broke the silence. "You know, I saw that horny rascal cozying up to Susan Cole. I thought there might be something going on between them."

"Yeah, I thought that, too," Jamie agreed.

Beth zeroed in on Rachel. "So, you say the man had a hard-on?"

"Yes, ma'am, he certainly did."

Beth grabbed her notepad and scribbled on it, feverishly taking notes. Jamie and Rachel exchanged hurried glances. Rachel wiped sweat off of her brow while her lips moved, formulating words with no sound. Jamie nodded, signaling she got the hint.

"Humph, there's another part to this story," Jamie said clearing her throat. Rachel braced for another one of Beth's explosions.

Beth stopped writing, and her head jerked up with intense anticipation in her green eyes. She slurred her words. "Yessssssss…please, go ahead."

"Anne told me Doctor Benny's last wife was a patient he treated in his private practice when he lived in Texas. He treated the woman for depression, and they had an affair."

"What a dog...then what happened?"

"Anne found out about the affair and reported him to the licensing board. He was jailed and released, and three months later the case was dismissed."

"Why was the case dismissed?" Beth asked.

Jamie drew in a deep breath. "Apparently, he and the patient got married and she refused to testify against him."

"That dirty dog!" Beth grabbed her phone and began dialing a number. Jamie stopped her.

"Wait, there's more." Jamie gestured for Beth to hang up the phone, and she complied.

"Okay, I'm listening."

"Rachel, tell her what you saw and heard last night," Jamie urged.

Rachel inhaled deeply. She didn't want to tell Beth, but she knew she had to. "Okay, here it goes...um, last night, I heard moaning in the employee lounge."

"Huh, huh, go on," said Beth.

"The door was closed, and I opened it to see what was going on. On the floor, I saw Doctor Hornsby and John Easley having sex."

Beth shot out of her chair and shouted. "Rachel, what the hell? You saw what?"

"I saw John and Doctor Hornsby getting it on in the employee lounge last night," Rachel repeated.

"Tell her about the barking," Jamie urged her, getting excited.

Beth cocked her head to the side, looking puzzled. "Barking? What barking?"

"Every time John said 'give it to me woman,' Doctor Hornsby barked like a Chihuahua!"

Beth screamed. "I knew it, I knew it, I knew it! I knew those two were having sex!" She slapped one hand over her mouth and whispered. "Did you say Doctor Hornsby was barking?"

"Um, yes, I guess she was turned on," Rachel calmly replied.

Beth's eyes went wild. "Who in the hell barks during sex?"

"Doctor Hornsby does!" Rachel and Jamie responded in unison. All three women fell out laughing.

"So, you knew about their relationship," Jamie said.

"Of course. The evening nurses told me about it, but no one had proof," Beth said.

Jamie was curious. "So, what did they say?"

"The nurses complained that Doctor Hornsby sometimes disappears and doesn't answer her pages. Hours later, she would show up looking frazzled and smelling like sex. This behavior has been going on for months!"

"Well, I'll be damned." Jamie stood on her feet momentarily, patting her butt. She flopped back in the chair.

"Beth, I've got a theory," Rachel interrupted with caution.

"What's that?"

"Was John on duty the night Susan Cole disappeared?"

Beth sank back in her seat, leaning forward and placing one elbow on the desk. She propped her chin in her hand, looking thoughtful. "I believe so."

"Is it possible whoever helped Susan Cole escaped knew John was preoccupied with Doctor Hornsby? I mean, John wasn't around when Susan left, and he didn't see the person who left with her."

Beth winked at Rachel. "Miss Thomas, you've got an excellent point." She paused and said. "Someone definitely escorted her off the unit. I always suspected Doctor Benny."

"That's why we came to you," Jamie said.

"Are you going to notify Doctor Beebe?" Rachel asked.

"Most definitely," Beth said with a bit of vindictiveness in her voice.

"I don't want him to lose his job. I just..."

Beth cut Rachel off. "Miss Thomas, stop worrying. It's not your fight. I appreciate your information. You and Jamie can leave now."

"Yes, ma'am," both social workers responded at the same time. When Rachel got up to leave, she heard a loud rip. Rachel glanced at her seat and panicked. Part of her pants was stuck to the seat. Turning ruby red with tears in her eyes, Rachel reached back and felt air and underwear.

"Oh, no, I've got a big hole in the seat of my pants! There's something sticky in this chair!"

Jamie lurched up and patted her butt. "My pants feel sticky, too!" Facing Beth, Jamie frowned. "What the hell did you put in these chairs to make our butts wet and sticky?" she demanded.

"Calm down," Beth chuckled.

"You think this is funny?" Jamie screeched. "Our butts are sticky and wet, and you think this is funny!"

"It's probably juice or soda on the seats. It's an accident. Calm down." Beth dismissively waved her off, laughing.

"Seriously?" Jamie said.

With a gleam in her eye and half-heartedly apologetic, Beth said, "Look, I'm sorry. There's nothing worse than a wet, sticky ass!"

Rachel and Jamie exchanged twisted glances, looking shocked at first, and then laughing. "Beth, you're a nut!" Jamie said, shaking her head.

"It takes one to know one," Beth cracked back.

"So long, Beth," Jamie huffed under her breath as she opened the door and hurried out with Rachel right behind her. "I've got to do something about these pants!"

"See you two later," Beth called out. She threw her head back and laughed as Rachel closed the door. "Now that some funny shit!"

Rachel and Jamie lingered in front of the door and heard Beth crooning on the phone, "Goood afternoon, Carl. I have some exciting news to share with you!"

Rachel and Jamie took the stairs to the ground floor to see Sally, who was in the nursing office. The office housed Sally's desk, and on the far wall sat a row of lockers for the nurses to store their personal belongings. The walls were virtually naked. Only a large calendar and monthly schedule hung near the door. Rachel and Jamie busted through the door, catching Sally by surprise.

"What's going on?" she gasped.

"We need your blow-dryer," Jamie said.

"Why, what happened?" Sally opened her desk drawer, took her blow-dryer out, and handed it to Jamie. Jamie turned it on, and she and Rachel took turns using it to dry their pants. Tears streamed down Sally's cheeks as Rachel told her about their meeting with Beth. Sally laughed so hard, she took a tissue from her smock pocket and sat on the sofa, wiping her face, giggling and mumbling, "Wet, sticky asses…wet, sticky asses."

Rachel, tearful and angry, lashed out at Sally. "Stop laughing at us! This is embarrassing! It's not funny!"

"Stop being a baby!" Jamie teased. "Be glad it was soda and not pee in those chairs!"

Sally giggled harder, and Rachel glared at Jamie with wet eyes. "I'm not a baby! I've got a right to my feelings!"

"Whatever!" Jamie muttered under her breath, rolling her eyes.

"So, did you tell Beth about Doctor Benny?" Sally asked, now more composed as she gently massaged her sore abdomen.

"We sure did, and Beth is going to tell Doctor Beebe." Jamie flopped in a nearby chair by Sally's desk and folded her arms.

Sally clapped her hands hard. "I can't wait for this shit to hit the fan!"

"I can't, either!" Jamie chuckled. The two women looked at Rachel and gasped. She had stripped to her underwear and was holding her ripped pants. "Does anyone have a needle and thread?" she asked, blinking her big brown eyes.

"Girl, what the hell are you doing, giving us a strip show?" Jamie joked

Finally, a grin appeared on Rachel's face. "Funny. But do either of you have a needle and thread?"

Sally leaped to her feet. "I do! Give me one minute." Sally reached in her desk drawer and took out her sewing kit. She handed it to Rachel. "Here, help yourself."

"Thank you." Rachel took the sewing kit and flopped on the couch. With her ripped pants on her lap, Rachel threaded the needle.

The door swung opened and Robbie Banks poked his head in. "Please, please, please lower your voices. I can't hear the little angels singing opera in my head," he pleaded with puppy-dogged eyes.

The three women stared at Robbie with their mouths hanging open, surprised he even heard them laughing with the door shut. Robbie closed the door, and the women bowled over in laughter.

Rachel smiled, finishing up her pants. Satisfied with her repair, she stood up and slid her pants on. "Sally, thanks for the needle and thread. You're definitely a lifesaver."

"Glad to help," Sally said. Soft knocking drew their attention to the door, and Sally glanced at the clock hanging on the wall. "Sorry, ladies, but I've got a meeting."

"Oh, no problem," said Rachel. There was another knock on the door, this time harder than the first. Rachel stepped to the door and yanked it open. Three nurses, all about five feet three inches tall, stood in the hall staring at her. "Is Sally here?" one of the nurses asked in a silvery voice.

"She's expecting you," Rachel replied, stepping aside. The three women marched in, one behind the other like tin soldiers in a parade. Rachel stepped out into the hall and Jamie quickly followed.

Sally walked over and stood in the doorway, hollering after them, "See you ladies later and stay out of trouble!"

Jamie waved, hurrying down the hall after Rachel. Catching up with her, the two women gave each other a high five. "I guess we accomplished our goal this morning," Rachel grinned.

"Well, done. Now let's see how the dominoes fall."

Later in the afternoon while Rachel was in her office, the phone rang. Rachel answered it on the first ring, and her dad was on the line.

"Hi, there, sweetheart. I'm coming to Salter's Point for a two-day conference. Let's meet for lunch tomorrow."

"Wonderful! I can't wait to see you." Thrilled her father was coming for a visit, Rachel excitedly asked. "Is there any place you would like to eat in particular?"

"No, go ahead and pick the restaurant," he responded in his usual husky voice. "I've no preference."

"Cool. Can I invite one of my coworkers?"

"Sure, fine with me."

"What time?"

"Is eleven-thirty too early?"

Rachel chuckled. "No. I'll call you later and give you the name and the address of the restaurant."

"Okay. Talk to you later."

Rachel hung up. It had been six months since she'd seen her father, and she couldn't wait to visit with him and tell him about the fight she witnessed on the unit. Eager to hear his opinion, she laughed to herself, knowing full well even her father would think a fight between coworkers and all of the other events were crazy.

Chapter Eight

Friday, November 16th

Rachel waited for her father in a booth near the entrance of Ming-Chang Kicks, a famous hole-in-the-wall five minutes from the hospital. She selected the place because the food was not only authentic, but spicy and delicious. The ambiance was simple, with red wallpaper throughout. Green ivy plants in light blue porcelain pots hung from the ceiling, and two black Buddha figurines sat on the counter in the lobby. Some patrons ordered takeout, while other customers like Rachel chose to eat in.

Rachel fidgeted in her seat with excitement. Although most of the time Beth scared her to death, Rachel was pleasantly surprised when the supervisor agreed to let her off for a couple of hours. She only hoped her father would be on time and not get lost. She had a lot to tell him, and she needed the full two hours.

The restaurant's warm vibe and delectable, savory aromas made her stomach growl with anticipation. She'd eaten little for breakfast, only a slice of toast and a boiled egg followed by a big cup of her favorite Café Verona coffee.

While Rachel was scanning the menu, Jamie moseyed in. Her burnt-orange wool suit coat was wrinkled and had cat hair clinging to the front. The dark circles under her eyes made her look tired.

"Hey, girl," Jamie greeted her, stepping briskly to the booth and glancing at her watch. "I'm here on time!"

"Yes, you are. So glad you came." Rachel's mouth curved into a sunny smile.

"I wouldn't miss meeting your dad for the world," Jamie smiled as she slid into the booth.

Rachel's sunny smile faded. She could smell the alcohol on Jamie's breath, and it was kicking. Steaming inside, Rachel lit into Jamie with an abrasive, accusatory voice. "Girl, have you been drinking? And look at you, there's cat hair all over you."

"Girl, mind your own business," Jamie frowned, brushing the front of her coat with both hands. She grabbed the menu, looking it over. "Have you ordered yet?"

"No, I'm waiting for my dad." Rachel cringed, rubbing her nose.

"Have you decided what you want?"

"I'm ordering my favorite, Szechuan Chicken."

"Good choice," Jamie said, looking around. "Where's the waitress? I need a drink."

Rachel tapped her fingers hard on the table and cleared her throat. "Really, Jamie? Do you have to drink in front of my dad?"

"What's wrong with that? We're all adults here," Jamie huffed.

"But it's my dad," Rachel pouted with her shoulders sagging.

Jamie threw her hands up in the air, huffing loudly. "All right, I won't drink in front of your dad."

"Thank you." Rachel sighed with relief. She hoped her father wouldn't notice the alcohol smell on Jamie. The sickly, sour odor was loud and offensive.

At the appointed time, precisely at eleven-thirty, DeWayne Thomas' lanky six-foot-two-inch frame entered the restaurant doorway. He looked splendid in his navy-blue suit, and his wavy black hair swept away from his face looked striking against his chocolate complexion. He strolled into the lobby, stroking his thin black mustache as his deep-set brown eyes scanned the place like a hawk.

Rachel popped out of her seat and wildly waved at him to catch his attention, and he picked up his pace, strolling swiftly across the room.

"How's my sweet girl?" he roared with his arms spread wide, grabbing Rachel and pulling her toward him into a bear hug.

"So glad to see you, Dad!" Rachel squealed, wrapping her arms around his lanky body. They rocked back and forth, embracing each other while Jamie looked on, grinning like a possum.

"Let me look at you." Her father clasped her shoulders as he gently nudged her back, lovingly staring into her welcoming eyes. "You look like you've grown a notch," he teased.

"No, Dad, I stopped growing years ago. I'm still five foot two," Rachel giggled.

"Who do we have here?" he asked, looking over at Jamie.

Jamie stood on her feet, leaned over the table, and offered her hand. "I'm Jamie Lee. I work with your daughter."

"Glad to meet you." He smiled warmly as he shook Jamie's hand. "I understand you've been teaching Rachel some clinical skills."

Jamie looked at Rachel and chuckled. "I'm doing my best. She's a quick learner."

He laughed. "That she is."

Rachel slid into the booth, and her father sat next to her. He grabbed a menu and began checking out the choices. "What's good to eat here?" he asked.

"I usually get the Szechuan Chicken. It's my favorite," Rachel said.

"Beef and Broccoli is my favorite," Jamie piped in.

At that moment, a short woman with brown eyes and dark brown braids bounced over to their table. She had on blue jeans, black adidas tennis shoes, and a short-sleeved tee shirt. The waitress took her notepad out of her apron pocket. "What can I get you?" she asked in a bored voice, eyeing Rachel's father.

"You ladies go first," he gestured.

"Beef and Broccoli with a glass of water," Jamie said.

119

"Szechuan Chicken for me," Rachel blurted out. "And a glass of water with lemons."

"I'll take what she ordered," her dad said, nodding his head in Rachel's direction. The waitress scribbled the orders on her pad and gathered up the menus. "Anything else?"

"No, I don't think so," Rachel smiled.

Jamie batted her eyelashes. "Professor Thomas, do you mind if I order a drink. I had a stressful morning."

His expression was dull. "Young lady, should you be drinking during business hours?"

Jamie smirked. "Probably not, but it calms my nerves."

Rachel shrank back in her seat, quivering inside. She was so angry, she wanted to reach over and slap Jamie. She nudged her dad's foot underneath the table, and he flashed her a weak smile.

"Suit yourself, young lady," he said, sounding annoyed.

"Bring me a shot of Jack Daniels," Jamie told the waitress.

"Will do." The waitress took off after she wrote the order.

Rachel scooted over a notch, giving her dad more room. He leaned forward and folded his arms on the table. "So, what's been going on? Have they found the missing patient yet?"

"No, Dad, not yet," Rachel eagerly replied.

"Do you know how she escaped?"

Jamie scratched her nose, looking at Rachel wary-eyed. "We have our theories, but we can't talk about it. It's confidential."

"Ladies, fair enough."

"You're not going to believe what happen the other day," Rachel interjected, changing the subject.

"Well, tell me."

A silly grin came over Rachel's face and she cracked up laughing. "The hospital attorney and a bunch of nurses got into a fight on the Admissions Unit. Even one of the doctors got involved."

Her dad fell back in his seat, furrowing his brow. "They got into a fistfight?"

"Yeah, a fistfight…rolling on the floor, pulling each other's hair, on and on," Rachel told him with big eyes.

Confusion fell on her father's handsome face. "What started the fight?"

"A patient hit the charge nurse with his cane. The nurse snatched the cane from him, and the patient fell on the floor. Hiram came out of nowhere, he's the attorney, and punched the nurse right in the nose. Everything exploded."

Jamie offered her two cents. "Professor Thomas, Hiram is crazy. There's no ifs, ands, or buts about it!"

He folded his arms across his chest with a baffled expression on his face. "You've got to be kidding me!"

"No, Dad, I'm not."

"Professor Thomas, a lot of people working in that hospital have loose screws," Jamie laughed.

He gave Jamie the side-eye. "Miss Lee, physically fighting each other is a bit much."

Soon the waitress returned with their drinks and meals, setting everything on the table. "Can I get you guys anything else?"

"No," everyone chimed in at once. The waitress bounced off, leaving the three of them to their meals. They dug in, eating in silence for a few minutes. All of a sudden, a man's loud voice drew their eyes to the lobby. Jamie groaned.

"Here comes trouble!"

Hiram stood at the counter, looking like a mad scientist with his long blond wiry locks tangled like a mop on his head. His wire-framed glasses sat lopsided on his nose, and his blue tweed coat was crumpled at the bottom. The white gym socks he wore stood out because his tan slacks were three inches too short, and his black penny loafers were caked with dried dirt.

Rachel nudged her father's elbow. "Who in the hell is that?" he asked, narrowing his eyes.

"The hospital attorney I told you about," Rachel calmly replied with a gleam in her eye.

"You've got to be kidding me! He looks like a clown!"

Rachel and Jamie cracked up. "Dad, he always looks hilarious," Rachel said.

"He goes to court looking like that?"

"All the time," Jamie giggled. They stared at Hiram, not saying a word, watching him order takeout as he danced in place.

"Hiram wants an order of Egg Foo Young and a can of Pepsi to go," Hiram loudly growled tapping a tune on the counter with his ink pen.

Rachel noticed her father frown and turn away. "That man acts like a toddler," he said, picking up a piece of chicken and shoving it in his mouth.

"That's not the half of it," Jamie said under her breath.

He rolled his eyes and shook his head. "Hiram is a little too much."

"Oh, boy, here he comes. Brace yourselves," Rachel warned. She picked up her chopsticks and stabbed at her chicken.

Hiram's lips parted into a wide grin as he pranced to their table, twisting his butt. When he arrived at the table, he waggled his eyebrows. He stood on the side of the booth where Rachel and her father sat. "Hiram is glad to see you guys here," he smirked.

Rachel placed her hand on her dad's shoulder. "Hiram, this is my father, DeWayne Thomas. He came for a visit."

"How wonderful! Hiram is glad to meet you, sir," he bowed with his head touching his knees, stretching out one hand.

Bemused by Hiram's behavior, Rachel's father reached over the table and reluctantly shook his hand. "Glad to meet you, too."

"My pleasure," Hiram bowed again. His hazel eyes drifted Jamie's way and he poked out his bottom lip. "Missy, you invited Sugar Tits to lunch with your pappy and didn't include Hiram? Hiram is pissed!"

Rachel snickered out loud. She couldn't help herself.

Rachel's father was floored. "Excuse me, who are you calling Sugar Tits?"

"Her!" Hiram shouted, pointing at Jamie.

"Don't you think that's a little out of line?"

Hiram raised an eyebrow, jolting his hip to the side as he slapped his right hand on his waist. "No, because Sugar Tits is her nickname!"

Rachel glanced at Jamie, and she noticed veins throbbing in her neck. She was as red as a chili pepper and seething with rage.

Jamie snatched her whiskey, gulped it down, and threw the empty shot glass at Hiram's chest. When she shot out of her seat, the table tipped, causing Rachel and her dad to jerk back. Jamie didn't notice. "Hiram, go somewhere! We don't have time for your silly mess!" she screamed.

Hiram gasped, blinking his eyes dramatically and tilting his body backward. "Oh, sweet Sugar Tits, such anger, such venom thrown at Hiram all at once for no reason!"

"I'm out of here!" Jamie grumbled as she scanned the area for a waitress. She noticed one walking in the general area, and she raised her arm, snapping her fingers. The waitress saw her and came right over.

"What's the matter?" she asked, her eyes round.

"Please bring me a to-go box and another shot of whiskey!"

"Jamie!" Rachel gasped. "I don't…"

Her father cut his eyes at her and placed his finger over his lips. Rachel stopped talking.

"I'm sorry, Professor Thomas," Jamie apologized. "I can't deal with this nitwit!"

"Nitwit? Hiram is not a nitwit!"

Jamie looked at the waitress with her eyes narrowing. "Please get me a box to go before I kill this fool!"

"Certainly!" the waitress said. She took off running to the kitchen while Hiram and Jamie glared at each other.

Fidgety and embarrassed, Rachel had enough. "Hiram, if you don't mind, I'd like to spend some time alone with my dad. I have some family stuff to discuss with him," she fibbed.

"Hiram gets that. But what about Sugar Tits? Is she leaving?"

Jamie slammed her fist on the table so hard, Rachel and her dad bounced up and down in their seats.

"It's Jamie, not Sugar Tits!" She gritted her teeth.

"Time for Hiram to leave." He shrugged his shoulders, backing up.

"Good riddance!" Jamie snorted.

Hiram spun around on his heels and pranced to the counter, twisting his behind. The waitress gave him his bag of food as he danced toward the exit. "Have a nice day, everybody!" he yelled as he slipped out the door.

Jamie wrung her hands. "Geez, he gets on my last nerve!"

"You shouldn't let him get to you like that. He's just looking for attention."

"Dad, I tried to tell her that many times." Rachel nodded her head.

The waitress appeared with Jamie's to-go box and her shot of whiskey. After the waitress set the items on the table, Jamie grabbed the whiskey and swallowed it all at once. She coughed, clearing her throat while Rachel covered her face with her hands.

"Really, Jamie," she grumbled, "I wish you wouldn't do this."

"Stop worrying. I'm fine," Jamie insisted. She scraped her leftovers into the to-go box and tossed a twenty-dollar bill on the table. "Professor Thomas, I've got to go, but it was nice meeting you."

"You, too." He pressed his lips together with a slight frown.

Narrowed-eyed, Rachel was skeptical. "Are you going to be all right?"

"Absolutely! See you at work." Jamie grabbed her box and hurried away from the table.

Rachel looked at her dad, and he shook his head in disbelief. "I've seen nothing like this before. Those two are nuts!"

"I told you," Rachel giggled, feeling vindicated. "Now, do you still want me to stay at the hospital for two whole years?"

"Sweetheart, I don't know." Her father adjusted his tie, looking worried. "If the rest of your coworkers act like those two, you might want to reconsider."

Rachel fell out laughing. "Actually, I like working there. I've decided I'm going to stay for a while."

"Okay, but be careful. You don't want craziness rubbing off on you."

"I'll be extra careful, I promise," Rachel laughed.

"Anything else happening in that crazy place?"

"Wellll…I witnessed a doctor having sex with one of the security guards one evening," Rachel calmly revealed.

"Excuse me? What did you say?" Her father's eyes looked like they were going to pop out of their sockets.

"Yep! They were on the floor in the breakroom getting it on. And Dad, let me tell you, Doctor Hornsby yelped like a little Chihuahua."

Her father roared with laughter, causing several customers to turn and look at him.

"Dad!" Rachel gasped, red in the face. "People are looking at us. You're laughing too loud."

"Hell, I can't help it. That's some crazy shit!"

Rachel lowered her head and snickered. "That's not the half of it."

"You got more?"

"Yep."

"Let's hear it." Her father sighed, reaching for his napkin and wiping the perspiration off his face. He grabbed his glass of water, sipping it down.

"One of the doctors flirted with a female patient right in front me during an interview, and boy did I let him have it."

"What do you mean, he flirted?"

"Well, the man called the woman naughty and, Dad, he even had the nerve to get hard."

Her father blew out his cheeks, choking on his water, coughing his heart out. "Did I hear you right?" he asked in a strained voice. "Damn, child, what kind of a place do you work for?"

"A looney bin," Rachel giggled.

Her father fell back in his seat, flabbergasted. "Rachel, my dear, please be careful. Don't let these crazy fools make you crazy like them."

"Don't worry, Dad, I won't," Rachel laughed.

Susan Cole laid sprawled out on a leather couch in the living room munching on popcorn and watching *One Life to Live*, her favorite soap opera, on Doctor Benny's twenty-inch television. She was dressed in a pink nightie and her blond hair was arranged in a ponytail. During the Crest commercial, she hopped up and hurriedly wiped the leather couch and its matching love seat with a damp cloth. She also wiped down the television and the shiny black console it sat on. Then when the soap opera came back on, Susan flopped on the couch and lay down.

While watching the television, Susan's eyes drifted to the six-foot-tall bookcase in the corner. It was filled with books and medical journals, piquing Susan's curiosity. Susan hopped up and went over to the bookcase. She grabbed a journal, leafing through the pages. Soon Susan came across an article on depression, and she returned to the couch and sat. She forgot about *One Life to Live* as she read the article, spelled-bound. *My! The symptoms described in this article sounds just like what I've been experiencing!*

For two hours, Susan made herself comfortable on the couch, reading every journal article on depression. After she finished, Susan realized for the first time in her life just how ill she had been all these years. Now enlightened, and with a new appreciation for George Benny, Susan smiled widely. *George deserves an award. He's treated me like a queen and brought me out of my pit of hell.*

Susan knew she lacked for nothing. No man, not even her own father, had shown her such kindness. At times, she felt like a leech, and she told George so. He would reassure her, covering her face with warm wet kisses until she felt better. The truth was, Susan felt the world owed her everything. After all, she had suffered so many atrocities in her life.

Susan got up and moseyed to the bathroom. She took her hair down and brushed it, then she twisted it in a big knot on top of her head. The scar on her forehead caught her attention. It reminded her of one of her darkest moments. She'd been having an affair with her boss, Picasso, and one evening his fiancé came home early and found them in bed together. The fiancé beat her to within an inch of her life, and after she recovered, she moved to Salter's Point to get a fresh start. But, as usual, life didn't turn out as she'd planned, and she'd ended up at Salter's Point Regional.

When Susan first laid eyes on Doctor George Benny, she was smitten. She adored his bedside manner and loved his kind, self-deprecating demeanor. Soon, she and the doctor became sexually involved, and Susan looked forward to their daily romantic escapades in his office. She was thrilled when he asked her to move in with him. It was an opportunity she couldn't resist. For several weeks, they planned her escape, executing their plan early one morning. The scenario went off without a hitch, and now Susan spent most days watching game shows and soap operas, and cooking meals for George. Once in a while, she would flip the channel to KIRO News to watch current events in the area. Susan was always surprised to learn her disappearance was still a riveting news story. Authorities were still looking for her after all this time.

Although she loved George Benny to the bone, Susan often felt like a prisoner in exile. Caught up in her own drama, her own sad story, stuck in the house, never going out for fear of being exposed. It was an awful way to live, and sometimes she felt lonely, isolated, stuck in an existence she never imagined. But when George came home, those dark thoughts magically disappeared. He was her knight in shining armor, and he had given her a new perspective on life.

This evening she'd make him lasagna and a big Caesar salad to show her appreciation. Susan glanced at her watch and noticed it was four o'clock. George would be home in two hours. Susan washed and dried her hands, then dashed out of the bathroom to the kitchen. For the rest of the afternoon until George came home, Susan prepared dinner.

Hiram, Doctor Benny, and Rachel were in the conference room waiting for Robbie Banks' commitment hearing to start. Rachel reflected on lunch with her father, and his words, *don't end up crazy like them*, rang in her ears. Court hearings were held in the conference room Monday through Friday.

Judge Dike Bigger, who'd arrived earlier, quietly sat at the end of the conference table reviewing notes. Completely bald and short in stature, Judge Bigger had commanding brown eyes and a brown bushy mustache. He looked the part in his long flowing black robe and his gavel sitting on the table in front of him. He was a no-nonsense legal scholar, and he often made decisions expeditiously. He was well-respected among his peers in the community.

On his left, Hiram sat quietly picking his nose. He pulled out a booger and flicked it across the room. Rachel turned her head, groaning with disgust. Doctor Benny was too engrossed in Robbie's notes to notice.

The door flew open, and a nurse escorted Robbie into the room. Robbie took a seat at the end of the table directly facing the judge. He sat on his legs, looking somber with his big onyx eyes. His unruly red hair was tied into a ponytail. Quiet as a mouse, Robbie checked out his opposition. He stared at the judge, watching his every move.

Soon, the judge nodded his head in Hiram's direction and the attorney slid out of his seat. Hiram pranced over to Robbie's side and stood behind him, his large hairy hands gripping the back of Robbie's chair. Eager and determined to persuade Judge Bigger to dismiss Robbie's case, Hiram began his argument as he playfully wiggled his eyebrows.

"Your Honor, this young man is stable. The medicine he takes works. Therefore, he no longer needs hospitalization. He is ready to go home."

"Your Honor?" Doctor Benny shifted in his seat. "Although Robbie is stabilized on Haldol and his voices are no longer prominent, he's certainly not out of the woods. He requires additional monitoring and observation. So, I would like to keep him in the hospital a little longer."

"Objection!" Hiram yelled, flipping his hair back. "Your Honor, you can see with your own eyes the doctor is lying. Look how calm he is. For the past three days, the staff has documented in his chart.

Zero somersaults! Robbie should be allowed to return home. Please dismiss this case!"

"Oh, get a grip," Doctor Benny groaned. "You can't be serious."

Judge Bigger pounded the desk with his gavel and shouted. "Order in the court!"

Both Hiram and the doctor clammed up while Rachel looked on. Judge Bigger peered at Robbie over his black-framed glasses. For five minutes, he studied the quiet young man's face, then he asked, "Mister Banks, are you willing to stay on your medication to keep the voices away?"

Robbie tilted his head backward and screamed like a hyena. The judge reared back with his eyes big and round in his eyeglasses. White as a sheet, Judge Bigger wildly gestured for Hiram to sit, and the attorney reluctantly complied.

"I agree with the doctor," the judge's voice trembled. "This young man needs additional monitoring."

"But, Your Honor," Hiram argued, "Robbie doesn't hear any voices telling him to flip or perform somersaults! He's been free from this condition for the past three days! The man is cured!"

"Yes, but…"

Out of the blue, Robbie leaped to his feet and climbed on the table. He stood upright, leaping into the air, twirling around twice with his feet over his head. Finally, he landed safely on the judge's end of the table. Judge Bigger had already scooted his chair out of the way to keep from getting kicked.

Shaken, the judge hoarsely yelled, "This man is completely out of control! *Someone better grab this man right now!*"

Red-faced, Hiram jerked Robbie's arm and dragged him off the table. "Dude, sit down!"

Robbie sat in a chair and folded his legs. He looked up at Hiram, blinking his long eyelashes and poking his bottom lip out. Pissed, Hiram turned his back and made eye contact with Judge Bigger.

"I'm sorry, Your Honor. I didn't know this would happen."

"I'll bet." Doctor Benny smirked under his breath. Quiet, but desperately trying to hold back laughter, Rachel tightly held one hand over her mouth.

However, the judge wasn't receptive to Hiram's apology. Instead, he reached for his gavel and pounded on the table. Hiram drew back wide-eyed.

"Mister Gottchalks, I don't think going home is in Mister Banks' best interest at this time. Therefore, I order Robbie Banks to remain in this hospital for an additional fourteen days. This is my final ruling. This court is adjourned!"

Doctor Benny grinned like the Cheshire Cat. "Thank you, Your Honor."

The judge rose from his seat, tossed the gavel on the table, and dashed out of the conference room, leaving Hiram speechless, defeated, and licking his wounds. For a brief moment, silence engulfed the room. Hiram abruptly stood up and gestured for Robbie to follow him. Robbie unfolded his legs and bolted from his chair. He winked at Doctor Benny, then he leaped into the air, his long body twirling before he landed safely on his feet again.

Hiram was furious. "Dude, will you stop that! Haven't you embarrassed Hiram enough?"

Robbie giggled like a little kid. Hiram swung the door open. "Let's go!"

Robbie backflipped out the door with Hiram running after him, growling at the top of his voice. "Hiram demands you stop this nonsense right now! Stop it!"

Rachel and Doctor Benny broke out into laughter. Barely getting out the words, Rachel squealed, "I love beating Hiram at his own game! He's such a baby!"

"Yeah, we whipped his pompous ass," the doctor joked, feeling satisfied. They laughed and basked in their victory until Rachel noticed the time. Overall, she liked Doctor Benny. For a minute, she felt guilty telling Beth about his unsavory conduct with Mary Peters. Rachel took a deep breath, brushing her thoughts aside, deciding in the end that she'd made the right call. Rachel bolted out of her seat and hurried to the door.

"I've got to go!"

"Where are you going?"

"I've got a telephone interview with a family member. I can't be late." Before Doctor Benny could ask her another question, Rachel was out the door.

Chapter Nine

Thursday, November 22nd – Thanksgiving

The moment Rachel open the unit door, the delightful, delicious citrus, nutty scent of baked turkey engulfed her nostrils. The enticing smell came from the kitchen located at the back of the dining room. Jamie had told her earlier the chef would be roasting three twenty-five-pound turkeys in the hospital's industrial oven.

As soon as Rachel arrived in the dining area, she saw dietary staff busily preparing the patient dining room for the big feast ahead. Male and female cooks wearing big floppy white hats spread orange tablecloths on substantial round tables. Housekeeping staff in tan uniforms dusted and scrubbed the chairs, end tables, and blinds. Even patients got into the act, decorating tables with fancy silverware along with elaborate displays of pilgrims, Indians, miniature turkeys, and bright orange pumpkins.

Hiram, covered with red and brown feathers from his neck to his ankles, sniffed the air like a dog, inhaling the delicious aroma as he pranced around the dining room. Decked out in a turkey costume, Hiram told everyone that he was dressed for the occasion. With his red-feathered tail bouncing up and down like a floppy ball, Hiram pranced in and out of patient rooms for two whole hours alerting patients to their upcoming court hearings after the holiday.

While he was at it, Hiram danced a little jig. Patients enamored with his dancing skills soon joined in. They clapped and danced with him in the hall, mimicking his every move. Pleased with their interaction, Hiram wasted no time amplifying the silliness, wiggling his behind, jumping in the air, and squatting every two to three minutes. Patients copied him, not missing a beat.

When Hiram saw Rachel coming toward him, he quickly switched tothe Funky Chicken. He danced up to her, forcing Rachel to stop in her tracks. She fell out laughing, waving her hands trying to brush him away.

"Hiram, what are you doing? You're so freaking crazy!"

"It's Thanksgiving, missy! Time to celebrate!"

He danced in a circle around Rachel, and she whirled around in place, trying to keep up as her head spun.

"Will you stop it? You're making me dizzy!" she giggled. Hiram stopped dancing. He threw both hands on his hips, looking at her with his lips clamped tight. Rachel could see his hazel eyes blinking erratically through the holes of his mask. "Stop staring at me, you nitwit! You're giving me the creeps!"

Hiram laughed.

Out of nowhere, loud laughter came from the nursing station, and Rachel and Hiram turned to look. "I wonder what's going on?" Rachel asked.

"Hell, if Hiram knows," the attorney smirked as he took off to the nursing station. Rachel caught up with him as Hiram opened the gate, and she followed him inside. Jamie, who decided at the last minute to come to work on Thanksgiving day, stood with Sally, and several nurses in a big circle, laughing their heads off.

Sally held up a piece of paper, fumbling her words. "Oh, I can't...I can't..." as laughter gurgled deep in her throat. Rachel walked over to her.

"What the hell is going on here? What's so damn funny?"

"Yeah, Hiram also wants to know what's so damn funny." He stood close to Rachel with both hands on his hips and his purple beak twisted on his face. Beet red with sweat dripping down her face, Sally took one look at Hiram and stooped over with laughter. Jamie shook her head and laughed.

"Girl, ignore this fool and tell me what's so funny!" Rachel demanded.

Unable to talk, Sally kept on giggling. Jamie stepped in.

"Obviously, you two haven't been to your mailbox this morning."

"Why, what happened?"

"Doctor Beebe put out a crazy memo. You've got to read it. It's so damn funny and off the wall. I think the man has lost his marbles." Jamie reached into her coat pocket and gave Rachel a copy of the memo. Rachel read it and howled with laughter.

"Let me see that." Hiram snatched the memo away from Rachel and began reading it out loud so everyone could hear him, putting on a show, adding drama to his words as everyone gave him their full attention.

To: My South Campus Hospital Staff
From: Doctor Carl Beebe
Important Subject: Unprofessional Behavior in the Workplace

It has come to my attention that some staff in this hospital were engaging in unorthodox sex and barking in the employee lounge during shift hours. Under no circumstances should there be unorthodox sex or unnecessary barking in the employee lounge or the office of the said person during on-call or shift hours. Please see your supervisor if you have any further questions concerning this matter. In the meantime, keep your sexual escapades and barking to yourself. Thank you.

Everyone roared with laughter.

"What does Doctor Beebe mean by unorthodox sex?" Rachel squealed with eyes wet with tears.

"Beats me!" Jamie chuckled, rubbing her eyes.

"Who was barking?" someone asked. "Can someone explain what Doctor Beebe is talking about?"

"I have no idea," answered a social worker standing behind her.

"What is this barking? Does anyone know anything about this barking?" a nurse asked.

"No," several people answered her at once.

Rachel, Jamie, and Sally giggled hysterically as they glanced at each other. None of them revealed the name of the person responsible for the barking. Instead, the three women remained silent, keeping their little secret to themselves, and Doctor Hornsby's barking continued to be a baffling, talked-about mystery for many years.

Waving the memo in the air, Hiram stepped up and stood on the seat of a chair. "Hiram has an idea, everybody! Let's give good old Doctor Beebe a written reply!"

Everyone cheered and stomped their feet in agreement. Sally yelled out. "Who's going to write it? Any volunteers?"

"Hiram will!" the attorney shouted as he hopped off the seat and ran to a typewriter sitting on the counter. Shoving his turkey mask up over his head, Hiram searched the desk for typing paper. Everyone soon joined in helping Hiram look. Hiram found a package under the counter, tore it open, and carefully threaded a piece of paper through the typewriter's roller. He straightened his shoulders and started typing. Snickers and comedic comments circulated through the crowd. Hiram typed and recited the words out loud.

To: Our Dear Doctor Beebe
From: South Campus Hospital Staff
Important Subject: Unorthodox Sex with Barking During Off Hours

We, the staff at South Campus Hospital, are responding to the memo you sent us this morning. Since we're banned from barking and having unorthodox sex in the employee lounge during shift hours, can we bark and have unorthodox sex during OFF hours instead? Also, can you clarify for us what you mean by unorthodox sex, and who was barking? Furthermore, since you do not approve of unorthodox sex, does orthodox sex meet your approval, and if so, can we perform it in the employee lounge during shift and on-call hours? Is barking allowed? We, the staff, appreciate your prompt response. Our professional work depends on it. Thank you for your assistance with this matter.

Hiram poked his chest out. "Tell Hiram, how does this sound?"

"Splendid," said Sally as everyone nodded in agreement. Once Hiram checked the memo, he stood on his feet.

"Hiram feels everyone should sign it before Hiram leaves it in Doctor Beebe's mailbox."

Hiram passed the memo off, and it made its way through the crowd. After every staff person signed it, the note was back in Hiram's hands. He danced a jig on his way to the exit. "Hiram is on his way, everybody. Hiram will be right back."

Everyone clapped as Hiram danced to the door. Once he reached the exit, he turned and faced the crowd, wiggling his red and brown tail. He pulled the turkey mask over his face and repeatedly bowed. Staff yelped with laughter and a nurse ran up and unlocked the steel door, shoving it open. Hiram pranced out the door as loud laughter erupted behind him.

Rachel spent most of the morning with Doctor Benny interviewing new admissions. It was eleven thirty when they finished their last interview. Mentally exhausted, Rachel exhaled deeply and closed her notebook. "Doctor Benny, I'm tired. I need a break."

"Why don't you go to lunch? Meet me back here at one o'clock. Then we can decide which patients to take to court tomorrow."

"Cool." Rachel left his office, and her stomach growled. She thought about the roasted turkey she had been smelling all day, and she couldn't wait to eat it. After all, Rachel hadn't eaten since six o'clock in the morning.

As soon as Rachel walked into her office, she called Jamie, who answered on the first ring.

"Jamie Lee, here."

"Girl, it's time for lunch. I have an idea I need to discuss with you."

"Okay, but let's eat in my office. I don't feel like going to the dining room."

"Why? It's Thanksgiving, Jamie! I want to eat in the dining room with the staff and patients."

Rachel heard Jamie let out a long sigh. "Okay, if you insist."

"What's wrong?"

"I guess I'm feeling bummed about Anne and me."

"Girl, what happened now?"

"We got into another tiff last night over her coming home late. I came to work this morning because we both needed space. This holiday is turning out to be so depressing."

"Well, staying in your office and thinking about your argument will make you even more depressed. I think it's better if you're around people."

"I'll guess you're right. I'll meet you in the dining room in a second."

"Cool." Rachel hung up the phone and walked out, locking the door behind her. Within minutes, she was standing in line in the dining area. Jamie and Peepers soon joined her, and Rachel wondered why Jamie was wearing her heavy black coat. She noticed Jamie was clutching something bulky against her breast.

"I'm here. Boy, I'm hungry!"

"Girl, I am too," Rachel gave Jamie the side-eye and momentarily looked down at Peepers, who was staring at her with his golden gaze. When their eyes met, he took off, disappearing down the hall.

"Peepers lives a pampered life," Rachel chuckled.

"He sure does."

Still eyeing Jamie's jacket, Rachel asked. "Jamie, what are you hiding inside your coat?"

"My pint of Jack Daniels."

Rachel dropped her shoulders, letting out a harsh breath. Jamie's drinking was getting out of control. *This woman has a severe problem. My friend needs help! I need to talk to Sally about getting her some help as soon as possible.*

The line moved fast and food was everywhere. The delicious, citrus, nutty aroma of roasted turkey drew Rachel to the table with the three twenty-five-pound turkeys. "Mmmm, I can't wait to eat. It smells so good."

Rachel grabbed a plate and utensils. She piled her plate with slices of white turkey breast and dumped a scoop of cornbread dressing on top. Then she moseyed over to another table and served herself some collard greens, potato salad, and cranberry sauce. Jamie followed her lead, piling her plate with food and confiscating a little extra meat for Peepers when she thought no one was looking.

"Jamie, I see you," Rachel giggled.

"The cat's got to eat."

"Girl, whatever."

After they filled their plates with food, they both grabbed a can of soda and a slice of sweet potato pie. Satisfied they had everything, they found a table next to a window and sat. Jamie wrapped Peeper's turkey meat in a napkin and stuffed it in her pocket. "I'll give this to Peepers later on."

"Spoiled cat," Rachel laughed. "Let's pray." Rachel bowed her head and clasped her hands tightly together. Jamie bowed her head, closing her eyes while Rachel gave thanks. After Rachel finished, the two women tore into their food. Rachel closed her eyes, chewing slowly and savoring each spicy, moist turkey morsel. For a minute, she thought she was in heaven until Jamie's loud smacking interrupted her concentration.

"Boy, you eat loud!"

"I can't help it. This turkey is so good." Jamie laughed with a mouth full of food. She paused a moment to swallow. "So, tell me, what's this idea you have?"

"I was thinking about conducting a weekly group or class on the unit."

Jamie grabbed her roll and took a bite. She gave Rachel a funny face and shook her head. "Remember, this is the Admissions Unit. Groups don't generally work on a unit like this one."

"Why not?" Rachel stared at Jamie.

"There's no time. We see new admissions every day. You know we have to work them up for court. Besides, I hate groups."

"Oh, now the real reason comes out," Rachel chuckled.

"So, what type of group are you thinking about facilitating?"

"Something simple, like a cooking class."

Jamie fell out laughing. "Girl, please!"

"What's so damn funny?"

"Please, these patients are too psychotic to participate in a cooking class. Hell, they can barely put two decent sentences together that make sense. A cooking class? I don't think so."

"Well, you have a point, but I'm willing to try." Rachel took another bite of turkey. "I think I'll start with simple recipes."

Jamie cracked up again. "Simple recipes, eh? Sounds like a crock of baloney!"

"Jamie!"

"I'm sorry, I can't help it. You're so naïve."

"Oh please, stop being so negative!" Rachel grumbled.

Jamie sampled her potato salad. "You need to get Beth's approval."

"I figured that. So, you think a group is a bad idea."

"No, I just don't see how you can do one on a busy unit like ours."

"Well, I'd like to try. Besides, the patients need something more constructive to do than take smoke breaks every four hours. The class will focus on peer socialization, camaraderie, and learning a life skill. At least that is my goal."

"Smoking breaks provide the same goal," Jamie smirked.

"Yes, but knowing how to cook a healthy meal doesn't put one's life in jeopardy as smoking does."

"Yes, you're right."

"I think I'll type up a plan after I meet with Doctor Benny." Rachel reached for her can of Sprite. She tore off the tab and took two sips.

"I think you'll need to start small. No more than six patients in a group."

"I plan to select patients stabilized on their medications."

"Good idea. Make sure you pick a day other than Friday. Fridays, you know, are our busiest days."

"Yes, I'm aware."

"So, if Beth approves this group, have you decided on your first meal?"

"Yes, blueberry pancakes."

"Now, that sounds delicious. Be sure to save me some," Jamie grinned.

"Okay." Rachel sipped on her Sprite and glanced at her watch. It was twelve-fifty, and lunch was almost over. She hurriedly ate the rest of her meal and finished her Sprite. Then she stood on her feet. "Got to go. I have a meeting with Doctor Benny in two minutes."

"Tell that slippery horny dog I said hi," Jamie joked. Rachel fell out laughing. She picked up her dishes. "I'm going to drop these off at the kitchen on my way out. See you later."

"Adios," Jamie grinned.

The meeting with Doctor Benny was short. Rachel learned he had already selected the patients he wanted to take to court. Pleased to have the rest of the afternoon to herself, Rachel went straight to her office. Once there, Rachel hung a *Do Not Disturb, In A Meeting* sign on the front of the door and shut the door behind her. For the rest of the afternoon, Rachel worked on her group plan, and around four-thirty she was finished. Rachel gathered her belongings and left her office. Before she left the hospital to go home, Rachel dropped her plan in Beth's mailbox.

Later that evening, Rachel called her parents. Her mother answered the phone after the third ring. "Happy Thanksgiving, Mom!"

"Well, hello, darling. Happy Thanksgiving to you, too!" her mother crooned in a silvery voice. "How are things at work? Your father told me you work with some peculiar characters."

Rachel laughed. "Mom, that's an understatement. Is Dad around?"

"Yes, he is. You want to talk to him?"

"Yes, ma'am." Rachel heard her mother yelled for her dad to pick up the phone. The phone clicked, and her father's husky voice came on the line.

"Hi there, sweetheart! How's life treating you?"

"Do you remember during our lunch I told you about the two employees, a doctor and a security guard, who were having sex on the floor and barking?" Rachel giggled.

"Yes, I remember," her father sighed.

"There's something else."

"Go on."

"This happened today. After the medical chief heard about those two having sex in the lounge, he sent the staff a memo addressing the situation. Dad, it was so hilarious!"

"Well, what did it say?"

Rachel drew in a deep breath and read the memo to her father. He fell out into a donkey laugh, panting, his throat gurgling, trying to catch his breath, sputtering out words, coughing as he attempted to clear his throat. "That's the...that's the funniest shit I ever heard!"

"I know, right?" Rachel giggled. "The staff decided to answer the memo and guess who wrote the response."

"I don't want to think about it," her dad said, sounding hoarse.

"Hiram!"

"Damn, what did he say?"

Rachel read the memo to him and heard her father gasping for air on the phone as he erupted in laughter. "Sweet girl, all I know you work with a bunch of crazy-ass knuckleheads," he joked.

"Dad, look at it this way. By the time I leave this place, I'll be able to work anywhere and survive."

"You got that right!"

Friday, November 23rd

The next morning, Rachel raced to the mailroom and found her plan signed by Beth in her box. Her lips curled into a smile when she picked up the paper and read *Approved* stamped across the top. Ecstatic, Rachel couldn't wait to tell Jamie. She raced to her office, dropping her coat, handbag, and lunch bag on her desk. Then she locked the door and ran to Jamie's office, her breathing ragged by the time she arrived. Jamie was in the hall, locking her office door. She twisted her face up, frowning when she saw Rachel.

"Girl, whose chasing you this morning? Why all the running?"

"I'm so excited. Beth approved my group!"

Jamie rolled her eyes. "Well, isn't that spanking-ass wonder-ful!"

Rachel tucked her plan under one arm and pouted. "Why are you so sarcastic? I thought you'd be thrilled."

"I'm sorry. I'm just in a bad mood."

"Why, what's wrong?"

"Doctor James called. He wants to go over patients. I barely had a chance to sit and drink my coffee, and here he calls with this early morning meeting shit."

Rachel giggled. "I hear he's a taskmaster and easy on the eyes."

"You haven't met him yet?"

"Nope!"

"You will. The fact that he's easy on the eyes doesn't change my urge to want to wring his taskmaster's neck!" Jamie steamed.

Rachel mocked her. "Well, good luck with your meeting with the handsome Doctor James. I can't wait to meet him."

Jamie made an obscene gesture with her middle finger as she took off down the hall.

Rachel laughed. "Jamie, you're such a sourpuss!"

Two hours later, Rachel was holed up in the kitchen talking to Tom Wheatly, the head cook. She told him about the group and her plan to have it on a bi-weekly basis. Rachel was all ears when Tom offered his two cents. As she listened intently, Rachel couldn't help thinking how strange Tom's features looked. Tom had wide expressive gray eyes and ears like an elephant. Tall, burly, and bald on top, Tom had hair growing above his ear lobes. He always donned a big white chef's hat and wore a double-breasted white coat with gold buttons. To offset his outfit, Tom wore gray checkered pants with shiny black shoes. He had a voice that sounded scratchy and gritty, which reminded Rachel of fingernails scraping on a chalkboard.

"Miss Thomas," he croaked, "I will cordon off a section in the dining area near the kitchen. That way, if you need anything I'll be close by."

"Great." Rachel scribbled on her checklist. "The group will have six patients. I'll need four tables, three for the patients, and one for me. Two patients can share each table."

"No problem. I'll set everything up and make sure you have everything you need."

"Thanks so much." Rachel smiled as she checked off her list.

"So, when do you want to start this class?"

"Next Wednesday."

"Wednesday, it is." Tom smiled, hesitating for a moment. "Have you decided what you're going to cook?"

"Yes, blueberry pancakes. My recipe. I'll need a pot of cooked quinoa, vanilla extract, a large package of frozen blueberries, eggs, oil, milk, and five small boxes of Log Cabin Buttermilk Pancake Mix."

"Wow, quinoa, that's a twist," Tom chuckled.

"Yeah, I made it up. Quinoa makes the pancakes moist and fluffy."

"I see. Well, I'll make sure I have those items available."

"Thank you so much."

"My pleasure."

Rachel left the kitchen feeling proud of herself and excited about her new venture. However, she had one more task to do. She needed to select six patients. Not sure which ones to choose, Rachel stood at the nursing station counter contemplating. It wasn't long before Sally walked up.

"A penny for your thoughts."

"Oh, hi, Sally." Rachel turned to face her. "I'm trying to decide which patients are stable enough to participate in a cooking class."

Sally raised an eyebrow. "A cooking class? Whose bright idea was that?"

"Mine." Rachel frowned.

Sally slapped her hand over her mouth. "Oh, I'm sorry, I didn't mean to..."

"Don't worry, Jamie has already said her piece. You might as well say yours."

"I just want to say it's hard to get psychotic patients together to work on a task, especially one like cooking."

"That's why I want to select stable patients. At least after taking medications for a week, their thought processes should be more organized."

"Well, let me help." Sally walked around the counter, opened the gate, and went into the nursing station. She sat at the counter and began leafing through the book of patient care plans. "I hope you have a pen and paper with you."

"I do." Rachel hovered over the counter with her checklist, ready to jot down the names.

"Lucy Cornwell, Cootie Mockingbird, Cathy Skeleton, and June Bug Lewis." Sally paused.

"I need two more names."

"How about Robbie Banks and Mary Peters?"

Rachel jerked her head back with big eyes. "I know Robbie is better, but Mary... she's still in her own world of different personalities.

The last time I checked, she was dressed like a little girl, wearing pigtails and sucking on her thumb."

"She's better. Especially since Robbie has been paying her some attention. He always sits with her during meals."

"Okay, I'll add them to the list."

Sally closed the patient book and rose to her feet. "I'll update their care plans so the nurses will remember to bring them to your class."

"The class is next Wednesday morning at ten."

"Marvelous, my dear! So, what are you cooking?"

"Blueberry pancakes. Would you like me to save you some?"

Sally shook her head violently, making a face. "Darling, I don't like to eat anything flat, round and squishy."

Rachel's mouth sagged open. "Sally, huh?"

"Forget it, darling, it's too difficult to explain. I'll talk to you later." With that, Sally left the nursing station before Rachel could formulate another word.

Chapter Ten

Wednesday, November 28th

"Tom, there are two electrical outlets on the wall outside of the kitchen. I think it's best to put the table with the pancake griddles there," Rachel suggested.

"I agree."

Tom helped Rachel push the rectangular table against the wall. After he covered the table with a white linen cloth, he lined up three large pancake griddles on it and plugged them into the wall outlet. Thunder popped and roared outside, prompting Rachel to glanced at the big window across the room. Thick icy sleet trickled down the clear glass in big waves. Despite the dreary morning, Rachel felt pumped. She could hardly wait for her group to start.

Rachel meticulously arranged items around the pancake griddles. On one side, she had a large mixing bowl, a wooden spoon, and the ingredients for her blueberry pancakes. On the other side of the table, she had a dish of butter, a large pan, a spatula, paper plates, utensils, and syrup. Rachel made herself comfortable at the end of the table and watched Tom as he finished up.

Tom covered the remaining three tables with white linen cloths and arranged them in front of Rachel in a u-shaped pattern. Each table had two metal chairs, as well as the ingredients and equipment to make blueberry pancakes. On every table, there was a mixing bowl, a wooden spoon, a spatula, a box of log cabin pancake mix, a bottle of vanilla extract, a bowl of sugar, a pint of milk, a bottle of safflower oil, half cup of quinoa, and a container of fresh blueberries.

"I thought you'd like fresh blueberries instead of the frozen ones," Tom mentioned.

Rachel's face brightened, pleased with Tom's gesture. "You're so thoughtful. Pancakes taste so much better with the fresh ones."

Precisely at nine-fifty, the patients began trickling in. Lucy Cornwell and Cootie Mockingbird took their seats at the table on the right. A minute or two later, Cathy Skeleton and June Bug Lewis came in. They sat at the center table directly across from Rachel. When the clock in the tower struck ten, Robbie Banks and Mary Peters walked into the dining room holding hands.

Mary's long pigtails swished like a broom on her shoulders, and the pink party dress she was wearing had a big bow in the back. Mary had on matching bobby socks with a pair of tan hospital slippers. Robbie had on denim overalls with his tan hospital slippers, and his dark hair was tied back into a ponytail. Robbie graciously pulled out a chair, and Mary sat. She scooted closer to the table, then tightly clasped her hands on the top.

Robbie wrenched a chair from the table and flopped in it, crossing his legs. Robbie's lips moved nonstop with no sound coming out. Rachel thought Robbie heard voices, and she wondered if he had taken his medicine. Worried, she decided to check with him after class.

Once everyone was seated, Rachel rose to her feet.

"Good morning, everyone! Welcome to the first cooking class at Salter's Point Regional!"

"Good morning," everyone mumbled in unison.

"I'm glad you're here. I hope you find this class helpful in your daily life. You have an opportunity to learn how to cook and make new friends. So, relax and have some fun."

"Are we going to make pancakes?" Mary stared at the pancake box on the table.

"Yes, blueberry pancakes."

"Yummy!"

"Yummy is right. Let's get started!" Rachel picked up her box of pancake mix and held it up for everyone to see. "On the back, there's a recipe for six to ten pancakes. We'll use that recipe. Everything you need is on the table. First, measure out a cup of pancake mix and put it in the bowl..."

As Rachel continued with instructions, everyone loosened up. They all talked and laughed amongst themselves, except for Robbie Banks. Instead, Robbie stared at the table, talking to himself. Once in a while, he glared at Mary, who was vigorously stirring her pancake batter in the bowl. He flinched when Rachel suddenly clapped her hands.

"Okay, everyone. It's time to add quinoa."

"What is quinoa? It sure looks weird." June Bug wrinkled up his freckled nose as he poked his finger in the grain.

"Quinoa is the oldest grain in the world. It's been around since the beginning of time. It's a good source of protein."

Cathy's hollow blue eyes carefully inspected the quinoa, slowly turning the cup in her small hand. "This stuff smells funny."

Rachel laughed. "It does have a fragrant light odor when cooked."

"Why cook it?" Lucy held the quinoa to her nose, sniffing it.

"Quinoa makes the pancakes moist and fluffy. You'll see."

"Can you put syrup on these pancakes?" Cootie blurted out. "I like syrup on my pancakes."

"Of course. I have syrup here on the table."

"Can we add the smelly stuff now? I'm getting hungry!" June Bug's brown eyes were big.

"Yes, go ahead. After you stir in the quinoa, add your blueberries and stir gently."

Robbie shot out of his seat and stood over Mary with his hands on his hips. "DON'T YOU DARE PUT THAT DOO-DOO IN OUR PANCAKES!" he yelled.

Everyone turned to look, including Rachel.

"Robbie, have a seat and stop yelling."

"I SAID, DON'T PUT THAT..."

"Okay, I won't." Mary pouted with watery eyes. Robbie scowled, rocking on his heels with his arms folded on his chest. Concerned, Rachel rushed over.

"Robbie, what's wrong? Why are you yelling at Mary?"

"He thinks blueberries are rabbit doo-doo. He won't let me put them in the pancake batter," Mary whined in a baby voice.

Rachel's mouth sagged open. "Rabbit doo-doo? How so?"

"They're round and dark like rabbit doo-doo!" Robbie looked sideways then turned around to glance behind him as if expecting someone to attack him. Rachel could tell Robbie was paranoid.

"Robbie, you look stressed. Have you taken your medicine today?"

"Yes."

"No, he hasn't. He never takes his medicine. He holds it under his tongue like this." Mary opened her mouth wide and rolled her tongue like a tube. "Robbie spits his medicine out when the nurse isn't looking."

Robbie's face was chili-pepper red. He gave Mary a nasty look.

"You liar! I did take my medicine!" he shouted.

Mary shook her head. "No, he didn't."

"Robbie, how long has it been since you took your medicine?"

Robbie pursed his lips tightly together, refusing to answer.

"Well, if you're not going to answer, I'll have to tell Doctor Benny."

Robbie kicked his chair on the floor. He reached over the table and snatched the bowl out of Mary's hands. He dumped the batter over her head and set the pan back on the table. Robbie stomped out of the dining room, leaving Mary dripping in pancake batter.

At first, Mary blinked, not sure what happened. When it finally dawned on her what Robbie did, she pouted and broke out in tears.

Rachel stooped over and hugged her. "Mary, I'm so sorry this happened. Robbie is having a bad day."

A nurse sitting at the nursing station witnessed everything and came right over carrying towels. Mary bawled as the nurse wiped her face, hands, and hair. The unit door opened and slammed shut. Doctor Benny walked down the hall, and when he arrived in the dining room he immediately rushed over.

"What's wrong? What the hell happened?"

"Help me take Mary to her room," the nurse calmly replied. "I'll explain everything there."

"Very well." Doctor Benny followed the nurse and Mary to her room.

Rachel whirled around and noticed the group staring at her. She clapped her hands, clearing her throat as she returned to her table.

"Okay, everybody, let's get back to work. We have blueberry pancakes to cook and eat."

"Whoopee!" Cootie yelled, clapping his hands.

"If you have already added and stirred in your blueberries, bring your bowl to my table and let's cook pancakes."

Cootie was the first to go to the table with his bowl. "I want to go first. I'm hungry." He grinned.

"I see," Rachel chuckled as she turned the temperature dial to four hundred on the griddles. Rachel doused each griddle with butter, and the yellow substance sizzled as it changed to a brown color. The patients gathered around, holding their bowls, waiting to cook their pancakes. "The griddles are ready, so let's cook some pancakes." Rachel reached for a measuring cup and held it up. "This is a half cup. I'm going to measure out a half of cup of pancake batter and pour it on the griddle."

Everyone watched Rachel as she carefully scooped out the pancake batter, measuring enough to fill the cup then pour it on the griddle. The pancake hissed, cooking in the butter as Rachel scooped out more mixture. "Hurry, grab your measuring cups on the tables over there and cook your pancakes."

The patients gathered around the three tables, taking turns flipping their pancakes on the griddles. As soon as Cootie finished cooking his pancakes, he drowned his cakes with syrup. Cootie cut his pancakes in bite-sized pieces then carried his plate back to his table. He plopped his butt in the chair and stuffed his mouth with a pancake.

"This is good," he mumbled as the pancake spilled from the corners of his mouth. Soon everyone joined him, returning to their tables with a stack of pancakes on their plate. They sat and ate their pancakes, looking satisfied and content. Rachel, pleased her class was going well despite Robbie's earlier outburst, visited each table smiling

"So, is everyone enjoying their pancakes?"

"Yessss…" They all responded in unison.

"Good. In two weeks, there will be another class." Rachel pointed to the bulletin board on the back wall next to the kitchen. "I'll post the time, day, and next recipe here on this board. So, don't miss out. Be sure to sign up." Rachel checked her watch. The time was ten-fifty. "Time to clean up, everyone. Class is almost over."

"Can we take the rest of our pancakes to our rooms to save for later?" asked Cathy.

"Cathy, you know having food in your room is against the rules."

"I don't want to throw my pancakes away. They're so good," she pouted.

"I want to keep mine too," Lucy blurted out.

"I tell you what. I'll have Mister Wheatly bring out some foil. Then you can wrap your pancakes, put your name on it, and the nurses can serve it to you as a snack later."

"Cool." As everyone began cleaning up, Rachel stood in the kitchen doorway, waving her hand, trying to get Tom's attention. He was frying a batch of hamburgers for lunch, and finally, he noticed Rachel. His face looked hot and flush with sweat dripping off his brow.

"Yes, Miss Thomas? How can I help?"

"Tom, I need a roll of foil. The patients want to save their pancakes."

"Sure." Tom wiped his hands and brow on a dishtowel. He opened a drawer, took out a box of foil, and brought it to Rachel.

"Thank you so much."

"No problem."

Rachel walked around each table, handing out sheets of foil. Everyone wrapped their pancakes, and Rachel noticed Cootie stuffing his pancakes in his pants pocket.

"Cootie, I see you over there. Bring your pancakes up here, please."

"Do I have to?"

"Yes, sir, you do." Rachel's mouth curved into a half smile.

"Ugh, okay." Cootie grimaced, trudging up to Rachel in slow motion. He dropped his wrapped pancakes in Rachel's hand and pouted. "Here!"

"Thank you, Cootie."

Cootie spun around on his heels and stomped out of the dining room in a huff. Everyone else finished cleaning up. They brought their wrapped pancakes to Rachel and she wrote their names on the foil with a black marker. Lucy, June Bug, Cathy, and Cootie left the dining room as soon as they finished, walking out in single file. Rachel sighed, dropping her shoulders.

"Whew, this was a lot of work. Maybe I can get Jamie to help me next time."

Later, around noon, Rachel and Jamie were in the cafeteria selecting their lunches. Rachel grabbed a chicken salad while Jamie chose a hamburger and fries. She looked at Rachel's salad and awe crossed her face. "Girl, you eat like a rabbit."

Rachel laughed. "I have to keep my sexy figure."

"If you say so."

Doctor Beebe rolled into the cafeteria and went straight to the coffee stand, whizzing by Rachel and Jamie, who were standing in the line waiting to pay for their lunch.

"Damn, he's in a hurry," Jamie chuckled.

"And he's madder than a hornet!" Rachel added with wide eyes. Her eyes drifted to the stuffed bag hanging on the back of Doctor Beebe's wheelchair. "I wondered what's in that bag?" Rachel asked.

"Maybe he's got our memo in that bag."

"Do you think he'll respond with another memo?" Rachel stepped forward in the line.

Jamie laughed. "Probably not. He's a man with little appetite for confronting others."

They watched Doctor Beebe go to the front of the line and pay for his coffee. He took off, speeding through the cafeteria and out the door like a mad demon. Rachel and Jamie hollered with laughter.

"The man acts like he's spooked," Jamie joked, sitting her tray on the counter to pay for her meal.

"Spooked, hell? He's nuttier than a fruitcake," Rachel smirked. She paid for her meal and found a table in the corner of the cafeteria. Jamie soon followed her, and the two social workers settled in and immediately attacked their meals.

"How did your class go this morning?"

"Pretty well, for the most part. Robbie and Mary got into a tiff, but the rest of the class turned out fine."

Jamie raised an eyebrow. "Why? What happened?"

"Robbie was so paranoid. He thought the blueberries were rabbit doo-doo. He tried to keep Mary from mixing the berries into the pancake batter and poured it over her head."

Jamie howled. "It sounds like he's not taking his medications."

"I thought that too." Rachel took a bite of her salad. "Do you mind helping me with the class next time? It was a lot of work, and I can use the help."

"Sure."

"Did you tell Anne about our meeting with Beth?" Rachel asked, switching gears.

"Yes, I did." Jamie hesitated, reaching for her glass of tea and taking a sip. "We haven't been talking much these days."

"Oh, I'm sorry. What did she say?" Rachel was more interested in hearing about George Benny.

"She doesn't want her name connected to Doctor Benny's problems. I can't say I blame her."

"Uh, I can see her point," said Rachel. A few minutes passed, and Rachel pointedly asked. "So, how are things with you and Anne, anyway?"

154

Jamie glanced at her plate. She hesitated again, and Rachel could see she was trying to find the right words.

"We're fine."

"Just fine?" Rachel raised an eyebrow, not buying Jamie's answer.

"We talked, but I still get the feeling she's messing around."

"Really? How so?"

Jamie's eyes watered. She dropped her shoulders and blew out her lips, looking pitiful. "She comes home late from work almost every day, and she never offers me an explanation. If I question her, it only starts an argument."

Rachel refrained from commenting. She didn't want to hear Jamie's whining. For a while, the two women ate in silence. Then out of the blue, Jamie spewed anger Rachel's way.

"Anne thinks I drink too much! She's demanding I go to alcohol treatment."

Rachel wasn't in the mood for Jamie's excuses. "I agree with her. You're already going down a slippery slope. Alcohol will not only ruin your relationship but your whole life."

"Oh, please. You two are overreacting," Jamie groaned, making a face. "I'm fine."

"Fine, my ass!" Rachel glanced at the ceiling, dropping her fork onto her plate.

"Don't come off like that! I've got everything under control."

"If you say so. It's your life." Rachel knew better, but arguing with Jamie was fruitless. She changed the subject to keep from getting angrier. "Sally mentioned to me that she'd like us to meet at Sully's for dinner on Friday evening. Do you know anything about it?"

"Mm-hm. And Anne agreed to come."

Rachel forced a smile. "Well, it's about time I meet the infamous Anne Cleveland!"

"Smart aleck!" Jamie shot back as she rose from the table.

"I'm just saying!" Rachel finished her lunch and stood on her feet. She watched Jamie take off to the exit.

155

"Are you coming or not?" Jamie's voice was loud, not looking back.

"I'm coming," she chuckled.

"What's so funny?"

"Nothing!" Rachel caught up with her in the hall, and they went opposite directions. "See you later," Rachel waved.

Jamie didn't respond. She kept walking without saying another word.

Rachel returned to the Admissions Unit, settling in at the nursing station to chart. She heard fussing in the dining area and stopped charting. She stood up and saw Country Fry Taylor, a petite little woman with black pigtails. Her name came about after her alcoholic-obsessed mother took her home from the hospital without giving her a name. When the nurse called from the hospital two days later to ask for a name to put on the birth certificate, her mother, high off gin and coke, told the nurse she had named her newborn daughter Country Fry Taylor.

Leroy Page stood over a frowning Country Fry as she sat at the table with her bag of Doritos. He looked like a bean pole in his dingy white long johns, and his shoulder-length brown hair was stringy and greasy.

"You can't sit here. You smell like somebody's garbage, and that stink is going to get on me!" Country Fry pouted.

"No, it won't," he snarled.

"You need a bath! You stink!" Country Fry moved her chair around the table, distancing herself from Leroy. She glared at him with burning dark brown eyes.

"But I like you," Leroy innocently declared like a little boy, ignoring the fact his body odor turned her off. "Why can't I sit with you?"

"Leroy, are you deaf? For the last time, you stink. You smell like garbage!"

"It's just your imagination," he half-heartedly joked.

Country Fry scoffed. "You're looney tunes!"

"Takes one to know one!" he shot back.

Country Fry bolted out of her seat and snatched her bag of

Doritos from the table. She stomped passed Leroy and quickly disappeared down the corridor. Leroy pulled out a chair and sat. He folded his hands in his lap and dropped his head. Feeling sorry for the poor man, Rachel walked over.

"Hey, Leroy, what's going on?"

"Oh, nothing, I'm cool." Leroy sounded boyish and kept his head down, refusing to look at Rachel.

"Well, you don't look fine to me." Rachel pulled out a chair and sat next to Leroy. She wrinkled her nose, covering it with her hand. Leroy smelled like a carton of sour milk. "I want to hear what's troubling you."

"Do you?" Leroy raised his head, making eye contact with Rachel. His chocolate brown eyes flickered with tears.

"I do," Rachel softly replied.

Leroy straightened in his seat. "I like Country Fry. She's cute. I want her to like me, too."

"Okay, but..."

Rachel leaned back in her chair, and before she could finish her thought, Leroy innocently asked. "Is it too late to take a shower? I don't want to smell like somebody's garbage!"

Rachel almost fell out of her seat, but she caught herself before she burst out into wild laughter. "No, Leroy, it's not too late to take a shower. I'll get one of the nurses to help you," she softly chuckled.

"Thank you." Leroy broke out into a cheesy grin. Rachel left her seat and went to find a nurse. A few minutes later, she was back with Sally by her side. "The head nurse is going to assist you with your shower."

"Cool beans!" Leroy shouted, clapping his hands.

Sally rolled her eyes and shook her head. "Come with me, young man."

Leroy jumped to his feet. He followed Sally, hopping up and down like a cocker spaniel alongside her as they headed down the hallway.

"Sally, will you make sure I don't smell like somebody's garbage? I want to sit next to Country Fry."

Sally fell out into a horsey laugh. She shook her head, welcoming the comedic relief. "Leroy, I promise, by the time you're done with your bath, you won't smell like somebody's garbage!"

Chapter Eleven

Friday, November 30th

Rachel arrived at Sully's Bar and Grill precisely at five-thirty. She was the first one there and wondered where Jamie, Sally, and Anne were. She stood in the lobby, scoping out the restaurant, looking for an empty booth with a window. Disappointed that all the tables were filled with customers, Rachel strolled over to the bar. The popular haunt had rave reviews, and Rachel was eager to see if the restaurant lived up to its hype. She flung her purse on the bar counter and climbed onto a stool.

Checking out her surroundings, a cloud of thick gray smoke hovered like a blanket over the bar and the smelly tobacco burned her nostrils. The soft circular lights in the ceiling gave the place a romantic glow. Men and women sitting at the bar with bleary red eyes puffed on thin cigarettes and fat cigars. They swayed and grooved to the jazzy tempo coming from the jukebox in the far left corner. On the center floor, men and women mingled together at tables, conversing with one another while sipping their favorite highballs. Two waitresses dressed in white blouses and short black skirts bounced back and forth between customers taking orders and busily scribbling on their pads.

In the shadows at the far end of the bar, Rachel noticed a woman who looked familiar to her sitting quietly nursing a drink.

Although it was fairly dark, Rachel could see the woman had blond curly locks hanging off her shoulders and her thin lips were ruby red. The woman mindlessly sipped on her drink, staring straight ahead. She seemed to be in her own little world, oblivious to everyone around her until she and Rachel locked eyes. Wide-eyed, the woman looked away as if she recognized Rachel. Based on her reaction, Rachel wondered if they had met before. *Mm…it's possible.*

Brushing her thoughts aside, Rachel flagged the waitress down. She came right over, and the young lady was no more than four feet tall. On each side of her head was a curly black ponytail neatly tied up in a red ribbon. Her eyes were round and gray, and when her pink lips parted into a smile, a decaying tooth emerged. The tooth was so black, it looked like a piece of coal. The waitress took out her pen and notepad, grinning like nobody's business.

"Hi there, what can I get you this evening?"

"A glass of merlot."

"Coming right up!" The waitress bounced off, leaving Rachel to her thoughts. She shifted her body weight on the stool, turning toward the door. Soon a conversation with Jamie came to mind. She recalled Jamie telling her that Anne had confronted her about her drinking, and Rachel felt vindicated. At least she wasn't the only one who thought Jamie had a drinking problem. However, despite agreeing with Anne, Rachel found the woman's thinking confusing. Why would Anne agree to dinner at a bar? Indeed, a venue like a bar defeated the purpose. Perplexed, Rachel went along with the plan, hoping this would be Jamie's last indulgence.

Finally, Rachel's wine arrived. After she paid the waitress, Rachel took a sip. The crisp, fruity flavor rolled over her palate, and she smiled with delight. *So very smooth, so very good.*

Before long, Sally, Jamie, and Anne strolled in laughing and teasing one another. Rachel slid off the barstool, waving wildly, catching Sally's attention.

"She's over there at the bar," she heard Sally shout. Sally took off, strutting like a giant stork.

"Wait up! What's your hurry?" Jamie waddled after Sally, trying to keep up.

Anne followed suit, and all three women arrived at the bar around the same time. Jamie, all smiles, jerked Anne toward her, throwing an arm around her shoulders.

"Girl, this is my other half, Anne Cleveland."

"I've heard a lot about you. I'm Rachel."

Anne rolled her eyes and scoffed. "Really? I've heard a lot about you too."

"Good things, I hope." Rachel wondered why Anne was so frosty toward her.

"Don't worry, nothing bad." Anne smiled demurely.

Sally climbed on a barstool and gestured for the bartender. "Ladies, I need a big glass of stiff bourbon! I mean stiff! Stiff like a dick!"

"Girl, me too, but minus the dick!" Jamie laughed. Anne folded her fat arms on the counter, looking disgusted.

Rachel hollered with laughter. "You two are so bad!" Anne rolled her eyes, unamused.

The bartender came over and the women ordered their drinks. Rachel sat back, checking out the infamous Anne Cleveland. She was taller than Jamie by about three inches. Plump and round in the mid-section, Anne had pouty red lips like the actress Marilyn Monroe, an olive complexion with light brown eyes like Jamie's, and brown hair styled in a pageboy haircut. She wore a wool sweater and her thick legs filled out a pair of black jeans. Anne climbed on a stool and crossed her legs, swinging one foot back and forth while Rachel admired the patent leather flats she was wearing.

"Do you come here often?" Rachel asked, trying to make conversation.

"Been here a few times," Anne coyly replied.

"This is my first time. Nice place so far."

"Mm-hmm."

Soon the waitress returned with their drinks, and Jamie requested a booth by the window. As soon as one became available, the waitress accompanied them to their table. The women settled in, and the waitress gave each of them a menu.

"Be right back for your order," the waitress said, running off. Anne and Rachel sat across from one another, and after Anne decided on her order, she zeroed in on Rachel.

"So, dear, how are you getting along at the funny farm these days?"

"I'm getting along fine." Rachel forced a smile. Leery of Anne, she was careful about how she answered. "It took a little time to adjust, but I'm doing well, thank you."

"I bet," Anne smirked.

Rachel bristled. "What does that mean?"

"Oh, nothing!" Anne haughtily replied, massaging and shrugging her shoulders.

"Anne can be sarcastic at times," Jamie interjected, trying to smooth out Anne's rough edges.

"Oh, I see," Rachel said, giving Anne the side-eye.

Jamie hurriedly changed the subject. "I think Doctor Beebe finally read the memo."

"Yeah, I heard he was speeding around the hospital like a raving maniac the other day," Sally said.

"What is this memo? What are you guys talking about?" Anne asked, squishing her face.

"Let me tell you," Sally said. She told the whole story, and Annie fell out laughing. The waitress returned for their dinner orders and left again. Thirty minutes later, their dinners arrived and the women dug in.

As the evening wore on, they gossiped about everyone they knew. No one was off limits, and soon Rachel found herself warming to Anne. Before long, everyone was giggling in hysterics and giddy with alcohol. Suddenly Jamie sprung out of her seat, wildly waving her chubby hands.

"Well, what do you know? The devil himself...there's Doctor Louis and his teenage wife!"

Everyone turned to look. Michael Louis, a tall, imposing man, was dressed in a tan tweed jacket with gray slacks. He was scoping out the place, searching for a table. His brown-framed eyeglasses took up his entire face. Gray-brown hair grew around his temples, and a brown, ratty toupee hid the bald spot on the crown of his head. A woman half his age with long thick auburn hair waited patiently by his side. She noticed Jamie waving like a lunatic, and she nudged her husband's elbow mumbling something. Michael glanced Jamie's way. He grabbed his wife's hand and came right over.

"Here, he comes!" Jamie excitedly giggled. "Rachel, get ready to meet the Colonel!"

"It's about time!" Rachel said as she checked out the doctor approaching the table. The doctor's toupee flapped in the air and Rachel giggled with her hand over her mouth. Too engrossed in their meals, Anne and Sally didn't notice. Still amused, Rachel's eyes drifted to Michael's face, and his skin was badly broken out. The deep crevices in his cheeks looked like empty holes in a smelly sponge. "He's not very attractive," Rachel whispered to Anne.

"You can say that again," Anne said.

Michael arrived at the table, flashing a crooked grin. "Good Evening, ladies!" he roared. Rachel thought he looked like Herman Munster.

"Hi, Doctor Louis," they all responded in unison.

All eyes fell on his wife, who was all smiles. Michael turned sideways, pulling her closer in. He wrapped his thick arm around his wife's tiny waist. A petite woman, the doctor's wife had expressive deep-set green eyes.

"Ladies, meet Sierra, my lovely wife," he boasted.

"Nice to meet you," Sierra greeted them in a raspy voice.

"Nice to meet you too," the women replied, refusing to look at each other, fearful their facial expressions would reveal their real feelings.

Jamie leaned over and tapped Michael on the arm. She made a gesture at Rachel. "Doctor Louis, meet Rachel Thomas, our new social worker."

Michael's smile was warm. "Well, young lady, how are you? I hear you're doing a great job. Glad to have you onboard."

"Thank you, sir. I'm glad to finally meet you."

"Likewise," Michael growled as he diverted his attention to Anne. "Haven't seen you around lately. Are you still on North Campus?"

"Yep, I keep a low profile. It's safer that way," she joked.

"Smart." Michael roared with laughter.

"When are you planning to return to work?" Sally interrupted.

"On Monday." The four women exchanged quick glances, startled by the news. Not going unnoticed, Michael roared with laughter again. "Obviously, you ladies didn't see that one coming. I guess no one told you!"

"Nope," Sally frowned. "Not one damn soul!"

"Go figure," Jamie muttered.

A waitress came up to Michael and announced in a squeaky voice, "Sir, the table you requested is ready."

"Thank you." Michael looked at Sierra and stretched out his hand. "Shall we?"

"Yes, I'm starving."

"You ladies have a nice evening," Michael said.

"You, too," all four women replied at once. The waitress escorted Michael and his wife to the other side of the restaurant. As soon as he was seated and out of earshot, the four women cut loose.

"That woman is young enough to be his daughter," Rachel blurted out. "I think the old folks would call this *robbing the cradle*."

"Robbing the cradle, my foot. She's no baby! I bet she's given him a real workout, if you know what I mean," Jamie cackled.

"Yeah, that's why his old ass almost fell out and died. His heart and dick couldn't take the strain," Anne joked.

The women fell out in hysterics. Rachel giggled so hard her stomach hurt. "The visual is too much, too much! I can't stand it!"

Soon the waitress returned to the table.

"Bring me a shot of Jack Daniels," Jamie demanded. Anne shot Jamie a dirty look, which Jamie immediately dismissed, sticking her tongue out. "Lighten up. It's Friday. Just one more...I promise this is the last one."

"Fine," Anne scoffed.

Jamie turned her attention to the waitress. "Bring me two shots!"

"Coming right up," the waitress replied as she scribbled down Jamie's order and bounced off. Silence gripped the table. No one said a word for fifteen minutes.

Finally, Rachel broke the impasse. "How long have those two been married?"

"Who are you talking about?" Jamie leaned back in her seat, folding her chubby arms on her chest.

"Doctor Louis and Sierra, silly!"

"Two years. He adores that woman," Sally interjected out of the blue.

"Does he have any children?" Rachel was eager to know if Doctor Louis had a daughter Sierra's age. If he did, she wondered how he could justify marrying a woman so young.

"No, he doesn't, and either does she," Sally revealed.

Rachel sighed with relief. "I guess they see themselves as the perfect match made in heaven."

"Maybe," said Jamie.

"What do you mean?"

"He can be a tyrant at times. He's not called 'the Colonel' for nothing. The man has definitely earned every bit of his nickname," Jamie said. The women laughed.

As the ten o'clock hour approached, more and more customers packed the restaurant. A man dressed in a well-made blue suit stood on the horse-shoe shaped stage making a plea for karaoke volunteers. Feeling sleepy and with her head swimming from the effects of too much wine, Rachel jerked her head back trying to keep her eyes open when she saw Jamie leave her seat and climbed on stage. She snatched the mike out of the man's hand and screamed into the microphone, slurring her words.

"I want to sing "Purple Rain," everybody!"

Rachel gasped, horrified. *What is she doing up there? Has she lost her mind?* Jamie screeched into the mike, belting out Prince's song in a shrill tone offending every ear in the room. Everyone around the restaurant stopped talking and stared at her with horrified looks. Seconds later, *boos* erupted around the room, and Rachel, Sally, and Anne shook their heads in disgust. The *boos* caught Jamie off guard, and she stopped performing and threw the mike on the floor. She stumbled from the stage, and Anne and Rachel rushed to her side, grabbing her before she fell on her butt. They assisted Jamie upright and Anne, with a pained look on her face, lit into Jamie.

"It's time to go home."

"I don't want to go home!" Jamie wailed, jerking her arm from Anne's grasp. "I'm having fun here!"

"You're doing nothing but embarrassing yourself!" Anne hissed in her ear as she and Rachel dragged Jamie back to their booth.

"Leave me alone!" Jamie jerked away and fell in the booth. She straightened herself up and snapped her fingers. A waitress scurrying by the table stopped to see what Jamie wanted. Her laser-sharp light green eyes glowered at Jamie.

"Lady, can I get you something?"

"Um, you sure can…bring me another shot of that nasty cheap whiskey you got!"

The waitress backed away, startled by Jamie's comment.

Anne's temper flared. "Jamie, how embarrassing. You're not getting another drink! I'm taking you home!"

"I demand another drink!" Jamie shouted with her red eyes bulging.

Anne whirled her body around, facing the waitress and glaring at her. "Do Not Bring This Woman Another Drink! You hear me?"

The waitress threw up her hands. "Okay, I get it, you don't have to yell!"

Livid, Jamie mocked the waitress, her face chili-pepper red. "Didn't you hear me, you little wench? Get me another drink!"

"Excuse me? What did you call me?" The waitress lurched forward heading Jamie's way.

Sensing disaster, Rachel jumped in front of the waitress. "Why don't you go and bring us the bill, and we'll take care of our friend?" Rachel calmly suggested.

"You need to get her out of here." The waitress grimaced, rolling up her sleeves and tightening her fists.

"We're working on it," Rachel said. The waitress reluctantly followed Rachel's suggestion, leaving the women alone to figure out what to do next.

Sally spoke first. "Anne and I will take Jamie to the car, and you settle the bill."

"Okay," Rachel agreed. Anne and Sally reached in their handbags and pulled out their wallets. They took out twenty-dollar bills and each gave Rachel forty dollars. "Thanks, ladies."

"No problem," Anne said. They each took Jamie by the arm and dragged her out the door. Jamie screamed bloody murder punctuated with a colorful array of profanities, jerking and twisting her body trying to loosen Annie and Sally's grip on her.

Meanwhile, Rachel stood at the bar and paid the bill. While waiting for her change, Rachel's eyes drifted to the end of the bar, and saw the blonde still sitting there nursing her drink. Rachel could see her more clearly from where she now stood. The woman's blue eyes, transfixed and vacant, stared at the crowd while she sipped on her glass of red wine. Rachel wondered how many drinks she'd consumed, now that it was ten-thirty in the evening. *What's her story? Why is she here? Is she waiting for someone? Damn, she looks familiar!*

The woman lifted her glass and held it to her lips a little too long. An eternity passed before the woman returned the wine glass to the counter again, empty. The bartender returned with her change and Rachel momentarily took her eyes off the blonde. After she finished counting up her money, she looked up, and the blonde was gone. *Strange…where did she go so fast? So very strange!*

With the woman nowhere in sight, Rachel flung her handbag over her shoulder. She left the restaurant, shaking her head.

Susan Cole left the restroom and returned to the bar wearing her blue cashmere jacket. The bartender came over and stood in front of her.

"Ma'am, would you like something else before you go?"

"No, sir... Just bring the bill."

"Will do." The bartender made out the bill and brought it to her. After she looked it over, she reached in her handbag and took out fifty dollars.

"Keep the change," she smiled.

"Why thank you, madam. Is there anything else I can get you before you leave tonight? A meal to go, a cab, anything?"

"No, that will be all, thank you. You have a lovely evening."

Moments later, Susan waited for the bus in front of Sully's, shaking like a leaf. Although she was cold, she reveled in her last minutes of freedom. With her teeth chattering in her head, the chilly night wind howled around her, and her hands, stiff from the cold, fumbled to button her jacket. After struggling for several minutes, she managed to thread every button.

Warm but feeling down, Susan dreaded going home to George. On the brink of losing what little sanity she still had, Susan had left the house without telling him. She knew he would be angry once he found out. He had an explosive temper, and it scared her. Despite her apprehension, Susan adored George. She appreciated the doctor making her life more comfortable than what she had before, but she was bored. Besides, she had no job and nowhere else to go. So, as each day passed, George's home became her personal prison. Alone and isolated, Susan longed for adult conversation. Ignoring the consequences of her actions, Susan had decided to venture out on her own.

After Susan showered and dressed, she'd taken the bus to Sully's. Her evening at the popular haunt proved refreshing. Glad to be around people, Susan stayed most of the evening. She enjoyed drinking wine and listening to the jazz music playing from the jukebox. By the time Susan glanced at her watch, she realized she had lost track of time. It was almost eleven and George would be on his way home. So, Susan settled the bill and promptly left.

As she waited for the bus, Susan reflected on her experience at Sully's. Susan swore Picasso Cooper's fiancé was sitting at the bar.

But when Susan locked eyes with the woman, she wasn't sure. She looked away, embarrassed, thinking she must have been mistaken. Susan hoped the woman didn't notice.

When the bus arrived, Susan saw it was empty and was thrilled. She hated crowded buses and smelling musty people sitting around her. The doors slid open, and Susan climbed on. She found a seat in the middle and made herself comfortable. Glancing at her watch again, Susan sighed heavily. George would beat her home, and she wasn't looking forward to his wrath.

Five blocks from the house, Susan stepped off the bus. She was alone and scared, no soul in sight. On high alert, Susan hurried down the cobblestone sidewalk. Saint Salmon Street snaked through the quaint neighborhood, and the moon, full and bright, lit up her path giving her needed light. Otherwise, it would've been pitch black for her to navigate unfamiliar surroundings. As Susan stepped swiftly down the street, she occasionally glanced behind her, paranoid someone might be following her. Susan stepped up her pace, and before long she was into a brisk jog.

Only two blocks from George's home, Susan noticed a man in a knit skullcap sitting in a 1968 blue Ford Mustang across the street underneath a streetlight. He stared at Susan as she passed, spooking her out. With her adrenalin on speed dial, Susan took off running. She ran so fast, she almost crashed into George's gate, stopping herself in the nick of time. Susan shoved the gate back and ran to the porch, hopping up several stairs in her rush to the door. She stood at the door, trembling and fumbling around in her purse. *Where is my key? I need my key!* The door flew open, and Susan lurched back.

"You scared me!" she screeched.

"Where the hell have you been?" George barked with icy blue eyes. He jerked her inside and slammed the door.

"You're hurting me! You're hurting my arm!" Susan tried to pull away, but his grip was too tight. Tears welled in her eyes.

"I'm asking you again. Where have you been?"

"I had to get out of here! I had cabin fever!"

George snarled. "Do you realize what you've done? People are still looking for you! What were you thinking?"

"I was bored. I got tired of being stuck in this house day after day!" Susan cried with rivers of tears streaming down her cheeks. Once he loosened his grip, Susan pulled off her jacket and threw it on the floor. She plopped her butt on the couch, rocking back and forth like a little kid, wringing her hands, weeping.

George sat next to her and gave her a big hug. He covered her face with soft kisses. "I'm sorry for yelling, but I was worried about you."

Susan melted. "I know," she sniffled. Susan hugged him back and kissed his lips. He shoved her back on the couch and raised her skirt over her waist. With his hand between her thighs, George caressed her sweet spot. Dripping wet, Susan moaned. George ripped her panties off and threw them on the floor. Excited, Susan tugged at his belt. She successfully unbuckled it and zipped his pants down. George leaped up and his pants and belt fell to the floor. He hovered over her and unbuttoned her blouse, slipping it over her shoulders, exposing her bare breasts. He kissed each one, greedily taking in each nipple, sucking on it like a hungry newborn.

Wrapped in each other's arms, Susan's legs hugged his hips as each thrust slammed inside her like a sledgehammer. Jerky and rough, Susan enjoyed his lovemaking, moaning out loud until they both reached a climax. Collapsed in each other's arms, they breathed heavily with their eyes closed, their hearts beating in rhythm.

Suddenly, George sat straight up. "I heard something!" He moved off of Susan and sat on the edge of the couch. Suspicious, he slipped on his pants while he stared intently at the door.

"What are you talking about?" Susan rose halfway up and flung her arms around his waist, holding him back.

"I heard someone running down the stairs outside!" George broke away from Susan and stood up. He grabbed his shirt and rushed to the window. George peered out, but he didn't see a thing.

"I think you're paranoid," Susan said.

"I guess you're right." George turned to face her and grinned, showing his stained yellow grill. "I have something to tell you, and I hope you like it."

"What is it?" Susan snatched her panties from the floor and slipped them on.

"I've decided to take some time off."

"Why?" Susan asked with big eyes.

"I need a break and I thought it would be nice for you and me to take a trip."

"Where to?" Susan hopped up and down like an excited toddler.

"To France. Paris, to be exact. I bought airline tickets and we're leaving in three days."

"France? Did you say France?" Susan clapped her hands like a little girl. "I've never been overseas before. I'm so excited! I can't wait!"

Susan fell in George's arms, wrapping her arms and legs around his upper body. He held her up as she covered his face with kisses. George whirled around in a circle while Susan giggled hysterically. "Stop, you're making me dizzy!"

George stopped turning and put Susan down. She swayed back and forth, leaning into him. "Are you okay?" he asked.

"I'm fine." She snatched the remainder of her clothes off the floor. "I'm going upstairs to pack. I can't wait!"

"Do you have a passport?" It suddenly dawned on him he hadn't asked her this critical detail.

"Yes, silly! I've just never used it. Now I get to!" Susan ran upstairs and briefly looked out the window. Her heart pounded in her chest when she noticed the man in the Mustang watching the house. *Who is that? What's he doing here?*

She pressed her nose against the cold glass, squinting. The man switched on his headlights and took off down the street. Susan tried to make out the license plate, but it was too dark. She wondered if she should tell George about the man, but she thought better of it. She went to her closet and pulled out two dresses.

"George!" Susan yelled down the stairs.

"What?" he groaned.

"I need your opinion on something."

"Just a minute, I'll be right up."

She heard George secure the front door and his feet pounding up the stairs.

Rachel sat in her bed with her knees bent, scribbling in her diary. She often wrote the day's funniest events in her journal, thinking one day she might write a book. Journaling not only relieved her anxiety but helped her to relax. Although Jamie's behavior at Sully's was embarrassing to everyone involved, Rachel couldn't help worrying about her. Jamie was falling off a cliff and she didn't know what to do about it. Her alcoholic episodes were out of control, and Rachel worried she was driving under the influence. *Something has to be done before she kills herself or somebody else. Maybe a thirty-day rehab program will do the trick. But how am I going to convince Jamie to go?*

Jamie was strong-willed and could be quite cantankerous to deal with at times. She always insisted on her way of doing things. Rachel needed a game plan. Maybe she could convince Jamie to go with Sally's and Anne's help. She glanced at the clock sitting on the nightstand, and it was eleven-ten. Her father was probably still up in his home office preparing his lesson plan for the next day. Rachel reached for the phone and dialed his number. He picked up on the second ring.

"Hello?"

"Hi, Dad, sorry I'm calling so late," Rachel sighed.

"No problem. What's wrong?"

"I'm worried about Jamie," Rachel calmly replied as she held the phone tight on her ear with her shoulder. She closed her diary and lay it on top of the nightstand.

She heard her father take a long, deep breath. "What's going on with Jamie, besides just being weird?"

"Dad!"

"I'm sorry. Go ahead."

"Well, you know she drinks a lot."

"Yeah, and…"

"Her drinking has gotten worse. We all went out to dinner this evening, and she acted like a fool while we were there," Rachel said in a somber voice.

"Really? What happened?"

"Jamie had too many drinks. She volunteered to sing one of Prince's songs during karaoke hour, and she sounded like a sick dog and fell on her butt. Sally, Anne, and I had to help her up," Rachel explained with strain in her voice.

"So, she was drunk as a skunk," her father joked.

Rachel's mouth dropped. She was surprised by her father's snide comment. "Dad, it's not funny. Jamie needs help!"

"Jamie needs rehab," DeWayne quipped. "Have you spoken to her about it?"

"No, I was thinking about it." Rachel blew out her cheeks and sighed.

"Do you know what an intervention is?"

"No."

"It's a useful approach to force alcoholic or drug-addicted clients to go to rehab."

Rachel leaned forward. "How does it work?"

"It's simple, really. First, the family reserves a bed at a rehab. Second, they band together along with a few friends and confront the client. Each person tells the client how the drinking has adversely impacted their relationship with him or her. The goal is to convince the client to go to rehab voluntarily. Most of the time, it works."

"I love the idea. In fact, I was just thinking I should talk to Sally and Anne about coming up with a game plan. Your suggestion is splendid. But I'm afraid Jamie won't go," Rachel fretted.

"Try it. You and your coworkers set aside some time to meet with Jamie and tell her how you feel."

"I don't know, Dad." Rachel sighed heavily, shaking her head, not convinced her father's suggestion would work.

"Stop doubting. You'll never know until you try."

"Okay, I'll try it. I'll have to talk this over with Sally."

"Keep me posted, sweetheart."

"I will. And thanks, Dad."

"No problem." Her father hung up, and Rachel placed the phone in its cradle. She turned off the light on the nightstand and scooted under her comforter. With her father's suggestion seared in her mind, she closed her eyes. A few minutes later, she was snoring.

Chapter Twelve

Monday, December 3rd

Rachel drove into the hospital's parking lot thirty minutes before her shift. She parked her Toyota on the right side of the parking lot so she could have a full view of the hospital. Rachel sat in her car, listening to the Jackson Five's Christmas Album on her car's tape recorder. When Michael Jackson's jazzy rendition of "Santa Claus Is Coming to Town" came on, Rachel snapped her fingers and sang along.

A cold winter wind whistled violently from the north, and snow flurries swirled in the sky. Twigs, crumpled paper, and dead shrubs blew across the hospital's parking lot. Rachel saw Doctor Louis drive in and park his black four-door Mercedes sixty yards from the hospital entrance. Rachel shook her head, puckering her lips. *He's got a lot of nerve parking so far away from the hospital!! What's he's trying to do, keep people from scratching up his expensive Mercedes? Dude, please!*

She scooted down in her seat so he wouldn't see her. Rachel watched him as he slapped the sun visor down to checked himself in the mirror. When the doctor tried to brush down the wisps of hair sticking up from his dusky brown, ratty toupee, Rachel cracked up laughing. Doctor Louis smoothed out his thick mustache, giving extra attention to the little gray hairs on his deep crater face. *Oh please, stop the vanity. You're not that attractive, dude!*

Rachel knew Doctor Louis had been off work because of his recent heart attack. His wife, Sierra, took care of him, and Rachel wondered if the doctor was truly up to the task. He shoved the sun visor back in place, opened the door, and stepped out of his Mercedes. The strong freezing wind slammed him against the vehicle, and it took all of his physical strength to shut the door. Rachel laughed, tickled that the doctor was having such a hard time on his first day back to work. She watched him like a hawk as he tried to shut his car door. Finally, by the third try, he was successful.

Shivering, the freezing wind ripped through his coat and clothes straight to the bone. Doctor Louis buttoned his long black wool coat and then adjusted the fuzzy earmuffs over his ears. He headed out, drifting along the parking lot, and the wind hurled his thick body this way and that. The wind blew off his ratty toupee and it floated and swirled in the air like a balloon. Rachel howled with laughter so hard, her stomach ached. She rubbed her tummy while she watched Doctor Louis struggle against the wind. When the wind finally died down, the hairpiece dropped to the ground. Rachel laughed again, holding her stomach. *Poor guy, I can't wait to tell Jamie and Sally about this funny shit!*

Frazzled, Doctor Louis took off and ran after his cherished hairpiece. A menacing big black crow beat him to the punch, swooping down out of nowhere. The crow snatched the ratty hairpiece off the ground and flew to a nearby pine tree, settling on a broad branch. The bird dropped its prize possession in a nest of muddy twigs, and it laughed at the doctor with its annoying hoarse caw. Rachel laughed out loud, immediately slapping her hand over her mouth. She noticed the doctor's face had turned as red as a chili pepper. He shook his fist violently at the crow. "You damn, crazy bird! If I had my gun, I would shoot your ass out of that tree!"

The crow laughed again, twitching its head sideways, cooing and cawing as it danced on the edge of its nest. The doctor scoffed. "Oh, shut the hell up, you dense, crazy bird!"

Bent over in hysterics, tears leaked out the corners of Rachel's eyes. She inhaled deeply, taking short breaths, trying desperately to regain her composure. As she watched, the doctor returned to his Mercedes, and the blistering wind knocked him around like a tennis ball. When he finally made it to his car and unlocked the door, opening it, he leaned over and stuck his head inside. A brisk wind slammed the door against his backside, and he fell in the driver's seat, bumping his head on the steering wheel. Rachel almost peed on herself from laughing so hard. Perspiration beaded on her face, and she grabbed her handbag, taking out a tissue. She patted her face, being careful not to mess up her makeup. *Man, I can't take much more of this! This shit is too funny!*

Doctor Louis massaged his temple as he sat in his car seat and pulled the door shut. He reached over, opened the glove department, and took out his black wool hat. He pulled it over his pale bald head, opened the door, and stepped out. He locked his Mercedes and started across the parking lot to the hospital entrance. Rachel ducked so the doctor couldn't see her as he passed by her car. She waited until Doctor Louis went inside. Then she opened her car door and got out. Rachel took off, catching up with him in the lobby. She stayed behind, following him at a safe distance as he stomped past Joyce and a janitor, refusing to say a word to anybody. Joyce frowned.

"So, Doctor, we're not speaking this morning?" the secretary called out to him.

He kept walking, ignoring her.

"Good morning, Doctor Louis!" she shouted at the top of her lungs as she winked at Rachel. "I said, good morning!"

"Humph," he grumbled, dismissing her with a wave. Joyce dropped her shoulders and shook her head. "The grumpy old Colonel is back. It's going to be a long, trying day."

Rachel slapped her hand over her mouth to stifle her laugh. Doctor Louis maintained his brisk pace until he arrived at the mailroom. He went inside, and Rachel watched him from the hall through the window. He frowned at his box of overflowing messages and then stuffed the notes into his briefcase. Doctor Louis stomped out of the mailroom, slamming the door behind him. He stomped past Rachel, never looking her way as he headed down the hall. *Man, how rude! What a sourpuss!*

Once he arrived at his office, Doctor Louis stood in the hall, fiddling with his keys. Rachel hurried past him to her office, stopping at her door. She turned and smiled at the doctor. "Good morning, Doctor Louis! You're here! Glad to see you!"

Still refusing to look her way, the doctor hurriedly unlocked his office door and growled. "What's so damn good about this shitty morning?" He shoved the door open, went inside, and slammed the door so hard the frame shook.

Rachel flinched with her mouth gaped open. *Geez, what a grouch! I hope he's not going to be like this for the rest of the day! Lord Jesus, help me!*

Rachel unlocked her office door and stepped inside. She closed the door and settled in at her desk. Soon, she heard loud knocking on her door, and it flew open. Sally's smiling face appeared in front of her. "Good morning! Can I come in?"

"Sure, girl. Have a seat," Rachel beckoned.

Sally strutted in and closed the door. She plopped her behind in a chair and crossed her legs. "So, how was your weekend?"

"Fine," Rachel smiled. "And yours?"

"Groovy. The kids were home from college and we had a grand old time."

"Well, good," Rachel said. "So, any new gossip I need to know?"

"No new gossip, but I do have something to tell you," Sally chuckled.

Rachel's eyes widen. "So, what is it?"

"Doctor Benny called out sick, and Doctor Everett James will be covering for him. Have you met Doctor James?"

"No, I don't believe so. I heard he is handsome."

"Oooo, girl! That man is easy on the eyes! A hell of a hunk!" Sally blinked her eyes in a seductive manner.

Rachel chuckled. "Girl, I hope the man is not hard to work with, that's all."

"He's okay, but he's a perfectionist," Sally warned.

Apprehensive, Rachel leaned over and sighed. She held her chin in her right hand with her elbow pressed on the desk. "Well, I hope he's not a grouch like Doctor Louis."

"Why? Did something happen?" Sally asked, raising an eyebrow.

"Doctor Louis came in here just now in a bad mood! I was sitting in my car in the parking lot listening to Christmas music, and he drove in. Girl, you should've seen him. It was so funny."

"Why, what happened?"

"When he got out of his car, his toupee blew off his head. A big crow swooped down, snatched it, and flew back to its nest. I swear that bird did that shit on purpose. The damn bird even laughed at him. Girl, it was the funniest shit, I laughed my head off!"

Sally gave Rachel a wary look. "You say the crow laughed at Doctor Louis? Have you been drinking, dear?"

"No, I'm not making this up!"

"If you say so." Sally rolled her eyes heavenward as she leaned back on the sofa. "No wonder the man is in a bad mood." They both laughed, then Sally said, "That man is something else. I'm afraid you'll have to get used to his moods."

"Ugh, I don't want to, but you're right." Rachel chuckled. Jamie crossed her mind. "Sally, have you seen Jamie this morning?"

"Oh, I forgot to tell you...she called out sick."

"I hope she's okay. I'm worried about her," Rachel said with her eyebrows furrowing.

"I am, too," Sally replied. "Anne and I talked. We're going to arrange an intervention with Jamie. Are you in?"

Rachel's face brightened. "Hell yeah, my dad suggested an intervention. Just let me know when!"

"Most definitely." Sally stood and hurried to the door. "It's time for our meeting. Are you coming?"

"I'm right behind you." Rachel slid out of her seat and followed Sally out the door.

179

Nurses, doctors, and social workers gathered in the conference room for the morning report. Doctor Louis, still wearing his wool hat, sat at the head of the conference table scowling. When Rachel entered the room, she couldn't help notice the tension in the air. She glanced over at Doctor Louis, and right away she knew why. His brooding and intimidating presence had already set the tone. Everyone sat with somber expressions on their faces whispering to one another. Rachel inhaled deeply as she selected a chair in a corner in the back of the room. She wanted to be invisible and unnoticed. She didn't want anyone calling on her to answer questions.

Standing in the doorway wearing dark sunglasses was the man with the giant afro she'd seen in the parking lot a few weeks ago dressed in military style. Rachel recognized him immediately as he strolled into the room. He took a seat next to Doctor Louis, and the two men shook hands. Rachel's eyes were as big as saucers. *So, this is the Doctor James everybody thinks is so handsome!*

Rachel carefully checked him out, studying his face. He had high cheekbones, and his smooth ebony complexion was flawless. *Mmmmmm...this dude is a bona fide hunk! But why the sunglasses? Are the lights too bright in the room? What is his deal? Damn, I just don't get it!*

"Greetings, everyone!" Doctor Louis' voice boomed like thunder as he peered over his eyeglasses, glancing around the table. "I know everyone is glad to see me back!"

Faint forced chuckles broke out around the room. Doctor James didn't crack a smile. Michael parted his lips into his crooked grin and turned, facing the doctor. "For those of you who haven't met Doctor James, he's the assistant medical chief of East Campus. He's covering for Doctor Benny while he's out for a couple of days."

Rachel sat back in her chair and twisted her nose up. *Doctor Louis is so passive-aggressive. Why is he introducing this guy to everyone? He knows full well everybody here knows who this guy is except for me! So dumb!* Rachel checked Doctor James out on the sly. She wished he would take off his sunglasses so she could see his eyes. When he spoke, his voice rumbled like a small earthquake, and when he smiled, straight white teeth emerged.

"Good morning, everyone! As Doctor Louis has informed you, I'll be covering for Doctor Benny. There is no reason to change your routine on my account. Just carry on as usual."

So, he's flexible. How refreshing! To keep from staring at the handsome doctor, Rachel focused on Doctor Louis as he went over the patient list. Some of the information on the list provoked laughter among the staff. Michael told the team about a patient who heard Chinese voices pointing out his ethnicity was Caucasian, but he spoke and understood only English. He also informed staff about another patient who feared green aliens were hijacking his brain. Police brought him to the hospital after his neighbors complained he was running in their yards shooting at squirrels with his little BB gun. Another patient was picked up in downtown Seattle for mooning pedestrians on Third Avenue. Doctor Louis made a particular point of telling staff this man had tattoos and pimples on his butt. The team howled with laughter.

Keenly aware she was being observed, Rachel looked up and caught Doctor James staring right at her. He smiled, and Rachel looked away, suddenly embarrassed. When the meeting was over, Rachel bolted out of her seat and walked swiftly to the door, but Doctor Louis stopped her.

"Miss Thomas," he called out.

Panicky, Rachel spun around and looked the doctor dead in the eye. "Yes, sir," she answered.

"Do you mind meeting me in my office at ten thirty to interview these new patients?"

Rachel glanced at her watch and saw she had an hour to play with. "Sure, no problem. I'll meet you then." And without hesitation, Rachel dashed out the door.

She hurried to the Admissions Unit, unlocking the steel door and going in. She walked down the hall to the nursing station and found a chair at the end of the counter. She plopped her butt in the chair, making herself comfortable. From the nursing station, she had a view of the patients' dining area.

Heavy gray smoke hung stagnant in the air. Patients paced back and forth, puffing on cigarettes, and Rachel coughed repeatedly from the suffocating smoke. Despite her discomfort, Rachel remained in her seat. She was days behind and determined to finish her charting. She kept coughing and hacking, fighting with the smoke around her. Suddenly a deep voice rumbled from behind her, and Rachel lurched forward. Her heart jumped in her chest as she turned to see who it was.

"I'm sorry. I didn't mean to scare you." It was Doctor James.

"Um…I didn't realize you were standing there." Rachel melted when she saw he was without his sunglasses. He had mesmerizing oval-shaped dark brown eyes she found sexy. He stared at her, and she stared back, covering her mouth as she coughed. Rachel waved cigarette smoke away from her face and felt she needed to explain herself. "I'm allergic."

"Cigarette smoke can be a pain in the ass if you're not a smoker."

"It's nauseating, and I hate it. It ends up in your clothes, your hair…well anyway, I don't mean to burden you with my issues."

"Not a problem. By the way, I don't believe we've officially met. My name is Everett James," he grinned.

"Um…my name is Rachel Thomas," she stammered, feeling uneasy again.

Doctor James smiled. "Glad to meet you. I certainly look forward to working with such a lovely lady."

Rachel felt her cheeks getting hot, and her heart fluttered in her chest. Embarrassed and pleased at the same time by his compliment, she found herself drawn to him. She glanced at her watch. It was ten-thirty. Time to meet with Doctor Louis.

"Listen, it's nice to meet you, but I've got to go. I need to get some fresh air, and Doctor Louis is waiting for me."

"Right. You and he have some interesting patients to interview."

"Yep, See, you around." Rachel waved as she dashed out of the nursing station. On her way to Doctor Louis' office, she fell out laughing to herself. *I think I'd better keep my distance. I could get into some serious trouble with that man!*

Only five minutes late, Rachel knocked on Doctor Louis' door. She braced herself, anticipating his anger, but when he opened the door he greeted her with his warm crooked smile. "Great, you're here. I was just getting started."

He whirled around and returned to his desk. Rachel walked in and shut the door. Sitting in front of her was a puny little man with icy blue eyes and a stringy blond ponytail. He dangled his legs over the armrest of his chair and Rachel noticed his overalls were wrinkled. When she walked past him, a whiff of musk assaulted her nostrils, and she frowned, wrinkling up her nose. Rachel joined Sally on the sofa, and Sally smiled, keeping her lips tight, trying not to laugh out loud.

The musk and the cigarette smoke took over Doctor Louis' office. He smashed his cigarette out in an ashtray, which was already overflowing with cigarette butts. For several minutes, no one spoke. The doctor's loud wheezing and coughing broke up the silence. He had a bad smoker's cough, and Rachel shook her head with amazement. *One would think he would give up smoking after his heart attack. But fools will be fools, my mother would say.*

Minutes passed before Doctor Louis finished reviewing the chart, and as he closed the record, he looked at Sally and Rachel.

"Ladies, this here is Bobby Pickett. They found him downtown on Third Avenue mooning pedestrians. The nurses believe he suffers from amnesia because when they questioned him about the incident, he couldn't remember."

"Hi Bobby, my name is Rachel Thomas, your social worker." Rachel smiled. Bobby just stared at her.

"I'm Sally Dobbins, the head nurse on the unit," Sally said.

Bobby nodded his head, but he still didn't say a word.

Annoyed, Doctor Louis snapped at him. "Does the cat have your tongue, son?"

Bobby made a face and looked up at the ceiling. "No, sir."

"I'm going to ask you some questions, and I want you to answer to the best of your ability."

"If you insist," Bobby flippantly answered, glancing around the room.

Doctor Louis let out a sharp sigh. "Tell us where you came from."

"New York."

"How long have you been here in Washington State?" Doctor Louis leaned forward and folded his arms on the desk.

"A few days...maybe a week." Bobby's icy blue eyes drifted to his lap.

"What made you decide to come here?"

"I needed a change in scenery."

Doctor Louis glanced up at the ceiingand fell back in his chair. "So, let me get this straight. You traveled three thousand miles across the country for a change in scenery? Are you kidding me? How did you get here?"

"I hitchhiked," Bobby flippantly replied.

"You hitchhiked?" Doctor Louis rolled his eyes heavenward again. "So, you were dropped off on Third Avenue downtown and decided to pull down your pants to show people on the street your pimply, tattooed behind. Interesting."

Unable to hold back, Rachel and Sally fell out laughing. Bobby winked at them with a smirk on his face.

"You think what you did was funny."

"Hell, it was fucking hilarious!"

Doctor Louis frowned, shifting position in his seat, shaking his head. "I reviewed your chart. You told the admissions nurse you've never been diagnosed with a mental illness. Is that true?"

"Yep!"

"I don't believe you."

"Why not?"

"People who pull down their pants on the street in front of thousands of people aren't exactly what I call sane."

Bobby grinned, wickedly showing two jagged front teeth. "I never said I was sane."

"Apparently not," the doctor agreed. "Have you ever heard voices, had racing thoughts, or felt suicidal or killed anyone?"

"Whoa, slow down, doc! I'm not crazy!"

Doctor Louis laughed. "Son, I think you're crazy as hell!"

Bobby glared at the doctor. "You're the crazy one!"

"How so?"

"You have crazy looking eyes and you look spooky in that wool hat."

"You think you're tough and scary, don't you?"

Bobby straightened up and slid his legs off the armrest. "Old man, I'm tougher and scarier than you think."

Chuckling out loud, Doctor Louis said, "So, you hitchhiked across the country for a change in scenery? I'm sorry son, I just don't believe that garbage!"

Rachel and Sally exchanged glances trying not to bust out laughing. Sally looked down and furiously scribbled on her notepad.

"Who cares what you think, old man!" Bobby hissed as he folded his arms across his chest. "You don't know what I've been through."

"Oh, did you go through something? Tell me about it." The doctor's tone was sarcastic.

Bobby looked away, refusing to look at the doctor.

However, Doctor Louis refused to put up with Bobby's antics. "Look at me, son…I said, look at me!"

Bobby provocatively bucked his icy blue eyes. "Old geezer, are you satisfied? See, I'm looking at you!"

"You're running from something, aren't you? Who are you hiding from?"

"Doc, all you're doing is fishing for information and harassing me."

Doctor Louis shrugged his shoulders. "Son, your story just doesn't add up."

"Well, you're wrong, old man!" Bobby tapped his fingers hard on the chair armrest.

Doctor Louis took note. "What's wrong, son? You seemed a little agitated."

"What do you want from me?"

"I want you to tell me the truth, the plain truth."

"I don't have anything else to say to you."

"Very well then, you can go back to the unit." Doctor Louis rose on his feet and walked to the door. He opened it and turned to face Bobby. "You can go now."

Bobby stood up. "How long will I have to be here?"

"I'll let you know in a few hours."

As soon as Bobby walked out, Doctor Louis shut the door. "He's a lying, and he's hiding something!"

Rachel arched an eyebrow, getting concerned. "What do you think is going on with him?"

"He's hotter than a loaded pistol. He's running from the law. There's no rhyme or reason why he's here. Call the sheriff and see if this asshole has any outstanding warrants."

Rachel hopped off the sofa and ran to the door. "I'll get right on it!" She opened the door and ran out.

Back in her office, Rachel tapped her fingers on the desk. On hold with the phone receiver pressed to her ear, classical music played in the background. Several minutes passed before Rachel heard a gritty female voice on the line.

"This is Sheriff Beatrice. How can I help you?"

"This is Rachel Thomas, a social worker from Salter's Point Regional. I need an emergency background check on a patient we have here in the hospital."

"The name, ma'am?"

"His name is Bobby Pickett." Rachel heard a click, and classical music played in her ear again. She inhaled sharply, frustrated to be on hold again.

Five minutes later, Sheriff Beatrice's gritty voice came back on the line. "Hello. Are you still there?"

"I'm here."

"It looks like you've got a convicted serial killer in your midst. Bobby Pickett is really John 'Pimple Butt' Lewis. He escaped two weeks ago from the federal prison in New York, and the FBI has been looking for him ever since. You say he's still there?"

"Yes, ma'am!" Rachel responded with big eyes. "A serial killer? Who did he kill?"

"Prostitutes," the sheriff said. "A hell of a lot of prostitutes. He had mommy issues. His momma was a prostitute. He killed her too."

Rachel gasped and fell back in her seat, flabbergasted. "What should we do?"

"Keep him there. I'll send the FBI over." A dial tone blared in her ear. The sheriff had hung up.

"Unbelievable! Doctor Louis was right!" Rachel stood up and hurried to the door. Jamie crossed her mind, and she stopped in her tracks. "I'll try to call Jamie after we take care of Pimple Butt."

She left her office and went next door. Rachel knocked and entered Doctor Louis's office at the same time. He looked up at her and growled, "So, little lady, what did you find out?"

Rachel stood in front of him with her notes in her hand. "Doctor Louis, Bobby Pickett's real name is John 'Pimple Butt' Lewis."

Sally, still sitting on the couch, snickered out loud. "Girl, you've got to be kidding me."

"No, that's what the sheriff told me."

"So, do you suppose he got his name from the pimples and tattoos on his pasty butt?" Doctor Louis loved being sarcastic.

Rachel smiled. "Now, sir, I wouldn't know."

"With a name like John 'Pimple Butt' Lewis…One would think his momma was high on crack when she came up with that name," Doctor Louis joked.

Rachel and Sally giggled hysterically. "You were right," Rachel said, barely getting her words out from giggling so hard. "Two weeks ago, John escaped from a prison in New York. He's a convicted serial killer serving time for killing prostitutes, including his own mother."

Sally's eyes were like hockey pocks. "Oh, my God! Are they coming to get him?"

"Yes, Sally, they are."

Doctor Louis reached for his phone. "I'm notifying security. But whatever you do, don't tip Pimple Butt off."

"While we're waiting, do you want to interview another patient?" Rachel was worried she wouldn't get off on time. They still had six patients to interview before her shift was over at four thirty.

"No, not right now. Let's take care of Pimple Butt first." Security apparently came on the line, and Doctor Louis demanded, "I need two officers on the Admissions Unit right now…"

Rachel dropped her shoulders, disappointed to learn she would be leaving work late. She headed to the door, leaving the doctor to his call. "I'll see you two later." She opened the door and drifted out. Rachel returned to her office and sat at her desk. She called Jamie, and there was no answer. *Geeze, where is she? I hope she's okay.* Rachel hung up and grabbed one of the charts she was working on. *I might as well chart while I'm waiting.*

An hour later, Rachel heard people running in the hallway. She slid out of her chair, rushed to the door, and swung it open. She peeked out and saw six tall men dressed in black suits and wearing dark sunglasses swarming the Admissions Unit like a pack of flies. Rachel glanced at her watch and noticed she'd called the sheriff an hour ago. *Damn, what took these cats so long?*

Unnervingly quiet, the men scoured the area searching for their prized prisoner. Nurses stood around, looking helpless with their mouths hanging open, wondering who these men were. Rachel stood in her doorway, deciding it was safer to stay close to her office. John Lewis emerged from his room, pimping down the hall, gazing into everyone's room. When he saw the six FBI agents coming his way, he took off sprinting toward the exit like a roadrunner. One agent saw him and yelled. "There he is!"

John hoofed it down the hall like a man on speed. Up ahead, someone had left the unit door ajar, and John, an award-winning high school sprinter, amped up his pace. As soon as he quickened his pace, a black suit came out of nowhere, shoving his butt onto the floor. John slid across the cold, laminated-tiled floor and slammed into a cement wall. He apparently blacked out for a moment, and when John woke up his wrists were in handcuffs. Blood trickled from his forehead. Two FBI agents jerked him up and stood him on his feet. Red-faced and wincing with pain, Bobby sneered at the two agents. They pinned his arms firmly against his back and shoved him forward down the hall. One agent shouted. "Walk, man, walk! I said, walk!"

John grunted as he jerked back and forth between the agents. They shoved him toward the exit, and the other four agents followed. Staff stared with their mouths hanging open, and patients watching the scene clapped, cheered, and whistled. Rachel had trouble containing her excitement. She bounced on her feet, gawking at the FBI agents as they escorted John to the exit. The unusual entourage took up the entire hallway as they passed through. "I can't believe they finally got him," Rachel gasped with one hand over her lips. And before she had a chance to blink an eye, the FBI agents had carried John "Pimple Butt" Lewis out the door.

Rachel went back into her office and shut the door. Jamie crossed her mind again. *Mm mm...let me check on her one more time.* Rachel dialed Jamie's number, but the phone rang and rang. Frustrated, Rachel hung up and sat at her desk. *Maybe I should visit her after work. I need to see she's all right.*

Rachel returned to Doctor Louis' office and spent the rest of the afternoon interviewing patients. Then she returned to her office to work on assessments late into the evening. Mentally exhausted, she called it quits around six thirty. Rachel picked up the phone and tried calling Jamie again, but she never answered. Worried, Rachel grabbed her jacket and handbag, turned off the lights, and ran out the door. Rachel rushed by the reception desk and waved at Joyce on her way out. "See you tomorrow," she yelled as she ran through the exit. Rachel groaned when she felt her stomach growling. She suddenly realized she hadn't eaten all day. *I'll stop by Sully's and get a bite to eat before I go over to Jamie's.*

Rachel unlocked her car and hopped inside. She turned the ignition on, backed out, and turned her vehicle toward the road. She waved at Darth Vader as she passed through the iron gate. He returned the favor, surprising her, and despite his welcoming wave, he managed to maintain his usual stone face. Rachel stepped on the accelerator and took off driving ten miles over the speed limit. Before long, Rachel had parked in front of Sully's and was heading up the sidewalk to the restaurant. She stopped, reaching into her wallet for some money. Unable to find any, Rachel swore she had a twenty-dollar bill hidden in her purse. Panicked, her heart bumped in her chest as she stood racking her brain, trying to remember where she left that twenty-dollar bill. Finally, Rachel remembered it was tucked away in her car cubby hole. Rachel returned to her car, unlocked the door, and flipped up the lid to the cubby hole. She sighed with relief when she found the twenty-dollar bill right where she'd left it. *This should be enough to get a turkey burger with some fries.*

Rachel tucked the bill in her wallet and got out of the car, slamming the door. She made a beeline into the restaurant and stood in the lobby. The growling in her stomach grew more intense when the smell of cooked food coming from the kitchen teased her nostrils. She searched the restaurant for the takeout counter, noticing the sign at the end of the bar. Right away, she stepped in that direction only to be derailed in her tracks. Her mouth flew open, and she couldn't believe her eyes.

Anne Cleveland and Rachel's ex-fiancée, Picasso Cooper, were engaged in a sensual lip lock. Rachel hadn't seen or spoken to Picasso since she found him in bed with a woman named Susan three years ago. The vivid memory of that horrible night came right back to her. The incident almost caused her to lose her mind and life.

Rachel remembered coming home early from class that evening. She opened her apartment door and stepped inside. She heard grunts and moaning, and the unusual noises lead her straight to the bedroom. She almost fainted when she found Picasso in bed with another woman. Rachel remembered going to the cabinet and retrieving Picasso's gun. She shot at him, barely missing him, and the bullet went through the wall instead. It left a hole, a souvenir for Picasso to remembered her by. Full of rage, Rachel recalled Susan snatching up her clothes and hopping out of bed. She ran to the door with Rachel chasing after her. Rachel grabbed the woman's hair and threw her on the floor like a rag doll. She beat the woman until welts and bruises show up on her skin. Later, after she cooled off, Rachel learned Susan was Picasso's secretary. She never knew the secretary's last name, nor did she bother to find out.

The whole incident landed her in jail overnight, but both Picasso and Susan dropped the charges. Later she heard from a friend that Susan laid in intensive care for two weeks, and after she was discharged, she quit her job and left town.

A shrill voice screeched from behind, jarring Rachel out of her thoughts. "Ma'am, are you okay?"

Rachel spun around, and a waitress with sunken green eyes stared back at her. On top of her small head was a big curly red bun. Rachel took a step back.

"Yes, I'm fine. Why do you ask?"

"You seemed a million miles away," the waitress observed.

"I probably was. I've got a lot on my mind."

"Do you want a table?"

"Yes. No, I mean no. I'll order something from the bar."

"Suit yourself," the waitress said, walking off. Rachel turned around, giving Picasso and Anne her full attention. With her heart pounding in her chest, Rachel took baby steps toward the bar. She leaned against the counter, standing a foot away. She tapped her fingers on the counter, which drew Anne's attention. Anne's face turned beet red when she recognized Rachel. She slid off Picasso's lap, looking wild-eyed.

"Hey girl, here to get a drink?"

Rachel shot Anne the evil eye. "After what I just witnessed, I definitely need one," she sharply replied.

Picasso pivoted around on his stool, and his full lips fell open. His brown eyes were huge.

"Rachel!" he squeaked. "What are you doing here?"

"I should be asking you that very same question," she shot back.

With eyes big as an owl, Anne was beside herself. "Picasso, you know Rachel?"

"He sure does," Rachel answered for him.

"Where did you two... I mean, how do you know her?" Anne stammered.

"What difference does it make? You're nothing but a lying, cheating witch!" Rachel charged.

"I beg your pardon?" Anne cut her eyes at Rachel.

"You heard me! I didn't stutter! Aren't you supposed to be with Jamie?" Rachel glared at Anne, looking her up and down.

"It's none of your business…"

Picasso stepped in, throwing his hand up. "Anne, let me handle this. Look, Rachel, we don't want any trouble. We're friends having a drink, that's all."

"Friends? Are you kidding me? How dare you!" Anne's light brown eyes looked like daggers. She looked like she wanted to slap the mess out of Picasso.

Tickled by Anne's reaction, Rachel laughed out loud. "I see he's got you fooled. He has you thinking you're 'it' on a stick! Girl, the man's playing you!"

"What are you talking about?"

"You don't know him like I do," Rachel said.

"Oh, really?" Anne jerked back, erratically blinking her eyes. She stood there with her hands on her hips.

"Let me enlighten you. Picasso and I were once engaged to be married. We used to live together. Now chew on that!"

Anne punched Picasso in the chest.

"Ow!" he hollered.

"Ow is right! So, Rachel is the woman you told me about!"

"Yes, what do you want me to say?" Picasso frowned as he rubbed his chest.

"I just don't believe this!" Anne briefly closed her eyes, swaying forward, almost tumbling over, she leaned against the bar counter.

"Are you okay?" Picasso's brow crinkled up. He tried to help Anne onto the stool, but she pushed him away.

"I'm fine. Leave me alone!"

"Okay," he said, keeping a healthy distance.

"So, Picasso, what did you tell this witch about me?" Rachel asked with burning eyes.

"It doesn't matter!"

"It does matter. You've no business telling this wench anything about me!"

Anne bolted from her stool. "Stop calling me names! Face it, Rachel, you and Picasso are over!"

"I know you're not talking to me like that, you, fat slut! Stay out of this if you know what's good for you!" Rachel flung her handbag on the counter. She stood there with fists balled up, ready to rumble. She wanted to beat the stew out of them.

"I see why you and Picasso aren't together. You're such a bit—"

"Watch it!" Rachel hissed, lunging toward her.

Picasso jumped between them, frowning. "We're not doing this!"

Rachel backed off. "Tell her to shut her mouth!"

Tears welled in Anne's eyes. "Rachel, why are you pestering him? What has he done to you?"

"A lot, and it's none of your business. But I must warn you, Picasso is a cheat! He can't be trusted."

Picasso threw his hands up, incensed. "Why are you dogging me out like this?"

"You're a cheat, a chump, and she needs to know who she's dealing with!"

"Rachel, I'm not interested…"

Rachel's voice was eerily cold. "Don't you say another word to me, Anne."

Picasso reached for Anne, grabbing her arm. "Baby, come over here by me. She's not going to hurt you." Anne leaned into him, inserting her arm into his.

Rachel rolled her eyes. "Oh, how sweet the two of you look. Girl, he can't protect you, and he knows it."

"Are you threatening her?" Picasso asked, with his eyebrows furrowing.

Rachel's laugh was wicked. "What do you think?"

The bartender heard Rachel's threat, and he immediately rushed over. Worried a fight might break out, he offered Rachel assistance.

"Ma'am, would you like to order something before you leave?"

"I certainly do. Could you please bring me a cold glass of water? I'm thirsty."

"Coming right up!" The bartender took off, disappearing around the bar.

Fidgety, Picasso danced back and forth on his feet.

"What's the matter with you?" Rachel charged. "You can't take the scrutiny?"

"Look, ladies, you're making me feel uncomfortable. Let's have a drink, call a truce, and forget this ever happened."

Rachel scoffed, rolling her eyes heavenward. "Oh, come on, you can't be serious!"

"Of course, I'm serious! What more do you want?" Picasso looked irritated.

Rachel shrugged her shoulders. "An apology would help."

Anne broke out with mirthless laughter. "Really? An apology? Where is that going to get you?"

"I told you to stay out of this!" Rachel steamed.

"Let's not have any animosity between us," Picasso suggested.

The bartender returned with Rachel's water. She took the glass from him, grinning cunningly, and took a sip.

"Okay, you're right...it's been three years. I should be over this." Out of the blue, Rachel threw the water in Picasso's face. He lunged forward, shaking his hands. Water dripped off his hands, face, and shirt. Rachel cracked up laughing. "Now, I feel a hell of a lot better!"

Rachel picked up her handbag and flung it over her shoulder. She laughed out loud as she made her way across the restaurant and out the door.

Anne followed and caught up with Rachel in her car backing out. She frantically waved her arms, signaling for Rachel to stop. Hot with rage, Rachel brought her Toyota to a screeching halt. She rolled down the window, and she stared at Anne with burning eyes. "You are a two-timing whore. What the hell do you want now?"

"I swear, I didn't know about you and Picasso. I'm sorry! You can't hold this against me. I didn't know!" Anne shook her head, looking frazzled.

"Oh, I don't. But Jamie will once she finds out you're cheating on her!"

"Please don't tell her," Anne pleaded. "It will break her heart."

"Break her heart? You should be ashamed of yourself!"

"I'll tell her when the time is right. I promise."

Rachel exploded. "Witch, you've got two seconds before I run over your fat ass!"

"You wouldn't dare!"

Rachel didn't say another word. Instead, she backed up and turned her Toyota around. She zoomed out of the parking lot, speeding down the road with her thoughts all over the place. Jamie had been right. Anne was seeing someone. But Rachel never thought it would be her ex-fiancée

She never expected to run into Picasso again. Rachel despised him, especially now. Anne was right. She shouldn't tell Jamie about Anne dating Picasso. She wasn't interested in hurting Jamie. Besides, she had her own demons to contend with, a rawness she thought had disappeared. A nervous wreck, Rachel fell back in her seat, sighing deeply. She glanced at the clock on the dashboard. The time was seven thirty.

"Well, Jamie, here I come." Rachel took another harsh breath. She peered out the rearview mirror making sure there were no police around. Satisfied, Rachel stomped on the gas and sped down the highway like a bat out of hell.

By the time Rachel reached Jamie's home, it was eight o'clock. Jamie lived in a small newly built brick house with a short driveway. Her beloved 1966 Mustang took up the entire driveway. Rachel parked her Toyota on the street in front of Jamie's house and got out. She stepped briskly to Jamie's door and rang the doorbell repeatedly. Hard footsteps approached the door and stopped.

"Who is it?" came a loud, rough, scratchy voice from behind the door.

"It's me, Rachel!"

The door swung open, and Jamie stood there, staring at Rachel with black mascara smeared around her angry bloodshot eyes.

"Damn it, are you trying to destroy my doorbell? You rang the hell out of it a dozen times!"

Rachel chuckled out loud. "Girl, you look like a raccoon in those wrinkled up polka dot pajamas."

"Well, hello to you, too," Jamie smirked as she erratically blinked her eyes. Barefooted, she turned her back on Rachel and left her outside. "What do you want?" she hollered back at her.

Ignoring Jamie's frosty attitude, Rachel stepped inside and closed the door. The place smelled like stale cigarette smoke. "I was worry about you," she hollered back, coughing.

"Why? Don't you see, I'm fine." Jamie shoved papers out of a chair and plopped her butt in it. An ashtray piled with cigarette butts sat on an end table. "Excuse the mess. I wasn't expecting company, as you can see."

"No problem," Rachel coughed as she made herself comfortable on the couch. "I was worried about you, and so was Sally."

"Oh, whoopee! Your concern is touching. Don't you see I'm still fucking kicking it!"

Rachel cracked a smile. "Girl, stop it, you look a damn mess."

"I know I do. I had a hell of a hangover this weekend."

"I'm not surprised. You were drunk as a skunk!" Rachel coughed and giggled at the same time.

Jamie fell back in her chair and massaged her temples. "You're right. I guess I was."

"Are you feeling better now?"

"I feel marvelous!" Jamie answered with sarcasm.

"No need to get smart," Rachel shot back. She studied Jamie's face and noticed her eyes were puffy. "What's wrong? Have you been crying?"

Jamie placed her hand over her chest, blinking. "Crying? What do you mean?"

"Yes, I said, crying. Don't be funny with me. Something's going on."

Jamie's eyes watered. "Anne left me. She wrote me this note telling me she'd moved out."

"What a bitch! I should've run over her when I had the chance," Rachel angrily mumbled under her breath, recalling how good it felt to scare the hell out of Anne.

"What are you mumbling about over there?"

"Oh, nothing," Rachel said, feeling empathy for Jamie. She remembered from her own experience how devastating a betrayal could be. She wanted to tell Jamie about Anne and Picasso, but she didn't dare. She didn't want to add to Jamie's misery. Besides, Rachel knew Jamie would drink herself into a stupor once she found out, and she didn't want that either. "So, tell me what's in the note."

Jamie leaped from her chair and ran to the kitchen. "I'll get it for you." Within seconds she was back, handing the note to Rachel.

Smoldering inside, Rachel took the note and read it. After she finished, she gave Jamie the note back. "Do you've any idea who Anne is seeing?"

"No," Jamie frowned.

"I know you don't want to hear this, but it sounds like your relationship with Anne is over."

"I know," Jamie whined with watery eyes. She reached for the tissue box sitting on the glass coffee table in front of her. Sniffling, she snatched a tissue and dabbed at her tear-filled eyes.

Furious for her friend, Rachel stood on her feet and began pacing back and forth like a wild animal. "Girl, let me tell you something. Anne needs to suffer. She needs her butt kicked!"

Jamie cracked up laughing. "Girl, please!"

"I'm serious. You need to hunt her down like a dog and whip her fat behind!"

Jamie rubbed her swollen, red eyes. "Girl, you're nuttier and crazier than a fruitcake! But you're right, Anne deserves a beat down."

"You're damn right she does!"

"Seriously, if you were me, what would you do?"

"Well, I was only kidding about beating her butt. However, if it was me, I would never speak to the woman again," Rachel said in a matter-of-fact tone.

"Remind me not to get on your bad side anytime soon," Jamie joked.

Rachel smiled slyly. "I'm afraid I've got a bit of a temper."

"Yeah, you do," Jamie chuckled. The smile left her face, and her expression turned doleful. "Have you ever been cheated on?" she asked.

Rachel paused for a moment. It felt like her cheeks were burning up. Jamie's pointed question caught her by surprise. Struggling to find the right words to answer Jamie's question honestly, Rachel threw caution to the wind and simply told her the truth. "As a matter of fact, I was. It happened a few years ago."

"Tell me about it." Jamie straightened, drew her legs up, and placed her feet on the edge of the chair. She clasped her hands around both knees.

"I was engaged to a man named Picasso Cooper. One night, I came home and found Picasso in bed with another woman. I was going to shoot him, but luckily for me, he talked me out of it."

Jamie's mouth dropped open, and her eyes grew round. "Girl, get out of here! You were going to shoot the man? Really?"

"Girl, I wanted to," Rachel said. "I was so angry and hurt. Actually, to be honest, I did try to shoot him, but the bullet ricocheted off the wall." Rachel folded her arms and fell back on the couch.

"What happened next?"

"Well, I kind of beat that Susan girl up. The neighbor called the police, and I spent the night in jail. After Picasso and Susan dropped the charges..." Rachel paused in mid-sentence. The blonde she saw at Sully's immediately came to mind. She frowned, looking perplexed as she tapped her chin with her index finger. *Hmmm, could that be her? No, it couldn't be. Susan had long, straight hair, not short curly hair.*

Jamie snapped her fingers and bucked her eyes. "Hello, hello? Earth to Rachel!"

"I'm sorry, I was in deep thought."

"Yeah, I can tell. So, finish the story."

"Um, well, I packed my bags and moved in with my parents."

"Wow, what a story!" Jamie smirked. "So, what's the heifer's name again?"

"Susan," Rachel quipped. "But I never got around to finding out her last name.

"Probably best," Jamie concluded. The two women laughed, and Rachel could see Jamie was feeling better. Jamie scooted out of her chair and stood on her feet. "My goodness, my manners are piss-poor! Rachel, can I get you something to drink?"

"Actually, I'm hungry. I need food!"

"How about a grilled cheese sandwich?" Jamie took off, heading to the kitchen.

"A grilled cheese sandwich sounds wonderful!" Excited to finally get something to eat, Rachel followed Jamie to the kitchen and parked herself at the table. "I haven't eaten all day. I could literally eat a horse."

"Sounds like you need two sandwiches," Jamie joked with all smiles. As Jamie busily prepared the sandwiches, Peepers crept into the kitchen and stood by his bowl of dried tuna. Attracted to the tuna debris, a small fly crawled up and down each side of the bowl. Peepers stuck his head in the bowl, and the fly flew off. Rachel took notice.

"I think Peepers is hungry. You need to feed him."

Jamie looked over at the big cat. "I will after I finish these sandwiches."

Still sore over her little encounter with Picasso and Anne, Rachel again entertained telling Jamie about it, but decided it wasn't the best decision. *Picasso and Anne together? Who would have thought!*

"It's done," Jamie announced, interrupting her deepest thoughts. Jamie brought the grilled cheese sandwiches to the table and placed them in front of her. "Honey, eat up! You look famished!"

"I am," Rachel laughed as she blessed her food in a hurry. Rachel grabbed one of her sandwiches and took a big bite. Chewing slowly, Rachel savored the buttery, cheesy flavor. "Mmmmmm, this is so good."

"Glad you like it," Jamie said, looking pleased. After Jamie fed Peepers, she joined Rachel at the table, and the two women gobbled down their sandwiches. They laughed, gossiped, and shared stories for a long while. Then at ten thirty, Rachel got up and went home.

Chapter Thirteen

Tuesday, December 4th

It was eight thirty when Rachel woke up and discovered she was late to work. Still exhausted from staying late at Jamie's the night before, Rachel showered and hurriedly dressed. After she called Beth to tell her she was going to be late, Rachel grabbed her coat and purse and ran out the door. Forty-five minutes later, she rolled into the hospital parking lot and parked. A red Fiat screeched past her vehicle and abruptly parked near the entrance of the hospital. "I guess I'm not the only one running late," Rachel chuckled as she strained her neck to see who it was.

The door flew open, and out stepped Doctor James. His afro appeared more significant than ever, and he was dressed in his usual bizarre attire. He swaggered to the building, leaving his car door wide open. *I can't believe he walked off and left his car like that! What a scatterbrain. I'll wait a few minutes and see if he comes back.*

Rachel waited five minutes, then got out and secured her Toyota. She walked over to the Fiat, muttering to herself. "I guess he's not coming back. He's a straight-up scatterbrain."

Rachel secured the lock and closed the doctor's car door. Once she entered the building, Rachel made a mad dash to her office. She threw off her coat, dropped her purse, and made several phone calls. Satisfied the pressing issues on her caseload were taken care of, Rachel left her office and strolled to the nursing station. When she opened the gate and walked in, Doctor James was reviewing charts and writing orders at the counter.

"Good morning, Doctor James," she cheerfully greeted him.

He twisted around and gazed at her with his sultry oval-shaped dark brown eyes. "Good morning to you, Miss Thomas," he said.

Damn, he's fine. Rachel melted. She twirled her index fingers, avoiding his gaze as she looked into the dining room. Patients paced back and forth like zombies, smoking cigarettes and staring at the floor.

"Doctor James, are you aware you left your car door open?"

"Oh, I did? I've got a lot on my mind," he chuckled.

"I see." Rachel's eyes drifted to his, and she noticed he was checking her out. "Doctor James, may I ask what you're looking at?"

"I must say, you look stunning this morning."

Rachel gushed, feeling embarrassed. "Thank you." Wearing red always brought her compliments, especially when she wore a dress. Still focused on the doctor leaving his car door open, Rachel wanted to make sure he'd heard her. "Doctor James, did you hear what I said earlier? You left your car door open. I closed the door and locked it for you."

"Oh, yes, yes, yes, thank you for taking care of me. I appreciate it." He grinned, showing straight white teeth.

"You're welcome, and I like your car. It's cute."

"That car has been with me for a long time." At that moment, a sly look came over his dark smooth face. "Can I take you for a spin sometime?"

Rachel dragged a chair from under the counter. She smoothed her dress and sat. Her hand trembled as she pulled a record out of the chart rack. Noticing her discomfort, Doctor James grinned.

"You know, I don't bite."

"Who said you did?" Rachel nervously giggled.

"Let's get to know each other better. After all, we'll be working together. How about dinner sometime soon?" Doctor James wasn't giving up. It was clear to Rachel he was taking a liking to her.

"Uh, no, I don't think so. I don't make it a habit to mix business with pleasure," Rachel shyly answered.

Doctor James gave Rachel a naughty grin. "So, you're playing hard to get, I see."

"No, I don't date at work," she snapped back with stone-cold confidence.

"Well, you're a smart young lady," he winked. Rachel's heart skipped several beats as she basked in his compliments, all the while very leery of his intentions. Mildly intimidated by his straightforwardness, Rachel threw caution to the wind. She longed to know more about him, so she put on her social worker's interviewing hat and attempted to find out more.

"Doctor James, I've got some questions to ask you."

"Shoot," he said.

"Are you married?"

"No, I'm single. What about you, Miss Thomas? What's your status?"

Come on, dude! You're not allowed to flip the script on me! Answer the question. "I'm asking the questions, here, Doctor, not you!"

"Feisty, I see." He stared at her, his sultry gaze more intense than ever. Rachel looked away, embarrassed.

"I don't mean to make you feel uncomfortable, but I like a woman who speaks her mind."

What a liar! See if you like this question! "So, Doctor James, why do you dress in army clothes all of the time? Were you in the military?"

He broke out in a hearty laugh and said. "No, but I used to belong to the Black Panther Party years ago. I find the style comfortable." He hesitated a moment. "You don't like the way I dress, pretty lady?"

"Well, it's different." Rachel was brutally honest to a fault. She couldn't help herself.

"If I dress more to your standards, would you consider going to dinner with me?"

He's a smooth one, but I've got his number. "We just met, so let's keep this professional."

"Very well."

Rachel slid out of her chair. "See you around. I've got a lot of work to do."

"You have a nice day," he grinned.

Rachel took off, leaving the doctor in the nursing station. She liked the doctor's handsome looks and the sexy way he tried to seduce her, but a romance with him was definitely out of the question. Office romances rarely work, she reasoned. "I'm staying as far away from him as possible. This way, I won't get myself into trouble," Rachel laughed to herself, knowing full well she was kidding herself. The attraction between them was inevitable, and Rachel had an inkling their relationship would change over time.

At Sea-Tac Airport, George and Susan boarded their flight to Paris. Susan gave George her bag and he stuffed their carry-ons in the luggage bin. Susan settled in a seat next to the window and glanced at her watch. It was one ten. George fell in his seat and buckled his seat belt.

"The plane takes off in twenty minutes. Are you ready for this long flight?" he asked, looking over at Susan.

"I'm sure I am. I can't wait to see Paris. I'm so excited," she giggled like a schoolgirl.

"There's a lot to see in Paris."

"I want to see the Eiffel Tower first! Will you take me?"

"You'll see it when we take a taxi into town. The Eiffel Tower can be viewed anywhere in Paris."

Susan clapped her hands like a little girl. "Splendid, so splendid!"

Passengers dressed in all kinds of styles moved like snails through the aisle, stopping momentarily to shove their luggage in the overhead bins. The cabin was crowded and stinky, and each passenger took their time settling in their assigned seats.

George leaned over and whispered in Susan's ear, "It sure stinks in here. Some of these people need a bath. I'm afraid it's going to be an uncomfortable flight."

"Relax, George, you can't do anything about it. Stop fretting," she softly giggled.

"I guess not," he smiled.

Out of nowhere, a musical bass voice boomed over the loudspeaker. "This is your pilot speaking. Good morning ladies and gentlemen, and welcome to flight seven hundred on Delta Airlines. We will be leaving shortly. Please take your seats and buckle up!"

Flight attendants dashed up and down the aisle, assisting late stragglers with their luggage. Two flight attendants at opposite ends of the aisle reviewed emergency procedures. Susan slid back the shade on her window and pressed her nose to the glass.

"It's still raining," she said.

"It rains a lot in Paris, too"

"Where are we staying?" Susan remembered she hadn't asked about their lodging previously.

"I'm renting an apartment. I plan to be there for a while."

Susan whipped her head around, blinking at George with wide eyes. "We're staying in an apartment? How long will we be in Paris?"

"Forever," he calmly said.

"Why are you just telling me this? What about your work?"

George took her hand, leaning over to kiss her on the cheek. "Calm down, my sweetheart. I can work over there."

"If you say so," she sighed, leaning back in her seat. Susan glanced down the aisle, and her mouth fell open. She saw a police officer with a German shepherd conversing with one of the flight attendants. The officer crept down the aisle checking out each passenger. His dog trotted beside him, sniffing the floor. Breathing hard, with her heart bouncing in her chest, Susan took a quick look at George. He took off his eyeglasses and dragged his hand over his face, groaning.

"Yikes! A police officer is coming our way."

"Yep, I know." Susan reached forward, retrieving a magazine from the pocket of the seat in front of her. She leafed through the pages pretending to be interested in the content. Sneaking a peek at George, Susan noticed sweat beading on his forehead. He lurched up and peered over the seat in front of him, then fell back in his seat. Susan noticed his face was red and flush. She had never seen him this nervous before. Tickled and surprise at once, she reached over and lightly touched his arm. He flinched.

"Geez, what's wrong with you? Are you all right? You seemed jumpy," she softly chuckled.

"Shush, I'm fine," he snapped back at her with perspiration dripping from his face. Susan left him alone, returning to her reading. It wasn't long before the officer passed by. He stopped when his dog ferociously sniffed around George's feet.

"Good morning," the officer said with a stone face.

George humbly cleared his throat, sounding hoarse. "Good morning, sir!"

"Are you all right?" asked the officer staring at him with concern in his eyes.

"I'm fine. I just have a tickle in my throat." George gently massaged his Adam's apple and cautiously asked, "Officer, is there a problem on the plane?"

"Not so far. Just checking for contraband."

"Oh," George said. Susan noticed the features in his face relaxed a little.

The officer's honey-colored eyes zeroed in on Susan, and she averted her eyes back to her magazine. "Good morning, ma'am!"

Susan didn't flinch. Instead, she looked up briefly and smiled. "Good morning, officer," she cheerfully replied.

He stared at her for a long moment. "You look familiar. Have we met?"

"I don't believe so." Inwardly nervous but outwardly calm, Susan dropped the magazine in the seat pocket in front of her. She reached under the seat and grabbed her handbag. Susan snapped opened her handbag and dug deep inside, taking out her Chap-Stick. "My lips are dry," she announced.

While Susan applied her lip balm, the officer craned his neck to get a better look at her. Placing his index finger on his brow, he questioned her. "Ma'am, I swear I've seen you on television before. Are you a celebrity of some sort?"

George crossed his legs repeatedly but kept his mouth shut. Susan, cool as a cucumber, batted her short eyelashes. "Officer, I think you're mistaken. I'm no celebrity. I'm just a regular girl," she lightly chuckled.

"Well, you sure are pretty enough to be a celebrity. Sorry to bother you."

"No problem," Susan blushed. Satisfied, the officer moved on to the back of the plane where his dog was sniffing around "Whew, that was close," Susan said.

"It sure was." George whistled out a long deep sigh.

"I see why you wanted me to stay in the house. It was a good thing he mistook me as a celebrity. Otherwise, you would've been in deep doo-doo!"

"I know, you don't have to tell me." George leaned over his armrest and gazed down the aisle. As the officer made his way back down the aisle, George straightened in his seat.

When the officer passed by them again, he smiled at Susan and George. "Have a nice flight, you two!"

"Thank you," George replied. Once the officer arrived at the front of the plane, he spun around and took one more look at the passengers. Satisfied, the officer tipped his hat and exited the plane. George dropped his shoulders, breathing a sigh of relief. Wet dew glistened on his face.

Susan reached over and wiped his cheek. "Honey, you're sweating bullets! He's gone. You can relax now."

"I guess the whole incident shook me up."

"Well, we're in the clear. Let's get some rest, we've got a long flight ahead." Susan nuzzled up to him, placing her head on his shoulder. At a loss for words, George just smiled. The plane taxied out of the gate, and George kissed Susan on the forehead.

"We're off! Paris, here we come!"

The flight attendants hurriedly took their seats, and the pilot's deep bass voice roared over the loudspeaker. "Ladies and Gents, we will be in the air in a few minutes. This is a twelve-hour flight destined to Paris, France. Buckle up, everyone, and enjoy your flight! Flight attendants prepare for takeoff!"

As the plane gained speed on the runway, George and Susan held hands thinking about their incredible journey together. They shared a lingering and passionate kiss as the plane climbed thirty thousand feet into the air. Years would go by before George Benny and Susan Cole were ever heard from again.

Sally and Rachel were taking a break in Rachel's office. Sally leaned back on the sofa and sipped on her coffee. "Does Jamie know we want to meet with her?"

"Yup, I called her several times this morning. I left three messages on her telephone recorder. I told her the meeting was at eleven fifteen."

Sally checked her watch. "Well, she's got five minutes."

A second later, Jamie opened the door and stuck her head in. "I'm here. What's up?"

"Girl, come in, how are you?" Rachel greeted her, waving her inside.

Jamie stepped in and closed the door. She dropped her shoulders, moving like a big turtle to the sofa where Sally sat. She flopped down next to Sally with her puffy, bloodshot eyes cast downward.

"Boy, you look a mess. Why are you dressed like that?" Sally asked with doleful eyes.

"I'm in mourning. I just lost the love of my life!" Jamie squeaked, raising her voice.

"We know, but we don't want to talk about Anne right now," Rachel gingerly informed her.

"Then, why all the phone calls?"

Bracing themselves, Sally and Rachel gave each other quick warning glances. Their looks weren't lost on Jamie, and she became extremely irritated. "What is it? What's on your minds?"

"We want to talk to you about your drinking," Rachel blurted out.

"Oh, I see." Jamie pouted, scooting down into the sofa and pursing her lips.

"Don't be salty with us. We're just trying to help you," Rachel said.

"I don't care!"

Suddenly, Sally bolted from the sofa, facing Jamie with her hands on her hips, sneering. "Every day, you come to work reeking of alcohol! Girl, you got a serious problem, and we demand you get help. It's time for you to sign up for rehab."

Jamie scoffed, twisting her face up. "Demand? Who are you talking to? Woman, my drinking is none of your damn business! Your ass drinks! Why are you on me?"

"I don't have—"

Rachel cut Sally off, gritting her teeth. "Jamie, don't you dare turn this around on Sally! Face it, you've got a problem. It's affecting your work and everybody else's work as well."

"Really?" Jamie's puffy, red bloodshot eyes burned with rage. "Tell me how my drinking is affecting your damn work, Rachel."

Rachel wildly bucked her eyes. "Glad too! When you and Anne fall out, you hide in your office all day drinking and sulking. You refuse to see patients, so I end up covering for you. The shit gets old. I have to do my work and yours too."

Overcome with emotion, Jamie fell back on the sofa and tears welled in her eyes. Jamie sobbed. "I don't want help. I want Anne."

"Remember, Anne left you because of your drinking," Sally quickly reminded her. Jamie dropped her head in her hands and balled like a baby.

"I miss her. I really do miss her!" Jamie's voice was muffled.

"I know, but you need alcohol treatment. It's time to sober up. If you do that, maybe you and Anne can get back together."

Rachel gave Sally a wary look. "Let's not make false promises," she said. Rachel stood on her feet and walked over to Jamie. She sat next to her, taking her hand. "Think about it, girl. There are a lot of good treatment programs out there. All we want is for you to be happy and well."

Jamie sighed heavily, dropping her shoulders. "Okay, I'll think about it," she said with her voice cracking. "But promise me, you two will give me time to think it over."

"Okay, we promise. But don't take too long. Otherwise, we'll have to jack you up again," Rachel smiled.

Jamie managed a half smile. "Believe me, I know you will."

An explosive pounding drew their eyes to the door. Rachel jumped up, rushed to the door, and swung it open.

In the hallway stood Beth tapping her foot on the hard floor. The supervisor wore purple three-inch ankle boots with gold buckles, and her fierce green eyes peered over her bifocals. "What's going on here?" She asked in a croaky voice as she waved for Rachel to move out of her way. Beth wobbled in and stood in the middle of the floor. Her eyes met Jamie's and a baffled look took over her features. "What's wrong with you? You look like a barracuda!"

"Hello to you, too," Jamie frowned.

"Are you going to answer my question?"

"Nothing is wrong with me. I'm fine."

Beth rolled her eyes. "Doctor Beebe is requesting all staff to report to the conference room for an emergency meeting in ten minutes."

"Why?" Jamie asked with droopy eyes.

"Don't ask why! Come and see for yourself." Beth wobbled to the door and then twisted around facing the three women. "The meeting starts in ten minutes. Do not be late." Beth walked out, slamming the door behind her.

"I wonder what's going on." Rachel grabbed her notebook and pen off the desk.

"Well, ladies, let's find out." Sally opened the door and walked out. Rachel and Jamie followed her.

On the way to the conference room, they passed by Doctor Hornsby's office. A rotten stench leaked from under the door and knocked them back on their heels.

"What is that smell?" Rachel gasped, fanning her nose.

"Hell, if I know," Jamie said, twisting her nose.

Sally knocked on Doctor Hornsby's door, but there was no answer. She pinched her nose, overwhelmed by the odor. "It smells like something died in there," she said with her voice muffled. "Has anyone seen Doctor Hornsby today?"

"No," Rachel and Jamie answered at the same time.

Sally knocked on the door again. Still no answer. "After the meeting, I'll get housekeeping to go inside and investigate."

"Good idea," Jamie said. The three women plugged their noses and hurried down the hall.

By the time they got to the conference room, all of the front and middle rows of seats were filled, and Rachel, Sally, and Jamie were forced to go to the back. They took seats against the wall among a group of nurses. The ladies chatted away like hens in a chicken coop.

A few feet to the right, Doctor James leaned against the wall checking everyone out as they came in. Dressed in his usual bizarre army outfit, he wore dark sunglasses and a black beret over his nicely groomed big afro.

Two feet over from him was Hiram sitting on the floor with his legs crossed in a pretzel position looking like a mad scientist with his hair wild all over his head. His shirt sleeves were rolled up to his bony elbows, and his red necktie was draped over his right shoulder.

Beth sat up front at a long rectangular table surrounded in cigarette smoke. She puffed on her Marlboro while observing staff taking their seats. Doctor Louis went over and whispered in her ear. A silly grin parted her lips as she listened intently to him. Nurses sitting around him gawked with amusement when Doctor Louis' greasy toupee slid to the front of his head. He reached up and shoved it back in place, and the nurses fell out giggling in hysterics. Doctor Louis ignored them.

"Did you guys see Doctor Louis' slimy rug? It almost fell off his bald head?" one nurse with a long dark brown ponytail asked.

Rachel scooted over and whispered in Sally's ear. "Doctor Louis just can't keep that rug straight on his head. He should consider not wearing it."

"I know, girl. It really does look ridiculous!" Sally chuckled.

"Foolish, more like it," Jamie said.

The nurses squirmed in their seats, getting antsy. Doctor Beebe looked tired as he rolled in, halting his wheelchair next to the podium. Doctor Louis soon joined him, and he reached up and patted his toupee. Satisfied the hairpiece was in place, Doctor Louis picked up the microphone.

"Good afternoon, everyone!" he growled with the microphone squeaking loud. Doctor Louis lower the volume, paused a moment, and then continued with his message. "We called this meeting because we have an announcement to make."

Loud whispers broke out, and Rachel glanced around the room. She didn't see Doctor Benny and wondered where he was. Rachel tapped Sally on the shoulder. "Where's Doctor Benny?"

"Who knows. He must still be out sick."

Puzzled, Rachel was not convinced. "Hmmm…something's not right, I know it."

"You're too cynical," Sally smiled.

"Maybe, I am." But Rachel had a feeling that something was amiss. It wasn't long before that feeling was verified.

Doctor Louis took a deep breath. "Doctor George Benny is no longer an employee at Salter's Point Regional."

"I told you something was up!" Rachel playfully slapped Sally on the arm.

"My word, what's going on here?" Sally asked with big eyes. Loud talking erupted around the room, and several social workers huddled together to converse more privately.

"SETTLE DOWN!" Doctor Louis yelled through the loud squeaky microphone. He flipped the switch on the microphone, lowering the volume again, and his toupee slipped slightly to the side of his head. Everyone in the room cracked up laughing, but Doctor Louis ignored it. He shoved the hairpiece back in place, carefully patting it down.

212

"You would think with all the trouble he's having keeping that piece of shit in place, he would just give up and go bald," Jamie observed.

Rachel shook her head and laughed. "Girl, I know."

Doctor Louis continued with his comments. "Management has learned that George Benny and Susan Cole have been living together for the past few weeks…"

Gasps of shock erupted across the room. Rachel, Sally, and Jamie exchanged knowing glances, not surprised by the disturbing news. After all, they had witnessed his inappropriate behavior with the female patients on the Admissions Unit.

"QUIET!" Doctor Louis shouted, getting inpatient. The chatter tapered down to mere whispers. Several social workers fidgeted in their seats, making childlike faces, and a male nurse bared down and blew out some gas. Seconds later, the smell of rotten eggs gripped the air, and staff sitting around him pinched their noses. Two social workers got up and made a beeline to the back. They took seats against the wall, plugging their noses.

Oblivious to the commotion, Doctor Louis continued with his disturbing news. "We believe Doctor Benny coerced Susan Cole into having an affair with him, so we filed papers for his arrest. However, he and Susan skipped town."

"George Benny, you scoundrel!" Hiram hopped up and pulled up his pants. "What a way to go! We old guys know how to put it down!"

The women cut their eyes at Hiram while the men gave him thunderous applause. Enjoying the brief spotlight, Hiram spun around in a circle, grinning and bowing his head. Across the room, Doctor Beebe and Doctor Louis glowered at him.

"All right, that's enough," Doctor Louis said, thwarting Hiram's thunder. Disappointed, Hiram dropped to the floor and sat, picking his nose. Giggles broke out around the room when Doctor Louis' toupee slid backward. Flustered but calm, Doctor Louis continued with his remarks. "The police are doing everything possible to find Doctor Benny and Susan Cole. Their story will be on the six o'clock news, so if you have questions, this is the time to ask."

"I have a question," Luther said, springing from his seat. He was a social worker with auburn hair.

"Go ahead," Doctor Louis said.

"Are you aware, sir, that your toupee has slid to the back of your head?"

Staff broke out in thunderous laughter, and Doctor Louis turned ashy gray. He tried desperately to straighten his toupee, but it kept sliding off his head. Everyone gasped when Doctor Louis threw the microphone down and snatched the wig off his head out of sheer frustration. He stuffed it in his coat pocket and stormed out of the room. Beth hopped out of her chair and ran after him.

"What does she think she's going to do?" Rachel asked, laughing her head off.

"Coddle his bruised ego," Jamie smirked.

"Stop it, you two are so bad," Sally giggled.

Doctor Beebe reached down and grabbed the microphone. He sat up in his chair and stared into the crowd with his face bloated like a red balloon. Not holding back his anger, he shouted into the microphone. "QUIET EVERYBODY! I SAID, QUIET!"

The laughter fizzled out. Doctor Beebe glared at Luther. "You need to apologize to Doctor Louis the next time you see him."

"Sure," Luther said with a smirk etched on his face. He returned to his seat as snickers continued to erupt around the room.

Visibly upset, Doctor Beebe blew into the microphone, speaking in a growling voice. "Now I'm opened to questions, not jokes. Do you have anything pertinent to ask me before I adjourn this meeting?"

"I do," Carmen answered in a baby voice. She slid out of her chair. Her big baby-blue eyes were wide with intrigue. "Doctor Beebe, do you plan to respond to the memo we sent you the other day?" she politely asked.

"What memo?" Doctor Beebe stared at her with fire in his eyes.

"The memo about staff participating in orthodox sex in the break room during work hours. We already know unorthodox sex is off limits," Carmen sweetly smiled.

Everyone roared with laughter, stomping their feet and giving each other high fives. Staff chanted in unison, "We Want Orthodox Sex! We Want Orthodox Sex!"

Rachel's mouth dropped open, shocked out of her wits. "I don't believe this! This place is downright crazy!"

"This whole meeting is out of control," Sally shouted over the loud laughter and chanting.

Red and puffed up, Doctor Beebe tossed the microphone across the room, barely missing a couple of nurses. Outdone, Doctor Beebe yelled. "This meeting is over!" He flipped his wheelchair around and rolled out of the conference room like a roadrunner on speed.

Carmen ran after him, her stride short and quick. "Doctor Beebe, wait up! You didn't answer my question!" she shouted in her baby voice.

Rachel, Sally, and Jamie looked at each other and, without saying a word, got up and walked out of the conference room. Rachel, still tickled over the meeting, fell out laughing. "Ladies, can you please tell me what just happened in there?"

"Girl, I wish I knew," Jamie chuckled.

"At least we know what happened to Susan Cole. The mystery has been solved," Sally added, giggling.

"Doctor Benny...what a dog," Rachel said.

"Yep, a straight-up yellow-tooth dog," Jamie joked.

Rachel was introspective. "Do you guys think the police will ever find him and Susan Cole?"

"I hope so," Sally answered.

Jamie shook her head. "Don't count on it. I'm afraid they're long gone!"

On the way back to their offices, Rachel, Jamie, and Sally ran into a group of patients standing in front of Doctor Hornsby's office. They looked horrified as they watch Peepers scratched violently at the door. The big cat growled, hissed, and bared his fangs because of the decaying, sour smell had taken over the whole hall. Sally gagged, covering her mouth to keep from puking.

She didn't yell, Sally yelped. "Someone, please call housekeeping right now!"

Rachel and Jamie pinched their noses, looking at each other. "Whatever it is, it should be buried in a cemetery somewhere," Jamie joked.

"Not funny," Rachel's forehead creased into a frown.

"Someone page Doctor Hornsby. We need her permission to open this door," Sally demanded.

A young nurse hurried to the nursing station, opened the gate, and ran in. She snatched the phone off the wall, paging housekeeping first, and then Doctor Hornsby. "Doctor Hornsby, please come to the Admissions Unit! Doctor Hornsby, please come to the Admissions Unit immediately!"

After five minutes, Doctor Hornsby emerged around the corner. She strolled to her office, taking her sweet time and grinning like a naughty little kid. The pungent smell didn't seem to bother her.

"What's all the commotion?" Doctor Hornsby innocently asked.

"Don't you smell it? It's enough to knock your britches off!" Sally responded.

"Sally, you look so pale. Maybe, you should go somewhere and lie down for a minute," the doctor teased with a gleam in her eye.

Ignoring her snarky comment, Sally's voice was subdued. "That awful odor is coming from your office, dear heart."

"Sally, what odor are you referring to?"

Sally was livid. "Grace, stop playing and unlock this door!"

"My, aren't we out of sorts this afternoon."

Sally balled up her fists, gritting her teeth. "All I'm trying to do is find out what is creating this odor."

"All right," Doctor Hornsby answered in a shrill voice. She looked around. The hall was crowded with patients and staff. Some patients in the crowd, overwhelmed by the putrid odor, gagged, coughed, or ran to the nearest bathroom to puke their guts out. Doctor Hornsby cackled like a wicked witch, amused by the whole scene she'd created.

This annoyed Sally. "You're getting on my nerves. Open the damn door, so we can see what's in your office," she demanded with her hands on her hips.

"Certainly," Doctor Hornsby said as she started for the door. The crowd split in half, moving to the side so she could get by. She hesitated when she saw Peepers' black claws scratching the door, leaving long splintered marks. The big cat noticed her approaching and flashed his fangs at her. The hair on his back stood straight up like a porcupine's as she came closer. Doctor Hornsby stopped in her tracks. Her eyes were huge. Keeping her eye on Peepers, she gingerly asked. "Will someone please move this cat so I can get into my office?"

Jamie grabbed Peepers and held her against her breast. She stood behind Doctor Hornsby as she unlocked the door. As soon as the doctor shoved the door open and went inside, the rotten odor slapped everyone in the face. Patients and nurses backed up, stumbling over each other, trying to distance themselves from the putrid smell. One patient puked right there in the middle of the floor. Another patient managed to run to a restroom across the hall, and her retching could be heard in the hallway. Peepers wiggled like a worm in Jamie's arms, trying to jump out. Jamie held onto him with a tight grip as she moved away from Doctor Hornsby's door.

"Oh my God, what do you have in there?" she gasped.

"Well, for the past week, I've been working on a little experiment." The doctor's voice trailed off as she walked to a cabinet.

Jamie stepped forward and stood outside the doorway. "An experiment? What are you talking about?"

"Let me show you." Doctor Hornsby opened the cabinet door and took out a Tupperware container.

Leery of what was inside, Jamie remained in the hall. Doctor Hornsby came to the doorway and opened the container.

"Lord, have mercy!" Jamie yelled. The rotten odor was so pronounced, Jamie almost dropped Peepers, and several nurses threw up on the floor. Peepers hissed, baring his teeth. Sally and Rachel pinched their noses. Doctor Hornsby hollered with laughter.

"Doctor Hornsby, what's so damn funny? What's wrong with you?" Sally glared at the doctor.

Giggling hysterically, Doctor Hornsby shoved the open container in Sally's face.

Sally jumped back. "My word, what is that?"

"Ladies and gents, this here is a human brain," Doctor Hornsby calmly announced as she lifted the container in the air, moving it back and forth. The shocked crowd gasped, looking at each other as they mouthed the words *human brain.*

Sally's face was white as a sheet. "A human brain? What are you doing with a human brain?"

"Studying it," Doctor Hornsby smiled.

"Studying it for what?" Rachel walked up and stood beside Sally with one hand covering her nose. Despite the odor, she wanted a closer look.

"I'm trying to find out how the human brain works when someone is mentally ill," Doctor Hornsby replied with a wicked expression on her face. She turned the container around clockwise, admiring it.

"Girl, someone needs to examine your damn head to find out what loose screws are missing," Jamie quipped.

Doctor Hornsby laughed. "Jamie, you're such a comedian!"

"Comedian, my ass. You're a crazy broad with loose screws," Jamie muttered under her breath, blinking her eyes.

Doctor Hornsby snapped the lid on the container. "I'm going to return this to the lab."

"You do that," Sally said, swaying a little. She staggered over to the wall, leaning against it. Rachel rushed over. "Sally, are you all right?"

Sally's eyes watered. She shook her head and cupped her mouth to keep from puking. Rachel felt her stomach gurgling. She, too, felt sick. "I think I need to go to the bathroom."

"Well, I didn't mean to upset anyone. It's an experiment, so relax." Doctor Hornsby took off, strolling down the hall, humming to herself.

Jamie ran to the bathroom, and Rachel followed her. Jamie dropped Peepers and threw up in the sink while Rachel released herself in the toilet. They remained there, retching until they had no more to give. They hyperventilated, taking deep breaths as they held their sore stomachs. Finally, Rachel came out of the stall and snatched a paper towel out of the dispenser. She wiped the sour spit from her lips and rinsed her mouth out with water.

"Why would anyone in their right mind keep a human brain in their office?"

"Doctor Hornsby is not in her right mind. She's a nut, crazy as hell," Jamie coughed.

"Do you think she did that shit on purpose so she could see us suffer?"

"Probably. I always thought she was a little sadistic," Jamie said. She looked down, and Peepers was rubbing up against her leg. His golden eyes stared back at her. Jamie reached down and gathered him up in her arms and headed to the door. "Well, I got to go. I have charting to do."

"Okay." Rachel followed Jamie out the door. "This sure has been a hell of an afternoon."

"You can say that again."

Glad to be home and relieved to be away from the hospital, Rachel wrapped herself in a blanket and curled up in her favorite recliner. She stared blankly at the television and finished watching the evening news. She was surprised to learn the woman she saw at Sully's the other evening was Susan Cole herself. However, she couldn't help thinking she had met Susan Cole before. Her face was familiar, a look forever etched in her distant mind. As she laid there, Rachel tried to remember, racking her brain to recall details. Bothered by the familiar face she knew she had met in the past, Rachel pondered where they'd met and the circumstances.

An aching pain gnawed at the center of her abdomen. She was still sore from all of the retching she'd done at work. The image of a human brain floating in rotten formaldehyde in a Tupperware container stayed on her mind. It turned her stomach, causing her to skip dinner. Weary and feeling low in energy, Rachel scooted out of her recliner and slowly trudged to her bedroom. She yawned and wiggled out of her work clothes. Rachel staggered to the shower, surprised how drained she felt, turned on the water, and waited for it to warm up.

She stepped into the shower, and the warm water felt good against her skin. She took her time bathing, enjoying the warm water on her body, then Susan Cole came to her mind again. As she stood there bathing, she tried to recall where she and Susan may have met in the past. After Rachel finished washing, she turned off the shower, opened the door, and stepped out. Grabbing her towel off the rack, Rachel dried herself off. She returned to the bedroom and shimmied into her red silk pajamas.

As she thought about Susan, a crude, awful memory crossed her mind. Rachel groaned as the memory became more vivid. *Damn, Damn, Damn!* Now she knew.

Susan Cole was the woman she found Picasso in bed with three years ago. The painful memory drudged up feelings she never wanted to experience again. Rachel winced when recalling that horrid night. She shivered when she remembered holding the gun in her hand with the intent to shoot. She never wished to take her anger out on Susan, only on Picasso, who was the real perpetrator. On that evening, life as she knew it had changed in a single instance. She was glad she came to her senses and didn't kill the cheating scoundrel. She never thought in a million years that she would run into Picasso or Susan again. Now her painful past had caught up with her.

Sleepy and worn out, Rachel sat on her bed and yawned. She reached over, turned off the lamp on the nightstand, and slid under her comforter, pulling it over her head. Five minutes later, she was sound asleep, dead to the world and everything wrong in it.

Chapter Fourteen

Monday, December 10th

When Rachel drove up to the hospital gate at seven thirty in the morning, her mouth dropped open. The guard she nicknamed Darth Vader stood in front of the entrance dressed in a Santa Claus outfit. Several people, shocked like her, slowed down to stared at the festive guard. Stoic and unmoved as always, the guard opened the gate and waved everyone in. When Rachel reached the gate and rolled down her window, she started to say something to him. However, when Darth Vader gave her a nasty glare, Rachel rolled up her window and drove on through, muttering to herself, "He has a lot of nerve dressing up as Santa Claus with such a mean attitude!"

As she chugged up the road toward South Campus Hospital, she noticed a huge Christmas wreath on the clock tower. The garland was threaded with twinkling lights and covered with massive red poinsettias. On the hospital grounds sat a lighted Santa Claus display with a red sleigh and twelve big reindeer. Black crows perched on the reindeer's backs honked at people as they rode by. Rachel drove onto the South Campus parking lot, and another large wreath hung above the hospital entrance. "Boy, they don't waste any time around here decorating for the Christmas holiday," she chuckled.

Rachel hurriedly parked, grabbed her handbag, opened the car door, and stepped out. After she locked her vehicle, Rachel dashed to the hospital entrance. Maintenance men dressed in heavy wool black jackets and baggy pants busily hung lights around the hospital windows. Rachel tapped the buzzer and walked in after the door slid opened. Warm air coming from the ceiling blew in her face. Rachel pulled off her red knit hat and watched Joyce at the reception counter struggling with a poster scripted with red and gold lettering. Several times, the receptionist tried to tape it across the desk, but the sign kept falling to the floor. Whenever Joyce taped one end of the poster on the counter, the other end would fall down. Joyce stomped her feet.

"Damn, I'm so tired of this shit! Why won't this damn poster stay up?"

Rachel laughed. Joyce looked a mess in her Missus Santa Claus dress that seemed to burst at the seams. Rachel rushed over, tossing her handbag on the counter.

"Hey, Joyce, let me help you." Rachel grabbed one end of the poster and held it in place so Joyce could secure her end.

"Thanks, Rachel. You're a gem."

"Glad to help."

After the poster was secured, Joyce and Rachel stepped back to inspect their handiwork. Rachel's lips curved into a bright smile after she read the poster's inscription.

"Wow, the hospital is hosting an employee Christmas potluck? Now, that's nice."

"Yep. Every year on the Tuesday before Christmas. Everyone brings their favorite dish or dessert, and the hospital administration supplies the meat, trimmings, drinks, and everything else."

"So cool. Will there be gift exchanges?"

"No, it's against the rules. The hospital stopped doing gift exchanges because people would get mad if they got a bad gift."

"Makes sense."

Joyce stepped forward and reached over the counter. She brought out a white sheet of paper and a black ink pen with yarn tied around it. She secured the sign on the top of the counter and tied the pen on a hook below the bar, allowing it to dangle.

"Now everything is set. You can sign up by writing your name on this sheet and the type of dish you plan to bring."

"Cool." Rachel grinned as she grabbed the pen, and wrote her name on the signup sheet. She hesitated a moment, placing her elbow on the counter, cradling her chin. With her other hand, she tapped her fingers on the desk in deep thought.

"Hmmm, what should I bring? Decisions, decisions, decisions."

Creases appeared on Joyce's forehead. "Girl, can you even cook? I can't imagine a girl like you spending any length of time in the kitchen."

"I beg your pardon, woman! Yes, I can cook, thank you!"

"Then pick something to bring and quit daydreaming!"

Rachel made a face. "You need to fix that attitude this morning. It doesn't match your outfit."

"Huh?" Joyce smoothed out her Missus Santa dress, inspecting it. "What's wrong with my outfit?"

"Nothing." Rachel giggled, realizing her joke went over Joyce's head.

Joyce groaned. "Will you pick something already!"

"Okay, how about rum cake?" Rachel stuck her tongue out at Joyce as she scribbled her selection on the signup sheet. She dropped the pen and grabbed her handbag. Joyce's eyes were huge.

"You can make a rum cake? From scratch?"

"Yes, ma'am, I sure can! Guaranteed to make your toes curl." Rachel laughed, whirling around. She took off across the lobby. "See you later, Missus Santa Claus Grouch!"

"Right back at you!" Joyce yelled.

Rachel turned and waved, then bolted around the corner and headed straight to the Admissions Unit.

Tuesday, December 11th

Rachel, Sally, and Jamie were in Jamie's office having their morning coffee. Sally and Rachel sat on the sofa while Jamie leaned back in her chair with her feet propped on the desk. In a corner, Peepers was hunched on his paws having breakfast, lapping up the warm milk Jamie gave him.

"Have you ladies decided what you're cooking for the Christmas potluck?" Rachel asked.

"I'm not cooking a damn thing." Jamie grimaced. "Albertsons will be doing my cooking."

"So, what do you plan to buy from Albertsons?"

"Fried chicken."

Sally squished up her face. "Why don't you bring dessert? Albertsons is one grocery store that makes a great dessert."

"What do you suggest?" Jamie put her feet down on the floor and stood up, walking to the coffee pot. She filled her cup with fresh coffee.

"Bring a fruitcake. It would be fitting to the occasion."

Rachel laughed out loud. She immediately slapped her hand on her mouth when she realized how loud she sounded. "Girl, that's funny!"

Sally blinked her long false eyelashes. "I only speak the truth, dear."

"I hate fruitcake," Jamie groaned. "It's like chewing bubble gum with fruit and nuts in it."

"Really, Jamie?"

"Well, yes, Rachel, fruitcake is gummy."

"Well, I'm bringing a rum cake."

"From Albertsons?" Sally's eyes widened.

"No, silly, I'm making it from scratch."

"You can bake, girl, really?"

"Yes, Sally, I can," Rachel scoffed. She set her coffee on the end table. "Why is it so damn surprising to everyone that I can cook?"

"You look too prissy to know how to cook, let alone bake."

"Too prissy, Jamie? What the hell are you talking about?"

Jamie smirked as she returned to her seat, sipping her coffee. "I'm just having a little trouble visualizing you as a Suzi Homemaker. It just doesn't fit you."

"Oh, please." Rachel huffed as she fell back on the sofa.

"I think I'll make some deviled eggs," Sally chuckled. "Hardworking fruitcakes need deviled eggs."

"Deviled eggs make me fart."

"Me too," Jamie giggled.

"Listen, ladies. I don't care if deviled eggs make you gas. I'm making them anyway."

All three women laughed, then a hard knock drew their eyes to the door.

"Come in," Jamie yelled.

The door opened, and Hiram pranced in.

"Good morning, ladies," he grinned with his wiry blonde locks wild on his head. "Hiram wants to know if you ladies are coming to the Christmas potluck."

"Why? Are you bringing gifts?" Jamie sneered.

"For you, Sugar Tits, I might just do that."

Jamie stood up, her face wolfish. "If you call me Sugar Tits one more time, I swear…"

"Hiram, there's no need to call anyone here insulting names," Sally scolded him, wagging her index finger.

"You're right. Please accept Hiram's apology, Jamie."

"So, Hiram, are you coming? And if so, what are you bringing?" Rachel asked.

"Yes, missy, I'm coming. I plan to bring sugar cookies."

"From the store, or are you going to bake them yourself?"

"Good question." Hiram tapped his chin with his forefinger as he looked up at the ceiling. "Let's see…what will Hiram do?" A moment later, he stated, "Hiram will make his cookies from scratch. Homemade cookies taste better."

"I agree." Rachel nodded.

Jamie gave Hiram the side-eye. "Hiram, I didn't know you could bake."

"Absolutely, but only on special occasions." He grinned as he turned and opened the door. "Well, Hiram's got to go. See you ladies later." He dashed out and slammed the door behind him.

"Sugar cookies, my foot! He'll be at Albertsons like the rest of us," Jamie smirked.

"All I know, I won't be eating his damn sugar cookies!" Sally scoffed.

"You guys are so hard on Hiram. I know he's not the cleanest guy in the world, but he probably makes a good cookie." Rachel leaned forward and crossed her legs.

"I don't care. This girl will not partake in anything he bakes."

"I don't blame you," Jamie said. "You'll probably get the runs after eating one of his cookies."

"Ewe!" Rachel frowned, uncrossing her legs and rising to her feet. "I got to go. I have work to do."

"Me, too." Sally followed Rachel out the door.

"See you around," Rachel waved as she took off down the hall in the opposite direction.

Tuesday, December 18th

Rachel woke up to a town covered with snow. She stared out her apartment window, in awe of the glistening white stuff. The snow's blinding white seemed to break up the darkness. Soon the sky turned gold, blue, and gray, signaling the arrival of sunrise. Rachel glanced at the clock on the nightstand, and it was six o'clock. She switched on the lamp and began preparing for work.

Forty-five minutes later, she was appropriately dressed for the weather, sporting a red wool sweater, black wool pants, and a pair of ankle boots. After Rachel ate her breakfast, she slipped on her long red wool coat and snuggly pulled her red knit hat over her ears. After giving herself a full inspection in the floor-length mirror, she grabbed her shoulder bag on the way to the kitchen. She secured the rum cake she made in a cake container and strutted out the door.

On the way to work, the sunrise was on the horizon. The sun, a fiery orange ball, looked magnificent against a sky colored with gold, gray, and blue streaks. Admiring the colors, Rachel sped down the freeway. By the time she arrived at the hospital and parked, it was daylight. Rachel stepped out of her car, locking the door. She checked her watch, and it was seven forty-five. As Rachel walked to the hospital, she took her time. The parking lot was icy and covered with snow. She didn't want to slip and fall.

When Joyce saw her arrive at the door, the receptionist buzzed her in. Rachel entered the lobby and stomped her feet on the floor, shaking off ice and snow. Rachel's mouth flew open when she saw the reception counter. Six naked trolls were lined up on top, wearing green hats and red shoes with bells on the toes. Rachel bowled over with laughter as she approached the counter.

"Joyce, who…Joyce did Hiram…" She was unable to get the words out.

"Who else would it be!" Joyce's forehead wrinkled into a frown. She stood there with her hands on her hips, disgusted.

"You've got to admit, this is freaking hilarious!"

"No, I'm tired of Hiram taking over my workspace and ruining my display." Joyce flopped in her seat, and her chair creaked.

Rachel pulled off her hat and finger-combed her hair. "Joyce, your sense of humor is lacking."

"I have a sense of humor!" she shouted. "I just don't think Hiram is funny!"

"Whoa, settle down. No need to get loud."

"Sorry."

Rachel set her cake container on the counter. "Should I drop my rum cake off at the kitchen?"

"Leave it there. I'll drop it off for you."

"So thoughtful of you. Thank you." Rachel headed toward the Admissions Unit. "I'll be in my office if you need me. In the meantime, you and those trolls have a wonderful day," she yelled, not looking back.

"Oh, be quiet!" Rachel heard Joyce say as she opened the door to the Admissions Unit and ducked inside.

Later in the morning, precisely at eleven thirty, Rachel, Sally, and Jamie joined several nurses, doctors, and other social workers in line as they waited to enter the cafeteria. Kitchen aides scurried in and out carrying green and red linen cloths and baby red poinsettias. Peepers rubbed his head against Jamie's leg, purring with his eyes closed. Jamie stooped over and petted his head.

"Peepers wants some of that good roasted turkey," Jamie laughed.

Rachel shook her head and smiled.. "Mm-hm, Mm-hm, Peepers is spoiled." She stepped out of line, walking to the front where Cassie stood by the door. "Excuse me, Cassie, can I take a look? I want to see the setup."

"Oh, sure," Cassie said, stepping back.

Rachel stepped in front of her and poked her head in the door. She saw four large oblong tables covered with green linen cloths against the back wall next to the kitchen. The aides ran in and out of the kitchen, putting food and condiments on the tables. In a corner near the front of the cafeteria sat a medium-sized square stage. Four men with long scraggly hair and scruffy white beards warmed up their musical instruments. They all wore Santa Claus hats, faded blue jeans, and shiny black cowboy boots. Rachel twisted around and stared at Cassie with huge dark eyes.

"We have a band?"

"Yep. And Hiram is the lead singer."

"Get out of here!"

Cassie giggled, shaking her head. "No, I'm not kidding."

Rachel lingered for a moment watching the band warm up. One man blew long notes on his saxophone while another belted out a do-re-mi scale on the electric piano.

"Where's Hiram?"

"He's not here yet."

"I can't believe Hiram is the lead singer!" Rachel left Cassie and rejoined Jamie and Sally in line. "You guys aren't going to believe what Cassie just told me."

"What?" said Sally.

"There's a band setting up in the cafeteria, and Hiram is the lead singer."

The color in Jamie's face disappeared, and she turned pearly white. "Girl, what did you say? You're shitting me!"

"Nope!"

"Hilarious!" Sally giggled.

"I can't believe this..." Jamie rubbed her face, shaking her head.

Suddenly, Hiram appeared in the hall, rushing by them. His guitar case was hanging over his shoulder, and he wore a red plaid shirt, a pair of faded blue jeans, and knee-high black leather boots with bells. A Santa Claus hat sat on his wiry, messy hair.

Jamie wrinkled her forehead, groaning. "Where the hell, does he think he's going?"

"I told you, he's the lead singer," Rachel laughed.

Sally's blinked erratically, still trying to comprehend what Rachel said. "He looks pretty decent today. I wonder who convince him to change his clothes. Lead singer? I wonder what he sounds like."

"We'll soon find out," Rachel replied, looking at Sally. They both laughed, and all three women watched Hiram prance into the cafeteria.

"What's so damn funny?" Jamie folded her arms on her chest, disgusted. "Man, if he's in this band, I think I might just upchuck right here."

"Oh, Jamie, stop being a sourpuss. You know Hiram will give us a show." Rachel chuckled as she looked down at Jamie's suit pocket and noticed a large bulge. "Girl, what's that in your pocket?"

"None of your business!"

"Oh, please, I already know what it is." Rachel frowned while Sally looked on, keeping her mouth shut.

"Then why ask? You're so nosy."

"They pay me to be nosy! Besides, this is not Sully's. You can't drink on the job!" Sally gave Rachel a knowing nod.

"I know that! Will you mind your own business?"

Rachel rolled her eyes, huffing out a long sigh. Disgusted, she reluctantly dropped the subject. "I'm hungry. I hope the food is good."

"It usually is." Sally rolled back on her heels with a solemn expression on her face. "The management usually provides turkey, ham, and roast beef."

"Yum." Rachel moved forward in line. She turned to look at Jamie, who still had her hand stuffed tight in her pocket. "I know Jack Daniels is your date, but what did you bring to the potluck?"

Sally laughed softly, and Jamie gave Rachel a nasty look. "I took Sally's advice and brought four big fruitcakes."

"Come on, Jamie. Four fruitcakes? Really?"

"No, I'm not kidding. After all, we do work with a bunch of fruit loops, nuts, and knuckled heads. Look at that fool Hiram."

Rachel forced a chuckle. "Jamie, you're so crazy."

"I know it," Jamie half-smiled.

Rachel stood on her tiptoes, stretching her neck and trying to check out the end of the line. Doctors James, Louis, and Benny were huddled in a tight circle, talking. Doctor James had on his usual, an army jacket, jeans, and a black beret hat over his wild black afro. Rachel's eyes drifted to his feet and noticed he had on a pair of shiny black dress shoes.

"Well, well, well, the eye candy doctor left his combat boots at home. Today, he's got on a decent pair of shoes."

"Oh, really, let me see." Jamie twisted around and grinned when she saw Doctor James' shoes. "He's weird."

"Yep, he is, but handsome." Sally flickered her long false eyelashes. "Rachel, I think you and Doctor James would make a beautiful couple."

"Get real. I don't date coworkers!" Rachel huffed with big eyes as she jerked her head to the side.

"But he's so handsome."

"I don't care!" Rachel folded her arms, indignant.

"Sally, stop it! You know that man is too freaking crazy to be in a romantic relationship with anybody. He'd drive poor Rachel insane."

"No, he won't because I'm not going to be in a relationship with him or anybody else in this crazy hospital, so there! Please drop the subject!"

They all laughed while Rachel refocused her attention, this time on Doctor Louis. "Doctor Louis always wears a white lab coat. Why? None of the other doctors wear lab coats."

"The man is a retired colonel. He's used to being in some type of uniform." Jamie bounced on her feet. "He's not the only one with a lab coat. Have you forgotten Doctor Beebe and Doctor Hornsby wear them, too?"

"Oh, yeah, you're right." As the line moved forward, Rachel saw Beth maneuver herself in front of Doctor Louis. "Beth's here," Rachel announced, still scoping out the end of the line. "She's got on a lime-green dress with red ankle boots."

Sally took a step back to check out Beth's outfit and fell out laughing. "That woman is a character. And I must say Doctor Louis' toupee looks pretty damn decent today."

"He probably went out and got a new one," Jamie laughed. Soon they were inside the cafeteria. Peepers sniffed the air, taking in the delectable scents of Christmas cheer mixed with an array of honey-roasted turkey, freshly baked rolls, and mincemeat pies.

Rachel noticed Peepers and smiled. "Look at Peepers. He's so cute."

Like Peepers, she loved the delectable scent of Christmas and the dark spicy stickiness of mincemeat pie, which she knew most people loathed. Mincemeat pie was her favorite and the best part of the holiday.

The band began playing a jazzy, light tempo of "Rudolph, The Red-Nosed Reindeer," and loud, gravelly male voices jarred their auditory senses. The hair on Peepers' back stood up, and his yellow eyes were wild with fright. The cat ran out of the cafeteria, screeching. Rachel, Sally, and Jamie fell out laughing as they covered their ears. Hiram howled like a wounded dog, singing and strumming his guitar while his four hippie-looking bandmates danced and played their instruments.

Jamie dragged her hand over her entire face. "He scared the hell out of my Peepers. Rachel, you weren't kidding. He's up there trying to sing! What an embarrassment."

"I told you." Rachel fell over in hysterics.

Tears streamed down Sally's cheeks from laughing so hard. "Poor Peepers. I don't blame him for running out of here. I won't be able to stand this howling much longer, either. I may have to join him. Hiram's singing is too much for my noggin."

Jamie rolled her eyes, sighing heavily. "Let's get some food before I lose my damn appetite."

Rachel and Sally followed Jamie to the back of the room. Good smelling food was spread all over the tables. Rachel's eyes were as large as hockey pucks, stunned by the amount of food. There was stuffing, turkey, mashed potatoes, spiced roast beef, and a huge ham on the first table. Tom stood over the meat in his chef outfit, slicing it up.

On the second table, there was mincemeat pie and sweet potato pie, Jamie's fruitcakes, plum pudding, gingerbread cookies, Rachel's rum cake, and Hiram's sugar cookies. An elf dressed in red stood in the middle of the cookie plate. Rachel and Sally laughed out loud when they saw the little fella standing in the middle of the plate surrounded by sugar cookies.

Jamie scoffed, shaking her head as she moved on to the third table. The third table had potato salad, macaroni salad, tossed salad, Sally's deviled eggs, collard greens, green beans, steamed broccoli, lasagna, and various condiments. A stack of plates with eating utensils and sodas were on the fourth table.

"Ladies, this is not a potluck. This is a feast!" Rachel said as she walked over and grabbed herself a plate with a knife and fork.

"Yep, you can say that again." Jamie grabbed her plate and began serving herself lasagna. Rachel and Sally grazed the vegetable and salad table, piling their plates high with green beans, collard greens, and potato and macaroni salads. The three women met at the meat table and stacked their plates with roast turkey, stuffing, ham, and a slice of roast beef. They stopped by the dessert and drink table, checking out their many selections. They each grabbed a dessert plate and balanced it on top of their plate of food.

"Sally, are you going to try Hiram's cookies? They look delicious," Rachel joked.

"Not this chick." Sally huffed as she grabbed a can of Lipton tea along with a slice of sweet potato pie. Sally walked off and found a table two feet from the stage. A male nurse sitting at the next table rose to his feet and pulled out a chair for her. "Thank you, darling."

"No problem," he smiled.

Rachel noticed the male nurse's chivalry toward Sally. "He's such a gentleman."

"Who?" asked Jamie.

"The male nurse who graciously pulled out a chair for Sally."

Soon Rachel and Jamie joined Sally at the table. Rachel balanced her plate of food and mincemeat pie in her right hand, and in her left she carried a can of Sprite. Jamie, on the other hand, bypassed the dessert table as well as the nonalcoholic drinks.

"Jamie, did you change your mind about dessert and a drink?"

Jamie grinned like a cheetah, gently patting her suit pocket with her left hand. "I have what I need right here."

"You're so crazy," Rachel muttered under her breath.

"Sally, why did you pick this table?" Jamie frowned, setting her plate of food on the table. "I don't want to be this close to Hiram."

"Hiram is not thinking about you! Girl, If I didn't know any better, I would say you're obsessed with the man."

"Ugh, how dare you?" Jamie plopped in her seat.

"Could have fooled me!"

Rachel arranged her plates directly in front of her. "Ladies, stop fussing! We're supposed to be celebrating and having fun."

"Here, here." Sally raised her can of tea in the air.

They sat together in silence, enjoying their meal and listening to music. Hiram's band played "Jingle Bells" in a calypso-like tempo, and Hiram dropped to one knee, strumming his guitar. He shook his head hard, and his hat fell off. His wild, wiry hair swayed in the air like Cab Calloway's.

Rachel giggled. "Look at Hiram, getting down up there!"

"Rock star in the making," Sally joked, taking a bite of her sweet potato pie.

Jamie ate her macaroni salad, talking with her mouth full. "You guys are delusional, and so is Hiram! Will you look at him? He sounds like a wounded bear!"

"Oh, Jamie, put a sock in it! You're just jealous!" Rachel rolled her eyes. She stood up and clapped her hands, cheering Hiram on.

"Oh, please. Is all of that clapping necessary?"

"Yes, ma'am! He deserves it." Rachel grinned, nodding her head with approval and clapping her heart out. The band took a break, and Rachel flopped back in her seat. She glanced around the cafeteria and noticed every table was filled with staff and patients. Two tables over from her, Rachel observed Robby scarfing down a slice of sweet potato pie, and next to him sat Mary, sipping on a can of Lipton iced tea. "Oh, how sweet. Robby and Mary finally made up. They're eating Christmas lunch together."

Sally twisted around in her seat to check out the couple while Jamie rolled her eyes heavenward, shaking her head and huffing. She took her napkin and covered her food, then scooted away from the table and stood up. "I can't take much more of this. I'm going to my office."

"Party pooper!" Rachel scoffed, wildly bucking her eyes.

"I second that." Sally shot Jamie a nasty look.

"I don't care what you two think. I'm going to my office. This scene is not for me. See you later!" Jamie grabbed her plate and promptly left the table.

"Boy, she's got a problem."

"I think it's the alcohol screwing with her mind." Sally squirmed in her seat.

"We should talk to her again about getting help. Sooner rather than later."

"I agree, but let's wait until after the holiday."

Rachel sipped her Sprite, sighing heavily. "Okay, we'll wait until after the holiday. But after that, we seriously have to talk to her about her drinking."

"Don't worry, we will."

Chapter Fifteen

Monday, December 24th – Christmas Eve

Rachel sat in her office drinking coffee while documenting last-minute notes on her cases. She was going away for Christmas and didn't want to leave Jamie a lot to do. She wasn't surprised when Jamie volunteered to cover for her. Rachel knew Jamie preferred to work during the holidays rather than be at home. As she finished each folder, Rachel added it to a plastic tray. She stood up, opened her drawer, and took out her dust rag. She lifted her desk calendar and wiped off the top of her desk, then wiped down her brass lamp. A knock on the door interrupted her cleaning, and she tossed her dust rag on the desk. "Come in!"

The door shot opened, and Jamie stood nervously in the doorway with Peepers in her arms. She tilted her head with her bottom lip poked out. "Hey girl, I just wanted to come by for a little chat before you take off for Christmas."

"Girl, you look so pitiful. Are you trying to make me feel guilty?" Rachel groaned, slumping her shoulders.

"Well, is it working?" Jamie's whole face lit up as her lips parted into a naughty grin.

"You're a mess!" Rachel giggled. "Do you have any special plans for the holiday?"

"No, not really," Jamie gave a dramatic sigh. "I guess Peepers and I will spend Christmas on the couch watching movies."

Suddenly, a crazy idea crossed Rachel's mind. "I have a better idea."

"What?"

"Order Christmas dinner in and invite Hiram over and…"

Jamie' whipped her head back, startling Peepers. He screeched and hopped out of her arms. "Girl look what you did? You scared poor Peepers to death! You're scaring the hell out of me! Have you lost your cotton-picking mind?"

Rachel laughed. "At least you won't be alone on Christmas."

"Girl, please, I'd rather be stuck in a pit of tar than be cooped up with that nitwit! No, thank you!"

"I'm just trying to help." Rachel sat in her seat and opened her desk drawer. She grabbed her dust rag, dropped it in the drawer, and closed it. Rachel moved her lips with no sound coming out as she gave Jamie a crazy look, taunting her. *Invite Hiram over for Christmas dinner. Invite Hiram over for Christmas dinner.*

Jamie threw her hands up in desperation. "Stop it! I have enough problems. I'm not having dinner with that troll." Jamie wrenched a chair away from the wall and sat directly across from Rachel. "So, do you have any cases that need following up on while you're gone?"

Rachel pointed to the plastic tray on her desk. "I only have ten cases, and there shouldn't be any pressing issues."

Jamie gave her the thumbs up. "Bless you, my child." She reached over and grabbed the stack of folders on Rachel's desk. "When will you be back to work?"

"January second."

"Why are you waiting to leave on Christmas morning?" Jamie leaned back and folded her arms across her chest.

"It's cheaper to fly on the holiday. I usually fly out of Oakland International Airport instead of San Francisco because I save at least a hundred dollars."

"Quite a discount."

"It certainly is."

Jamie got up, went to the door, and open it. Peepers ran out, and both women laughed. "Do you suppose he had somewhere to go?" Jamie snickered.

"Beats me, but he sure was in a hurry," Rachel giggled. She hopped out of her seat, walked over to Jamie, and wrapped her arms around her.

Jamie stiffened with her eyes bugged out. "What the hell was that for?"

"Don't be like that!" Rachel hugged her tighter. "I don't want you to be depressed while I'm gone. Will you please try to have a nice Christmas?"

"I'll try," Jamie grinned. "Now, let go of me before you squeeze my titties out of place."

Rachel let her go and laughed. "Girl, please, stop being so damn dramatic."

"I have to be. It adds character." Jamie winked. She turned around to go out the door, then hesitated and turned back around, grinning. "Merry Christmas, my friend. I'll see your silly little butt next year."

"Girl, bye," Rachel laughed as she shoved Jamie out the door.

Tuesday, December 25th – Christmas Day

Rachel's plane arrived on time at Oakland International Airport at eight in the morning. As soon as Rachel deplaned, she took off her red jacket. The temperature was seventy degrees, twenty degrees higher than Seattle. Rachel wiped the sweat off her brow as she hurried up the walkway and entered the terminal. A bouncy rendition of "Jingle Bells" blasted through speakers in the ceiling. Rachel eyed the bathroom and stopped there to freshen up. She opened her handbag, took out a tissue, and dabbed her face. After

Rachel finished applying a new coat of red lipstick and finger-combed her curls, she promptly walked out of the bathroom.

The airport was mostly vacant except for a few stragglers like herself. She checked her watch again. Rachel told her parents she would be home by ten. She rode the escalator down to baggage claim and scanned each of the six evenly spaced carrousels, looking for her flight number. She spotted it posted on carrousel one and hurried over.

While she was waiting for her suitcase, a naked skinny man with dark hair on his back sprinted by her wearing a Santa Claus hat and black boots. Police officers in black ran after him, hollering for him to stop. The man kept running, soon disappearing through the exit. Rachel stood there with her mouth open for a moment, then fell out into a donkey laugh. *Insanity is everywhere! Hell, I can't get away from it!*

It wasn't long before her bag came down the chute and onto the carousel. She ran over, pulled her bag over the railing, then stood it upright on its wheels. Rachel rolled her luggage out the door to the shuttles. She had reserved a car at Hertz as she planned to visit EM, her college friend in Sausalito, while at home. Rachel pulled her luggage behind her as she rushed over to the Hertz shuttle. The driver grabbed her suitcase and tossed it on the rack while Rachel climbed up the steps and settled in a seat on the second row.

The shuttle was clean as a whistle, and it smelled like Lysol. The driver's radio was on a classical music station, piping a traditional version of "Silent Night" through the speakers on the dashboard. Rachel found the soft, musical sound of the piano and the whining strokes of the violin strings soothing to her soul. She shut her eyes and scooted down in her seat, meditating on the music for the rest of the short ride.

The Hertz representative gave Rachel a Toyota 4-door hatchback with a stereo system. After he brought her the car and they both inspected it, he finally gave her the keys. Rachel tossed her luggage and jacket in the back, slid into the driver's seat, and turned on the ignition. Rachel checked her watch as the radio came on, bombarding her ears with Christmas music. *I've got one hour left to get to my parents' house.*

Rachel took off, following the signs to Interstate 5, merged onto the highway, and stomped on the accelerator. Eager to see the joy on her parents' faces when they opened the presents she'd bought them, Rachel couldn't drive fast enough to get home. Rachel was proud of herself. Her days of being broke were behind her, and she finally had money to splurge on her parents. She glanced at the speedometer and discovered she was twenty miles over the limit. She slowed down just before passing a police car parked in a nearby cut on the side of the road.

Thirty minutes later, she was on the Bay Bridge, driving into San Francisco. Foggy as usual, the city was damp and chilly. The change in temperature always boggled her mind when she was growing up. *Boy, I've never understood why the temperature changes so drastically when driving from one city to the next.*

As she drove through the city, on her left she saw the Golden Gate Bridge. Most of the iconic structure was immersed with thick white clouds, and the bridge's orange steel arches looked spiritual and magnificent in the overcast sky. As she admired the bridge, the dense, white fog seemed to swallow her up as she merged into traffic onto Interstate 99. Like the rest of the traffic, she slowed down and crept the rest of the way. It took Rachel fifteen minutes to drive across the bridge to Marin County, where the sun was shining bright on the other side.

Rachel checked her watch and was pleased that she'd made good time. With hardly anyone on the freeway, Rachel pressed her foot on the accelerator and sped down the road at fifty-five miles per hour. On her left, there was a rocky embankment, and to her right was the Pacific Ocean below. Massive waves splashed on the rocky shore, and Rachel's mouth flew open when she noticed black otters sunning themselves on the rocks. *Wow, those little fellas are cute!*

At nine fifty she parked in front of her parents' house, grabbed her handbag, jacket, and luggage, and pulled her suitcase over the brick walkway leading up to the Mediterranean-style house. Seeing the rounded bell gables, flat stucco walls, and red tile roof always made her feel at home. Rachel hurried up the brick steps and dropped her luggage on the porch. She rang the bell, heard it chime, and opened the door. The sulfur smell of collard greens cooking in the kitchen smacked her in the face, and Rachel twisted her nose up, bothered by the unpleasant odor.

"Merry Christmas, everybody! I'm home!" Rachel rolled her luggage inside and shut the door.

"Rachel is that you?" she heard her mother yell from the kitchen.

"Yes, ma'am, I'm here!"

Rachel's mother walked into the living room with her arms stretched out, smiling warmly. Her green eyes matched the green in her Santa Claus sweater, and she had on stylish straight-legged red pants. Rachel's mother's fiery, red hair complemented her caramel complexion. Her name was Juanita, but she preferred to be called Nita.

"So glad to see you!" She hugged Rachel tightly around the neck and kissed her cheek, leaving a smear of red lipstick. She released Rachel and pointed in the direction of the kitchen. "I'm cooking your favorite dish, collard greens."

"I can smell them. I love me some collard greens!" Rachel laughed.

Her father moseyed in, dressed in a red wool pullover sweater and khaki slacks. He hugged Rachel, then pushed her back, resting his big hands on her shoulders. His questioning brown eyes met hers.

"So, how's everything? Any news to tell me?"

"Plenty, but I'll tell you all about it after we open the presents."

"You've always been excited about opening presents ever since you were a little girl," her father chuckled.

"Dad, I'm excited. This time, I got presents for you and Mom, and I can't wait for you to open them."

"Well, what are we waiting for? Let's get this show on the road!"

"I second that!" her mother crooned as she and Rachel hugged each other around the waist. Rachel's eyes danced in their sockets when she zeroed in on the Christmas tree. It stood in front of the big dome window, and its eight-foot height took up the entire space. The tree was brilliantly lit with a multitude of dazzling white lights, and the red and gold ornaments on the tree's branches sparkled from the lights' reflection. On the top of the tree sat an exquisite black angel in white lace, and underneath there were several presents neatly wrapped with red, gold, and green paper. Rachel was all smiles.

"How beautiful. I love the red and gold theme. So amazing!"

"Your mother deserves the credit. I had nothing to do with it." Her father chuckled, rocking back on his heels.

"I know that's right," Rachel laughed. She sat in one of the two fluffy leopard-print chairs by the eighteenth-century fireplace. Exquisitely tiled with black and crème colors, it had a large poinsettia wreath draped on its oak mantle. Bright flames warmed the entire room, and the rapid speed of the ceiling fan's fig-leaf wood spools pushed warm air down from the ceiling. A leopard rug covered the fresh lemon-scented wood floor, and a black leather couch sat against the wall across from the Christmas tree. Rachel's mother loved everything African, and it showed throughout the house. Her mother sat in the other leopard-print chair, and her father stood next to the tree. He grabbed the first present, and Rachel raised an index finger, stopping him.

"Wait! I have to get your presents. They're in my suitcase."

She ran to her suitcase by the front door and took out two gifts wrapped in red striped paper. Rachel placed the presents under the tree and returned to her seat. Satisfied, she held her palm out.

"Dad, go ahead."

"Are you sure?"

"Yes!" Rachel fidgeted in her seat, excited. "Hurry up!"

"Slow your roll, young lady!" her dad laughed. He reached under the tree, brought out a tremendous gift wrapped in blue paper with little snowmen, and handed it to Rachel.

Her lips parted into a wide grin. "Is this for me? Oh, you shouldn't have!"

Her mother cracked up laughing. "Girl, you're crazy!"

Rachel looked at the name tag and saw that the gift was from her dad. She ripped off the paper, and her mouth dropped open.

"Oh, my goodness, this is so beautiful! I needed a bag like this!" Rachel rubbed the soft camel leather on the shoulder bag, and her mouth flew open when she noticed the bag's flap and saw her initials scripted in gold. "Dad, this is so nice. I love it!"

"Good, I'm glad." He reached under the tree and brought out a small box wrapped in shiny gold paper. He gave it to his wife and stood in front of her, wide-legged with his arms folded.

Rachel scooted to the edge of her seat, stretching her neck, trying to see around her father. "Dad, could you move over some? I want to see Mom open her gift."

"Gladly." He moved to the side, allowing Rachel full view.

Her mother carefully unwrapped the box, opened the lid, and her eyes widened. "My word, DeWayne, how much did this cost?"

Grinning like the Cheshire Cat, he calmly replied. "None of your damn business. Just put it on."

Rachel leaped out of her seat and went to stand by her mother's side to admire the opal and diamond ring. "Wow, very pretty."

"I'll say," her mother agreed.

"Well, we still have lots of presents to open..."

Rachel cut her dad off, and her dark brown eyes twinkled. "Before you open any more presents, I want you and Mom to open the presents I got you." She stepped briskly to the tree, grabbed her presents, and gave one to her dad and the other to her mother. Rachel plopped her butt in the leopard-print chair and crossed her legs with her hands clasped over one knee. The corners of her lips rose, and her teeth shone as she anticipated her parents' reactions.

Her parents tore into their gifts, ripping the paper off and throwing it on the floor. Her mother held up her green silk pajamas.

"Oh, how nice! And my favorite color! Thank you, my dear!"

Her father shrugged his shoulders back and forth as he pulled the navy-blue sweater around his muscular torso. Pleased it fit well, he broke out in a wide grin, showing his party teeth. "You did good!"

Rachel hopped up, clapping her hands. "I'm so glad you like them!"

"We love them, thank you," her mother beamed.

For the next hour, they laughed, talked, and open gifts. After they finished, Rachel's mother went to the kitchen, leaving Rachel and her dad alone. Rachel decided to use the time to talk about work.

"So, Dad, a lot has happened since we last talked."

"Well, tell me about it." He leaned back in his chair and crossed his legs at the ankles. He rested his hands on his abdomen and made a steeple with his fingers, giving Rachel his full attention. "So, how's Jamie?"

"She and Anne broke up a few weeks ago."

"Oh, I'm sorry to hear that."

"But wait until you hear this..." Rachel paused, pressing her hands to her cheeks, feeling flushed. She fell back in the chair and rested. "Do you remember my ex-fiancé, Picasso?"

Her father sucked in a sharp breath and frowned. "Now, how could I forget that scoundrel? What about him?"

"I ran into him at Sully's a few weeks ago. He's was hanging in the bar with Anne."

Her father's pupils flared. "You mean to tell me that asshole lives in Salter's Point?"

"Yep, he moved there last year."

"So, what's he doing in Salter's Point?"

"Um, I don't know. I guess the man works there. But Dad, listen." Rachel hesitated and scooted to the edge of her seat, and her eyes narrowed. "Remember Susan, the woman I found him in bed with three years ago?"

"Yesssss..."

"Well, it turns out, she was the missing patient."

"Damn!"

"I know, but get this. I found out that she and Doctor Benny were lovers and he's the one who helped her escape from the hospital. They ran off together, and no one knows where they are."

Deep creases appeared on her dad's forehead, and he sat straight up in his chair. Lowering his voice and sounding like the character Arnold on *Diff'rent Strokes*, his lower lip quivered. "Rachel, whatcha talking about, girl?"

"Dad, it's true." She tucked a curl behind her ear. "Susan and Doctor Benny were lovers, and the two of them ran off together."

"That's insane!"

"I know. And you know what else?"

Her dad lowered his head into his hands and groaned, shaking his head. "Go ahead, tell me."

"A doctor I met a few days ago kept a human brain in a Tupperware container in her office. The damn thing stunk up the place so bad that everyone got sick and puked their guts out."

Her dad's expression went blank, and his eyes were round, with long blinks. "This stuff you're telling me right now, no one...no one I know would ever believe this nonsense."

Rachel fell out into a belly laugh. "Dad, it's a psychiatric hospital, a looney bin. You know weird stuff happens there!"

"Running off with your patient is not weird, it's unethical."

"I know, Dad," Rachel softly replied. She heard the telephone ringing in the kitchen and stopped. A few moments later, her mother appeared in the living room entryway, wiping her hands on a dishtowel.

"Rachel, it's EM. She wants to speak to you."

"Great, I'll take the call in the den."

"Okay." Her mother turned and left the room.

Rachel leaned forward and stood on her feet. "I guess we'll finish this conversation later."

Her father glanced at the ceiling. "I can't wait."

Rachel chuckled and stepped briskly down the short hall to the kitchen. As she passed through the kitchen, the smell of baked ham and sweet potato pie tickled her nostrils. She looked forward to eating Christmas dinner. Rachel walked into the den. She loved hanging out there. It had a view of the Pacific Ocean, and on a clear day one could view the Golden Gate Bridge in its full glory. She sat in a high-backed Victorian-style chair next to a marble end table, picked up the phone, and brought it to her ear.

"Merry Christmas, EM!"

"Girl, what's happening?" Her voice was scratchy from years of smoking, but the last time Rachel spoke to EM, she had quit.

"Nothing much!"

"How're your parents?"

"They're fine. And your mom, how's she doing?"

"Great. She's still working at Children's Services, but she plans to retire next year."

"I know she's happy."

"She is." Rachel heard EM draw in a long breath then slowly exhale, she knew right away her friend was smoking.

"I thought you quit!"

"Quit what?"

"Quit smoking!"

EM hesitated. "Rach, you can tell I'm smoking right now?"

"Yep!" Rachel smirked.

"I tried to quit, but it's so hard." EM groaned. "But..."

Rachel cut her off. "Girl, you're a social worker. Social workers are full of resources. Don't you know where to go to sign up for those quit-smoking classes?"

"I sure do, but I can't go. I'm afraid I might see some of my clients there, and you know that's a no go," EM whined.

"Then get your doctor to write you a prescription for some of that nicotine gum. I hear that helps."

EM sighed heavily. "I suppose."

Rachel wasn't going to let her friend off the hook that easy. "EM, I mean it. Smoking is hazardous to your health! You can get cancer!"

"I know, Rach. Stop being a taskmaster!"

"I can't help it," Rachel giggled. "Girl, what day do you want to meet for lunch?"

"How about tomorrow at one o'clock?"

"Fine. I'll drive to Sausalito and we can meet at that little restaurant called Fish and Chips."

"Cool, see you then!" EM disconnected the call. Rachel placed the phone on its receiver and heard her mother and dad raising their voices at each other in the kitchen. She hurried to the kitchen and found her mother wrapping foil over the sweet potato pie she'd just baked. Her father was at the table eating a slice of that pie.

"Um, excuse me," Rachel cleared her throat. "What are you two arguing about?"

Rachel saw heat in her mother's eyes. "Your dad cut my pie before it had a chance to cool. Look at him over there, stuffing his face like a big squirrel," she grumbled.

Rachel huffed, slapping her hands on her hips. "Dad, really. You couldn't wait until after dinner?"

Her father shoved a piece of pie in his mouth, and he shook his head with satisfaction on his face. "Man, Nita, you put your foot in this pie! I believe this pie is one of your best!"

Her mother scoffed, rolling her eyes heavenward as she grabbed the pie off the counter. She disappeared into the dining room and returned a moment later. Rachel gave her father a crazy look. "Dad, really, you should have waited.

"I tried, but the pie smelled so good."

Her mother opened the oven door and checked on the ham. "Your father is going to fool around and get diabetes! You know it runs in his family!" her mother quipped.

"What about your family? Your crazy brother has diabetes," her father shot back.

"Uh, oh. I'm not getting in this fight." Rachel made a beeline for the exit. "I'll be back later. I'm going upstairs to unpack."

"Okay, dear," her mother said.

Tired, Rachel returned to the living room, and grabbed her

suitcase, handbag, and jacket and went upstairs to her room. *I'll get settled and take a little nap before Christmas dinner.*

Wednesday, December 26th

Late the next morning, Rachel showered, dried herself off, and slipped on her black jeans. She put on her beige silk blouse with the ruffled collar and slipped into her black leather ankle boots. After she ate a light breakfast, she threw on her red jacket, grabbed the leather shoulder bag her dad had given her, and left the house. Rachel hopped in her rental car and drove to Sausalito.

When she left San Francisco at noon, it was a chilly sixty degrees. By the time she arrived in Sausalito forty-five minutes later, the weather was a lot warmer. Rachel stopped at a traffic light, took her seatbelt off, and quickly slipped out of her jacket. Then she rolled down the window and the light turned green. Rachel put her belt back on, and took off, staying on the same road to Sausalito.

Rachel drove through the city, and she saw several different sized boats bobbing up and down in the bay. Sausalito, known for its Richardson Bay houseboat community, was simply beautiful. On her right, substantial palm trees lined the paved sidewalks, and people lingered and meandered in and out restaurants and stores. Soon Rachel eyed Fish and Chips, and she merged over to the right, slowing down. The restaurant was a quaint little place with leafy vines hanging on each side of the white-painted glass door. Two couples sat in outdoor wood seating in front of the establishment. Rachel parked a few yards up the street and looked around, turning off the ignition. When Rachel got out of the car, she saw EM entered the restaurant. Rachel threw her bag over her shoulder as she hurried to the restaurant, opened the door, and walked into the waiting area.

"EM!"

EM twisted around, and her whole face brightened. She stretched her arms out as Rachel rushed toward her. "Hey, girl! I'm so glad to see you!"

Rachel wrapped her arm around EM's neck. "Girl, how long has it been?"

"Not since about a year after we both got out of graduate school." EM laughed. The two women released each other, and EM took one look at Rachel and grinned. "Well, you certainly look good, girl!"

"So do you!"

EM, a full-figured woman, was three inches taller than Rachel, and she had beautiful long, thick sandy-black hair. EM didn't wear much makeup, but her dark brown face lit up when she smiled. EM wore a red checkered shirt tucked into baggy blue jeans with a black belt. She had on brown leather loafers, and her long thick black hair was in a bushy ponytail. Rachel always dressed a little dressier and sexier than EM, who preferred the casual, low essential look. A waitress with a fluffy red bob and sky-blue eyes walked up to them.

"Welcome, ladies! You can sit anywhere."

"Thank you," they both said. Rachel followed EM to a table next to a window where they pulled out their chairs and sat. They settled in, and a few minutes later their waitress came to the table and took their orders. EM ordered a hamburger, fries, and a coke, and Rachel ordered fried oysters, fries, and a Sprite. The waitress left, and they looked at each other. EM spoke first.

"Tell me about that crazy place. The last time we talked, you told me about a missing patient."

"You're not going to believe this, but I recently found out that Susan was the missing patient. You know the woman I caught Picasso in bed with when we were engaged."

EM fell back in her seat and her mouth dropped open. "Girl, get out of here!"

"No girl, I'm not kidding! It's true."

"Freaking unbelievable! Where is she now? Did they ever find her?"

Rachel leaned forward and folded her arms on the table. "Yeah, the girl was living with the doctor I was assigned too. They left town together three weeks ago, and no one has seen them since."

"Girl, that's crazy!"

"Yep!"

"So, are the police looking for them?"

"Uh, as far as I know. But I don't think they'll find them."

"Speaking of Picasso, have you heard from him?" EM reached in her handbag and took out a pack of Newport cigarettes and matches. She looked at Rachel with pleading dark brown eyes.

Rachel sighed heavily, giving her a dismissive wave. "Go ahead, girl, just don't blow the shit in my face."

"I won't." EM lit her cigarette. She took a puff, then pursed her lips, turning her head away. "Rach, you didn't answer my question," she snorted.

"Yes, I spoke to Picasso. I ran into him at a bar in Salter's Point a few weeks ago. He works up there."

EM's forehead furrowed, and she tapped her cigarette with her index finger. Ashes fell in the ashtray as she talked. "Do you think he followed you there?"

"No, girl. It's just a coincidence, that's all."

"Okay, if you say so."

Rachel's whole face twisted up. "Oh, stop being sarcastic. It is what it is."

"All right, girl, calm down!"

The waitress bought their food and set it on the table. "Can I bring you ladies anything else?"

"No," both women replied. The waitress walked off, leaving Rachel and EM to their meals. EM reached over and snuffed out her cigarette in an ashtray, then she grabbed her hamburger and sunk her teeth in. Rachel doused her oysters in hot sauce, then grabbed her fork, stabbed into an oyster, and shoved it in her mouth. Rachel savored the fried crunch followed by the briny, copper, gooey taste oozing in her mouth. After she swallowed it, she went for another one.

"These oysters are cooked perfectly," she beamed.

EM wrinkled up her nose. "I don't see how you can stand eating those nasty things."

"You've got to have the stomach for them," Rachel chuckled.

"Well, I've some news to tell you."

"What?"

"I got a teaching position at San Jose State University. I'll be teaching government and social services policy in the spring." EM proudly grinned.

Rachel dropped her fork, and her mouth sagged open. "EM, that's wonderful news! You always wanted to teach."

"Yeah, girl, I know."

"I think you'll make a fabulous professor with your brainy, smart self!" Rachel teased.

"Oh, stop being sarcastic! You're just jealous!"

"A little," Rachel laughed. "We should celebrate! How about a drink?"

"Good idea!"

Rachel twisted around and made eye contact with the waitress. The waitress came right over and they both order a glass of merlot. After the waitress left, they continued eating their meal.

"Why don't you join me? You can teach mental health. I can talk to the dean and get you a position. Then you can come home and leave that crazy place."

"That would be nice, but I can't leave right now. I need more experience before I can teach mental health. "

"Rach, don't you miss home?"

Rachel sighed. She placed one elbow on the table, resting her chin in her hand. "Sometimes, and believe me, I thought about coming home and getting a job here, but..."

"But what?"

"I probably should stay at Salter's Point for at least two years. You know, get more experience."

"Well, if you change your mind, my friend, the offer is still open."

"Thank you. I'll keep it in mind."

They ate their lunch, had dessert, and for the rest of the afternoon they lingered at the restaurant, drinking wine, chatting, and laughing at each other's jokes. Then at five-thirty, they said their goodbyes, and Rachel drove back to San Francisco.

Rachel spent the rest of her time, relaxing, going on afternoon shopping trips with her mother, and spending evenings in long discussions with her dad talking about work and life. Before she knew it, her holiday trip was over, and on Saturday morning Rachel said goodbye to her parents. She drove back to Oakland, dropped the rental car off, and boarded her flight at eleven forty-five. By three o'clock, Rachel was back in Salter's Point.

Chapter Sixteen

Monday, January 7th

Rachel sat in her office twirling her pen between her fingers as she stared at the stack of charts sitting on her desk. During the holiday break, the hospital had had more admissions than usual, and Rachel discovered her caseload had grown from five to fifteen patients. She was a little perturbed when she visited Jamie in her office earlier, only to discovered she was glassy-eyed drunk. Instead of giving her an update on her cases, Jamie preferred to talk about Anne. She listened to Jamie whined over Anne for a few minutes until she asked Rachel to cover for her. Rachel angrily declined, grabbed her cases from Jamie's desk, and promptly walked out the door. Feeling guilty, Rachel replayed their conversation over and over in her head.

"Listen I've got a lot to do. Can we talk about this later?"

Jamie gazed at her with red puppy-dog eyes. "I was hoping you could cover for me today. I can't concentrate. I'm so depressed."

"I'm sorry, Jamie, I can't this time," Rachel said with a stern face. "This is my first day back and I've got a lot to catch up on."

"Fine!"

As Jamie's angry face lingered in the back of her mind, Rachel gathered her charts and went to the nursing station. She settled in a chair next to the chart rack and, again, Jamie crossed her mind.

Rachel wondered why the woman refused to get help. Her drinking was getting worse and worse, and Rachel had no idea how to help her. Frustrated, Rachel sighed heavily, shaking her head.

She returned to reviewing her charts, and a moment later Doctor James swaggered in and took a seat at the counter. She noticed he wasn't wearing his usual army beret or his sunglasses. His huge afro looked significantly wild and unruly and Rachel wondered if this was intentional or if he forgot to comb his hair.

"Good morning," he said with a toothy, pearly white smile. "Busy?"

"The answer to your question is yes. I'm busy. I'm always busy," Rachel cracked, half smiling.

"At least it makes the day go by faster." Doctor James scooted his chair closer to the chart rack and grabbed a chart.

"So, I take it you're here to oversee Doctor Benny's caseload."

He gave her a sly grin. "Yes, that means we'll be working much closer together."

Rachel turned away, that was the last thing she needed to hear. She knew they were attracted to each other, but she wanted to keep their relationship strictly professional. The whole premise was evaporating before her eyes. Rachel frowned.

"Is something wrong?"

"So, how is this going to work?"

"Excuse me?"

"I mean, are you going to handle the admissions, too?" Rachel needed to know how much time she would be spending with him so she could come up with a game plan.

"No, Doctor Louis and I will split the admissions until Doctor Beebe hires another doctor."

Rachel sighed with relief. *The situation was temporary.* "Well, I guess you know about Mosquito Bellamy, a new admission who came in last evening."

"Yep, I'm going to review his chart right now. I hear he's upset about being here." Doctor James opened Mosquito's chart.

"Yes, he's been talking nonsense to the nurses all morning, asking to leave."

A faint tapping noise drew their eyes to the front of the counter. A medium height, thin man with a shiny bald head tapped on the counter with his long tan fingers. Long eyelashes fringed his beady brown eyes, and he stared at Doctor James and Rachel, not saying a word. He hummed in a weird tone, tapping his fingers. Rachel swore he sounded like a bumble bee.

"Can I help you?" Doctor James asked.

"Huh, huh, my name is Mosquito Bellamy, and I want to see a doctor so that I can get the hell out of here…" His voice trailed off into a hum.

Doctor James stood up and extended his hand. "I'm Doctor James. I'll see you in a few minutes."

Mosquito grasped the doctor's hand and shook it hard, grinning. "Cool beans! I'll be in my room." He dropped the doctor's hand and sprinted across the dining room.

"He's quite a character," Rachel mused.

"I'll say." Doctor James sat, taking a few minutes to review Mosquito's chart, jotting some notes in his notebook. "It appears his primary problem is mostly drugs, not a mental illness."

Rachel raised an eyebrow. "Maybe he could benefit from a rehab referral."

"You're right, but let me evaluate him first to make sure."

"Absolutely."

Doctor James stood up and gazed down at Rachel. "Do you want to come with me? I'd like to hear your opinion."

"Why not?" Rachel smiled. She followed the doctor across the dining room and through the hall. Mosquito's room, located at the end of the hallway, was next to the men's restroom. Doctor James knocked and entered Mosquito's room at the same time with Rachel right on his heels.

"Can we come in?"

Mosquito's eyes were birdlike, zeroing in on Rachel. "Who you be, girl?" he asked with a bashful expression on his thin, narrow face. Rachel frowned, surprised Mosquito asked such a dubious question since he just saw her at the nursing station. Propped up on one side holding his head in one hand, Mosquito Bellamy was a peculiar looking fellow with his bright beady brown eyes and shiny, pointed bald head. He reminded Rachel of an insect and she wanted to laugh out loud, but she didn't.

"Mister Bellamy, I'm Rachel Thomas, one of the social workers on the unit. We met at the nursing station a minute ago. Nice to meet you."

"Huh, huh," he hummed.

Doctor James sat at the end of the bed, and Rachel pulled up a chair next to him. "I hear you're a little upset about being here," Doctor James said.

"Doc let me tell you something! That raunchy little ho sold me some bad stuff," he snorted.

"Bad stuff? What bad stuff?" Doctor James crossed his legs and laid the notebook on his lap.

"Man, I'm talking about weed. I paid good money for that weed, and the shit was bad! I mean bad!" Mosquito sat up and set his feet on the floor. He flicked his earlobe as he talked. "Man, don't ever let a little ho sell you any bad shit."

Doctor James raised his eyebrows, trying not to laugh. "Explain to me what happened."

"Man, let me tell you, I smoked the shit, and it tasted like sardines." Mosquito snapped the straps on his faded blue overalls and rolled his shoulders back. "After I finished the joint, I heard Japanese voices cussing in my head. Man, it freaked me the fuck out!"

"Let me get this straight. You heard Japanese voices cussing in your head? Do you even speak or understand Japanese?" Doctor Louis was clearly having trouble keeping a straight face.

"No, doc, I don't. But they were there, cussing loud like a motherfucker." Mosquito rubbed his long thin hands together.

"How do you know the voices were cussing in Japanese?"

Mosquito bucked his beady eyes. "Well, they weren't cussing in English, that's all I can tell you."

Rachel covered her mouth and felt her face flushing trying not to burst out with laughter.

Doctor James lowered his head, pinching the bridge of his nose. "Tell me, what happened next?"

"I went to the po-po station and told those suckers that little raunchy ho sold me some bad shit." Mosquito was jerking his neck in a circular motion.

Doctor James hesitated, shaking his head and rubbing his eyes. "Brother, excuse me, you went where?"

"I went to the po-po station," Mosquito repeated, twisting his thin lips.

"Will you tell me, what possessed you to do that?"

"Absolutely! I needed the po-po to help me get my money back…" Mosquito smacked his forehead. "Look man that crazy little ho ripped me off! What do you expect me to do? Let her?"

Doctor James shook his head again. Not only was Mosquito Bellamy a pothead, but he was dense. "Let me see if I understand you correctly." Doctor James shifted in his seat. "You went to the police station to snitch on yourself, is that correct?"

"That's right, I had to get my money back. I knew the po-po could help me."

Doctor James shrugged his shoulders. "Well, did you get your money back?"

"Doc let me tell you what those fuckers did. They asked me if I had weed on me, and I told them yeah. I pulled the shit out of my pocket, and those fuckers arrested me right on the spot! Man, I'm telling you, it pissed me the fuck off!"

Doctor James and Rachel fell out laughing.

Mosquito scratched his bald head, staring at them with his beady eyes looking confused. "What's so funny? I'm telling you the truth, man! I had to do something to protect my rights."

"I hear you, man, but snitching on yourself is not protecting your rights." The doctor laughed, shaking his head.

"Doc, all I wanted is my money back so I can buy some good shit." Mosquito fell back on the bed, rubbing his temples. "Doc, can you do something about these Japanese voices cussing in my head? They're so distracting."

"The voices will go away after the weed wears off. Once you're back to normal, we'll transfer you to drug rehab."

Mosquito dove from the bed. "Listen, doc. I don't need any rehab. What I need is some good shit to get rid of these voices."

Doctor James laughed. "Mister Bellamy, I think you need to give up the good shit and go to rehab."

Mosquito fell on the bed and poked his bottom lip out. "How long do I have to stay?"

"A month." Doctor James stood on his feet.

"Oh, shit!" Mosquito fell back on the bed bending his knees and swinging one leg over the other.

"What's the matter?" Doctor James asked with his hands on his hips.

"I forgot to tell you doc. I've got air in my urine stream. Can you fix it while I'm here?"

"You've got what?" Everett frowned.

"Air in my urine stream."

"Air in your urine stream...how so?"

Mosquito sat up with a grave look on his face. "Doc, when I urinate, my pee comes out in bubbles."

Rachel almost choked on her own salvia, trying hard to hold back her laughter. Mosquito glanced at her and Rachel stared at the floor, rolling her lips inward.

"What's wrong with her?" Mosquito looked perplexed.

Doctor James chuckled. "Don't worry about it. In the meantime, I'll ask Doctor Hornsby to come by to see you."

"She'll check my pee and give me some medicine?"

"I certainly hope so," Doctor James smiled.

"Thanks, doc."

"No problem. Delighted to help." Doctor James waved at Mosquito as he glided out the door.

"Bye, Mosquito," Rachel chuckled, barely getting the words out. She followed Doctor James into the hallway and closed Mosquito's door. They walked to the nursing station together, laughing. "That Mosquito Bellamy is a strange little dude, and quite a character," Rachel giggled.

"And he's not too bright, either. That's the silliest shit I ever heard," Doctor James roared. They settled at the nursing station, reviewing records until Ricky Beaver pranced up to the counter. Dressed in a dirty white tee-shirt with no sleeves, Ricky clutched the edge of the counter, with his fingers badly stained with brown tobacco. His large gray eyes and dark freckles complimented his round face. Ricky broke out in a childlike snaggletooth grin as he swayed on his feet. When he spoke, he shouted in a high-pitched voice.

"What's everybody laughing about?"

"Ricky, can I get you something?" Doctor James asked.

"Yeah, a cigarette."

"No, it's not time yet. You have to wait until ten o'clock." Everett twisted around and glanced at the clock on the wall. "Ricky, you only have fifteen more minutes to wait."

Deep wrinkles lined Ricky's forehead as he glowered at the doctor. Mad, he busted out singing to the tune of "Mary Had A Little Lamb."

"Niig-gaa, your hair looks wild, your hair looks wild, your hair looks wild! Niig-gaa, your hair looks wild..."

Taken aback, Doctor James shot out of his seat and his smooth dark face twisted up like a prune. Rachel held her breath as the doctor's deep voice rumbled like a volcano. "What did you call me?"

Ricky edged away from the counter. He gave Doctor James the finger, and threw his head back, laughing. He took off, skipping around the dining room, singing at the top of his lungs. "Niig-gaa , your hair looks wild, your hair looks wild, your hair looks wild! Niig-gaa, your hair looks wild..."

Doctor James growled with fire in his eyes, "I'm going to lock your ass up."

"No, you're not!" Ricky shouted from across the room as he ran down the hall. Doctor James reached for the telephone and called security. Rachel froze in her seat when she heard the doctor tell security to put Ricky in seclusion.

She waited for Doctor James to hang up the phone, then she spoke in a low, trembling voice, but louder than she intended. "Have you lost your mind?"

Doctor James blinked twice and sat. He gripped the arm of his chair and it took him a minute to respond. When he did, his deep voice was quiet, spiteful, and dangerous. "No, Miss Thomas, I haven't lost my mind. When security arrives, Ricky is going in seclusion."

Rachel wilted in her chair, at a loss for words. She felt a flash of irritation, but she knew better than to challenge him. She kept quiet, too conflicted to say another word despite the nagging urge to do otherwise. Security rushed in, swarming around the nursing station.

The lead guard hovered over the counter and stared at them with piercing blue eyes. "Which one of you is Doctor James?" he asked in a brittle voice.

"I am." Doctor James stood up with hostility glowing in his eyes. His body shook, he was so angry. "I want Ricky Beaver taken to seclusion right now."

"Why, what happened?"

Doctor James clenched his jaw. "I don't need to give you an explanation. I'm ordering it, and he needs to go now!"

"Okay, sir, what's his room number?" The guard distanced himself from the doctor.

Doctor James's nostrils flared. "One sixteen," he said. The lead guard took off along with the rest of the security staff. Doctor James and Rachel heard screaming and cursing as two security guards dragged Ricky into the hall. Red as an apple, Ricky kicked and screamed. A guard following behind them swung a string of keys in the air. He opened the steel gray door to the seclusion room, and the other two guards shoved Ricky inside and slammed the door. The guard with the keys locked it, and Ricky pounded on the door with his fists, cursing and spitting. "I'm going to sue every one of you assholes when I get out of here! You just wait!"

Security left Ricky to his fit of rage. All of them vanished from the unit except for the lead guard, who returned to the nursing station.

"Doctor James, Ricky Beaver is in seclusion, just as you ordered."

"Good," Doctor James said with a quiet rage.

"Can you tell me what the poor man did?" The guard shoved his right hand in his pants pocket while he held on to his holster with his left.

Doctor James kept his frustration in check. "I prefer not to talk about it."

"Fine. Let me know if you need anything else."

"Don't worry. I will."

The guard left the unit, and Doctor James flipped Ricky's record open and charted.

Despite being annoyed by his behavior, Rachel had empathy for the doctor. "Are you all right?"

"I'm fine," he quipped as he scribbled hard in Ricky's chart.

Rachel squared her shoulders. "Don't you think you overreacted a little?" The rage in the doctor's face was clear. She was wasting time trying to console him. Rachel stood on her feet, stacking charts on the counter. "I'm going to my office to finish my charting."

When he didn't respond, Rachel gathered her stack of charts and quietly walked out of the nursing station. Leaving him alone to his rage, she didn't speak to him for the rest of the day.

As Rachel entered her office, her phone was ringing off the hook. She laid the charts on her desk and answered it on the fourth ring. "This is Rachel Thomas. Can I help you?"

"It's me." Jamie's voice sounded broken.

"What's wrong?"

"I need to talk to you. Can you come to my office?"

"Sure, I'll be right there." Rachel hung up, and within minutes was pounding on Jamie's door.

"Come in," a feeble voice came from within.

Rachel eased the door open and stepped inside. She shut the door and hurried to the couch, plopping her butt next to Peepers. He yawned, showing his black tonsils and his pearly white teeth.

"Girl, what's up?" Rachel asked, slouching her shoulders when she saw Jamie's wet, red face.

"Anne stopped by. She told me she's seeing someone."

"Oh, my, I'm so sorry." Rachel clutched her blouse, hating to see Jamie so hurt and feeling bad for being so mean to her earlier.

"I'm sorry, too."

"Is there anything I can do? Like, get one of my gangster friends to kick her butt?"

Jamie snickered amid her tears. "You're so silly. No, girl!" She snatched a tissue out of the Kleenex box and wiped her face. "However, I do have a favor to ask you."

"Oh, what is it?" *She's going to ask me to cover for her again.*

"I need a few days off. I can't work like this. I need time to get myself together. Will you please cover my caseload?"

"Sure, I'll cover. But what do you mean, get yourself together?" *Is she finally going to rehab?*

"I need time alone...you know, to deal with the breakup. My emotional energy is so spent, I'm no use to my patients."

Damn, no rehab! Please! "You're right. You're in no condition to deal with patients right now." Rachel sighed with disappointment.

"So, will you cover my caseload?"

"I said I will."

"Are you sure?"

"Girl, yes, take your butt home." Rachel dismissively waved her off. "I'll handle things here."

Jamie sighed. "Thanks, girl. I appreciate it."

"You're welcome. Any cases that need immediate attention?"

Jamie slipped on her reading glasses and grabbed her caseload list. "There's one. He's scheduled for court in the morning."

"What's his name?"

Jamie snickered under her breath. "Peter Pan."

"Who?" Rachel flicked her earlobe forward.

"His real name is Michael Barrie, but he only answers to Peter Pan."

Rachel cracked up laughing. "Are you serious?"

"Yep."

"Is that the same knock-kneed dude I hear dresses like an elf?"

"Yep, that's him," Jamie chuckled.

"Are you recommending long-term hospitalization?"

"I sure am. The little dude is out of his tree."

Rachel took a glimpse of her watch and immediately stood up. "I need to get back to work. I've got a lot of charting to do." She hesitated, looming forward. "Are you going to be okay?"

"I think so," Jamie replied with red eyes.

"You think so? Are you sure?" Rachel cocked her head to the side, not sure Jamie was being truthful.

"Yes, yes, yes. Go on, girl, I'm fine." Jamie shooed her away.

"Okay, but if you need to..."

Jamie raised her voice. "Go, I said."

Rachel headed to the door and opened it. She looked back at Jamie. "Call me if you need to talk."

"I will," Jamie said, rubbing her eyes.

Rachel walked out and closed the door. She strolled to her office, taking her sweet time. She wondered if Jamie could manage alone at home. Jamie didn't have many friends, and except for herself, Anne, and Sally, she really had no one. Worried, Rachel feared Jamie would drink herself into a stupor and not have the sense to stop. With these thoughts brewing in her mind, Rachel decided she needed a plan to keep her friend in check.

I'll visit her every day. That way, I can keep an eye on her silly butt. She won't like it, but I don't care.

After Rachel ate lunch, she made a few phone calls. When she was done, Rachel began her charting. A half an hour later, Rachel heard poetic, silvery whistling in the hallway. To her, it sounded like a flute or a clarinet. Curious, she stopped charting and laid her pen on the desk. She rose out of her seat and stepped to the door. The light, airy music got louder, and Rachel opened the door and stuck her head out. The music seemed to be coming from the patients' dining room.

Rachel locked her office door and made her way there, walked past the nursing station and into the dining room. Her pupils grew huge when she saw a little man the size of a large toddler playing the flute. Dressed in a green elf outfit, the man played "Mary Had A Little Lamb." His bright green eyes sparkled and on his square-shaped face was a thick gray handlebar mustache. Rachel knew exactly who he was, Michael Barrie, aka Peter Pan. *Cute!*

As Michael play louder, patients circled around him. They clapped wildly, singing and dancing in place. A six-foot man dressed in a clown suit caught Rachel's attention. He was dancing a jig on top of a dining room table. Rachel's mouth fell open as she stared at the clown, thinking he looked familiar. Rachel swore he looked like one of the nurses. Intrigued, Rachel proceeded with caution to the table to get a better look. When the clown saw Rachel coming, he jumped off the table and ran toward her. Scared, Rachel's eyes flickered, and she turned away and ran.

"Hey Rachel, where are you going? It's Hiram!" the clown yelled in a reedy voice.

Rachel stopped and whipped around. She gave Hiram the once-over and bowled over in laughter. "Damn, you scared me!"

Hiram whirled around showing off his clown suit, excited. "You got to like it. Isn't it sweet?"

Rachel held her stomach, laughing her head off as tears rolled down her face.

The attorney inched up closer to her and stood by her side. He reached over and gently patted her back. "Are you all right, missy?"

Rachel straightened up, inhaling deep breaths. "I'm fine," she coughed, breathing heavily. She wiped her eyes as she checked out Hiram again. "Dude, what possessed you to dress like a clown today? It's not Halloween!"

"Hiram is trying to help Peter Pan entertain the patients." The attorney spread his arms wide. "Look at them, they're having such a marvelous time."

Hiram bounced on his toes when Peter Pan revved up his flute again. Peter changed the song to "Puff the Magic Dragon," and Hiram's eyebrows waggled as he wiggled his butt doing the jig. He took off, skipping around the room, and Peter Pan joined him along with the rest of the patients. They all formed a line, dancing the jig, clapping, and singing, with some of them badly off key.

"Hiram, you're such a crazy fool," Rachel muttered, scratching her nose, laughing. Sensing the situation would soon ravel out of control, Rachel searched the dining room for nursing staff. When she didn't see any, she hurried to the nursing station and paged the team. While she waited for some nurses to show up, Rachel drummed her fingers on the counter and watched Hiram and Peter Pan hop up and down like jackrabbits. She was relieved when four nurses appeared in the dining room.

"What's going on here?" one nurse with black curly hair asked.

Rachel walked over. "See the man in the green suit? He's causing a ruckus in the dining room. He has everyone hypnotized, even Hiram."

The nurse rolled her chocolate brown eyes. "Is that Hiram in the clown suit?"

"Yep, it is."

"He's so out of his element," the nurse chuckled.

"No, I think he's in his element," Rachel joked. The nurse laughed.

"What's the little dude's name?" another nurse asked. Her red ponytail swung back and forth as she stretched her neck trying to see.

"Peter Pan," Rachel snickered.

"Get out of here!" The nurse's eyelashes fluttered nonstop.

"No, I'm not kidding. The man calls himself Peter Pan, but his real name is Michael Barrie."

The nurse with the red ponytail forced her way through the crowd and snatched Peter Pan's flute right out of his hand. Startled, the little guy's eyes welled up. He stomped across the room to a corner and fell on his butt on the cold floor. He nibbled on his bottom lip as a tear rolled down his cheek. Rachel giggled when he shoved a thumb in his mouth.

Hiram, still high on the music, skipped over to her. "What's up, missy? Why did you ruin our fun time?"

"I didn't want the situation getting out of control."

"Hiram had everything covered. We're just having fun."

Rachel glanced up at the ceiling. "It's done, Hiram. Get over it!" Rachel turned away and left him in the dining room.

Back in her office, Rachel locked her door and sat at her desk. Luckily Michael Barrie's chart was available, and she'd grabbed it on her way to her office. She opened it up and giggled to herself. "Peter Pan, Michael Barrie, whatever you prefer to call yourself, your little butt is staying in the hospital for sure." Rachel picked up her pen and wrote a lengthy note on Michael "Peter Pan" Barrie.

Jamie remained barricaded in her office until long after the rest of the staff had left for the day. She worked feverishly updating her patient charts. She didn't want Rachel doing extra work. Finally, by seven, she finished everything and called Beth, leaving a message on the recorder that she would be out for a few days. Worn out, Jamie threw her blue jacket on, locked up, and hurried down the hall. Outside, the crisp fresh air felt good against her face. She buttoned her jacket as she stepped briskly to her rust-colored Ford Mustang, a classic nineteen sixty-six model.

Jamie gazed up at the clear night sky, bright with white stars twinkling like Christmas lights. Jamie made it to her car, unlocked the door, and hopped in. She turned on the ignition and sat there while the car warmed up. Her life flashed before her, and she cringed. Her childhood conflicts with her deceased mother and feelings about her sexuality brought back painful memories she didn't want to revisit. Memories of her marriage also came to mind, and she winced when she recalled the hurt on her ex's face when she told him she was leaving him five years ago for a woman.

Jamie gripped the steering wheel and twisted her body so she could see out the rear window. She backed out of her parking space and whipped her Mustang around. She zoomed out of the parking lot and down the hill, waving at Darth Vader as she passed through the gate. Jamie turned left, speeding down Salter's Point Boulevard. Twenty minutes from home, Jamie remembered she'd left Peepers at the hospital. With tires screeching, Jamie made a quick U-turn and zoomed back to the hospital.

Ten minutes later, she was speeding through the iron gate again and up the hill to South Campus. Jamie gazed out the window. The moon's significant glow shone on the rose bushes along the edge of the curb, accenting their bright red color. When she reached the parking lot, Jamie noticed a mixed-race couple standing next to a black Mercedes. They kissed, then the man opened the door for the woman to climb inside. He closed the door and the woman rolled the window down halfway, blowing him a kiss. Nosy, Jamie slowed down and squinted, trying to see who the couple were. Her mouth fell open when she recognized Anne, the love of her life. Instantly her whole body fell limp and it felt like the wind had been knocked right out of her. Jamie knew Anne didn't see her. She was too focused on her man. Huge tears fell from her light brown eyes as she watched the Mercedes leave the parking lot. *Damn Anne, how could you? How could you do this to me? Anne, Anne, Anne…*

Blind with tears and sobbing hysterically, Jamie managed to park her Mustang. She snapped the glove compartment open and grabbed her tissue pack. Tearing the package open, she snatched a tissue and dabbed her face. Jamie snapped the glove compartment door in place and stuffed the tissue pack in her coat pocket. She opened the car door and dragged herself out. Jamie locked the door and shuffled along the parking lot, dropping her head as tears fell from her eyes. Jamie unlocked the door with her key, the sliding door opened, and she walked inside. Immediately, she searched for Peepers. Jamie wanted to find him and go home.

"Peepers, where are you?" she called out in a burbling voice. "Where are you?"

Jamie turned around and spotted Peepers on the windowpane in the lobby licking his black fur.

"There you are, you crazy cat," she mumbled with her face brightening a little. Jamie shuffled over and gathered Peepers up in her arms. She held him close to her chest as she carried him to her office. Once in her office, Peepers leaped out of Jamie's arms. He crept to the sofa, hopped up on it, and laid down, closing his eyes. Jamie sat in her chair, rocking back and forth, her face crimson as she fought back more tears.

Jamie pulled her top drawer out and reached for her bottle of Jack Daniels. She scrutinized the container, thrilled to know she had a half bottle left. Jamie twisted the cap open and finished off the whiskey, coughing repeatedly as the bitter liquor cleared her throat. She threw the empty bottle in the trashcan, waking up Peepers. He flipped on his side and sat up, looking startled. Jamie's shoulders sagged as she sat, big tears streamed down her cheeks. Peepers stared at her as he cocked his head to the side. Woozy, Jamie wiped her face with her jacket sleeve and laid her head on the desk. She closed her tear-filled eyes, trying to shut out the cruel world.

Barefooted with wet, cold sand between her toes, Jamie danced on Salter's Point Beach with her arms stretched out and her face tilted toward the bright blue sky, basking in the sun's warm rays. Cold ocean waves splashed over her bare feet, and the water soon accumulated around her ankles. Jamie danced happily through the rippling waves, splashing water everywhere. She loved the faint fishy smell of the ocean and the crisp cold water on her feet and legs. Giant white seagulls flew overhead, laughing with one another. Tickled, Jamie giggled like a small schoolgirl, feeling good, feeling free. Free from all of the problems, burdens, and worries in her troubling life. She knelt on her knees, scooping up sand dollars from the wet sand. Using her coat sleeve, she wiped them off and carefully stuffed the seashells in her pocket. She was taking them home to add to her growing collection.

At midnight, the soft chiming of the clock in the hospital tower jerked Jamie awake from her beautiful, stimulating dream. Her sore, puffy, bloodshot eyes darted around the room, confused. She'd slept four hours and forgotten where she was. The four walls of her cold drafty office shocked her back to reality. Sleepy, Jamie yawned like a baby lion as she raked her stubby fingers through her salt-and-pepper hair. Disgusted with herself, she slid one hand over her face while curse words fell from her dry, cracked whiskey-smelling lips.

"Damn it," she groaned. "I'm still fucking here. Why aren't I at home in bed?"

Jamie's eyes drifted across the room to Peepers, who was curled up in a big furry ball, snoring on the couch. Jamie rested her hands on the desk, supporting herself as she struggled to her feet. Her head spun, forcing her to lean against the counter until the dizzy spell subsided. She pulled open her desk drawer and took out her notepad and pen, tossing the items on her desk. She swayed on her feet, feeling woozy again. Jamie scribbled some words on a piece of paper and ripped the note off the pad. She stuffed it in her coat pocket as she lazily dragged herself over to the couch. Jamie gathered Peepers in her arms and rubbed her nose in his thick warm fur. The cat yawned as Jamie shuffled to the door. With one free hand, she opened it and walked out. After locking the door, she hurried down the dimly lit, shadowy hallway. As Jamie clipped along, again, her head spun. She tripped over her feet and stumbled, almost dropping Peepers on the floor. Crudely disgusted, Jamie grumbled, "Why do I always do this to myself?"

With the big cat's head buried in her bosom, Jamie continued down the corridor, keeping her eyes on the floor. She stopped by the mailroom, dropping off the note she'd written in Rachel's mailbox. Jamie shuffled out of the room and headed straight through the lobby. As soon as she exited the building, Anne crossed her mind. She cringed when the image of Anne kissing that man replayed in her head. Tearful, Jamie clutched Peepers tighter against her bosom, mourning her recent loss. *I guess I fucked up! She's not coming back.*

Jamie shivered and her whole body trembled. Although she wore a heavy coat, the frigid night air seemed to rip right through her straight to the bone. Despite the prickly cold air, it felt good on her face. Now fully awake and more alert, Jamie gazed at the concrete slab parking lot and marveled at its ghoulish appearance. The streetlights added more drama to its overall creepy look. Jamie opened her eyes wide so she could get a good look at the night heavens. White stars twinkled on the horizon and the crescent moon seemed to shine more brightly than usual. Jamie trudged on, clutching the big cat closer to her. His sizzling body heat kept her toasty and warm.

Miniature bats flew overhead and settled on the edge of the hospital's roof. The creatures flipped over with their heads pointed downward with their webbed claw feet tightly gripping the roof's ledge. Suspended, the bats swayed back and forth in the cold night air. Jamie heard coyotes howling and owls hooting in evergreen trees. Unfazed by the wildlife noises, Jamie pressed on. Determined to get home, she longed to be in the comfort of her own surroundings, in bed with the covers over her head, shutting out her sad, troubling thoughts. Shutting out the world.

Finally, she reached her Mustang, unlocked it, opened the door, and dropped Peepers inside. Peepers crept over to the passenger's side and made himself comfortable in the center of the seat. Jamie slid in and slammed the door, starting the ignition. The seatbelt light came on, and Jamie ignored it. She always wore her seatbelt, but tonight she was too emotionally tapped out to bother with it. Jamie waited a few seconds for the car to warm up. She stomped on the accelerator and backed out, zooming out of the parking lot and down the road, passing the rose garden, North Campus, and finally out the iron gate. The gate was wide open, and she drove through it then took off down the street.

The speed limit was forty-five, and Jamie was over the limit by ten. Eager to get home, she kept up that speed, making every green traffic light before the lights turned red. While Peepers slept in the seat next to her, the silence in the car annoyed her. It reminded her she had nobody and was destined to face life alone. To drown out the silence, Jamie turned on the radio. Led Zeppelin's hit song

"Stairway to Heaven" played over the airwaves. In love with the song, Jamie turned up the volume and sang along to fight off the drowsiness she was feeling.

Suddenly an invisible hand jerked her awake before she realized she'd nodded off. She veered toward the side of the road and narrowly missed running into some bushes. Her heart pounded in her chest as she straightened her Mustang. She sighed with gratitude. *Damn, that was a close call!*

Jamie rolled the window down and stuck her head out. The frigid cold air whipped across her face. She ducked her head back inside when she began her descent down the steep road. Dark as coal, the road had no streetlights, and it was curvy, requiring her full attention. Jamie slowed down and switched her headlights to high beam. She looked out the window, trying to see the valley below, but it was too dark. It looked like a black hole, a bottomless dark pit.

Out of nowhere, Jamie felt dizzy again and her head spun. Pain throbbed around her temples and she reached up and massaged her forehead. *Damn, another headache? I can't seem to get rid of them.*

As she navigated the steep road, her head spun. Her eyeballs ached, making it challenging to focus on the road. Jamie swerved from lane to lane and almost side-swiped a black BMW coming up the other way. The driver's horn sounded like a train whistle as he sped passed her. The man frown, shaking his thick fist while his lips moved like a meat grinder. Jamie could tell he was cussing at her and she returned the favor by flipping him the finger. Never at a loss for words, Jamie yelled out, "Oh, go to hell, you, sorry asshole!"

Slowing down a tad, Jamie glanced at the radio and changed the station.

Trying to sleep, but sensing danger from being jerked back and forth, Peepers' golden eyes flew open and he immediately sat up.

When his mistress screamed and the car slammed into something, Peepers gripped the seat with his claws and the fur on his back bristled. Trying his best to stay in one place as the car jerked and swerved, his body slammed against the door when Jamie jerked the steering wheel. The car crashed into something again, and Peepers screeched in terror, leaping onto his mistress' lap. He clutched the front of her jacket as her head hit the windshield. Glass shattered into pieces around them, and blood ran down Jamie's face. Peepers whined with distress, ferociously licking her bloody chin.

His mistress screamed again when the car started to spin in a circle. Peepers hissed when his body slammed against the dashboard, then hard into the passenger's seat. He whined loud when he heard Jamie cry out, "Jesus, please help me! Please!"

Peepers whimpered as he tried to silently respond to Jamie, gazing at her as he desperately gripped the seat, trying to hold on. Blood freely dripped from a gaping hole on her forehead and into her eyes. The car slammed into something immovably solid, and the car flipped and spun. Peepers flew out the shattered windshield, screeching with terror, his legs spread wide, flailing in the air. He miraculously landed on his feet and saw the car tumble down the side of the cliff, bouncing several times off the rocky terrain. It disappeared into the dark pit below, and within seconds an explosion erupted, creating a fiery blaze that lit that up the entire valley. Startled bats roosting in the trees flew out into the darkness.

Terrified, Peepers clung to the edge of the cliff. With his long claws gripping a crumbling ledge, he fought for his life, clawing and crawling until he managed to pull himself up over the rocky ridge. There he rested, lying on his belly as he gazed down into the fiery, smoky valley, growling. He zeroed in on Jamie's car, then stood up on all fours. He wailed as he watched the fiery blaze consumed his mistress, his shrill cry rippling through the valley.

Soon firetrucks and police vehicles arrived, stopped a few inches from the cliff's edge above him. Police stood on the side of the cliff, coughing and choking from the thick, black smoke. Firefighters scrambled out of their trucks and scaled down the rocky cliff, pulling long flat hoses from their vehicles. Some ran toward the burning carnage, but the flames were so hot, they had to retreat. Suddenly, the car exploded again, raging flames shooting into the sky.

"Get back! Get Back! Get Back!" the firefighters screamed as they ran for cover.

Peepers huddled on his ledge for a long time, watching as the firefighters poured water on the fiery blaze. Finally, the flames died down, leaving patches of red hot sizzling embers and gray smoke. All that was left of Jamie's vehicle was bent, melted metal. All that was left of his mistress was gently placed in a large black bag and carefully carried up the cliff to a waiting ambulance.

What will happen to me without my mistress? When Peepers uttered an agonized, mewling wail of distress, a firefighter caught sight of him and started climbing toward him. By the time the firefighter reached Peepers' ledge, he had already fled, seeking solace in the black night.

Chapter Seventeen

Tuesday, January 8th

Rachel sat in her kitchen with a cup of coffee warming her fingers. She took a bite of freshly warmed cinnamon roll and thought about the day ahead. It took some doing to find the last packages of sugar, and then she'd discovered a forgotten bag of expresso coffee in the corner cabinet. She decided to take it to Jamie after work. *This will lift her spirits! After all, it's her favorite!*

Rachel sniffed her coffee, breathing in the sweet, nutty scent. She took several sips and set the coffee mug on the table. She reached over and flipped on her eighteen-inch black and white television and turned it to KIRO News. Breaking news flashed on the screen prompting Rachel to turned up the volume. She almost choked on her cinnamon roll when the newscaster reported a fire in the valley the night before. The newscaster showed pictures of the devastation. The valley, once beautified with green vegetation and tall evergreen trees, was now a dark, desolate abyss of burned land.

Rachel slapped one hand over her mouth when the newscaster told the television audience about the unidentified driver who was killed in the fire. Apparently, the driver's car accidentally went off the edge of the cliff. "My goodness, what a terrible way to go," Rachel gasped.

She wondered what caused the driver to run off the cliff. She wanted to avoid making the same mistake. After all, she took that same road to work every day. With those thoughts lingering in her mind, Rachel finished her breakfast. She went to the bathroom, hurriedly brushed her teeth and put on her red lipstick. Satisfied that she looked pretty decent, Rachel returned to her bedroom, grabbed her handbag, and went to the kitchen. She grabbed Jamie's coffee and stuffed it in her handbag, then glanced at the clock. It was seven thirty. She grabbed her coat out of the closet, slipped it on, flung her handbag over her shoulder, and promptly walked out the door.

It took only forty-five minutes for Rachel to drive to Salter's Point Cliff. The traffic was unusually light for a Tuesday morning. As she drove up the winding road to the hospital, the sun emerged over the horizon. It broke out in its fiery orange haze, and it wasn't long before the star's bright rays turned into a yellow inferno that reflected on the road, temporarily blinding Rachel as she carefully navigated the steep slope. She reached up and slapped the sun visor down, blocking the sunlight out of her face. Rachel tapped on the brakes to slow down, and her heart sank when she laid eyes on the valley's destruction.

Once-majestic evergreen trees looked like charred matchsticks stuck in the rocky, crisped ground, and the valley's vegetation, ususally a vibrant green, had turned black. Smoldering black-gray smoke crept over the charred, desolate land, and ashes floated in the air like dirty flakes of snow, showering onto everything, sprinkling on the black, lifeless ground.

Rachel swallowed hard. She couldn't believe her eyes. *This is horrible, so horrible!*

When Rachel parked her Toyota in the hospital parking lot, she noticed a group of nurses standing outside next to the sliding door. *Why is everyone standing outside?* Eager to find out, Rachel slid out of her car with her handbag on her arm and locked the door. As she walked toward the building, she heard one of the nurses whimpering. Her pupils grew huge when she noticed Joyce standing amongst the crowd crying. Concerned, Rachel immediately walked over to her.

"What's going on here? Why is everybody crying?" Rachel's voice was brittle.

278

"It's Jamie…" Joyce's voice cracked. "She's gone!"

Rachel's eyebrows scrunched together. "What do you mean she's gone?"

"She's dead. There was an accident. Her car ran off—"

Rachel shook her head hard and threw her hand up. The devastating words pouring out Joyce's lips were too much to hear.

"Stop! Don't say another word!" Rachel yelped. With her heart thumping hard in her chest, Rachel took off and ran through the lobby and the unit, not stopping until she reached her office. She hurriedly unlocked the door and rushed inside, then picked up the phone and called Jamie's home number. After the phone rang many times and the answering machine clicked on, Rachel heard Jamie's recorded voice and felt her heart fall into her stomach. *"This is Jamie. You know what to do. So, do it!"* Rachel hung up and pressed her hand on her throat, panting and inhaling deep breaths. *Jamie dead? No way! This must be a terrible mistake.*

Rachel glanced at the clock on her desk. It was eight forty-five. Jamie was usually at work by now, so Rachel grabbed the phone and called her office. The phone's harsh ring irritated her, and Rachel hung up when no one answered. She sat in her chair, staring at her desk as she wrapped her fingers in her long curly hair, unsure what to do.

Rachel laid her head on the desk, feeling numb. She couldn't cry, and it bothered her. *There's something wrong with me. Why aren't I crying? Jamie was my best buddy, my friend. I should be crying!*

Rachel lifted her head when she heard sobbing. A red-faced Sally stood in the doorway with tears streaming down her cheeks. Rachel jumped to her feet and ran to Sally with open arms. The two women hugged, rocking back and forth while Sally bawled. Unable to conjure up a tear, Rachel felt even more guilty.

"Sally, I can't even cry! Something is wrong with me, Sally! I can't even cry!"

Sally stepped back and wiped tears off her face with the back of her hand. She placed both hands on Rachel's shoulders and said in a soft voice, "Girl, you're in shock, that's all."

"Do you know what happened?" Rachel stared into Sally's face, searching for answers.

"No, not really. All I know is she ran off the road on Salter's Point Cliff last night."

Rachel's face brightened a little. "So, we really don't know. It's not confirmed." She was hoping everyone was wrong, and Jamie was alive, drunk somewhere.

"Well, the guard reported he saw her leave the hospital late last night. When did you last talk with her?"

"Yesterday. She was pretty bummed by Anne's visit."

Sally bucked her eyes. "Anne came to see her?"

"Yup, and she told Jamie she was seeing someone else. Of course, she was devastated after hearing that news." Rachel sighed deeply. "She asked me to cover for her so she could take some time off."

"Anne is such a bitch!" Sally hissed as she marched over to the couch and flopped on a cushion. Rachel shut the door and returned to her seat. She turned on the lamp, and the two women sat in silence, alone in their thoughts. Rachel snuck a glance at Sally, and her eyes were shut with her head bowed. Rachel could see her lips were moving, but no sound was coming out. Assuming Sally was praying, Rachel joined in, lowering her head. They both prayed in silence with their lips moving at the same time. A knock rumbled on the door interrupting their tender moment. "Let me see who this is," Sally said as she rose off the couch and stepped to the door, swinging it open.

Beth Jones stood in the hallway looking pale as a ghost. "Good morning, ladies," she said in a monotone voice. "I'm sure by now you've heard about Jamie."

"Yes," Sally mumbled as water welled in her eyes. She left Beth in the hallway and sat on the couch.

"Doctor Beebe has scheduled a meeting in the conference room in ten minutes. He will update the staff on the details of Jamie's death," Beth said as she stood in the doorway.

Rachel propped her chin in her hand and stared at Beth with a blank look. "Beth, are you sure Jamie is gone?" Rachel erratically blinked her eyes.

Beth nodded her head in the affirmative as a tear ran down her cheek. She reached up and wiped it off. "Rachel, she's gone. She's not coming back."

Rachel set her palms flat on her desk as she fell back in her chair. She closed her eyes and shook her head as she spoke in a falsetto voice. "I don't believe it. I just don't believe it. It's not true, it's just not true!"

Beth walked over to her and patted her back. "I know all of this is hard. It's hard for all of us."

Rachel hugged herself and didn't say another word.

Beth glanced at her wristwatch as she stepped to the door. "The meeting is about to start. If you want more information, I suggest you ladies attend."

Beth walked out, leaving the door wide open. Sally stood on her feet looking worried. "Should I call Anne and tell her?"

Rachel slammed her fist on the desk, and Sally jerked back. "No! She probably knows already and, personally, I don't have much to say to her!"

Sally threw her hands up. "Okay, okay, you don't have to yell."

Rachel rose out of her seat and headed to the door. "Let's go. I don't want to be late." Sally walked out first and Rachel joined her, locking the door. No words passed between them as they hurried down the hall.

When Rachel and Sally walked into the conference room, the place was so quiet one could hear a pin drop. A full house, nursing and social work staff were either standing shoulder to shoulder against the wall or jammed up together sitting in metal chairs. Most of the doctors sat around the conference table with solemn faces. Quiet and introspective, none of them uttered a word. In a corner across the room, Hiram sat with his legs crossed like a pretzel, twirling his fat thumbs as he stared blankly at his lap. Cassie Marks, a social worker, tiptoed around the room holding a Kleenex box, offering tissues. Anne wasn't there. Rachel and Sally navigated the crowd and saw two metal chairs in the back of the room. They hurried and took those seats, and sat, crossing their legs.

Doctor Beebe rolled in and parked his wheelchair in front of the podium. Red in the face and visibly upset, he reached for the microphone and cleared his throat.

"Humph…Good morning. I'm sure everyone has heard the devastating news about Jamie Lee." Doctor Beebe took a deep breath. "I'm sorry to report that Jamie was killed last night in a car accident."

Silence gripped the room. Everyone's face was twisted with awkwardness and sadness. No one crumpled, wailed, or burst into tears. Instead, they handled their grief like robots, unemotional, non-committal, and indifferent.

Doctor Beebe's voice trembled as he explained the dastardly news. "The police told us Jamie's car went off Salter's Point Cliff. No one knows why, but they are investigating."

"Do you think she had a heart attack?" Cassie asked with a weak voice.

"I don't know. It's being investigated."

"Was she drunk? Everybody knows she liked her whiskey," Buddy Carlson, a male social worker, pointed out.

Rachel spun her head around and lashed out at Buddy. "How dare you assume such nonsense? Who do you think you are?"

"Calm down, I'm just asking a question." Buddy stiffened and looked away with his mouth set in a hard line.

Doctor Beebe stepped in to smooth the situation over. "Let's not make any assumptions. The police will do a thorough investigation, and we'll know the details soon enough."

Sally reached over and rubbed Rachel's back. "Do you know if anyone has been in touch with her family?" she asked.

"Yes, yes, yes," Doctor Beebe exclaimed. "They will notify us when funeral arrangements are set. Are there any other questions or concerns?"

"What about her cat?" Cassie asked, looking around. "Where's Peepers? I haven't seen him this morning." Negative murmurs erupted throughout the room.

Doctor Beebe sighed. "Nobody knows what happened to Peepers. He'll probably show up soon."

The only noise in the room was the faint ticking of the clock on the wall. Glued to their seats and lost in their thoughts, no one wanted to move. A male nurse abruptly jumped to his feet and walked out. Everyone soon followed, forming a single line as they quietly exited the large room. Rachel and Sally left and stood in the hall.

"Speaking of Peepers, let's check Jamie's office and see if he's in there," Rachel suggested. "She may have forgotten him when she left last night,"

Sally snapped her fingers. "Good idea, but we'll need the master key to get into her office."

"Let's ask Beth." Rachel went back into the conference room and saw Beth talking to Doctor Beebe. She rushed over. "Humph, sorry to interrupt, but Beth can I borrow you for a few minutes?"

Beth breathed out a dramatic sigh. "What do you need?"

"Can we borrow your master key to open Jamie's office? We want to see if Peepers is inside."

Beth's face brightened a little. "Well, that's a thought. Why don't I come with you?"

"That would be great!"

"Carl, we'll talk later?"

"Absolutely." Doctor Beebe waved her off as Beth and Rachel left. He yelled after them, "I want to know if that cat is in there!"

"Will do," Beth hollered back. They joined Sally in the hall and all three women rushed off. Rachel felt her heart beating wildly in her chest as she swiftly walked to Jamie's office. When they finally arrived, Rachel held her breath. Beth unlocked the door, and Jamie's office was dark and eerily quiet. She flipped the light switch on and walked inside. Rachel and Sally followed her in and looked around, but Peepers wasn't there.

Rachel fell on the sofa and buried her head in her hands and cried. "No, not Peepers! No, not Peepers!"

Sally rushed over and plopped herself next to Rachel patting her back. "Peepers could be anywhere! Don't think like that!"

"She's right. He's probably out somewhere on the grounds hunting," Beth offered.

Rachel lifted her head and her eyes glistened with tears. "I guess I wanted Peepers to be here. At least with him being here, everything about Jamie isn't permanently gone."

"I hear you." Sally gave her a big hug and Rachel broke away and stood on her feet. She headed straight to the door. "I'm going to my office. I need some time alone."

"We all do," Beth softly said as Rachel walked out the door.

With her head swimming with confusion, Rachel stopped by the mailroom to check her box. Her eyes stopped cold at Jamie Lee's box. Her body shook and she fell limp, releasing a fountain of tears. Rachel grabbed her messages, leaning against the counter. She sorted through every message, throwing away the ones she didn't need. Teary, with a lump in her throat, a crumpled note in her stack almost took her breath away.

Rachel swallowed hard as she carefully unfolded the note. Blind with tears, she read Jamie's note, and her heart sank.

"I need peace. I must get away. I'm going to another place and I may never come back."

The words ripped her soul apart. *Why, Jamie, why? What are you saying?*

She jolted off her feet when a deep booming voice came from behind, interrupting her thoughts.

"Are you all right?" Doctor James asked with concern in his dark brown eyes. He was holding a box of Kleenex.

"You scared the hell out of me!" Rachel reached over and snatched a tissue out of the box and dabbed her face.

"I'm sorry, I didn't mean to scare you."

Rachel folded the note. "This note is from Jamie," she quietly offered. "It was a little disturbing."

Everett raised an eyebrow. "Oh? What do you mean?"

Rachel handed him the note. "See for yourself."

Everett hunched forward, receiving the note, and read it. A line appeared between his nicely groomed brows, and he lifted his shoulder into a half shrug,

"Very disturbing. It's almost like she knew she was going to die." He gave her the note.

"Don't say that!" Rachel raised her voice. "Doctor Beebe is right. We need to wait until the police complete their investigation."

"You're right. I don't mean to upset you. I'm sure the police will have something soon."

"I hope so." Rachel rushed past him on her way to the door.

"Are you going to be okay? Is there anything I can do for you?" he called out.

"No, I need time alone. But thanks anyway." Rachel lowered her head, holding back tears. Then without hesitation, she walked out the door.

Back in her office, Rachel collapsed in her chair. Her whole face crumpled, and she burst into tears as the reality of Jamie's death finally sunk in. *Why? Why? Why? Why did Jamie have to die? What will I do without her? We're sidekicks, colleagues, friends. Now she's gone.* Rachel squeezed her eyes shut as she leaned over her desk, cradling her head in her arms. Memories of the good times and laughter they shared flooded her mind, bringing on more tears. For five long minutes, Rachel cried her heart out, and her chest hurt from the constant hard heaving. She laid on her desk, sniffling for a long time, trying to decide what she should do next.

Rachel raised her head and glanced at the clock on her desk. It was nearly ten thirty, and she was due in court soon to give her testimony on Michael Barrie. Exhausted, Rachel needed a cup of coffee to get herself going. When she looked across the room at the coffee pot on the medal stand, Rachel saw she was out of coffee. She twisted her face as curse words fell from her lips. "Damn, Damn, Damn, I forgot to go to the store!"

She reached for her handbag and pulled the snaps apart. Nestled in the middle of her bag, along with her lipstick, powder compact, and comb, was Jamie's espresso coffee. Rachel's shoulders slumped when she saw it. Her eyes swam with tears, devastated she never had the chance to give Jamie her favorite coffee. As tears streamed down her cheeks, Rachel unclipped the bag, sticking her nose inside to smell the coffee's rich, bitter aroma. She decided to have a cup of expresso in honor of her friend's short life.

After she prepared the coffee, Rachel stood there, watching it perk. The coffee's soft gurgling and its rich floral, earthy aroma were comforting to her. Halfway through the perking, Rachel grabbed the canister, poured herself a cup, and set the canister back on the burner. She didn't bother adding creamer or sugar, deciding to endure the bitter taste instead, just like Jamie would've preferred it. Wisps of steam crept in front of her face as she gently blew on the hot liquid. She held her cup away from her face and declared, "Here's to you, Jamie, my friend. You always loved yourself a good cup of coffee. Rest in peace." So, with watery eyes, Rachel sat at her desk, quietly reminiscing, sipping her friend's favorite brand of coffee for the very last time.

Regardless of her grief, Rachel worked through the rest of the day on autopilot, mostly staying in her office, avoiding everyone. When the end of her shift finally came, Rachel threw on her coat, grabbed her handbag, turned off the light, and left her office. She was eager to get home, and dreaded driving past the place where Jamie had died, but she knew she had to because it was her usual route home.

Dread quickly turned to anger. She was mad she lost a friend. Mad she lost a mentor. Mad that Jamie was still young enough to enjoy the many pleasures of life. The realization of Jamie not coming back severely pained her soul. She had to move on and deal with her grief.

Rachel drove her car down the curvy slope, and her heart tightened in her chest. It felt as if someone was wrapping a rubber band around it. In an effort to soothe her pain, Rachel massaged her aching chest. Soon the desolate valley came into view, and the destruction of it took her breath away. Overwhelmed with emotion,

Rachel wept. Blind with tears, she parked her Toyota on the side of the road and got out. She took baby steps around the front of the car and her body shook as she stood at the railing. The black smoot covering the valley floor made her shuddered.

Eerily quiet, the valley was lifeless except for a few black crows flying above. Rachel could still see the smoke suspended in the air, hanging like a thick, gray veil over the ruined valley. Dense clumps of ash covered the ground. Rachel wondered if God had seen fit to spare Jamie's pain before her car went off the cliff and crashed into the valley. She certainly hoped so.

Rachel didn't know how long she stood there, gazing at the valley, mourning over her friend. By the time she settled in her car and drove home, it was after dusk.

At her apartment, she flopped on the couch, tossed her handbag on the coffee table, and reached for the phone. Her hand trembled as she dialed her parents' number. Once her father's voice came on the line, she broke down crying.

"Rachel is that you? What's the matter?"

Rachel sobbed into the phone for a few seconds before she answered. "Jamie died," she blurted out in halting sobs. "She...she...she's gone...I can't believe it!"

"What? I can't understand you. Take a deep breath and tell me what happened," her father firmly urged.

"It's Jamie..." Rachel hesitated.

"Yes, what about Jamie?"

"She was killed! Jamie's gone!"

A brief silence fell on the line. Rachel cupped the phone tight against her mouth. "Dad, did you hear me? Are you still there?"

"Yes, I'm here," he said in a low, quiet voice.

Big tears streamed down Rachel's cheeks and onto her lap. She held her hand over her mouth to muffle her deep halting sighs.

"I'm so sorry," she heard her father say. "I wish I was there to give you a big hug." His reassuring voice lifted her spirits a little.

"I wish you were here, too," she sniffled.

"Are you able to tell me what happened?"

Rachel's voice cracked as she told her dad about the accident. "Jamie's car ran off Salter's Point Cliff and crashed into the valley last night."

"Ugh, how awful."

"I just can't believe she's gone," Rachel sobbed. "It's so terrible! I drove by the valley today. It was pitch black. When I think about Jamie burning in that car..." Rachel's voice trailed off. Her sobs came in waves, uncontrollable and deep.

"Sweetheart, that's awful. I'm so sorry, so very sorry to hear that. Is there anything I can do? Like, come up there?"

Rachel swallowed hard, clearing her throat. "No, I think I can manage for now. Maybe I'll come home for a few days after the funeral."

"Okay, I'll send you money for an airline ticket."

"Thanks, Dad. I sure do appreciate it."

"No problem." He hesitated a moment. "Are you sure, you're going to be all right dealing with this by yourself?"

"Yes, Dad, I'll be okay," she answered in a weak voice.

Her father paused. "I can come up there, you know."

"No, no, no, Dad, it's not necessary." Rachel shook her head violently. "I have friends at work I can talk to."

"Okay, but keep me posted. I'm here for you."

"I know Dad, thanks." Rachel placed the phone in its cradle easy-like and fell back on the couch. She closed her eyes as tears leaked out, streaming down her face. Overwhelmed with grief, Rachel didn't move from the couch until the next morning.

Wednesday, January 9th

Rachel didn't get much sleep, so she called out sick to take time to get herself together. She wasn't in any emotional shape to see patients, especially mentally ill ones. Rachel showered and threw on her red sweats. She went to the kitchen and made herself a cup of coffee. With her back against the counter, Rachel contemplated how to spend her day honoring Jamie. She wasn't the least bit interested in sitting around moping and crying. She wanted to do something worthwhile.

Antsy, with no ideas in mind at first, Rachel finished her coffee, grabbed her purse, and strutted out the door. She had no idea where she was headed, but she hopped in her Toyota and took off down the road. To her surprise, Rachel found herself turning on the street where Jamie lived, and she decided she would stop by to see if Peepers was there,

Rachel pulled up in front of Jamie's house and parked. She was surprised to see a green Oldsmobile sitting in the driveway and wondered who it belonged to. *Maybe it's one of Jamie's family members.*

Determined to find out, Rachel grabbed her purse and got out of the car. She stepped briskly to the door and boldly rang the doorbell. Swift and heavy footsteps approached from the other side and abruptly stopped. The door swung open, and a man about half a foot taller than herself stared back at her with deep-set ocean-blue eyes. He had blond hair, which was thick and lustrous, but graying around the temples, and his suntanned face was sharp and well-defined, giving the impression he had weathered many storms. He wore wrinkled black overalls with Nike tennis shoes.

"Can I help you?" he asked in a gruff voice.

"I'm sorry…I…I don't mean to pry," Rachel stuttered, terrified. "My name is Rachel Thomas. I'm a friend of Jamie's, and I also worked with her at Salter's Point Regional Hospital."

The man's face brightened a little. "I'm John Lee, Jamie's husband."

Rachel jerked her head back and bucked her eyes, floored. "Oh, glad to meet you. Jamie didn't tell me she was married!"

"Yep, for ten long years." For a minute, he seemed to blank out, staring into space as if he was reminiscing, living in another time. When Rachel cleared her throat, he came to his senses. John took a step back and opened the door wide.

"Would you like to come in? I'm packing some of Jamie's things."

"Love to," Rachel said as she walked in and he closed the door behind her. She stood in the living room, inspecting the place. Clothes and shoes were sprawled everywhere on the couch and chairs. Cardboard boxes were scattered on the floor, some filled to the top with clothes, and others half-filled with Jamie's shoes. John had carefully folded Jamie's sweaters and packed them in a box.

"I see you're packing up Jamie's clothes. Are you taking them somewhere?"

"I thought I'd take them to the women's shelter in town. I certainly don't have any use for them," he gruffly answered.

"Sounds like a plan," Rachel smiled, pleased Jamie's clothing would be put to good use.

John stopped packing and walked swiftly toward the kitchen.

"Can I offer you anything? Coffee, juice, water? Anything?" Rachel took the liberty and followed him. The color drained from her face, unable to answer when she entered the kitchen. Cardboard boxes were everywhere, and Jamie's dishes and pots were out on the counter and table. Rage pulsated through her veins, and her cheeks burned. *Why is he packing everything up so soon? Jamie hasn't been dead for a good forty-eight hours, and he's already getting rid of her belongings! What's the rush?*

"I didn't hear your answer," John said, raising an eyebrow.

"I'm sorry," Rachel replied. "I guess I was taken aback by all of the packing. Why the rush?" *Oh, shit, I didn't mean to say that. Oh, well.*

"I realize this looks quick, but I don't have a lot of time. I pastor a church in Colorado and I'm leaving on a mission trip next week. Although we were separated, Jamie considered me her family. It was her desire that if something happened to her, I would take care of things."

Rachel's anger faded. "I understand. Please forgive me."

"No problem. So, what would you like to drink?"

"I know it's early, but a shot of whiskey would be fine."

John's eyebrows went up, hesitating, and he cracked up laughing. "A shot of whiskey? So, you're a whiskey drinker like my wife."

"No, not really. I prefer wine, if you must know." Rachel chuckled, batting her eyes.

"Then why the whiskey?"

Rachel shrugged her shoulders. "Maybe it's my way of honoring Jamie somehow."

"Perverse, but I love it!" John laughed. "Let's see if I can find some for you."

He went to the pantry, opened the door, and shoved some canned goods around. "I know Jamie must have some stashed away in here somewhere," he muttered to himself. Rachel checked John out. She had to admit Jamie had good taste. He was handsome despite his rugged, weathered looks and short stature, but John wasn't her kind of guy. She preferred a taller man, much like the suave, mysterious Doctor Everett James.

"You're in luck! Look what I found behind a big can of Crisco." John held the bottle up so Rachel could see it.

"Great," Rachel smiled as she pulled out a chair and sat at the table. "I just want a little bit. I'm not used to drinking whiskey."

"At your service." John went to the counter and twisted the cap open on the bottle. He found two shot glasses in the dish rack and poured the whiskey, filling both glasses to the rim. He brought the drinks to the table and sat, sliding one over to Rachel.

A box of photos caught his attention, and he pulled it in front of him. John grabbed the first picture he saw on the pile, and that was all it took for his eyes to water. He clutched the solid wooden frame tight in his hand, apparently reminiscing over a perfect moment in his past.

"This is Jamie and me when we first got married. The happiest memories hurt the most," he said in a low voice as he managed to restrain the flood of tears from within.

"You say you guys were married ten years?"

"Yes. Jamie and I grew up together. We were both from religious families, grew up Catholic. We talked about having our own church one day." He handed Rachel the photograph, and she looked at it. Rachel marveled at how Jamie's style had changed over the years, from dressing feminine to more manly. Thinner and looking happy, Jamie was cute in her little white dress, holding her bouquet of flowers. She had a big smile on her face as she gazed into her husband's eyes. John looked like a movie star in his double-breasted pinstriped suit. His hair was longer, but still swept back away from his handsome face.

"You know, Jamie never talked about her marriage much. What happened between you two? If you don't mind me asking." The photograph reflected happier times, and they were such an attractive couple.

"Anne Cleveland happened," John quipped in a sour tone, frowning. He almost looked wolfish as he briefly recalled his wife's betrayal. "Jamie met her at an aerobics class, and the rest is history. It took me a while to get over it," he said in a low, cracking voice.

"I bet." Rachel could see it was painful for John to talk about it and decided not to press him for more details, but John apparently needed to talk.

"Every time I called her and learned she was still with Anne, it would break my heart. I knew I couldn't live anywhere near the two of them. My ego couldn't take it."

"So, you and Jamie never divorced?"

"No, we never did."

"Well, if it's any consolation, Jamie and Anne broke up a month ago."

John's eyes widened as he fell back in his chair. "Really? What happened?"

"Anne will tell you they broke up because of her drinking, but the real story is, she fell in love with a man who happens to be my ex," Rachel answered with sourness in her voice.

"Damn!" John shook his head in disbelief.

"Damn is right," Rachel said, half smiling.

John looked down for a moment at his whiskey. He brought the glass to his lips and threw his head back. The bitter sensation of the liquor made his eyes water. John coughed, blowing out his cheeks as he swallowed and grunted. "Well, I guess we both got burned!" He looked over at Rachel and noticed she hadn't touched hers. "What are you waiting for? Drink up! It's in Jamie's honor."

"I know." Rachel sighed, taking a deep breath. She laid John's wedding photo back in the box and picked up her glass. Rachel took one sip, almost spitting the bitter-tasting liquor straight out of her mouth. She managed to hold it in, getting it down, screwing up her face as she swallowed. Rachel coughed repeatedly. "Damn, that's nasty!" she said in a dry, hoarse voice.

John's eyes gleamed with amusement as his mouth curved into a smile. "You weren't kidding. Whiskey is definitely not your drink."

"No, it's not." Rachel looked John dead in the face, scrutinizing him. "I don't believe I ever witnessed a pastor drinking alcohol." Rachel wanted him to know she disapproved of his behavior.

"They generally don't, but this one does," he smirked, winking at her. "Besides, I've got a lot on my mind."

"Well, alcohol isn't the solution."

"I'm well aware." John's smile slipped into a questioning frown. "So, is there a reason why you stopped by? You knew Jamie is no longer here."

Rachel's eyes watered. "I know. I guess I wanted to see if she was really gone, and I was hoping Peepers would be here."

"Peepers and Jamie are gone, I'm afraid." His face darkened a little.

They sat quietly for a while, each soul a million miles away in thoughts. Rachel flinched when John tapped his fingers hard on the table.

"Where are you with the funeral arrangements?" she asked.

"I'm almost done. Jamie is Catholic, so her funeral will be at Saint Mary's Church." A muscle in John's jaw twitched as he gazed down at the table misty-eyed.

Recognizing his vulnerability, Rachel felt empathy for the pastor. "Do you need any additional help with the planning? I don't mind helping," she softly offered.

"I'm fine. Jamie and I talked about this many times. She has a will. I'm following her wishes."

"When is the funeral?"

"This Saturday."

Rachel stood on her feet. "Okay. If you need anything, please let me know."

"You're so kind. Thank you," John smiled as he stood up. He escorted Rachel out of the kitchen and into the living room.

Rachel walked to the door and then abruptly turned around to face him. "I enjoyed meeting you, John. I wish it was under better circumstances," she said with a warm smile.

"I do, too. It was nice meeting you, Miss Thomas, my wife's friend."

She laughed, and John opened the door for her. Rachel waved as she walked out.

"See you soon," she hollered as she hurried to her car.

On her way home, Rachel stopped by the grocery store and bought a pint of chocolate ice cream. She thought about John and his heartbreak over Jamie. For a brief moment, she scolded Jamie for giving up on her marriage, but her scolding turned to sorrow when reality hit her again. *Damn, I'm going to miss that girl!*

Once she arrived home, Rachel went to the kitchen, opened her chocolate ice cream, and put two scoops in a plastic bowl. She put the rest in the freezer, then went to the living room and plopped on the couch. Exhausted from grieving, Rachel turned on the TV, inserted a movie in the VCR, and ate her bowl of ice cream. For the rest of the afternoon, she watched funny movies, and at dusk, she put on her pajamas and climbed into bed.

Chapter Eighteen

Saturday, January 12th

The days leading up to Jamie's funeral were rough for Rachel. Mornings were especially hard. Every time she passed Jamie's office, Rachel broke down crying. Her work suffered. She hardly saw patients. Emotionally spent, she reserved her energy for emergency patient needs only. Every morning she sat in her office with the door closed drinking coffee, staring at the wall, teary-eyed. With Jamie gone, she no longer looked forward to coming to work, and thoughts of resigning from her job frequently crossed her mind.

John called early Thursday morning and asked if she would help him clean out Jamie's office. She was hesitant at first, but she agreed. The task of sorting through and packing up Jamie's belongings made her misty-eyed and anxious. While they worked on Jamie's office, Rachel occasionally glanced over at John. He was stoic and unemotional during the whole process. She marveled at how well he was managing emotionally, and when she commented on it, he told her in his nonchalant way that he had a job to do. However, Rachel knew better. From the conversations they'd had over the past three days, it was clear that, like her, he was dying inside. It took them all day to clear out Jamie's office, and when Rachel closed and locked the door, turning the key over to Beth, she once again broke down and cried.

After a long trying week, Saturday finally came. Rachel arrived at the church forty minutes early and parked her car across the street. Looking stylish in her black cat-framed sunglasses and wearing her red trench raincoat over a form-fitting black lacey dress, Rachel got out of the car with her black patent handbag and umbrella tucked under her arm. She hated that black was affiliated with death. She chose to wear brighter colors to funerals instead. It was her way of protesting the long-held tradition.

Rachel looked up when the gray sky grumbled, threatening rain. It was cold and blistery, with the wind roaring from the east. Rachel locked her car door and buttoned up her coat. She stood on the sidewalk gazing at Saint Mary's Church.

In all of its gothic splendor, the church looked magnificent against the gray horizon with its high arched stained-glass windows and steep stone steps. Rachel flinched when thunder boomed up above and thick gray clouds darkened the sky. Rachel hurriedly put up her umbrella as torrential rain poured from the heavens with a roar. Bumper-to-bumper traffic crept down the street in front of her, and when Rachel saw an opening, she dashed across the street to the other side and ran up the church steps. She stood under the covering, gazing across the street as she closed her umbrella. A boom of thunder clapped in the heavens again, startling her and several other mourners scrambling out of their cars. The rain kept pouring, creating chaos as nurses, doctors, and social workers held up umbrellas in various colors as they ran toward the church for cover.

Rachel joined her colleagues and went inside. They packed the church, forming a single line in the center aisle as each person took seats in the nearest pew. Rachel saw John sitting in the front row by Jamie's casket and pushed through the crowd to get to him. When John saw her, he immediately stood up and his thin lips curved into a bleak smile. Dressed to the nines, John had on a double-breasted black suit and shiny Allen Edmonds loafers with multi-colored polka dot socks, a pop of color against the black he was wearing. He stretched his hand out and Rachel walked over and sat.

"Good morning, John. How are you holding up?"

"It's rough, but I'll manage," John replied as he sat next to her. Rachel patted his hand, and together they stared at Jamie's casket in silence. Black and sealed shut, a wreath of red roses sat on the top lid, and roses in large pots surrounded the casket's base. For the most part, Rachel thought the church was beautiful with its high gold-plated ceilings, rows of dark oak pews, and plush red carpeting. Behind the podium, choir seats made of shiny red silk added glamour to the gothic sanctuary. The whining, gloomy organ music she heard in the background simply got on her nerves. The musty smell of dusty prayer books and dying, dried out flowers made her sneeze. Rachel opened her purse, took out a tissue, and wiped her nose. People sitting around her, also affected by the musty odor, sneezed and wiped their noses with handkerchiefs or Kleenex. John leaned over and whispered in her ear. "Are you alright?"

"I'm fine, just allergic to dust."

Rachel wiped her nose, fighting back tears as she gazed at Jamie's casket. Loud murmurs and laughter broke out in the rear of the church. Rachel twisted around in her seat to check out the commotion, and her jaw dropped open. *Oh, my God! Look at this fool! Doesn't he know he looks like a lit-up Christmas tree?*

Hiram, in all of his hilarious glory, stood at the aisle entrance, decked out in an orange neon suit with green sequins, along with a matching wide sombrero hat. Hiram grinned like the Cheshire Cat as he strutted down the aisle, waving at people he knew. Rachel turned back around, shielding her face with one hand. *Lord, please don't let that fool see me. I don't want him sitting with me dressed like that!*

Hiram slid in a pew behind Rachel and John, reaching over and tapping her on the shoulder. Rachel cringed, horrified. She twisted around, glaring at him.

"Good morning, Hiram."

"Good morning, missy! You look lovely this dreary day!"

"Why, thank you, Hiram." Rachel half-heartedly smiled.

Hiram scratched his nose as he checked John out. "Hiram wants to know who's your friend?"

"This is Jamie's husband, John Lee..." Rachel trailed off.

Hiram reached up and slid his eyeglasses down his nose, raising his eyebrows and peering over the rims. "Jamie had a husband. Somebody actually married her. Well, Hiram be damned!"

"Shush!" Rachel hissed, placing one finger over her lips. John twisted around and glared at the attorney with icy ocean blue eyes, but kept his mouth clamped shut. Apparently, Hiram sensed the man didn't appreciate his comment. He straightened in his seat and crossed his legs, looking straight ahead and not saying another word. Rachel sighed with relief.

Soon Carl Beebe, Grace Hornsby, and Michael and Sierra Louis joined Hiram in the pew. Carl parked his wheelchair in the aisle next to the bench. Beth Jones hurried down the aisle and sat behind Michael and his wife. Beth wore a lacy black dress with matching knee-high boots, and a floppy black hat was tilted on the side of her head. She looked like a wicked witch with her big green eyes flashing through her bifocals. Sally, who was also dressed in black, sat next to Beth, dabbing her eyes with her handkerchief as she blinked back tears. Across the sanctuary, Everett James stood against the wall watching the crowd as they trickled in. He looked dapper in a gray suit, a nice change from his usual attire.

Out of the blue, loud whispers erupted around the sanctuary. Rachel twisted around in her seat again to see what the disturbance was and saw Anne Cleveland. Everybody in the church gawked at Anne as she stepped briskly down the aisle. Dressed in a gray coat with matching pants and wearing gray-tinted glasses, Anne abruptly stopped at the pew where Sally and Beth sat. She gestured for Sally to move over, who refused to budge. Sally didn't open her mouth. Instead, she gave Anne a dirty look, looking her up and down.

Beth leaned over and whispered in Sally's ear, "Let the woman sit down, please."

Reluctant and irritated, Sally moved over to make room for Anne, still not opening her mouth.

"Good morning," Anne greeted her, looking glum.

"Good morning," Sally coolly answered, looking straight ahead.

Rachel turned around in her seat and frowned. "She's got some nerve," she muttered under her breath.

"Huh, what did you say?" John leaned over so he could hear Rachel better.

"Oh, nothing, I'm just talking to myself," she smiled.

"I guess talking to yourself is okay, as long as you don't answer yourself. If you do, you need to check into that looney bin you work for."

Rachel chuckled, impressed with his sense of humor in such a distressing time. She'd hoped he wouldn't run into Anne, feeling it would be a disaster.

Men and women in gold-trimmed red robes quietly walked in single file and took seats in the choir stand. The priest walked in after the choir, taking his place at the podium. Short and frail, the priest wore a long flowing red robe with puffy gold sleeves and a red cap on his short silver-white hair. Pale with piercing gray eyes, he rubbed his thin hands together, checking out the crowd as they came in and took their seats. Apparently growing tired from standing, the priest left the podium and sat in a gold high-backed chair.

Once the church was full, the ushers shut the doors. The woman playing the organ looked like Dracula's wife with her wiry, long white hair down her back. Her bright sky-blue eyes were frighteningly eerie as she gazed out at the choir. Her long bony fingers slowly tapped out "Amazing Grace" while the choir painstakingly belted out the words. The song tugged at the heartstrings of every grieving soul in the church, and the choir's voices at times were drowned out by waves of sobs.

The choir sat down after the song was over. The priest stood on his feet, and with a somber look walked purposefully to the podium. As he tested the microphone, it gawked like a crow, forcing people in the congregation to cover their ears. "Sorry," he mumbled in an anxious voice as he turned the volume down. Once the microphone was adjusted, the priest scanned the congregation and began the eulogy.

"Good morning, family, friends, and colleagues. My name is Father Rob," he greeted everyone in an authoritative, baritone voice. "We're gathered…"

Surprised that Father Rob's voice was so profound for such a short, frail man, Rachel listened intently as the priest talked about Jamie's life. She glanced over at John, and he was whimpering. Grief was his master now, and it had taken over his soul. He was at the mercy of its whims as salty tears flowed unchecked from his ocean-blue eyes. Misty-eyed and feeling sorry for him, Rachel reached over and held his hand. He patted her hand in return, appreciative of her comfort. Father Rob solemnly moved on to a thought-provoking prayer, invoking more sobs from the congregation. As tears streamed down Rachel's face, the emptiness in her heart and the numbness pounding her brain threatened to engulf her. She flinched violently, trying to shake off the intrusive feelings. John looked at her with concern in his watery eyes.

"I'm fine," she patted his hand. "I just got a chill."

He nodded with understanding, turning his head as his eyes, again, fixed on Jamie's casket. Before long, the priest finished his prayer. He extended an invitation to Jamie's family and friends to come to the podium to offer their remarks. Anne bolted out of her seat and hurried down the aisle. Whispers broke out around the church as she grabbed the microphone to make her remarks.

"Jamie Lee, my dear friend and love. I adored her…"

"You're a bald-faced liar!" a woman hollered from the congregation. People turned around in their seats, looking for the disgruntled woman, while others giggled and whispered to the person sitting next to them. Red-faced and tearful, Anne continued with her remarks with her eyes cast down at the podium. She dabbed her eyes, sniffling as she talked.

"Like I was telling you, I adored Jamie. She was loving, sensitive, and she had such a great sense of humor. I can't tell you how much I will miss her. She was an important part of my life."

Stone-faced, John wouldn't look at Anne while Rachel, incensed, cringed in her seat.

"Stop lying!" a woman yelled again from the crowd. Rachel's mouth dropped open as she and John pivoted around in their places to see Cassie Marks up on her feet with her round black eyes like daggers. She glared at Anne, shaking her long index finger. "You're a damn liar, and you know it! You should be ashamed of yourself!"

A woman with big gray eyes tugged on the hem of Cassie's navy-blue dress. "Cassie, sit down. You're making a spectacle of yourself." Cassie reluctantly took her seat as loud whispers swirled around her. Red-faced, Anne stepped down from the podium and hurried down the aisle to her place. She grabbed her purse and stepped swiftly to the exit. The ushers standing on each side of the double doors shoved them open to let her out. Cheers erupted around the sanctuary.

Father Rob leaped out of his gold chair and rushed to the podium. He grabbed the microphone and yelled, "Please, people settled down. This is a funeral, not a sports stadium!"

Everyone settled down, and the church was quiet again. Rachel was stumped. *Did Cassie know Anne left Jamie for someone else? She had to know, otherwise why would she call Anne out like that?* Rachel and John straightened in their seats, looking at each other.

John raised an eyebrow. "Is she a friend of Jamie's?"

"Her name is Cassie Marks. She's also a social worker. We all worked together at the hospital."

"Well, I'm glad I'm not the only one who thinks Anne is a despicable human being."

Rachel smiled demurely, deciding to keep her opinion to herself.

John got up and spoke, and so did several coworkers. An hour later, the service was finally over. The pallbearers, men dressed in black double-breasted suits, carried Jamie's casket down the aisle. John followed, and soon everyone flowed out of the church in a single line. As the pallbearers loaded Jamie's coffin into the shiny black hearse waiting outside, Rachel took a detour to the bathroom. Cassie was there hovering over the sink, applying her purple lipstick.

"Oh, Cassie, I didn't expect to run into you in here." Rachel gasped with big eyes. "Girl, you lost your marbles today, didn't you?" Rachel reached in her handbag and took out her compact, prying it open.

"No, not really. I just wasn't going to sit there and listen to Anne's lies." Cassie replaced the cap of her lipstick tube and dropped it in her purse.

"So, you know about Anne and Jamie breaking up?" Rachel stared at Cassie through the mirror while she powdered her face.

"Yeah, Jamie told me about it two weeks ago. She told me Anne left her for someone else."

"Yep, she did." Rachel opened her handbag and dropped her compact in, then she took out her red lipstick. She colored her lips while Cassie looked on with her arms wrapped around her waist.

"Jamie's husband is quite a looker. I can't believe she traded him for that whale, Anne!"

Rachel chuckled. "Girl, I know. It's a long story."

"Are you going to the cemetery?"

"Yep, I have too." Rachel sighed as she snapped her lipstick container shut.

Cassie hurried to the door and opened it. "Well, I guess I'll see you there." She was gone before Rachel could say another word.

As Rachel stepped outside, the sky had cleared some, and the sun's fiery face was peeking through the clouds. A chilly, blustery wind rustled through the evergreen trees, and the majestic structures swayed back and forth with powerful passion. Branches tumbled to the ground, overpowered by the strong wind, and the breeze tousled Rachel's tight black curls as she ran down the stairs onto the sidewalk. Parked on the curb in his black four-door Mercedes, Hiram in all of his bizarre glory rolled down the window.

"Missy, do you need a ride to the cemetery?"

Rachel hesitated, not sure if she should ride with such a crazy man. If his driving was anything like his mental health, Rachel expected a rollercoaster ride.

"I'll pass," Rachel said as she teetered on the curb.

"Oh, come on," Hiram urged, sensing her reluctance. "Hiram promises to be a good boy."

Rachel dropped her shoulders and sighed. "Okay, but remember to drive like you got some sense."

"Don't worry, Hiram will!"

Rachel opened the door and hopped in. The black hearse carrying Jamie's body passed by them before Hiram pulled away from the curb. He maneuvered his Mercedes, getting in the front of the funeral procession, following the limousine down the street. Rachel gazed out the window. Stinging tears flooded her dark brown eyes. She twisted around in her seat, looking out the back window, and saw a long funeral procession traveling behind them, different model cars with sad faces inside.

The drive to Saint Mary's Cemetery, fifteen minutes away, was smooth. The limousine swished through the iron gate, parking its long body a few yards from the cemetery entrance. The limousine doors popped open, and four pallbearers hopped out simultaneously. They moved to the back of the limousine, and one man opened the hatch door, lifting it into the air. Two men pulled out a gurney, unfolding it. They sat the stretcher upright on the ground, grabbed Jamie's casket, and carefully lifted it out of the limousine. The men hoisted the big coffin onto the gurney and shoved it across the wet, grassy, hilly lawn.

John followed behind while everyone still sitting in their vehicles opened their doors and got out. The entourage came upon a rocky, steep path, and the pallbearers huffed and puffed as they carefully guided the gurney over it. The journey to Jamie's grave was long and tiring. Breathing heavily, mourners crept along whispering amongst themselves as they navigated the slippery, rocky path. Rachel picked up her pace, passing some of the mourners until she caught up with John and walked alongside him.

"I wondered where you were." He managed to smile, looking surprised.

"I stopped to take a potty break," she smiled back. It wasn't long before the sun faded behind dirty gray clouds, and seconds later, light sprinkles sprung from the sky. Frowning, Rachel put up her umbrella. "Ugh, I hate it when it rains."

John laughed. "Young lady, this is typical of the Great Northwest."

"Yes, I'm fully aware. But it's still annoying." It had stopped sprinkling by the time they reached Jamie's burial site covered by a green canopy in front of a huge evergreen tree. The pallbearers parked Jamie's coffin next to a freshly dug rectangular-shaped hole which had a pile of dirt on the side. The crowd jammed around each other, shoulder to shoulder, forming a large circle. Some of the mourners remained on the wet, grassy lawn jockeying for a closer spot so they could see the casket. John sat on a bench directly in front of Jamie's coffin, and Rachel closed her umbrella and joined him, crossing her legs with her handbag on her lap. Sally, Beth, and Cassie shoved their way through the thick crowd and took seats next to Rachel. By the time Father Rob arrived, everyone had settled in.

As the wind whistled and whipped around the canopy, the dark sky threatened more rain. Father Rob stood in front of Jamie's casket and opened his Bible to a hushed, somber audience. He looked over the crowd. There must have been at least one hundred people watching him, waiting patiently to hear his final remarks before Jamie was laid to rest.

Father Rob tightly clutched his bible as Psalm 23 elegantly slipped from his thin lips in a soft poetic melody. Faint sobs erupted in the audience while lightening cracked across the dark sky. Rachel felt tears coming on again, moved by Father Rob's rendition of her favorite bible passage. She first heard Psalm 23 in Sunday school when she was a little girl, and she often read it in times of trouble, giving her a sense of comfort and hope.

The pallbearers lowered Jamie's casket into the ground while Father Rob recited the final line of the Bible passage. He led the crowd in a brief prayer, and when he was done, he sat down. Rachel opened her handbag and took out a black rose. She stood up and tossed it on Jamie's casket. Overcome with grief, Rachel walked as fast as she could to the back of the crowd.

Once Jamie's casket was in the ground, John stood up and quietly left. One by one, the crowd followed him, silently returning to their vehicles as thunder rumbled in the heavens above. Not ready to go just yet, Rachel walked to the gravesite and stood there, dabbing her eyes with a tissue and shaking her head. The laughter and friendship she and Jamie had shared came to mind again. The thought of never seeing Jamie again gnawed at her like an aching sore.

"Jamie, Jamie, Jamie," Rachel whispered to herself. "You left us way too soon. Goodbye, my friend, goodbye. Rest in peace."

"Are you okay?" A deep, baritone voice came from behind her.

Rachel yelped, jumping off the ground two inches. She whirled around, stepping back, and her eyes met Doctor James'.

"You scared the hell out of me!" she frowned. "You're always sneaking up on me. You need to stop that! It's annoying!"

"Sorry, but I'm concerned about you, that's all. Are you all right?"

"Yes, I'm all right!" Every muscle in Rachel's face was tense. Mistrust, anger, and annoyance glared from the windows of her soul. "How about you, are you all right?" she asked in a nasty, sarcastic tone.

"Yes, I'm fine, and I want you to be fine as well," Doctor James politely answered, ignoring her frosty attitude.

Rachel hugged her waist and turned her back on the doctor. He moved closer to her, and the two of them stood side by side gazing at Jamie's coffin inside her grave. For several minutes, neither spoke. Then lightning cracked in the sky, a warning that another downpour was on the way.

Doctor James gently broke the silence. "Rachel, did you drive here?"

His question jarred her, and she looked around. Hiram was nowhere in sight, and Rachel burned inside. *That knucklehead left me! How rude!*

"Uh, no, I rode here with that crazy Hiram. Apparently, he left me. My car is parked at the church."

"I'd be happy to give you a lift to your car."

Rachel forced a smile. "That would be nice, thank you."

They stood at Jamie's gravesite a few moments longer, paying their respects. Thunder clapped in the sky, and Doctor James said, "I think we'd better go." Together they walked swiftly down the steep rocky path and over the wet, hilly lawn. A water droplet splashed on the doctor's nose, and he broke out in a slow jog. "You better hurry," he called out. "It's about to rain."

Rachel put up her umbrella as water droplets fell around her. Thunder crashed in the distance, startling Rachel, and she took off in a brisk jog. The sky opened up, drowning the universe with buckets of water. She reached the doctor's Fiat, opened the door, closed her umbrella, and hopped inside. Drenched, Rachel raked her fingers through her damp, curly hair. "Damn, I hate the rain!"

"Sorry, you got a little wet," Doctor James said, trying to be empathetic.

"This is normal. Another typical day in the Great Northwest," Rachel grumbled.

Doctor James grinned. He cranked the ignition while glancing at his rearview mirror. He gradually pulled his Fiat away from the curb, stepped on the gas, and sped out the cemetery gate. "How about going out to dinner sometime?" he slyly asked.

Rachel took a deep breath and rolled her eyes. "You don't give up, do you?"

"Nope!"

"Okay, let me think about it."

Doctor James laughed. "Don't take too long. I'm not going to wait forever."

Rachel shot him a mischievous grin. "You don't have a choice, Doctor James. You'll wait as long as it takes."

Chapter Nineteen

Monday, January 14th

Rachel was busy wrapping up details on her cases, making last-minute phone calls and plans. She hadn't been sleeping well. For several nights, she tossed and turned in bed, visions of the site where Jamie died burned into her mind. One night, she experienced a terrible nightmare where Jamie was engulfed in flames. She tried to save her, but she brutally failed. Rachel woke up, sitting straight up in her bed with beads of sweat dripping down her face and under her arms. She didn't go back to sleep, fearful she might experience the horrible dream again.

Her father sent her funds for an airline ticket as promised, and she was grateful. She longed for different surroundings. Since Jamie's death, not only did Rachel suffer insomnia, but her energy level was low. She would sit in her office most of the day with her door closed, either staring at the wall or the same page of her favorite magazine, Essence. When the phone rang, Rachel sometimes answered it, but sometimes she didn't. She only saw patients during court hearings or if they needed assistance with their discharge.

Working at Salter's Point Regional had become unbearable with Jamie gone. No more coffee breaks, no more entertaining fights with Hiram, no more girl talk. Rachel missed Jamie. She had been her friend and her mentor, and they'd been a team. Every time she passed Jamie's office, Rachel burst into tears. She was surprised when Beth approved her request for two weeks off with no questions asked. Cassie Marks agreed to cover her caseload while she was away. Rachel appreciated their understanding. After all, she'd only been employed at the hospital for three months.

Rachel's flight was scheduled to leave at one thirty, and she was determined to get her work done. She threw all of her energy into charting, making sure her documentation was complete and thorough. Unexpectedly, loud banging rattled her door.

"Come in," she shouted.

Sally's smiling face appeared around the door. "Hello, dear. Can I come in?"

"Sure." Rachel waved her in.

Sally mosey in and shut the door. Dressed in a flowing white blouse, black bell-bottomed pants, and black ankle boots, Sally flopped her ample behind on the sofa and crossed her legs. Stale cigarette smoke reeked from her clothing, and Rachel twisted up her nose in disgust. Sally didn't notice.

"I hear you're taking off for a few days."

Rachel's dark brown eyes widen. "My word, nothing is private around this place!"

"Was it supposed to be a secret?" Sally had her eyes fixed on Rachel.

"No, but…" Rachel dropped her shoulders. "Sally, I can't stay here another day. Every time I pass Jamie's office and that place where the accident happened, I boo-hoo like a baby. I'm so tired of crying."

"I know it's hard, dear. I've got those moments too."

Rachel's eyes were misty. "I'm thinking about quitting. I don't think I can stand it here. I see Jamie everywhere!"

"Rachel, you can't quit!" Sally lurched forward with watery eyes. "What will I do without you? I can't lose Jamie and you, too!"

"I'm sorry, Sally, but I'm seriously thinking about it."

Sally's face crumpled, and tears streamed down her cheeks.

"Don't cry," Rachel said as she stood on her feet and ran over to Sally. She sat next to her and rubbed Sally's back. They sat together for a long while, with no words passing between them. Sally's soft sniffling and the ticking clock on the wall were the only noises in the room. After a while, Rachel spoke in a quiet, reassuring voice.

"Sally, I haven't made up my mind yet. That's why I'm taking time off. I need to clear my head, talk it over with my parents so I can make the best decision."

"I understand." Sally hung her head, staring at her lap as big tears fell on her pants. Rachel grabbed a Kleenex box off the end table and placed it on Sally's lap. Sally snatched a tissue and blew her nose hard. It sounded like a foghorn.

"Damn, girl," Rachel shrieked. "You'll wake the dead blowing your nose like that."

They fell out laughing, and Sally vigorously rubbed her nose. "My husband always says I blow my nose like an old man."

"Well, he's right," Rachel joked.

Sally playfully slapped Rachel on her arm. "Stop making fun of me," she giggled. She rose to her feet. "I'm going to leave so you can finish your work. Can I call you? I'd like to check on you while you're gone."

"Sure, that would be nice." Rachel stood up and stepped to her desk. She grabbed her notepad, scribbled her parents' telephone number on it, and tore off the note. "Here. Try not to call before ten in the morning or after ten in the evening."

"Got it." Sally took the note and jammed it in her pants pocket. She stretched out her arms, looking pitiful with glistening eyes. Rachel grabbed Sally, hugging her tight.

"I sure will miss you," Sally sniffled as the two women rocked side to side.

"Me too," Rachel whispered. She let go of Sally and twisted the doorknob, opening the door. "Take care of yourself."

"Dear, you do the same." Sally walked out, shutting the door behind her. Rachel turned to lean back against the door. "This place is so depressing. I can't wait to get the hell out of here."

309

San Francisco was windy, sunny, and cold. Rachel stepped through the door of the airplane and onto the ramp. Shivering like a leaf, Rachel buttoned her jean jacket and hurried down the corridor into the airport. As she scanned the waiting crowd, Rachel spotted her father in a navy suit, waving at her. She took off with a brisk pace and shimmied her way through the crowd. Rachel fell in her father's arms, raising on her tiptoes to kiss him on the cheek.

"So glad to be home," she whispered in his ear. "I couldn't wait to get away from that place."

"I know," her father said as he patted Rachel on her back. Soft tears rolled down her cheeks, dropping on her dad's shoulder. He stepped back to look at her. "There, there, don't cry. I know Jamie's death threw you for a loop. It will be a while before you get over it," he said.

"I'll never get over it." Rachel blinked back tears. "No one close to me has ever died before. It's not a good feeling."

"Let's walk," her dad said as he threw his arm over Rachel's shoulders. "You made a good decision taking time off. Emotionally you need some downtime. Be around family. Talk things out."

Rachel reached up and wiped tears off her face. "Thanks, Dad, for being so understanding."

"Anything for you," he smiled. They arrived in the baggage claim and waited by the slowly revolving carousel.

"Dad, the red one is mine."

Her father grabbed the suitcase and pulled it over the railing. "Is this the only one you've got?" he asked.

"Huh, huh." Rachel carefully checked the nametag to make sure the suitcase belonged to her.

"Everything cool?"

"Yessir!"

"Well, let's go. Your mother is waiting for us."

Rachel and her dad walked out of the airport and crossed the street to the parking lot. Her father's black Mercedes was parked on the first floor. He tapped his remote, and the trunk clicked opened. He touched it again, unlocking the car doors. Rachel walked to the passenger's side of the vehicle, opened the door, and hopped in. Her father threw the suitcase in the trunk and closed the lid. He glided to his side of the car and opened the door. He slid in and slammed the door as he glanced at Rachel.

"Are we set, sweetheart?"

"We are," Rachel grinned.

"Then, let's get out of here," her father chuckled as he turned on the ignition.

Rachel enjoyed the ride home. By the time her father parked in front of the house, her stomach was growling.

"I'm hungry. I hope Mom cooked something good."

"She did," her father smiled. Rachel got out of the car, ran up the steps, and went inside.

She found her mother at the breakfast bar in the kitchen making a salad. Her fiery red hair twisted in a massive bun on the top of her head brought out her caramel complexion. She was wearing her favorite green raggedy sweatshirt over a pair of blue jeans.

"Hey, Mom! What's going on?"

Her mother grabbed a dishtowel and wiped her hands. She pivoted on one foot, and her face lit up when she saw her only child. Her green eyes danced as her lips parted into a warm, broad smile. "Hi, honey. Come here and give your momma a big hug."

Rachel hugged her mother's neck and smacked a wet kiss on her cheek. "Glad to be home."

"So good to see you," her mother crooned as she patted Rachel's back. Sizzling goodness drew Rachel's eyes to the stove. The aroma of the dish that had just been pulled from the oven took over the entire kitchen, and Rachel's mouth watered, anticipating the spicy, tangy, and delicious taste. Rachel let go of her mother and trotted to the stove.

"Mom, when is dinner? That lasagna looks so good."

"In a few minutes," her mother answered in a syrupy voice.

Her father came into the kitchen and sat at the end of the breakfast bar. "Your suitcase is in your room."

"Thank you." Rachel glanced at her watch. "Mom, do I have time to unpack before dinner?"

"Certainly," her mother laughed. "The lasagna has to cool some, and I need to finish this salad."

"Cool." Rachel went upstairs, and as she passed through the hallway, Rachel admired the African oil paintings hanging on the wall. Her favorite one was the little African girl weaving a basket as she sat in front of a straw hut draped with large green leaves. Her tight curls glisten in the hot sun. Rachel stopped momentarily to admire the painting. She noticed a tiny fly with silvery wings on the girl's bare shoulder. She was astonished to see it, never having noticed it before. The fly looked out of place. Lost. She remembered feeling lost and out of place when she started working at Salter's Point Regional. Jamie changed all of that, taking Rachel under her wing and showing her the ropes. Jamie's friendship, humor, and mentoring kept her from getting lost like the fly on the girl's shoulder. *Boy, I'm going to miss that woman! What a bummer!*

Rachel sighed heavily and continued down the hall to her room. The door was open, and she stepped inside. Her room was the same as she left it when she went off to college so many years ago. Rachel marveled at the simple style. The walls were painted light pink, and stuffed animals sat on a full-size heart-shaped white iron bed. The white comforter was trimmed in pink, and two full-sized pillows encased in ruffled pink pillowcases were stacked against the headboard. A few feet from the bed sat a cream dresser with six gold knobs. The dresser's mirror was shaped like a big heart, and Rachel smiled when she remembered convincing her father to buy her the furniture.

Rachel moseyed over to the window and gazed out. She could view the Golden Gate Bridge from her window, and a few feet from the house was a sandy beach with sparkling seashells. The entire scene was breathtaking, and Rachel sighed, taking it all in. The Bridge's bright orange color enhanced its visibility in the fog, and it complimented the surrounding natural habitat and the roaring Pacific Ocean. Today, the sky was flawless, a splendid blue backdrop that gave the famous bridge a regal appearance. Rachel sighed with appreciative awe. *Tomorrow, I'm taking a walk on the beach.*

Rachel hurriedly unpacked her clothes, hanging three dresses in the closet and folding her jeans and sweaters in the dresser drawer. The smell of lasagna caught her attention again, and Rachel left the room, leaving the door slightly ajar. She hurried through the hall and down the staircase, running into her father.

"I was just about to call you. Dinner is ready," he grinned.

"Oooo, I'm hungry!" Rachel rushed to the kitchen, leaving her father behind. The table was beautifully decorated with a black tablecloth and a large vase of fresh sunflowers. In front of each chair was a plate setting with shiny silverware. A bowl of green salad sat next to the pan of lasagna, along with a basket of French bread. Rachel pulled out a chair and sat.

"Someone's hungry," her mother laughed as she sat at the end of the table.

Her dad sat at the other end. "Let's pray."

They bowed their heads and prayed, and as soon as they finished, they served their plates and dug in. Rachel took a bite, shaking her head." Mm-hm, mm-hm, this is so freaking good!"

Her mother fell out laughing. "You're so dramatic."

They ate dinner and chatted for the rest of the evening. For a brief while, Rachel was happy. Jamie and Salter's Point Regional never cross her mind. By ten, Rachel was curled up in bed. She yawned, exhausted from the day, and drifted off to sleep. For the first time since Jamie's death, she slept until morning.

Rachel's days were filled with morning walks on the beach and afternoons shopping in the city with her mother. One afternoon during one of their shopping trips, Rachel and her mother went to Fisherman's Wharf in San Francisco. They ate lunch outside at Chowders on Pier Thirty-Nine, and Rachel ordered a big bowl of clam chowder. The chilly wind coming off the ocean made Rachel shiver. She buttoned her jacket up to her chin. Once the waitress set her bowl of soup on the table, Rachel said a quick prayer and dug in. The smooth, thick, fishy liquid felt good going down, warming her insides.

"Mm, mm, so good." Rachel's face lit up with delight.

"Is that all you're going to eat?" her mother asked as she arranged French fries around her fish sandwich.

Rachel grabbed a piece of French bread out of the basket. "The soup and bread will fill me up," she insisted.

Her mother rolled her eyes heavenward. "Hard to fathom, but okay."

The two women ate in silence as they gazed at the sailboats bobbing up and down along the ocean waves. Giant seagulls soared throughout the sky, and a red helicopter whirled at rapid speed toward the Golden Gate Bridge.

"I love this city," Rachel said, breaking the silence. "There's no city as beautiful as San Francisco."

Her mother raised an eyebrow. "My, it's sound like we're homesick. Are you thinking about moving back home?"

"Thinking about it. I haven't decided yet."

"I thought you like working at Salter's Point."

Rachel hunched her shoulders and took a deep breath. She laid her spoon on the table. "With Jamie gone, I just can't…"

"Look, honey, I know it's hard. Give yourself time. Losing a friend takes a while to get used to."

"I know," Rachel sighed as she grabbed her spoon again, and stirred her soup. She glanced up momentarily, and her eyes met her mother's. Her mother looked worried. "So, you think I should stay there and not move right now?"

"Yes, I think so." Her mom reached for Rachel's hand, patting it. "Honey, you've only had this job for three months. You should stay for the rest of the year. Besides, it looks better on your resume." She hesitated a moment. "Honey, that's my advice, but it's your decision."

"Mom, it's challenging working with a bunch of cuckoos who called themselves professionals. Sometimes it feels like I'm the only normal person there. At least when Jamie was around, I had someone with a little sense to talk to."

Wrinkles appeared on her mom's forehead and she erupted into a belly laugh. "Didn't you tell your father one time that Jamie smelled like whiskey and drank on the job? I don't believe she had much sense, either!"

"Mom!"

"Well, I call it like I see it, honey." Her mother blinked her green eyes.

Irritated, Rachel took up for Jamie. "Jamie was my friend. She taught me everything she knew about social work. Because of her, I have good interviewing skills and can write a damn good assessment."

"Young lady, be careful and watch your tone with me!" her mother quipped, grimacing. "You're not talking to one of those cuckoos at the hospital."

Rachel snickered. "Sorry, Mom. I didn't mean to cuss."

"Let's finish our lunch. We still have places to go before we return home."

"Right." Rachel dipped her spoon in her clam chowder and slurped it down. After her mother finished her fish sandwich and paid for their lunch, they left Chowders and took the cable car uptown. They shopped for the rest of the afternoon, and by the time they returned home, it was dusk.

Rachel was on the patio with her sunglasses on, reading the employment section of the classified ads. It was a sunny morning, but a cool sixty-five degrees, and Rachel had on her old heavy long-sleeved college sweatshirt with a pair of black jeans. Rachel loved being on the patio on clear days, relaxing in the long lawn chair with a blanket over her. She would gaze for hours at the ocean, watching the waves splash over the rocky embankment. She took several sips of coffee, being extra careful not to spill the hot steamy liquid on her lap. The coffee tasted good going down her throat, warming her insides from the chill.

The social work jobs she circled in the classified ads didn't interest her. Now that she was used to the exciting, unpredictable work environment at Salter's Point Regional, Rachel dreaded looking for a new job. She didn't mind working in an unpredictable work environment as long as the professionals working around her behaved like normal human beings.

The faint ringing of the telephone in the den caught her attention. Rachel barely heard her mother's voice as she talked on the phone. A few seconds later, her mom opened the sliding glass door.

"Rachel, honey, there's a call for you."

Rachel raised up and twisted around, looking over the top of the lawn chair. "Who's calling?"

"He didn't say."

Rachel raised an eyebrow. "Did you say a man was on the phone?"

"Yes, dear, I did." Her mother frowned, slapping one hand on her hip. "Stop asking me questions and get off your duff and answer the phone!" She shut the door and walked off.

Rachel threw off her blanket, scooted to the edge of the chair, and stood on her feet. "Damn, this better be important." She crossed the patio, opened the sliding door, stepped inside, and grabbed the telephone handset that was lying on the end table.

"Hello, who's calling?" she asked in a firm voice.

"Missy, are you trying to escape?" a gruff voice shouted. "When are you coming back?"

Rachel laughed. "Hiram, you crazy man, how did you get my phone number?"

"Sally gave it to me. So, missy, tell Hiram, what are you doing down there? When are you coming back?"

"Maybe never!" Rachel half-heartedly joked, but secretly she was serious.

"Never? What in the world does missy mean, never?" he growled.

"It's not the same since Jamie died."

"Missy, nothing is the same. Hiram misses Jamie too. But the rest of us poor souls are still alive and kicking, aching for some cute social worker like yourself to help us along this topsy-turvy road they call life. You have to come back. Look at what you're missing."

Rachel smiled. Hiram's persuasive powers were working on her. "Hiram, stop calling the patients "poor souls." They're people who are mentally challenged."

"Mentally challenged, huh? Hiram likes that phrase." Laughing like a school boy. There was a brief lag on the line. "Missy, are you still there? Talk to Hiram!"

"I am," Rachel answered in a low voice.

"You've been gone for almost two weeks. Hiram needs you to come back. Sally misses you. She's been walking around, whimpering like a sick mouse the whole time you've been gone. Hiram needs you to come back so she can stop gibbering!"

"Geeze, Hiram, give Sally a break."

"Hiram is trying. But Sally's whimpering sure gets on Hiram's nerves!" Hiram grunted.

"Hiram, I'm sorry. I'm really not cut out for this kind of work. I need less stress in my life. That job makes me feel like a fly in the wrong soup. And besides, Jamie's death and that crazy hospital have simply worn me out."

Hiram sighed heavily over the phone. "Hiram understands what you mean. It's hard working with these lunatics, who called themselves doctors and nurses. Hiram knows the shit gets on your nerves, but that's beside the point. Jamie would want you to stay. So, please don't leave? Pretty please..."

Rachel cracked up, shaking her head. She was touched by Hiram's words and his sudden display of affection. Hiram had his issues, but his heart was in the right place. Rachel found his practical approach quite entertaining. Suddenly she realized she missed the crazy attorney and the daily mayhem of the hospital. Maybe, just maybe, she could go back and work a couple more years. After all, that had been her original plan. Rachel took a deep breath and exhaled loudly into the phone.

"Hiram..."

"Yes, missy."

"Tell Sally I'll be back on Wednesday."

"Whoopee! Outstanding! Hiram knew you wouldn't let the troops down!"

Rachel held the handset away from her ear. "Hiram, stop yelling!"

"Hiram is sorry, missy! Hiram's excited to hear you're coming back."

"Okay, but I've got to go. In the meantime, you behave yourself."

Hiram's laugh was loud and shrill. Rachel slapped her hand over her ear to muffle out the sound. "Hiram will hold down this hell hole until you get back!"

"Damn, dude, you're so freaking loud!" Rachel groaned. "You're crazier than a loon."

"Missy, like the old folks say, it takes one to know one!"

Before she knew it, the dial tone screeched in her ear, and she hung up. "He's so off the wall!" Rachel giggled. Hiram never failed to make her laugh. He was a comedian, a funny, professional misfit. Rachel missed his crude humor and bizarre antics. "Hiram, I believe you're right. Jamie would want me to stay. So, thanks to you, I'll be back at that crazy hospital once again very soon. You can count on it."

Epilogue

Peepers knew what resided in the grounds near the big church, and remembered vividly the day his mistress had been placed there. Since that day, he'd been returning to her grave, sad, withered, and fragile, to lay near the headstone. Most days he basked in the warmth of the hazy sun for hours guarding her grave. When rain came, he sheltered under the huge evergreen tree.

As Peepers approached the gravesite, he watched for the old man with the bushy eyebrows, prepared to bolt if the man ran at him again. On the day his mistress was buried, the man had chased him away, waving his long arms and yelling, "Skat, cat!" But today, he approached slowly and placed a bowl on the ground near the headstone. Peepers growled, showing his sharp fangs. The man backed away and stood by quietly. The two watched one another, and then the old man gestured.

"Eat, big boy. I know you're hungry."

Smelling something vaguely familiar and weary of hunting for meager creatures to eat raw, Peepers stood up and crept to the bowl. He remembered his mistress eating something similar and recognized the chunks of meat floating in it. Famished, Peepers lapped up the soup, licking the bowl clean. Then he turned his face upward into the gentle breeze as if thanking his creator. With his tummy deeply satisfied, Peepers sprinted down the rocky path, back to the home he'd made on the cliff.

He returned the next day, and the day after that, each day finding a bowl of chicken soup waiting for him with a few flies teetering on the rim, the old man watching from a respectful distance. He returned for so many days, season after season, he nearly forgot what his days had been like before he lived in the hollow tree on the cliff.

Peepers had just finished licking the last bit of soup from his bowl and laid down to enjoy the warm sunshine, when he heard a familiar voice saying the name that his mistress used to call him.

"Peepers! Peepers! Where have you been all of this time?"

Too comfortable to rise from his basking, he turned his head and saw a well-dressed woman with curly black hair kneeling in the grass a few feet away. It was the woman that his mistress used to call Rachel.

"Peepers, it's me, Rachel. Boy, have I missed you, old buddy!"

She was speaking in a soft, comforting way that reminded him of Jamie. She held her arms out to him, and he suddenly remembered what it was like to be held by his mistress. He remembered how comfy and soft she was, what she smelled like, the vibration of her chest when she spoke into his fur and made funny sounds, the bliss when she scratched his chin and ears, the contentment of napping in his place on the couch in her office. Suddenly, he wanted all of those things again, more than he'd ever wanted anything else.

He rose from his resting place and crept toward the woman cautiously, stopping a few times to consider her closely. She rose and stepped toward him slowly with her hand outstretched, still speaking softly, until she was able to scratch him on the top of his head.

"I'm sure I can find you something better to eat than an old bowl of soup. Do you want to come with me?" She took a step back and made one of those tsk-ing sounds Jamie used to make. "Come on, buddy, let's go together." She turned and took a few steps, looking back to see if he would follow, still making soothing noises.

Something inside of him decided, and Peepers purposefully trotted after the woman, catching up to her just as she stopped at a car. When she opened the door and gestured for him to hop in, he was seized with a dreadful fear from long ago. He froze, uncertain, but the woman gently scooped him up the way his mistress used to, held him to her chest for a moment, snicking on the top of his head, and placed him inside the car. Just as he used to do, he climbed over to the other seat, turned a few times, and curled up in a circle, carefully tucking his tail under his chin. He watched warily as Rachel got in, closed the door, and started the car, and they moved forward. After a few moments, the comforting rumble of the engine soothed him to sleep.

Peepers woke when the car stopped and the engine shut off. Rachel got out and stood patiently by the open door while he casually yawned and had sufficiently stretched, and then hopped down onto the ground. She closed the door, picked him up, and took him inside a building he hadn't seen before. Once inside, he recognized it was a "home" like Jamie's, rather than a place like her "office."

Rachel set him down and went to the room where the food was kept, and after some fiddling around, she put a plate down on the floor. Peepers was feeling sufficiently safe and comfortable with the woman that he took a moment to sniff around a bit, making her wait an appropriate length of time before he sauntered over to the plate. Whatever it was, it smelled much better than the chicken soup he'd gotten used to. But, he took time to perform his obligatory "sniff the food" routine before beginning his second meal of the day. Before the first bite was swallowed, he rewarded his new mistress with a loud purr.

For Peepers, there would be no more flies in the wrong bowl of soup.

Rachel's Blueberry Quinoa Pancakes

Ingredients:

Your favorite pancake mix
1 cup cooked quinoa
1 teaspoon vanilla extract
1 teaspoon cinnamon
1 tablespoon sugar
1 cup fresh blueberries
butter

Heat skillet over medium heat or electric griddle to 375 degrees.

Prepare pancake mix as directed, then stir in quinoa, vanilla extract, cinnamon and sugar with a wooden spoon until the lumps disappear.

Add the blueberries being careful not to overmix.

Pour ¼ cup of batter for each pancake onto the lightly buttered griddle or skillet.

Cook for 90 seconds on the first side. Turn, and cook for another 60 seconds on the other side. For soft fluffy pancakes, avoid turning more than once.

Leftovers: Wrap in wax paper and freeze. Pancakes can remain in the freezer for one month.

About the Author

Anita Dixon Thomas is the author of *Whiskey and Merlot, A Love Story*. A Clinical Social Worker by day, a novelist on her spare time, she began writing her debut novel after she found an old journal one day while cleaning out her closet. A Seattle native and a movie buff, she loves to travel, cook and entertain friends. Currently residing in the boondocks in Powder Springs, Georgia, look for her next novel, *Strange Occurrences*, in late January 2021. You can visit her online at www.koolstorytelleranitadixonthomas.com.

Made in the USA
Monee, IL
18 April 2021